UNSAFE CONVICTIONS

Alison Taylor

ARROW

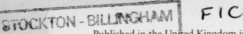
Published in the United Kingdom in 2000 by
Arrow Books

3 5 7 9 10 8 6 4 2

Copyright © Alison Taylor 1999

The right of Alison Taylor to be identified as the author
of this work has been asserted by her in accordance with
the Copyright, Designs and Patents Act, 1988

First published in the United Kingdom in 1999 by
William Heinemann

Arrow Books Limite
The Random House Group Limited
20 Vauxhall Bridge Road, London SW1V 2SA

Random House Australia (Pty) Limite
20 Alfred Street, Milsons Point, Sydney,
New South Wales 2061, Australia

Random House New Zealand Limite
18 Poland Road, Glenfield, Auckland 10, New Zealan

Random House (Pty) Limite
Endulini, 5a Jubilee Road, Parktown 2193, South Africa

The Random House Group Limited Reg. No. 954009
www.randomhouse.co.uk

A CIP record for this book is available from the British Library

Papers used by Random House UK Limited are natural,
recyclable products made from wood grown in sustainable forests.
The manufacturing processes conform to the environmental
regulations of the country of origin.

Typeset in Sabon and Times
by MATS, Southend-on-Sea, Essex

Printed and bound in Denmark by
Nørhaven A/S
ISBN 0 09 927208 3

Alison Taylor has a son and a daughter, and has lived
in North Wales for many years. Her interests include
baroque and classical music, art and riding. She
worked for many years for the former Gwynedd
County Council, but lost her job after reporting
suspected cases of abuse of children in care. This led
to a major police investigation and a Tribunal of
Inquiry. She is the author of three previous crime
novels, *Simeon's Bride*, *In Guilty Night* and *The
House of Women*.

Also by Alison Taylor

Simeon's Bride
In Guilty Night
The House of Women

To find out more about Alison Taylor's
novels, visit the Alison Taylor
website at **www.alison-taylor.freeserve.co.uk**

For Rachel

I

ASPECTS OF GUILT

Two years after Piers Stanton Smith received a life sentence for murdering his ex-wife, the Court of Appeal judged his conviction 'unsafe'. Accused of corruption, the police officers who sent him to prison are now themselves under investigation. In the first of three major articles, our chief reporter Gaynor Holbrook looks into the tragic background of this miscarriage of justice

On a chilly April afternoon, someone in Haughton battered thirty-six-year-old Trisha Stanton Smith into oblivion, drenched her home in petrol, and dropped a match. The autopsy on her charred remains proved that the cause of death was smoke inhalation. Ten days later, her thirty-one-year-old ex-husband was arrested for murder.

Haughton, where Trisha spent all her life, is a bleak, wind-swept town in the Pennine hills. Manchester and Sheffield are twenty-odd miles away, over snaking moorland roads that are often blocked by winter blizzards. At one time, the town's monumental mills reverberated to the thump and roar of King Cotton's massive machinery. Now, the vast empty walls echo to the drip of water through ruined roofs, the whine of bitter winds off the moors, and the scuttle of vermin.

Shortly before she died, Trisha lodged an alimony

claim against Smith. By then, he was married to Beryl Kay. She inherited one fortune from her grandfather, the owner of the town's largest clothes shop. She later made another one by selling the shop site to a supermarket chain.

Smith's trial began at Manchester Crown Court on a raw November day, and the public gallery was packed. Trisha's widowed father, Fred Jarvis, never saw his former son-in-law in the dock – he was still too distraught over the murder. But her sister, Linda Newton, was a key prosecution witness. Oddly, Beryl was never called, but she sat through every harrowing second of testimony.

The prosecution argued that Trisha had to die to stop the squalid secrets of her marriage reaching Beryl's ears. In her divorce petition, Trisha described eight years of terror as Smith's wife. She was beaten, humiliated, sexually debased, and dragged into debt. Ravaged by stress, she became too ill to work. As their income went from bad to worse, so did Smith's

behaviour. Then, she had to go into hospital for a gynaecological operation.

'I was still in dreadful pain when they sent me home,' she had written. 'I was crawling on the floor I hurt so much. He screamed at me to get up, but I couldn't, so he kicked me between my legs as hard as he could.'

One by one, the prosecution witnesses slashed Smith's reputation to shreds. He was not 'Piers Stanton Smith' from a small village in South Yorkshire, but plain Peter Smith from a corporation housing block in Sheffield. Then frail, elderly Henry Colclough spoke of the 'wickedly cruel' death his wife Joyce suffered in her blazing car, while ten-year-old Smith calmly watched.

'Joyce was his teacher. She was giving him a lift home from school, but something happened. She drove straight into a tree, and her legs were trapped under the dashboard. He got out, but when he saw the flames licking around the car, he stood and watched instead of running for help. He kept on watching, until she was dead.' Looking steadily at the blue-eyed man in the dock, Colclough added: 'I'll never forget that look in his eyes. Never! And it's still there. It makes my blood run cold.'

Linda Newton claimed her former brother-in-law was a closet homosexual as well as a violent monster. Relentlessly cross-examined by Smith's barrister, she had to admit that Trisha had her own flaws. But she was outraged by the suggestion that Trisha connived masochistically in her own pain. When it came to the advertisements Trisha placed in several lonely hearts columns while she was still married, Linda hung her head and refused to reply.

'According to your testimony, Mrs Newton,' the barrister said, 'your sister was completely demoralised by the violence and sexual humiliation she allegedly suffered at my client's hands. That picture of her sits very uneasily with that of a woman confident enough to solicit approaches from total strangers, and a woman who, for all we know, engaged sexually with one or more of them.' He then denounced the police investigation for not finding these men. 'Not one iota of forensic evidence links my client to the murder, whereas any one of these mystery lovers could have killed Trisha Stanton Smith.'

The climax of the trial was Smith's testimony on his own behalf. He talked about his deprived childhood, and his mother, who died many years ago. Then he described life with the unstable, neurotic Trisha, who devised her own ways of violence. He was asked why he did not defend her divorce petition. 'I had to get free of her. She was destroying my personality, like water dripping on stone. She often threatened to ruin me, and now she is doing, even from beyond the grave. How can I defend myself against that?'

Of course, he could not. Despite his lawyers' best efforts and even the claim of an alibi for the murder, the jury took less than an hour to find him guilty. As he was led down to begin a life sentence, Beryl collapsed. Linda, gloatingly, hissed: 'Rot in hell, you bastard!'

Smith's appeal was refused. He was forgotten by everyone except Beryl and Trisha's family. Then a young Roman Catholic priest called Father John Barclay returned to England.

Father Barclay had been assistant priest at St Michael's church in Haughton. Two days after Trisha died, he left to do missionary work in South America. He learned about Smith's arrest when an old newspaper came his way months later. But he knew that Smith was in church throughout the fatal afternoon, and therefore over five miles away from the blazing house. He immediately wrote a letter to the police. Not knowing who was in charge of the investigation, he sent the letter to Father Brett Fauvel, St Michael's parish priest, asking him to pass it on unopened.

He heard nothing more. The police did not contact him, and Father Fauvel did not reply. So Father Barclay assumed someone else had been arrested for Trisha's murder. Then he caught meningitis and hovered between life and death for many weeks. He was sent back to England to recuperate. When he found out Smith had been convicted, he approached the authorities. His evidence confirmed Smith's own alibi defence and secured his release. But for the police it opened up a can of worms. At the appeal hearing, Father Fauvel stated under oath that he personally handed Father Barclay's letter to Detective Inspector Barry Dugdale the day it arrived.

Dugdale, thirty-five, was in charge of probing Trisha's horrible death. He stolidly maintains that he did not receive Father Barclay's letter. He has been suspended from duty. His two assistants, Detective Sergeants Wendy Lewis, forty-two, and Colin Bowden, twenty-seven, are also under suspension.

Superintendent Neville Ryman, fifty-one, supervised the murder investigation from police headquarters in the county town of Ravensdale, an elegant spa on the edge of the Peak District. He is a

4

prominent Mason, and his wife Estelle works tirelessly for charity. Their daughter Shelley is a student. Ryman was an inspector in Haughton until his promotion.

The Home Office has now called in officers from North Wales to investigate what looks like blatant corruption among Haughton police. The North Wales team is headed by recently divorced Superintendent Michael McKenna, who is forty-five. Also on board are Detective Inspector Jack Tuttle, forty, Detective Constable Janet Evans, and Ellen Turner, their top administrator. They have a nasty job to do and, as things look at the moment, will probably recommend criminal prosecution of Dugdale and the others.

The authorities appeared to respond quickly to Smith's wrongful conviction. But the Haughton community has new worries. Trisha's murder file remains closed, despite clear evidence that her killer is still at large. And people are suspicious about Haughton police being investigated by brother officers.

Wanting to appear independent, McKenna refused to base his inquiry at the town's police station. He has been allocated a former police house in the village of Old Haughton. But his strings are already being jerked by the Police Federation, police lawyers and insurers, the Crown Prosecution Service, the Police Complaints Authority, and the Home Office. And he is an odd choice to head this kind of investigation. His own background is very murky. He was brought up in Holyhead, and went to Aberystwyth University, but he comes from an Irish Republican family. A relative was hanged by the British after the 1916 rebellion.

McKenna is now head of a divisional criminal investigation unit in North Wales. But his last promotion was mysteriously delayed. He has also been absent from his usual duties at times. I queried these absences with the Home Office. Very brusquely, I was told they concerned 'appropriate and legitimate police business'. But, as everyone knows, police business often gets very dirty.

Gaynor Holbrook's feature article in a mass-circulation newspaper was read with varying degrees of interest over many breakfast tables on Monday morning, not least by Jack Tuttle and Michael McKenna in their cramped billet on Old Haughton's Church Street.

The village of Old Haughton was a mile and a half from the town, by either of the two roads which began at the town centre traffic lights and, diverging to embrace a huge public park, met again on Church Street. One way took in rows of mean Victorian terraces and gaunt-faced mills, turned sharp left at the Junction Inn, and entered the village by an old stone cross. The other way left the town via a steep hill, then levelled out along the park's western boundary. Overlooked by St Michael's Roman Catholic church and the gleaming golden cross on its roof, the road swept downhill past the presbytery, the Roman Catholic primary school, and the high walls of the convent.

Narrow and meandering, Church Street was bounded on one side by tall iron railings, much in need of a coat of paint, that topped the deep retaining wall around the yard of All Saints Anglican parish church. Opposite was an uneven terrace of millstone grit dwellings, broken here and there by cobble-stoned alleyways. Some of the houses were ancient, with low, recessed doors and mullioned windows, the rest two-up and two-downs with back extensions and aspiring sash windows. At the end of the terrace, the weathered masonry of the sixteenth-century Bull Inn sagged against its neighbours.

With the apex of its tall steeple symbolically further from heaven than the footings of the Roman Catholic church, All Saints church lay in a deep depression. Dense-growing trees filled the yard, their roots now breaching old graves and toppling angels, and bramble, nettle and ivy climbed unchecked around tombs and monuments and tree boles. The ground was ankle deep in mouldering fallen leaves, while more had blown in drifts against graves and the church's dank north wall.

The two-up and two-down dwelling that once housed the village policeman had been transformed, inside and out. Steel grilles covered the windows, surveillance cameras were bolted to roof and back extension, and each stout outer door had its own staunch defences. In the front parlour were four desks, four black leather swivel chairs, two grey steel filing cabinets, a safe, four computers, various telephones, fax, tape and telex machines, and the video-recorders and monitors for the surveillance system. Freezing air wormed through holes newly drilled in the window frame to accommodate cables, and raw wood showed on the door frame where a security lock was fitted. The room was quiet, save for the rustle of paper, the occasional click of a cigarette lighter, and the hiss of a large gas fire which, turned up high, still left voids of bone-numbing cold in the corners. Outside, in the bleak monochrome of a winter morning, swags of cloud, bellied with snow, threatened the steeple, and rooks clawed their way like paper silhouettes through the bare dark trees, flapping, as a wind rising from the north-east snatched at their feathers.

Rubbing tired eyes, Jack reached the final page of the two-inch-thick transcript of McKenna's meeting in Ravensdale the previous week with the force's senior officers and the many other organisations with an interest in their activities. 'Must have been a very boring afternoon,' he commented. 'The lawyers did most of the talking. Still, I suppose they always do.' Suddenly, he shivered quite violently. 'Couldn't we take ourselves to the Bull as soon as it opens? They've got real fires, not to mention the food.'

'Maybe so, but there's no privacy,' McKenna replied. He selected another wad of paper from the many stacked on his desk, and handed it across. 'And that's the transcript of my interview last Friday with Superintendent Ryman.' While Jack grumbled to himself about 'bloody awful English weather', and even 'slave-drivers', McKenna returned to the towering pile of police statements before him, turning pages slowly, making notes, flagging pages and paragraphs here and there with small yellow stick-on labels. Shortly after eight thirty, he heard keys assault the deadbolts on the back door, and a woman's voice calling.

'Yoo-hoo! Anybody up?' Without waiting for a response, Rene Minshull barged into the office. 'There you are! Aren't you early birds! Have you had breakfast yet?'

'We have, thank you,' McKenna said.

'I'll make a pot of tea, then. Or would you rather have coffee? And I've got some nice currant teacakes for later.' Eyes darting around the room, she added: 'I won't bother cleaning in here today. You only got here last night, anyway. I'll do the beds and dust upstairs, and I was thinking of making shepherd's pie for your evening meal, if that's all right. A body needs something solid when the weather's like this. It's bitter outside.'

'Shepherd's pie will be fine.' McKenna smiled.

'And veg, of course,' Rene said. Pulling off thick woollen gloves, and stuffing them into her coat pocket, she added: 'The two ladies will be staying at the Bull, won't they? That's if they get here at all. There's snow on the way, and we could be cut off for days.' She smiled, exposing a fine set of false teeth. 'Never mind, eh? Happens most winters, and there's plenty of food in the shops, although what you'll do with all these fancy machines when the power's off I can't imagine.'

As she went from the room, closing the door quietly, Jack gazed thoughtfully in her wake. 'D'you remember those Greek plays we had to read in school? She's like the chorus, isn't she? Popping on-stage every so often to make a pointed comment, then disappearing into the wings until she's needed again. Let's hope she resists the temptation to twitter to the rest of the old-biddy network in between times.'

'Stop fretting.' McKenna reached for a cigarette. 'She's a policeman's widow. She'll know exactly when to talk, and when to keep her own counsel.'

'Unlike Ms Holbrook, then,' Jack said. 'You don't need a law degree to know she's well and truly breached the rules of *sub judice* with all this garbage. Why don't we shut her up with an injunction?'

'That's not the answer.' McKenna moved aside the statements. 'Injunctions will simply encourage more speculation about a cover-up, of which there's been far too much already.' Searching for an ashtray, he added: 'Anyway, her promised exclusive interview tomorrow with the grievously wronged Mr Smith should make for interesting reading. She writes with a clever mix of sensationalism and pseudo-intellectualism.'

'And poisonous innuendo,' Jack observed. 'She's thoroughly tainted your integrity with that rubbish about your ancestors. Not to mention what people will read into your delayed promotion and mystery absences from duty.'

9

'What she wrote about my ancestors is perfectly true, as you well know. How you read it depends on your own frames of reference, which was precisely her intention; and my integrity, as well as yours, is already compromised simply by our being here. Everyone we speak to will be hostile and evasive, if not downright dishonest, and the outcome will displease, disappoint, or anger someone. As Holbrook so clearly points out, we stand to get our hands very dirty.' Pausing to draw breath, McKenna went on: 'The police see us as their worst nightmare, the public see us as a corrupt arm of a corrupted body, and for the media we're simply page fodder until something juicier comes along. We'll get a warning shot fired across her bows, but it won't have much of an effect. She's on a roll, as the saying goes, and I expect she'll cross our path sooner rather than later. She's probably holed up somewhere where she can keep her eye on the tragedy queen, if, that is, she's not actually camping out on his doorstep.' Catching the expression on Jack's face, he scowled. 'And I don't want a lecture about my attitudes! In more honest times, Smith would be judged for the vicious pervert he undoubtedly is, instead of attracting maudlin sympathy from people who should know better.'

'Not a few psychologists believe some degree of violence is inevitable in marriage and other close relationships.'

'And comments like that simply encourage the outrages that Smith and his ilk choose to indulge.' McKenna's eyes sparked with anger. 'You see them on television, you read about them in the papers, and you find them in the dock, displaying their suppurating emotional wounds, and laying claim to debts society doesn't owe. It's a lifelong revenge trip against the world at large.'

'You can't jump to conclusions about Smith being a pervert because of what Linda Newton said at the trial,' Jack added mildly. 'And even if he is, it's not necessarily his fault. Research points clearly to a genetic or pre-natal predisposition towards homosexuality.'

'What he chose to do about it *is* his fault,' McKenna insisted. 'He married under false pretences, abused his wife, stole some of the best years of her life, and tried to pretend all the misery he caused wasn't his doing. Nobody held a gun to his head while he deceived and battered Trisha, and nobody twisted his arm to marry again. He's indulging a monumental and parasitic self-centredness, and I shudder to think what might befall Beryl when her gullibility and bank accounts dry up.' He paused, searching to express feelings which he believed were based on moral truth, but which, when voiced, seemed to be founded in bigotry. 'I'm not condemning homosexuality, Jack, but I abhor the hidden misery people like Smith cause. They demand every available social and material benefit on the grounds that their alleged affliction bestows greater rights than the rest of the world enjoys. Their orientation *might* be beyond their control, but how they deal with it most certainly is *not*.' Again, he stopped speaking, then said: 'Still, my feelings don't matter. He's laughing, all the way from the open prison door to the bank where he'll deposit his obese compensation cheque.'

The sudden roar of a vacuum cleaner overhead drowned the last of his words as Rene set about her chores, her footsteps thumping around the upstairs rooms. Each roar from the vacuum cleaner was preceded by a squeak from its wheels, then, as the church clock began to strike nine, chimes echoed weakly from an old-fashioned mantel clock above the gas fire.

'That blasted church clock's getting on my nerves already.' Jack sighed, gratefully changing the topic. 'It woke me up every hour last night. Not that I got a proper sleep, anyway. The bed's too small. I haven't slept in a single bed since I got married.'

'Maybe you're too large,' McKenna suggested blandly.

'You're just as tall!'

'But not so heavy.'

'I'm bigger built, that's all. I'm not into the heroin-chic look you and Janet favour.'

'I've always been scrawny. Janet's another matter, though.'

'She is, isn't she? And considering it's six months since that awful miscarriage, she should be back to her old self by now.'

'She'll never be back to her old self, and she can't come to terms with her new one.'

'She eats hardly anything, you know. I've watched her in the canteen. She picks at her food, then pushes it away like it's choking her.'

'She's feeding on her guilt,' McKenna said.

'Well, I hope you don't unconsciously encourage her. Religious guilt runs in your veins, too, instead of good red blood. You might be at opposite ends of the spiritual spectrum, but the guilt's the same.'

'My church was always more accommodating than the Welsh chapel of pregnancies out of wedlock.'

'You're still into self-castigation. You can't help yourself.' Jack regarded the other man, amusement flickering in his dark eyes. 'On those many occasions when you light another fag as soon as you've stubbed out the last, you mouth a couple of Hail Marys or something similar while you're flicking your lighter.'

'Don't be ridiculous!'

'And smoking's another bad habit you foster in

Janet. You should positively *dis*courage her, instead of offering the packet out of some twisted sense of good manners. Or', Jack added caustically, 'because of a mutual sympathy between addicts.' When McKenna failed to respond, he said: 'Perhaps we should get Ellen Turner to take her in hand.'

'What good would that do? We're not making any impression on Janet, so why should Ellen fare any better? She's a total stranger.'

'Exactly,' Jack said. 'She also makes the final decision about officers who are physically or mentally unsound and should be retired. In many ways, she's got more clout than our chief. She's certainly got more degrees. She could wield the big stick in Janet's face, couldn't she?' He paused, drumming his fingers on the desk. 'But more to the point, she's a woman, she's older, she's presumably wiser, and she's been there herself.'

'Been where?'

'Her first child arrived four months after that very posh wedding she had, so it was either extremely premature, or Ellen thoroughly enjoyed her engagement.' Jack grinned. 'And as she's now got two more kids, she and Andrew Turner QC must be at it like rabbits at every turn.'

'Not necessarily. It's not statistically improbable that they've had sexual relations on only three occasions.'

Rene had an instinct for people which had rarely let her down. She pottered around the kitchen, collecting utensils and the ingredients for shepherd's pie, while McKenna sat at the table, finishing a drink. He could have finished his drink in the front room, where the other man was making one telephone call after another, but she sensed that he wanted to talk to her, so, with just the odd, innocuous comment disturbing the comfortable quiet, she waited. He was very handsome, she thought, glancing at his fine-boned face, even if rather too thin, and his dark-auburn hair would make a saint green with envy. She suspected there was a real temper to go with that hair, but she had no intention of arousing his ire, for she wanted his mind clearly on the facts, not confused by ill feeling and annoyance. Only then was he likely to discover who scapegoated a decent, honest policeman, and had probably left the mortally wounded Trisha to suffocate in her blazing house. Counting potatoes into the sink, she covered them with warm water, pulled on rubber gloves, and reached for the peeler. 'You do realise I've known Barry Dugdale since he was in nappies, don't you? And you must've been told I see a lot of Fred Jarvis. And Linda, of course.' One peeled potato landed with a thud on the draining board. 'Fred's wife, Dorothy, was my best friend.' She sighed. 'She was a lovely young woman. Her dying the way she did was a tragedy. Linda was only eleven, and Trisha was just getting to that age when she should have been enjoying herself.' Another clean potato joined the first.

'What was wrong with her?'

'Breast cancer.' She scraped ferociously. 'It's a cruel way to go.'

'Between finding out you've got cancer and dying from it there's too much time for hope,' he said. 'My father had a tumour cut from his stomach and less than a year later, they found another one in his liver. He was barely fifty when he died.'

'And how old were you?' Rene asked, adding to the potato mound.

'Twenty.'

She nodded. 'Like Trisha, then.'

He lit a cigarette and while smoke drifted under her nostrils, reminding her quite forcibly of the scent that had always hung about her husband's clothes, she finished the potatoes, scooped the peel into the bin, rinsed the sink, then tipped in four large carrots, ready topped and tailed, and covered them with water.

'Have you seen Linda recently?' McKenna asked.

'Yesterday afternoon. And she asked me to tell you she wants to talk to you.' Holding each carrot in her left hand, she took off long, neat strips of orangey peel. 'She doesn't know what to do with herself since Smith came out of prison. She's hurt, and bitter, and grieving, and she's scared of him and, heaven knows, she's got good cause.' She picked up a chopping knife, and began expertly slicing the vegetables. 'And she hasn't a good word to say for young Father John, but that's to be expected, isn't it? He was the one to give Smith his "get out of gaol" card.' The carrots landed with a hollow sort of noise in a big steel colander, then danced under a jet of cold water, while she turned her attention to the potatoes. 'Mind you, if you took too much notice of Linda at the moment, you'd believe every priest ever to set foot in Haughton is a cheat, or a liar, or a drunk, or a pervert, and she says Father Brett's the worst of the lot.' The carrots went into a pan, while the colander was filled with potato chunks, and doused under more cold water. 'Then again, she's not the only one who doesn't like him. He's smarmy, and he's got a big opinion of himself, which isn't helped by the way some folk fawn over him, especially the women.'

'Why does Linda want to see me?'

'Like I said, she doesn't know what to do with herself.' She put the potatoes into another pan, sprinkled salt, lit the gas, then sat down opposite

McKenna, rubber gloves still on her hands, orange stains on the hatched palms and finger ends. 'To tell you the truth, I think she's hoping you'll somehow be able to send Smith back where he belongs. I told her that's not why you're here, and I said you're not here either to find whoever killed Trisha, more's the pity.' She fell silent, memory disturbing her features. 'Most folk think you wouldn't have far to look if you were, whatever that court decided. You'd go past the church, down the road as far as the Junction Inn, turn left, drive another mile, turn right, and there you'd be, right outside the gates of the house. Would you believe', she added, shaking her head, 'what that silly Beryl Kay's done? That house was called The Parsonage from the day it was built, which must be at least a hundred years before her grandfather bought it, and now she's changed the name to Piers Holme. My daughter noticed the other week when she was going past.'

'How many children have you got?' asked McKenna.

'Just the one. She'll be thirty in April. There's only a few weeks between her and Linda, you know. Dorothy and me used to take those two everywhere together.' Rene took off her rubber gloves and placed them neatly beside her. 'And what about you?'

'We didn't have children.'

'P'raps as well, seeing as you got divorced. D'you live alone, then?'

He nodded. 'Apart from two cats. Mr Tuttle's wife is looking after them.'

'Has Mr Tuttle got youngsters?'

'Twin girls. They're doing A levels this summer, and they both want to go to university.'

'*That*'ll cost,' she said feelingly. 'You could still get grants when my girl went, but we were forever baling her out. Then again, she was training to be a vet, and that's always an expensive business.' She glanced at him, knowing perfectly well he knew she was horse-trading information. 'The two ladies you're expecting,' she began. 'What about them?'

'Janet Evans is a detective constable,' he told her. 'She's twenty-seven, and she's not married. Ellen Turner's in her late thirties, and her husband's a barrister. They've got three children.'

'Is she a police officer as well?'

'No. She's in charge of administration for our force, but in this case, she'll be overseeing this investigation.'

Frowning, Rene said: 'I thought you were in charge.'

'I am.' He smiled.

'That's all right, then.' She rose and, picking up the gloves, added: 'I wouldn't dream of telling you how to do your job, but don't you forget one thing. If Smith really *didn't* kill Trisha, whoever did is going to get very worried now you're here. You need to watch out for people.'

'I've notified the various solicitors when we intend to interview Dugdale, Lewis and Bowden.' Jack pushed a list of times across the desk to McKenna. 'You said you want to see Ryman again, too.'

'He'll keep for a few days,' McKenna said. 'And make arrangements to interview Linda Newton as soon as possible.'

'With or without legal representation?'

'With.'

'Is an interview under caution really warranted? Because she was briefly Dugdale's flame many moons ago – and you've only got Ryman's word for that – it's jumping the gun to suspect her and Dugdale of conspiring to fit up Smith. And that's another idea

Ryman put in your head, isn't it? He probably dropped Linda into your lap to take your mind off the bloody awful job he did of supervising the investigation.'

'We leave no stone unturned, if we can help it.'

'Then shouldn't we add Fauvel to the first round of interviews? Our primary task is to find out whether Dugdale lied about that letter, or whether Fauvel did.'

'Our first priority is investigating what Dugdale, Lewis and Bowden actually did or didn't do, to resolve the uncertainty around them. Suspension can make people very panicky.'

'They'll have been offered counselling, I imagine.'

'That won't alter the fact that they see their future in the hands of total strangers, who could, for all they know, be under instruction simply to find, or fabricate, grounds for dismissal.'

'As in no one cares very much who's hacked to bits as long as the pound of flesh is forthcoming.' Drawing circles with his ball-point pen on a sheet of scrap paper, Jack asked: 'Exactly how much latitude do we have?'

'As long as we don't provide Smith with further grounds for complaint and, by extension, enhanced compensation, our hands are remarkably unfettered.' McKenna began sifting a pile of documents, in search of a pathology report. 'And bearing in mind you were quick to rebuke me for prejudging Smith's sexual orientation, don't leap to your own conclusions about Ryman's motives.'

'How did the top brass come over to you?' Jack asked. 'Well-practised in shrugging off allegations of corruption? Resentful because this applecart was tipped up so publicly? Scared we'll find a whole load of rotten apples, instead of just a few?'

'I had the impression of a well-run force doing its

best to provide a good public service. The senior ranks seem more distressed than anything, and not only because three of their officers had to be suspended. Linda Newton's not alone in believing Smith killed her sister, and the only real resentment I detected was over the fact that he's out of prison. Trisha's murder was a nasty affair, and it's left a very nasty taste.'

'So, contrary to what Holbrook's telling the world, the file on Trisha isn't closed?'

'No, but it's not officially reopened, either.'

'That won't please Rene,' Jack commented. 'Bearing in mind *her* connections and aspirations, at what point do we tell her to stay in the kitchen, as it were?'

'We don't. Like Smith, we're outsiders, so we need all the good press we can get. Having her on our side, thinking she's privy to what's going on even if she can't direct it, won't do us any harm.'

'That's an extraordinarily cynical view.'

'I've never been able to see the dividing line between realism and cynicism,' McKenna admitted. 'Perhaps it's something I should deal with. But don't belittle her potential. You could say she's powerful with the local knowledge.'

'And looking to grind her own axes, given the chance.'

'Which could be the same as ours.' Picking up a file of documents, McKenna rose. 'I'm going to explore the lie of this very strange land.' He glanced outside. 'Janet and Ellen should be here soon, as it's not snowing yet.'

'We're due to see Dugdale at two.'

'I'll be back long before then.'

3

The documents on the seat beside him, McKenna pulled away from the kerb outside the house, inched along Church Street past a row of parked cars, and made as if to follow Rene's instructions to reach Smith's place, but instead of going left at the Junction Inn, as soon as there was a break in the stream of morning traffic he went right.

Haughton had neither the slightly romantic edge of Gaynor Holbrook's description, nor the air of dereliction she cast upon it. Although the surrounding moorlands, visible at every turn, were near overwhelming, the interminable terraces of stone houses were smart with fresh paint, double-glazed windows, bright front doors, and doorsteps pumiced to a creamy white. The mills were far from idle, or empty of all but vermin life. King Cotton had given way to rubber mouldings, plastic extrusion, food canning, an industrial museum and, close to the town centre, women's lingerie, its wispy, ethereal products in a display case attached to one of the gate pillars.

The town centre, its grand Victorian buildings sand-blasted of industrial grime, was, to use a word he loathed for no discernible reason, bustling, and the shops, windows bright on this grey morning, packed with customers. Cars and trucks and buses stretched ahead as far as he could see, moving forward when the traffic lights changed, then coming to a halt while more traffic flowed across the intersection. Once clear of the lights, he followed an orange and brown double-decker bus down the road, past the new supermarket where Kay's drapery once stood, past more terraces, more shops, and more mills, different moorlands now on the horizon. The town was much larger than he had imagined, more prosperous, better served and, in this patch, clearly under regeneration, with new commercial investment and enclaves of modern chimneyless dwellings spreading like rashes over the lower reaches of the moors.

Dent Viaduct came into view, an enormous six-arched brick structure carrying the Manchester railway line, so lofty that the flimsy tracery of electricity wires and gantries along its top was wreathed in cloud. The road passed under one arch, beside a narrow, dirt-spumed river, then came to another fork, between an old-fashioned public house and a small riverside mill. The glass in its windows was smashed to bits, its roof a caved-in wreckage of slate and wood, and its walls sprouted withered weeds from a myriad cracks in the brickwork. A defunct wood-and-iron paddlewheel, green with moss and red with rust, rotted in the brown water. Car indicator blinking, McKenna turned right, drove by the mill's windowless frontage, and turned right again, along a narrow lane fringed on both sides by scrubby hedges, from which a few dead leaves still hung. Drawing to a halt beside a dusty holly bush bedecked with strips of plastic carrier bag, he picked up the documents, locked the car, and pulled on a sheepskin jacket.

Days of unthawed frost rimed the dead grass under the hedge and the lower branches of the holly bush, as if it were assailed by fungus. He could smell the chill off the river, and hear the trickling water. His breath plumed, and he felt the cold biting his ears and face, and creeping through the soles of his shoes. One hand thrust in the jacket pocket, the other holding the documents, he read as he walked, the words jerking out of focus with each step. Called to the burned-out house on that early April day, the pathologist who later dissected Trisha's remains had left a record of the scene as it unfolded before him, neatly printed on paper which bore the logo of the district hospital trust and his own impressive qualifications.

The time is 16.17, the weather is windless and fine, although the sky to the north is beginning to cloud over. Ambient temperature away from the house is 11.5 degrees Celsius and cooling.

The two-storey house lies at the end of an unmade lane, with only its pitched and slabbed roof visible from the road, as it is located in a depression some fifty yards from the river. Several police cars and official vehicles are parked along the verges of the lane, which is still muddy in places although there has been no rain for six days. The gardens are untended and mostly overgrown, with unclipped privet hedges, broken-down brick walls, and some saplings to the rear, on which newly emerged leaves hang in blackened shreds. There is a general air of neglect, which existed before fire debris worsened the view. A large crowd of people gathered prior to my arrival, doubtless attracted by flames and excitement, and they are now being kept back by police officers. Two fire tenders and an ambulance are outside the property, all hoses have been deployed, and a doctor and four paramedics are waiting at the front door, which is placed centrally with windows to each side. The fire, which was reported by anonymous telephone call at 15.07, has been extinguished, although much smoke is still about the ruined walls and roof. There is an overwhelming smell of petrol in the air, and the water running from the house and forming puddles in places shows traces of iridescence. The first fire tender arrived from Haughton

Station, some three miles distant, at 15.17, by which time the whole building was well alight, with flames shooting from windows and doors back and front, and through holes already burned in the roof.

Provided with a protective jacket and hard hat, I have been escorted into the house by the chief fire officer – I am told it is not safe to examine the rest of the building – and led into the ground-floor room to the right of the front door. This would appear to have been used as a sitting-room. There is a modern tiled fireplace on the exterior wall, and a door in the reveal wall leading to a lean-to kitchen, which runs the length of the rear wall. Such must have been the intensity of the blaze here that it is no longer possible to determine the state of the furnishings or decorations: everything is charred beyond recognition, with plaster stripped from the walls. The ceiling has collapsed, bringing with it the few contents of the room above, and daylight is visible through the many large holes in the roof.

The anonymous caller, a woman, said that a person was possibly in the burning house. The police have already traced the call to a nearby public telephone kiosk, and inform me that attempts are being made to isolate fingerprints from the apparatus: there is little hope of success, as the kiosk is well used and on a main thoroughfare. The tape-recording of the call will be examined later, and house-to-house enquiries made locally in an attempt to identify the caller. The fire crews from both tenders searched the building as soon as the flames had been brought under control, and found one body in the room where I now stand, underneath debris fallen from the ceiling and upstairs room. This debris has been moved sufficiently for me to carry out initial examination, but the whole area is saturated with water, and fouled with fire residues.

The body lies on its left side facing towards the fireplace, and has suffered severe heat contraction. From the nature of the burns to the visible parts of the body it is my immediate impression that the person made no attempt to escape the fire, and did not move voluntarily at any point, although there would have been a sufficiently fierce draught from the flames to disturb the body somewhat *in situ*. I therefore make an initial conclusion that the person was deeply unconscious, or deceased, before fire took hold. The right arm is bent sharply, and all flesh and muscle have been burned away, exposing the bone, which is charred. Similarly, flesh, muscle and hair are missing from the visible area of the head, exposing the skull, and the right eye socket is empty. I note that facial bones are shattered, although the body does not appear to have fallen against any hard surface or object, and was not felled by collapse of the ceiling. It is not possible to say at this stage whether the damage is due to heat fracture. The visible lower extremities of the body are similarly incinerated, bone exposed in the pelvic girdle, thigh, knee and shin. One buttock is completely consumed, the other partially so, and both feet charred inside the remains of what appear to be female leather shoes with a heel some 5cms in height. Filaments of melted synthetic fibres remain on the legs, suggesting the person wore stockings or tights, and there are further molten substances adhering to the torso and thighs.

I confirm that life is extinct. Still photographs of the body and surroundings have been taken by forensic and fire officers, and fire officers continue to take video film of the scene. Forensic scientists are waiting to begin their own examinations. In view of the fragility of the remains, I do not propose to disturb the body to make a further examination at this stage, and have ordered the remains to be taken to the mortuary, where I shall conduct a full autopsy later today. Removal of the body will be executed under my supervision and recorded on video film. The forensic scientists are under instruction to sample the residues of liquefied body fat and tissues under and around the remains, and the remnants of clothing. My own experience and that of the fire crews suggest that accelerants of some type, probably petrol, were laid at various sites to facilitate the fire, and from the nature of the burn injuries to the deceased, that at least one site was very close to the body. It is my view that identification of the deceased should be pursued via fingerprinting, if sufficient flesh remains on the left hand, and by dental and any other medical records. The condition of the body is such that not only would visual identification be uncertain, but the experience of viewing the body would prove too distressing for any relative.

Wilfred Ernest Spenser
Home Office Pathologist

McKenna leaned against the cold brick of the garden wall, looking at the shell of the house, which nature had partially reclaimed in the intervening months. Rain, driven by winds off the moors, had scoured the worst of the smoke stains from walls inside and out, and the saplings of which Dr Spenser wrote reared behind the building, bare branches clacking against the eaves. In the front garden, still littered with charred odds and ends, grass and brambles grew in a thick tangle, which was already creeping towards the walls.

He made his way up the path, slipping on icy, mossy flagstones, and went through the hole where the front door had hung. In rendering safe the building after the fire, the upper floor had been brought down completely, and only the ends of the rafters, below which he stood as if inside the rib-cage of a massive skeleton, still told of a roof. A huge, weathered mound of wood, stone, tile and rubble obscured the patch where Trisha's body had lain. Hands in pockets, he leaned against the wall, and noticed a broken Cornish-ware jug, then some patches of patterned carpet, their edges singed, and lengths of wood fashioned into a zigzag, which he realised must be part of the staircase, rammed side on into the mound. Wondering what else he might discern if he lingered, he turned away, to walk gingerly around the back, where a great sheet of corrugated iron hung off the lean-to kitchen roof like a guillotine waiting to fall. Here, where the saplings were obviously new recruits to an older thicket, which cut off air and light from the back of the house, he was sure he could still smell the fire. Mingled with it was the rancid odour of damp, curling off the slimy flagstoned path and around the base of the wall that was also green with moss. The corrugated iron squealed like a live thing as the wind caught one of its corners, and he stepped back, suddenly cowed by the misery of the place. Its horizons were overhung by the moors and the massive viaduct, and came to an utter dead stop as soon as he lifted his eyes. Walking slowly back to the car, looking over his shoulder now and then, he wondered too if Smith ever revisited the place he had once called home, but thought not.

Reversing the car, he twice rammed the scrawny hedge, ice-brittle twigs crackling under the wheels, then drove slowly to the end of the lane, to find his way barred by a supermarket trolley half filled with firewood, being pushed slowly to and fro by a rotund body dressed in padded jacket, scarves, a skirt, trousers, thick striped knee socks, and short black wellingtons. Dull eyes stared at him from under a knitted Fair Isle cap and, as he pulled on the handbrake, another body hove into view like a crow fluttering to earth, dressed in flapping garments. Bare head jerking, exposed shins blue with cold, arms gesticulating to the sky, the man uttered an unintelligible stream of words, snapped his mouth like a trap, stared at the car, then repeated both gestures and streaming words. At a total loss, McKenna waited, still under the woman's vapid scrutiny. Then a thin woman, clad in jeans and pale-coloured duffel coat with a fur-trimmed hood, appeared as if from the wings of a stage. She glanced at the car, and began to harry the others out of his way. As he turned into the road, he saw the little group trundling away to the right, the thin woman's hands on the shoulders of the others.

4

'Back at last!' Rene trilled, as McKenna came in through the rear door. 'I'll get the teacakes under the grill now. Mr Tuttle's had to wait for his elevenses, but I gave the two young ladies a hot drink as soon as they got here.'

27

'I went to have a look round the town.'

'And Trisha's place as well, I expect. Not that it was ever hers. Or his. They rented.'

'So I understand,' McKenna said.

'And she'd've had to go on renting, married to him. I reckon every penny she earned went on keeping him dressed up and idle, and when she lost her job I dare say most of their social security still went on him.'

'I saw two rather odd-looking people as I was driving away. And there was a woman with them.'

'Did she look normal?'

'Normal? Yes, I suppose so.'

'She must be one of the workers, then.'

'Where?'

'At the Willows. It was a nice house before they put the mental defectives there. If you ask me, they should be back in hospital, instead of wandering the streets on this community care thing everybody talks about.' Frowning, she looked up at him, her hair under the kitchen light peppery with grey. 'They weren't at Trisha's place, were they?'

'No. I saw them on the road.'

'Only I shouldn't think even mental defectives would be daft enough to go there. I can't think how you could stomach it on your own.'

After booking into their reserved rooms at the Bull Inn, Ellen and Janet returned to the Church Street house for lunch. Rene hovered over the table in the back parlour, serving lunch to her four charges, and tutting quietly as Janet picked here and there at her food but ate nothing of substance. She nodded with pleasure when small-boned, skinny Ellen consumed all that was put before her, and reached for more.

To McKenna, Janet looked ill. Shorn of all her old voluptuousness, her once luxuriant dark hair was fiercely cropped into an almost architectural shape, she had blue smudges under her eyes, and not an ounce of spare flesh on a body she now clothed in dark, austere garments that mimicked the garb of her chapel-minister father.

Rene broke into his thoughts. 'One of the young ladies can heat up the dinner when you're ready. I finish at five, but I could stay later some nights if you need me.'

'Where d'you live?' Ellen asked her, wiping cake crumbs from her lips.

'If you go past the Bull, then the corner shop and the Wheatsheaf, you'll come to a row of cottages. Mine's the second one.'

'Have you been there long?'

'Since I got wed. My husband worked out of the police station in town. The village policeman lived here, but that was in the days when we had local men who knew who to keep an eye on. Nowadays, they're just strangers in uniform.'

Ellen nodded. 'It's the same in our force. We need Welsh-speaking officers in some areas, but all this shunting around doesn't take that sort of thing into consideration.'

'Really?' Rene's eyes widened. 'I didn't know people still spoke Welsh. I thought it'd died out years ago.'

'It's actually on the increase, thanks mainly to a bunch of political activists who cause us no end of bother.'

'I *had* heard about fire bombs in holiday cottages,' Rene said, passing Ellen another slice of cake. 'There'd be bits on the news now and then, but I didn't understand why they were doing it. Seems like cutting off your own nose to spite your face, doesn't it?'

29

'Quite.' Ellen smiled at her. 'But you can't reason with people like that, can you?'

'Not usually,' Rene agreed. Chewing her mouth, she looked down at McKenna. 'D'you speak Welsh?'

'I do.'

'And what about you, Mr Tuttle?'

'I don't,' Jack admitted. 'But Janet does, of course.'

Looking again at McKenna, she added: 'And d'you actually speak Welsh to people?'

'If necessary. If they want to.'

'Can you write your reports in Welsh, as well?'

'We can, but all official documents must be bilingual.'

'How strange.' Rene seemed taken aback. 'You don't think of Wales as a *real* foreign country. I mean, you go there for holidays, but it's not like Spain or France, is it? And you don't *look* foreign. You look quite like anybody else.'

I

Waiting again for the town centre traffic lights to change, McKenna said: 'We might not look foreign to Rene, but the locals look decidedly alien to me.'

'Different racial types, sir,' Ellen offered from the back seat. 'Rene and her ilk come mostly from Saxon stock, with bits of Roman and Viking thrown into the pot, which could', she added thoughtfully, 'be relevant to us, because priorities, frames of reference, loves, hates, needs, wants and bugbears are different in different places, and those things govern behaviour.'

'If Dugdale deliberately withheld crucial alibi evidence, the outcome would be exactly the same wherever it happened,' Jack asserted.

'But if he did, his actions could have been dictated by arcane local factors,' McKenna said. The lights changed and, as the line of traffic jerked forward, he touched the indicator to turn left on to the Buxton road.

Ellen had a large-scale road map open on her lap. 'It's about two miles to Rowarth Rise estate, where Dugdale lives, and fifteen or so to Buxton, where Dr Spenser, the pathologist, lives. Will we be seeing him?'

'Probably not,' McKenna told her. 'His reports are very comprehensive, and there's been no dispute about his findings.'

31

'I found his scene-of-crime report far more harrowing than the autopsy report,' Ellen said. 'It was probably that warning against visual identification. When I was helping Rene wash up after lunch, she said Linda insisted on seeing Trisha's remains. Then she told people exactly what she'd seen, which could be why nobody can stop talking about it. Rene says Smith's an out and out monster, and if he's any sense, he'll get out of town while he's still got legs to walk on.'

'I trust you told her to warn the town off any lynch mob activity?' Jack broke his silence.

'Our being here focuses local attention,' McKenna said. 'Until we're gone, Smith will be the main topic of interest, and as he's shown no reluctance to make a public spectacle of himself, he can't complain if the public turns out to watch, and judges in the process.'

Rowarth Rise estate consisted of twenty or so detached and semi-detached modern houses, built of local stone and fronted by lozenge-shaped gardens. The pavement line followed the gardens, zigzagging along the side of the hill behind a row of old sycamore trees, their denuded branches stark against the overcast sky.

McKenna parked between other cars angled against the kerb, and, his briefcase leaden with papers, walked across frost-rimed grass to the unlatched garden gate, Jack beside him carrying the tape-recorder, Ellen with her laptop computer.

A small, bent, wispy-haired man in lawyer's pin-stripes opened the front door before they reached the step, and introduced himself. 'Rodney Hinchcliffe, Superintendent. I'm Detective Inspector Dugdale's legal representative.' When McKenna had introduced his own contingent, Hinchcliffe added: 'I really must protest about the way you've chosen to conduct this investigation. Turning a person's own home into an interrogation centre is quite inappropriate, especially when there are more than adequate facilities at the town's police station. Mrs Dugdale was forced to go out, and she's had to arrange to keep the children away until I contact her with the all clear.'

The hallway was carpeted in a warm, rosy pink, and McKenna carefully wiped his feet on the doormat before following the solicitor inside. 'I note your objections, Mr Hinchcliffe,' he said, 'but I'm sure you appreciate that using the local facilities could give rise to far graver concerns.'

'Such as?' Hinchcliffe demanded, stopping in his tracks.

'If this investigation is to succeed, we must remain as independent and as far removed from influence as possible. Our being based at Haughton police station could put us in danger of being drawn into institutional crisis and neurosis, and of adopting the distorted perspectives of others. In addition,' he went on, moving along the hall and forcing the solicitor to do likewise, 'the local officers would be aware of our every move, which, in my opinion, would place DI Dugdale and his colleagues at an even greater disadvantage, and under quite intolerable pressure.'

Frowning with annoyance, Hinchcliffe pushed open the door to what was obviously the family's sitting-room, where Dugdale stood before a large gas fire, wiping his hands nervously down his trouser legs, and not sure if a smile might, or might not, be appropriate.

Shocked by the man's gaunt appearance, McKenna thought he looked as if the stuffing had been literally knocked from his body, and tried to ignore the thought that guilt usually wore a different face. The apparatus of interview plugged in, switched on and readied, he announced the date, the time, the names and status of those present, then said: 'For the tape, Inspector Dugdale, please state your name, rank, and date of birth.'

Dugdale tried to speak, and failed, then cleared his throat, and tried once more. The words emerged slowly and falteringly, as if these essential details eluded his memory.

'Thank you,' McKenna said. 'I will now show you various statements made by yourself, and given by yourself, with regard to the investigation into Trisha Stanton Smith's death, the arrest and charge of Piers Stanton Smith, and statements made subsequent to the submissions of Father John Barclay. Please read these statements, and say if there is anything in them with which you now disagree, or which you wish to amend. At a later stage, I shall deal with your testimony at Smith's trial.'

As McKenna handed over each sheet of paper, some now dog-eared and grimy, Dugdale obeyed his instructions, then gave the papers to his solicitor. The rustle of papers, the rasp of breath and the hiss of fire grew oppressive, and Dugdale began to sweat, drawing his finger around the neck of his shirt. Jack and McKenna watched him, while Ellen gazed through the window at a moorland panorama, where the earth reflected the grey of the sky.

Taking the last sheet from his interrogator, Dugdale said, in a more certain voice: 'I don't disagree with anything, sir, and I don't wish to change anything.'

'You're sure?' McKenna asked.

'Positive.'

'Throughout the investigation, you reported to Superintendent Ryman at police headquarters in

Ravensdale. You also reported to the station commander in Haughton.'

'Yes, sir, but Mr Ryman decided what procedures should be taken.'

'Did you agree with Mr Ryman's command?'

Dugdale shifted in his chair, glancing at his solicitor. 'It wasn't really a matter of agreement or not, sir. For all practical purposes, what happened was up to me.'

'That's common procedure,' McKenna commented. 'Were there any specific issues on which you required Mr Ryman's consent, support, or co-operation?'

'Only Smith's arrest. He rubber-stamped it, so to speak.'

'Did he ever advise pursuit of specific lines of inquiry?'

'Well, no. He didn't know the people involved, he never visited the crime scene, and it was a long time since he'd worked in this area.'

'Headquarters set up a toll-free telephone line after the murder,' McKenna said. 'If someone lodged information on that line, or with Crimestoppers, who would receive the information? You or Mr Ryman?'

'It would have been relayed to me,' Dugdale said. 'But no one called, sir. There was a thorough trawl as soon as Father Barclay turned up. Nothing had been overlooked, and certainly not his letter.' He paused, then added: 'If we'd had it, believe me, Complaints and Discipline would have found it. They turned the station upside down, came here, then searched Wendy Lewis's house and Colin Bowden's flat.'

'Don't be naive,' McKenna chided. 'If you decided to frame Smith, you'd get rid of Father Barclay's letter first. Why didn't you interview Father Fauvel?'

'Because we had no call to consider him until the

papers for the appeal hearing arrived. As far as we were concerned, he was just the parish priest for the Catholics.'

'And of whose flock Smith had become a member.'

'He wasn't relevant.'

'He was very relevant in the end, wasn't he?'

'Look, sir, Brett Fauvel had months to come forward about this letter, only he didn't. He didn't mention it at the trial either, even though he was a character witness for Smith.'

'According to his testimony at appeal, he claims the letter was handed to you, unopened as Father Barclay instructed, and that as he heard nothing further, he assumed it was irrelevant.' McKenna glanced at his notes. 'Father Barclay had no idea who was running the investigation into Trisha's murder, or even if it were still active, but assumed, quite reasonably, that Father Fauvel *would* know, and would know who was in charge. In his affidavit for the appeal hearing Father Fauvel states that he called at the police station on the afternoon of the day he received the letter, and gave it to you.' Watching Dugdale speculatively, he added: 'He also states that you identified yourself to him. The detail in his statements, and their level of simplicity, have the ring of truth.'

'Then why didn't anyone else remember seeing him there?'

'Probably for the same reason that none of the women working at St Michael's church on the afternoon Trisha died could be certain they'd actually seen Smith there at the time. You know as well as I do how unreliable the public memory becomes when challenged, and especially so where someone like Father Fauvel is involved. He's very well known, apparently very distinctive, very prominently involved in all kinds of activities and, when he's wearing his social-worker hat, a fairly frequent visitor to what is a very busy police station. In other words, he could be seen anywhere in the area at any time, and therefore', McKenna concluded, 'few people are willing to commit themselves to *when* he might have been seen in a particular place.'

Hands trembling almost violently, Dugdale said: 'He did not give me any letter. I never saw him or spoke to him throughout the investigation.' He looked squarely at his interrogator. 'I'm calling him a liar, sir, priest or not.'

'What motive could he have?'

'I've no idea.'

Hinchcliffe leaned forward. 'Has it occurred to anyone, Superintendent, that this letter is nothing more than a myth, and that *both* these priests are lying?'

'That is an issue I shall have to pursue, although Father Barclay's actions speak of his being an honest man, and to our knowledge he has no stake in any aspect of Trisha's death or your client's investigation,' replied McKenna. 'Father Fauvel's statements on Smith's behalf indicate a regard quite contrary to the notion that he would allow an innocent man to go to prison.'

'I don't understand why Father Barclay didn't tell Father Fauvel what was in the letter,' Dugdale said. 'Why not, at the very least, make its importance clear?'

'I don't know.' McKenna was thoughtful. 'Perhaps he thought there was no need.' He shuffled his papers. 'Leaving aside Father Fauvel for the moment, were there other lines of inquiry you should have pursued?'

'You want the benefit of my hindsight, sir?' Dugdale's voice was bitter. 'We did what seemed right and necessary at the time.'

'Were you negligent?'

'No, sir. We probably missed odd things here and there, but that's inevitable in any investigation, and this one was a real mystery. Trisha was well-liked, she hadn't upset anyone, she didn't have any insurance, she didn't owe large amounts of money, no one seemed to benefit from her death, and she had no compromising knowledge about anyone apart from her ex-husband, so we began to wonder about Beryl. Wendy Lewis said she could have been pathologically jealous of Trisha.'

'Why should she be?'

'Second wives often worry that the husband will go back to the first,' Dugdale asserted. 'There's so much history between them. Apart from that, a failed marriage doesn't exactly point towards reliability, and Beryl already had more than enough to make her feel insecure.'

'Such as?'

'Wendy Lewis can give you a better perspective, sir. She researched Beryl's background very thoroughly.' He rubbed his forehead, and stared at the smears of moisture on his hand. 'But she spent all afternoon at the dentist's, having gold fillings done, so she had a cast-iron alibi, even though I'm sure she wouldn't balk at murder to protect Smith.'

'That brings us to these mysterious male escorts with whom Trisha allegedly took up,' McKenna said. 'Are they included in the "odd things" over which you were probably remiss?'

'No, sir.'

'But you didn't really look for them, did you?'

'There was nowhere to look. Everything in that house was destroyed: no address book, no record of any ads sent to papers or magazines, and no replies. We contacted every publication in the country which carries personal ads, and found where Trisha placed hers, but that was the end of the line.' He paused, gathering thoughts. 'The main attractions of personal ads are secrecy and anonymity. Any of the four million or so readers in the area could have replied to her box number. Mr X sends his letter to the paper, addressed to the box number, and it's sent on unopened. The paper has no idea who Mr X might be.'

'Why did you give up so easily, just because the obvious way failed? Why did you assume these men were both untraceable and innocent?' McKenna demanded. 'Wasn't Trisha ever seen with a man? Where did they go for outings? Surely Linda Newton knew about them?'

Dugdale flushed. 'Linda only knew what Trisha told her. People always keep secrets from each other, no matter how close they are. Trisha might've been embarrassed about advertising for company, or just ashamed of the types who replied. Personally, I think the all-round battering she had from Smith put her off men altogether.' He paused again, measuring his words. 'At the trial, Smith's barrister twisted the whole thing for his own ends, and shoved Linda into a corner. She knew about the ads, but she didn't know if Trisha had met any respondents. That was an assumption, for the benefit of the defence.'

'But as Smith's barrister so rightly pointed out,' McKenna said, 'simply for Trisha to advertise in the personal columns was hardly consistent with her alleged state of mind.' He watched Dugdale's face. 'Was it?'

'I don't know, sir. Trisha's not here to explain herself.'

Hinchcliffe roused himself once more. 'I feel obliged to draw your attention, Superintendent, to the quite exhaustive documentation relating to my client's search for these elusive letter writers. In my opinion, he did all that could be expected, and I would defy even yourself to have been any more successful. You will also note, I hope, my client's examination of the entirely plausible, if probably unprovable, possibility that Beryl Stanton Smith instigated the murder, and paid someone to do her dirty work while she gave herself a near-perfect alibi.'

McKenna nodded. 'I have Mr Dugdale's report to the Crown Prosecution Service. I also have a long list of people who gave what he described as "negative" statements.'

'Which I think you will find,' Hinchcliffe commented, 'constitutes most of those he interviewed, including the ladies busy in St Michael's church, Father Barclay's evidence notwithstanding. As is usual in such matters, no one saw, heard, or knew anything of significance, or even, relevance. Nor, I may add, was it possible to find a voice match with that of the recording of the 999 call about the fire.' He gazed at McKenna, pale eyes wide. 'What more could my client do, Superintendent? He isn't Superman, you know.'

Ignoring the solicitor's barbed remark, McKenna turned to Dugdale. 'In the CPS report you refer to Julie Broadbent, a care worker at the Willows, which I understand is a home for the mentally handicapped. You indicate that she was friendly with Trisha.'

'I think I wrote "acquainted with", sir, not "friendly with",' Dugdale said. 'Trisha had talked about working there. Now she had the freedom to choose, I suppose she was thinking about something with a purpose, instead of any old job to keep Smith in idleness.'

'Why did you report that Broadbent "appears to be holding back"?'

'Wendy Lewis and Colin Bowden interviewed her. They tried to talk to the residents, too, but as few of them can speak more than gobbledegook, it wasn't very productive.'

'Broadbent, please, Inspector.'

'That was their impression.' Pausing again, Dugdale clenched his fingers. 'It had to be recorded, even though it wasn't necessarily correct. As they aren't local, they didn't know about Julie's circumstances, and what they perceived as "holding back", and significant, was probably only her automatic response to the police.'

'Why?'

'She'd come to police attention in the past. Persistent truancy, a bit of teenage delinquency. That kind of thing.'

'Does she have a criminal record?'

'She was cautioned twice for under-age drinking, and once for shoplifting. That was the end of it, which is all to her credit, given her background,' Dugdale said. 'Her mother was the town tart, and she never knew her father, or any other family. She had no proper schooling, no guidance, no support, and no love, so it was no surprise when she went off the rails for a while.' There was something near outrage in his voice. 'No one ever gave her a fighting chance, and all you ever hear about her is "like mother, like daughter".'

'In other words, Broadbent has a piquant reputation?' McKenna asked.

'Which I don't believe she deserves,' Dugdale insisted. 'Unfortunately, it wasn't long before Wendy Lewis got wind of it, and she was all for crediting Julie with guilty knowledge on the assumption that she'd given Trisha a taste of the high life and introduced her to the scum who battered her face and set the house alight.'

'And as you will know,' Hinchcliffe added, 'my client also made an exhaustive, and to my mind, unnecessary, pursuit of *that* line of inquiry.'

McKenna ignored the solicitor's sarcasm. 'At what point did Smith begin to feature as a suspect, or did he only become so by default, as it were?'

'He featured from the day after she died, when we saw the divorce petition.'

'But according to Beryl, Smith made no secret of his shameful behaviour towards Trisha. Indeed, it's almost as if he gloried in challenging her to take the risk of marrying him. So, as he had nothing to hide, Trisha posed no danger to his new-found comfort.'

'I have to disagree, sir. Even now, Beryl probably knows only what Smith carefully calculated he couldn't keep hidden,' Dugdale said. 'And, of course, there was the fact that Trisha was planning to sue him for maintenance.'

'But why?' McKenna queried. 'He wasn't earning. Beryl had no liability, however rich she might be. Trisha would get nothing.'

'Beryl was giving him a hefty monthly allowance,' Dugdale said, 'as well as picking up the tab for all the bills, so, technically, he had an income to annexe. Once Trisha proved that, to all intents and purposes, Beryl would be forced to keep her, which Beryl wouldn't like one little bit.'

'So are you suggesting she issued some kind of ultimatum that provoked the murder?'

'Simply voicing her objections would be enough to make Smith fret that his new, and much fatter, milch cow might disappear into the distance if he didn't rid himself of the millstone round his neck.'

'Very colourfully put, Inspector, if the metaphor is somewhat mixed, but all assumption.'

'Smith had motive, opportunity, and means.

Anyone can get their hands on a can of petrol.'

'He doesn't drive, and there was no record of his buying petrol.'

'Beryl's garage was converted from the old stables. It's full of all sorts, including several spare petrol cans. She couldn't say if any were missing, or empty when they should have been full, and nor could her hired help.'

'I think you must agree, with or without the benefit of hindsight, that your reasoning was based on rather tenuous links. There was no physical or forensic evidence whatsoever linking Smith to the murder.'

'In a case like this, sir, the best you can hope for is circumstantial evidence. All in all, it was a very clever crime.'

'Where was Broadbent during the crucial period?'

'At the Willows. She lives in, and she spent the afternoon asleep in her flat because she was due on the night shift.'

'The Willows is no significant distance from the house.'

'The other staff say she never left the building.'

'Was her voice compared with the 999 call?'

'No, sir.'

'Perhaps it should have been,' McKenna told him. 'Now, I want to discuss Linda Newton. How well do you know her?'

Hinchcliffe sighed theatrically. 'Is that question *strictly* germane, Superintendent? As you've already been told, my client has known Linda Jarvis, as she was, since they both attended All Saints primary school, albeit that he was about to leave for senior school when she entered at the age of five.' He paused, summoning a little smile. 'To my mind, the issue is *not* relevant. My client is a local man, and is therefore acquainted with a great many local people, a fact

43

which, while often of great assistance in police business, is not significant to this case.'

'At one stage, your client's relationship with Linda Newton went far beyond mere acquaintance,' McKenna said.

Hinchcliffe snapped: 'Is this true?' When Dugdale nodded, he asked: 'Why on earth didn't you say so?'

'I didn't think it mattered,' Dugdale muttered.

'Of course it matters!' The lawyer almost squealed with exasperation. 'When did this happen?'

'A long time ago! Linda was about sixteen.'

'And as you were twenty-two,' McKenna added, 'her father thought the association was quite inappropriate. He ordered you to stop seeing her, didn't he?'

'Yes,' Dugdale admitted, 'but only because he was over-protective with both girls after their mother died. There was no ill feeling.' He paused. 'Nothing would have come of things, anyway, even if he hadn't interfered.'

'Was the relationship sexual?' McKenna asked.

Dugdale gazed at him, almost amused. 'We never got beyond sweaty hand-holding and whispering promises, because Rene Minshull had put the fear of God in both those girls about what she called "goings-on" out of wedlock.' Completely sober once more, he said: 'Not many get to the altar as pure as Linda, and the pity of it is that Trisha got there at all, chaste or not.'

'And you've remained friendly with Linda?'

'I have a very high regard for her, sir, and I get on well with the whole family, including her husband Craig, their two boys, and Fred Jarvis. I was also very fond of Trisha.'

'So when she fell victim to a vicious killer you would naturally do your best to nail that killer,'

McKenna suggested. 'You attended the post-mortem, and must have been quite appalled by her injuries.'

'Is that a question, or a statement, sir?'

'Whichever you wish, Inspector.'

Hinchcliffe intervened. 'I think my client is concerned with the implications.'

'Inspector Dugdale must accept that certain issues have yet to be explored, one of which is the possibility of collusion between himself and Linda Newton.' Turning to his notes, McKenna went on: 'Clearly, he had a long-standing relationship with the whole family. More pertinently, as other suspects were excluded, often on very dubious grounds, leaving Smith as the sole focus of police interest, it could be construed that Linda Newton was directing operations. As Inspector Dugdale is an experienced investigator, that could not have happened without his consent and co-operation. Linda had every reason to want her former brother-in-law punished and, given Inspector Dugdale's admitted affection for her, he may well have decided to oblige.'

'I see.' Hinchcliffe tapped his cheek with spindly arthritic fingers, staring first at Dugdale, then, with a frown, at McKenna. 'Tell me, Superintendent, in the wholly hypothetical, and most unlikely, event that criminal charges may be considered against any of the officers under suspension, are you in a position to offer them the usual opportunity to resign on health grounds?'

Face suffused with anger, Dugdale jumped to his feet and strode to the window. 'I will *not* resign! I've done nothing wrong!'

'You also failed to disclose your interest in Broadbent,' McKenna said.

His face now as grey as the sky beyond the window, Dugdale asked: 'Who told you?'

'My sources of information are not relevant,' McKenna replied. 'Rest assured they will be checked and double-checked, and the informant's motivation taken into consideration.'

'What else didn't you think fit to tell me?' Hinchcliffe demanded of his client.

'I used to go out with Julie.' Dugdale shambled back to his chair. 'I was seventeen, and she was sixteen. She'd left school, but I was still in the sixth form.'

'And was *that* a sexual relationship?' When Dugdale nodded, McKenna said: 'How long did it continue?'

'Off and on until I left school, I suppose.'

'Were you seriously involved?'

'I don't *know*!' His face was almost haggard. 'She was the first girl I'd ever been with.'

'So, you made your own contribution to pushing her "off the rails"?' McKenna persisted. 'Your own phrase, if I recall correctly.'

'Oh, really, Superintendent!' Hinchcliffe was becoming energised by the conflict. 'It's quite apparent this Broadbent girl made no secret of her inclinations, and my client can't have been the first, and obviously wasn't the last, to take advantage of what was on offer. If your case against him is reduced to chastising him over an adolescent sexual fling with a very willing girl who was also over the age of consent, I suggest you terminate these proceedings as of now.'

'As your client failed to disclose this relationship during the murder investigation, I do not accept that his professionalism was intact.'

'What difference would it have made if I *had* said?' A steely challenge gleamed in Dugdale's eyes as he confronted McKenna. 'Apart from making Julie's life harder than it already is? She had to haul herself through acres of shit to get where she is, and she's a right to be respected for it. Wendy Lewis, for one, had plenty of bitchy things to say about her, without my handing out even more ammunition.'

'Does Broadbent know Linda?' asked McKenna.

'Probably,' Dugdale replied. 'Julie knows a lot of people. She's local born and bred.'

Noting the way Dugdale stressed her name, McKenna began to replace the documents in his briefcase. 'For today, the interview is suspended. It is my duty to warn you that you must make no attempt to contact or communicate with any of the principals in this matter, and must avoid any chance or opportune meeting or discussion. Should you ignore my order, you will be arrested and held in custody pending the outcome of my investigation. Do you understand?' he added, looking at Dugdale.

'Yes.'

'And do you agree to comply?'

'My client is well aware of his vulnerable position, and will do whatever is necessary to expedite this most unfortunate and, I must say, most stressful business.' Before Dugdale could take the initiative, Hinchcliffe shepherded the visitors from the room, saying, as they reached the front door: 'Tell me, Superintendent, how long will this charade go on?'

'Charade?'

'While some of my client's actions might be open to mild criticism, you'll find the answers to the questions you *should* be asking lie well outside the knowledge of any police officer.'

'Please don't attempt to suborn me,' McKenna advised. 'Your motives can hardly be described as impartial, whereas my duties must be carried out without malice or favour, as you know.'

Hinchcliffe bared his teeth in a parody of a smile. 'Well, Superintendent, if such a noble ethic succeeds in informing your conduct, it'll be a first in the history of policing, won't it?'

'You're not here to be a silent witness to the proceedings, Jack.' Waiting at the kerb while Ellen, out of earshot, stowed the machinery on the back seat, McKenna began to nag his deputy. 'You left me to do all the work in there.'

'You didn't leave me much to say.'

'You're supposed to provide a balance. I go on the attack, you offer the listening ear.'

'I thought the "nasty copper, nice copper" routine was frowned upon these days?'

'It may well be, but it's still effective.'

'You were effective enough on your own with Dugdale,' Jack commented. 'Granted, he looks awful, but he's got plenty of fight in him, and he's not in the least apologetic.' Walking over to the car, he added: 'And my guess is that he's got nothing to apologise for.'

'You think?' McKenna demanded, striding after him. 'The case he put together against Smith was like a house of cards. No wonder it collapsed!'

I

Rene had gone for the day, leaving the Church Street house spick and span. Dinner over, they sat around the table, drinking freshly brewed coffee.

'Wendy Lewis is next on the list,' McKenna said. 'Janet's doing her interview.'

'She outranks me, sir,' Janet pointed out.

'Neither she nor her brief objected when that was put to them.' Lighting a cigarette, McKenna turned to Ellen. 'Because of the potential conflict of interest between Dugdale, Lewis and Bowden, the Police Federation made sure they have independent representation, but you'll need to check that Linda Newton's solicitor isn't hand in glove with Hinchcliffe or the Miss Pawsley who's representing Lewis.' He frowned. 'Who's Bowden's brief?'

'Anna Singh,' Janet said, toying with a cup of unsweetened black coffee.

'I also intend to interview Julie Broadbent under caution,' McKenna added, 'so whoever she instructs must be cleared of pre-existing interest in anyone else involved with the case.'

'We're seeing Lewis this evening,' Ellen said. 'Bowden's down for tomorrow morning, and Newton's on Wednesday. We could fit in Broadbent afterwards.'

'You know he can't talk to you! He *daren't*!' Susan Dugdale hissed into the telephone. 'Oh, Linda, what have you done?'

'I haven't done anything!' Linda snapped. 'I want to know why the police are after me. They're coming to see me on Wednesday, and I've got to have a solicitor.'

'They know you and Barry used to go out together.'

'Is that all? It was *years* ago!' Linda was astounded.

'They think you put Barry up to arresting Smith.'

'You're kidding!' She laughed.

'It's not funny!'

'No, it's bloody ridiculous. Wait till I tell Craig.'

'They asked him about Julie Broadbent, too,' Susan added.

'Why? What's Julie got to do with it?'

'Oh, I'm sure you know!' Susan's voice stung. 'He went out with her as well. Had a ride on the local bike, you might say.'

'Don't be so nasty, Susan. She wasn't really like that.'

'Wasn't she? The only difference between her and her mother is that she never charged for it. People called their house a slag-heap.'

'I know they did,' Linda agreed, 'but you shouldn't always believe what people say. Rene Minshull went on about them till she was blue in the face, saying Trisha and me would end up like Julie if we didn't keep ourselves to ourselves.'

'You must've heeded her, then, because Craig wouldn't have looked at you twice if he thought you couldn't keep your legs together.'

'Some people just don't stand a fair chance,' Linda said. 'That's the bottom line.' Then she put down the telephone.

'Who was that?' Dugdale asked, as his wife returned to the sitting-room.

'Linda. I told her you can't speak to her.'

'What did she want?'

'She's going to be interviewed under caution.'

'Hardly surprising. Everyone I've ever spoken to will probably get the same treatment.' He sighed. 'At least McKenna's being thorough.'

'And what's his thoroughness likely to unearth?' Susan asked.

'The truth, I hope.'

'But what *is* the truth?' she demanded. 'After what's been dragged up today, I don't know if I can believe a word you say!'

3

Wendy Lewis now lived alone in a pre-war bungalow with angular bay windows on each side of the front door, and a chimney poking from the centre of a pyramid-shaped roof, which topped the eaves like a lid. With others of its kind, the bungalow occupied a quiet, pleasant patch behind the playing fields of Haughton's comprehensive school. Until a month before Smith's arrest she had lived with her mother, but on a bitter March day, when wind and rain were thrashing the newly emerged daffodils and irises in the front garden, the old woman looked through the sitting-room window from her chair near the fire, smiled to herself, and died instantly from a massive heart attack, the smile still on her lips as the death rattle grew in her throat. Wendy found the stiffening corpse at midnight when she returned from a tedious tour of duty and, since that night, had not dared to alter, let alone destroy, a single element of the bungalow's fussy, over-decorated interior. The Sunday morning, four weeks before Smith's appeal hearing, when four purposeful, stony-faced officers from her force's Complaints and Discipline section breached her front door and tore the house apart looking for Father Barclay's letter stayed in her memory as if gouged there. She ran after them from room to room, her innards churning from gut to gullet, and when they had gone away, empty-handed and without a word, she sat on the floor in the middle of chaos, and wept.

She spent weeks rebuilding Mother's house, but even now she would find the odd thing out of place, and was compelled to abandon whatever she was engaged with to make the tiny reparations, as if Mother's shade watched her every move, and judged her every lapse. To some extent she resented her job for coming between her and her mother at the most poignant time in anyone's life, but she deeply resented the way she was orphaned without the least warning. Whether she ever knew and appreciated her mother as an individual was quite outside the range of her emotional literature.

Seated in the same room, and possibly in the same chair in which the old woman died, with her legs at an angle to escape the heat of the fire, Janet considered the possibility that Wendy Lewis had wandered through the investigation into Trisha's death in a state of shock, pushed and pulled in whichever directions others dictated or wanted. She looked her part, Janet thought. Approaching middle age was threading grey through her mousy hair, her lined face was rather sullen, and in her pale-lashed eyes there was the bitter gleam of perpetual disappointment. She blinked a great deal, and her eyes looked rather sore, making Janet wonder if she were taking sedatives or tranquillisers.

The other woman, by the table in the window bay where Ellen had her machinery primed, was, Janet suspected, playing the part written for the occasion. At least fifteen years older than her client, Frances Pawsley wore a thick tweed suit with the jacket buttoned tight over a well-corseted torso, thick stockings, heavy brown brogues, and the uncomfortable, overheated appearance of post-menopausal womanhood. The greying hair above her florid face was clipped almost as short as a man's. Her over-stuffed fingers meddled with the shiny red apples and freckled bananas in a green glass fruit bowl, pushed it aside, then began to nudge an inquisitive spider towards the open jaws of a Venus flytrap, in various stages of banqueting, rearing from a terracotta pot. Fleetingly, Janet wondered if Miss Pawsley and her client had other than a professional relationship, but could not decipher the many tantalisingly surreptitious looks that passed between them.

Tape-recorder buzzing and Ellen's fingers poised over the keyboard of her laptop, Janet completed the formalities of interview, then said: 'Now you've had the opportunity to reread your statements, Sergeant Lewis, is there anything you wish to amend or alter?'

'No.'

'Is there anything in the report which Inspector Dugdale submitted to the Crown Prosecution Service with which you disagree?'

'No.'

'Anything you feel was omitted?'

'No.'

'Do you have any reservations whatsoever about the investigation?'

'No.'

'Or about Smith's arrest?'

'No.'

'Are you then stating that you were, and are, perfectly happy with the conduct of the investigation, the conduct and motivations of the officers concerned, and the outcome?'

'Yes.'

'Prior to the appeal, did you have any knowledge of the letter that Father Fauvel apparently received from Father Barclay and allegedly handed to Inspector Dugdale?'

'No. I'd never even *heard* about it before the appeal papers were disclosed.'

'Do you know Father Fauvel?'

'Yes.'

'In what capacity?'

'As the Roman Catholic parish priest.'

'Have you ever spoken to him?'

'Yes.'

'How often?'

'I don't know.' Wendy reached for the cigarette packet lying on the kerb of the hearth, and fumbled inside. 'Lots of times. We're RC, and Mother went to Mass regularly.' Cigarette extracted, she pushed it between her lips, and struck a match, the flame wavering in the draught. 'I couldn't go as often as I should because of work, but he was a great comfort to me when Mother died so suddenly.'

Watching tears swell in the bloodshot eyes, Janet asked: 'On the basis of your own knowledge of the investigation, have you reached a conclusion, tentative or otherwise, about what might have happened to Father Barclay's letter?'

Before she could respond, Frances intervened. 'Superintendent McKenna's whole investigation really depends on a hypothesis, doesn't it? After all, no one's ever seen this famous letter.'

54

'But we do have Father Barclay's sworn testimony for the appeal, which satisfied three highly experienced judges,' Janet reminded her. 'We must assume he sent the letter.'

Frances smiled. 'As long as you don't forget that assumptions are always dangerous.' To Wendy, she said: 'You may answer, dear. We've already discussed what you'll say.'

Her agonised features betraying the conflict between faith and professional loyalty, Wendy drew a deep breath. 'I can't believe Father Brett would lie. I believe he handed over the letter, like he said. Why would he lie about it? He had nothing to gain. He wasn't even involved.'

'And you still maintain you don't wish to amend your statements?' asked Janet.

Frances stepped in once more. 'DC Evans wants to know why didn't you voice your doubts before the appeal, or when you were interviewed prior to suspension.'

'I couldn't think straight! I struggled with my conscience for weeks!' Wendy's voice shook. 'If I believed Mr Dugdale, I was as good as blaspheming, and if I believed Father Brett, I'd be ruining a man I've trusted for years.'

'How did you reach a decision?' Janet asked. 'What guidance did you take?'

'I took Wendy to my parish priest,' Frances replied. 'He's a stranger, but she could have confidence in him.'

'And do you believe you reached the right decision?' Janet added.

'Oh, please! Don't make me go over it again. I thought I'd go mad.'

'I think you can accept Wendy's decision, dear,' the solicitor told Janet. 'She suffered long enough and hard enough in the making of it.'

55

'Very well,' Janet conceded. 'Could you tell me how long you've known Father Fauvel?'

'Since Mother and I moved to Haughton, about ten years ago. After Daddy died, Mother wanted a clean break. She hated living in Manchester.'

'How long has Father Fauvel been here?'

'Oh, years,' Wendy said. 'At least twenty.'

'What made you join the police? You trained as a social worker, I understand.'

'Wendy *worked* in social work,' Frances said. 'But she wasn't qualified, and had little prospect of getting qualifications unless she financed her own training. Her parents couldn't afford to keep her while she studied, so rather than remain in a dead-end job, she applied to the police, where she's done very well, in my opinion. She's developed several specialisms, most notably in the management and investigation of crimes against women and children.'

'And I'm responsible for area child protection,' Wendy added to her solicitor's eulogy. 'It was because of my background that I interviewed the residents at the Willows. I'd worked with the mentally handicapped at one time.'

'What's their level of incapacity?' Janet asked. 'As they're not hospitalised, some at least must be capable of semi-independent living.'

'I wouldn't like to put it to the test,' Wendy replied forcefully. 'Most of them have multiple incapacity, including epilepsy, and I'd say seven are profoundly handicapped.' She tossed her cigarette stub into the fire. 'Today's polite term for them is "people with learning difficulties", which implies they're capable of being taught, but they're not. The Willows is a twenty-bed unit, and it's nearly always full. They've got three or four high grades who *could* exist in the community with proper support, but the last time residents were sent on the community care programme, they ended up dossing on the street.' Reaching for another cigarette, she added: 'Father Brett's disgusted about it, but unfortunately he doesn't make the decisions.'

'I thought the Area Health Trust ran the Willows,' Janet said.

'It's owned by the Roman Catholic Diocese, and run as a joint initiative with the Trust.'

'Who's responsible for staffing and general management?'

'A committee,' Wendy said. 'Father Brett's on it.'

'Those details aren't in Inspector Dugdale's report to the CPS,' Janet pointed out.

'Were they relevant?' Frances asked.

'Probably not,' Janet admitted. 'To return to the residents, did you think any of them might have pertinent information, whether they realised it or not?'

Wendy shook her head. 'I spent a lot of time with them, but there was nothing, which didn't surprise me.'

'Julie Broadbent was rather a different case, wasn't she? You felt she was being evasive.'

'And hostile,' Wendy added.

'But you're now aware of her background and teenage excursions into delinquency?'

'I wasn't at the time. Mr Dugdale said he didn't want to create prejudice.'

'Did he ever interview her?'

'Not as far as I know.'

'Do you accept that Broadbent's evasiveness is satisfactorily explained by her historical associations with the police?'

Drawing on her cigarette, Wendy gazed into the fire. 'No. Not really, and for several reasons, including my intuition.' She lodged the cigarette on the kerb of the hearth, held up the fingers of her left hand, and began to count off with her right. 'First, she sat in on most of the residents' interviews, and couldn't have been more helpful. Second, she'd have been checked out for a criminal record before she got the job there, so that secret was already out. Third,' she said, pushing down her middle finger, 'I got to know her quite well, because interviewing the mentally handicapped takes time and patience. She must have known I didn't pose a threat. And fourth, her teenage delinquencies didn't amount to much.'

'She might still be ashamed of them,' Janet suggested.

'She might,' Wendy conceded. 'She might have thought I'd sit in judgement on her, like a lot of women would and, for all I know, she could still be promiscuous. But none of that explains why she clammed up so fast.'

'At what point did that occur?'

'I can't say, because it wasn't until later I realised she had. I've racked my brains, but I can't pin-point the trigger.'

'Was Colin Bowden actively involved in the interviews?'

'He came along on occasion, but he was quite happy to leave things to me. To be honest, I think he felt completely out of his depth, which I accepted.'

Frances struggled to her feet, breath wheezing in her corseted chest. 'Don't know about you gels,' she said, disarmingly conspiratorial, 'but I need a drink, preferably alcoholic. I'll perc coffee for the rest of you.' She plodded to the door, adding: 'Interview suspended 19.34.'

The choice made for her, Ellen switched off the tape-recorder.

'Don't mind Frances,' Wendy said. 'She's been our solicitor for years, so she can't help treating me as if I'm still in ankle socks.' She smiled, rather sadly. 'She was an absolute brick when Mother died.'

'Was your mother ill for long?'

'She wasn't ill at all. I think I thought she'd live for ever, then she just went, like the light had gone out.'

'It must have been a dreadful shock,' Janet sympathised.

'Oh, it was! And I still miss her. I plan to do something, or I hear a bit of juicy gossip, and I still say to myself: "Oh, I can't wait to tell Mother." Then I remember she's not here any more, and it hits me like a fist in the chest. I even find myself feeling winded, at times.'

'You can ask if shock affected her professional judgement when the tape's switched back on.' Frances appeared in the doorway with a glass of neat whisky in her pudgy fingers. 'Personally, I think it did, but Wendy said she went on to auto pilot, as it were.' She returned to the kitchen, and Janet heard the clatter of crockery landing on a tin tray, and the sucking sound of a refrigerator being opened and closed. The aroma of percolating coffee seeped into the room.

'I wouldn't know, would I?' Wendy asked. 'If my judgement was affected. It's far too subjective, and Mother's death made such root-and-branch changes nothing could ever be the same. There's always going to be a before and after.'

'Were you dependent on her? Emotionally?'

'That's a silly question, if ever I heard one!' Frances clumped back into the room, put the tray on the table with another loud clatter, and resumed her seat. 'Of *course* she was dependent, and even though they had the odd row, they were still very, very close. Most of the arguments came about because it's always a struggle for a mother and daughter to redefine their relationship into something acceptable to two grown women.' She glanced at Ellen. 'You can switch on again now, dear. D'you like cream and sugar with your coffee?'

When Wendy made no attempt to take control of this simplest and least contentious of proceedings, Janet wondered if she always needed someone on whom to depend, and were therefore always vulnerable to more powerful personalities. As Frances handed over her coffee, black and steaming in a pretty china cup, she assessed the impressions gathered in the last hour, asking herself if Wendy Lewis's rather naive responses implied more than a somewhat immature personality under extreme stresses. 'You realise that your change of heart about the letter creates an entirely new set of circumstances, don't you?'

Wendy nodded.

'Does Father Fauvel have much day-to-day contact with the Willows?'

'As much as he can, but he's very busy,' Wendy said. 'He's the only priest permanently on the management committee, and he takes his turn on the various parish committees and so forth. The church is involved in a lot of community activities, far more than the Anglicans.'

'But they've only got the vicar and a curate,' Ellen said. 'Whereas, apart from the nuns and Father Fauvel, there are usually at least two junior priests lodged at the presbytery and doing something with the church.'

'Most people still think the Protestants aren't very well served,' Wendy commented snappishly.

Putting her cup in its matching saucer, Janet said: 'Inspector Dugdale said you'd researched Beryl

Stanton Smith's background. Although the relevant details are written up, I wonder if you could elaborate. What were your personal impressions of her?'

'Well,' Wendy began, slurping her coffee like a child, 'at first, I thought: "What's a woman like this doing with a loser like Smith?" Have you met him yet?' As Janet shook her head, she went on: 'When you do, you'll see what I mean, which is all I'm saying, because I don't want to give the impression we were so prejudiced about him it blinded us to the truth.' She blinked fiercely. 'I mean, Beryl's filthy rich. When she sold the shop site it was as good as winning the lottery jackpot. Her house is a gorgeous old rectory at the foot of the moors, and it's been the family home since her grandfather moved out here. He made pots of money before the war, and he and her father made pots more afterwards, so she led a charmed life. She went to a posh boarding-school in Derbyshire, had her own horses, and just about everything else that money could buy.' Wendy smiled, rather spitefully. 'The only thing she couldn't apparently get was a husband, so in the end, she bought one.'

'What brought you to that conclusion?'

'She's very spoiled and arrogant, although I'm not sure she's aware of it, and she just can't relate to people. Maybe all that money isolated her from reality, or simply turned her into a dreadful snob.'

'Their relationship could be based on genuine affection,' Janet suggested. 'Even love. Where did they meet?'

'At the shop, apparently. Smith met both of them there. Trisha was a salesgirl, and Beryl was cracking the whip. I don't know if he kept in regular contact with Beryl, but she was definitely on the scene before the divorce, offering a shoulder to cry on, if nothing else. She told me, in confidence, that she'll never forgive herself for standing by and doing nothing while Trisha ate into his very core like a "fat maggot".'

'Are you suggesting she deliberately encouraged the divorce by tempting him with a far more promising alternative?'

'I think that's the way it was.' Imagination triggered, Wendy added: 'It's a classic example of one person's needs dovetailing perfectly with someone else's.'

'Or the planned occupation of a mutually fertile feeding ground,' Janet commented.

'That's a very clever observation, dear.' Frances leaned forward to pat Janet's arm, and let her fat fingers loiter for a moment too long. 'But really not necessary and, to my mind, a way of showing off your superior education.' As her fingers drew away, almost reluctantly, she frowned. 'You should have more respect for the background of your fellow officers. Not many people can enjoy the privileges you had, and Wendy, for one, struggled to get where she is. Nothing was handed to *her* on a plate.'

Janet's self-control stopped her from engaging in the verbal skirmish Frances clearly hoped for. 'I see you've done your homework, Miss Pawsley,' she said, 'although I'm not sure every answer would earn a tick. However, I do apologise for any offence. None was intended, I assure you.'

'I'm glad to hear it.' Frances surveyed her, still frowning. 'I trust you'll make it clear to Superintendent McKenna that Wendy expects to get back to work very soon. Being under such a cloud is dreadful for her.'

'And for the other officers,' Janet replied, 'as Mr

McKenna has stressed.' She faced Wendy once more. 'Returning to Broadbent, Sergeant Lewis, did you challenge her about her evasiveness?'

Wendy shook her head. 'There was no point. She'd only have looked at me like I was stupid, then denied everything. She's tough when she wants to be.'

'Did she ever discuss Linda Newton?'

'No.'

'Did she indicate that she knew Inspector Dugdale?'

'What d'you mean?'

'Exactly what I say.'

Wendy shrugged. 'Not that I recall. Do they know each other? As friends, I mean?'

Without answering the question, Janet went on: 'Did Linda Newton discuss Broadbent at any time?'

'No.'

'Or Inspector Dugdale?'

'All the time. She made out they're thick as thieves, and got quite shirty when I turned up to talk to her. She was *always* asking for him. The rest of us didn't count in her book.'

'Did you discuss either woman with Inspector Dugdale?'

'Not really. Not in depth.'

'Why not?'

'He wouldn't. When I asked him how to handle Broadbent's secretiveness, he told me about her background, and said to leave it. When I said Linda was being funny with me, and demanding to talk to him, he just shrugged it off.' She stared. 'Is it important? Does it mean something? Should I have reported him at the time?'

'Reported him to whom?' Janet asked.

'Superintendent Ryman, of course.'

'But what could you have said, dear?' Frances asked. 'You can't very well report a hunch, can you?'

To Janet, she added: 'I think we should leave this kind of speculation out of the equation, don't you?'

'I'm not speculating,' Janet replied, 'although I suspect Sergeant Lewis is allowing imagination to colour her responses. At the beginning of this interview she had no reservations about Inspector Dugdale, but then admitted she believes he suppressed vital evidence. Now, she seems to be concocting a conspiracy theory involving him and Newton.'

'And is that not precisely in line with Superintendent McKenna's thinking?' Frances asked, snatching victory in the fight Janet assumed had been abandoned.

'I beg your pardon?'

'I think you heard me.'

'Where did you get that information, Miss Pawsley?'

'Goodness me, we don't disclose our sources,' Frances said, pursing her mouth. 'You should know better than to ask, but quite frankly, my dear, I'm not sure you do. In fact, I'm not even sure you should be here. Wendy outranks you.'

'When that issue was put to you both, you had no objections.'

'We didn't realise how *young* you are,' Frances replied. 'More importantly, I imagined you'd be infinitely more experienced. After all, every police force has its complement of highly experienced officers in the lower ranks, but as it is, I think you're completely out of your depth.'

'Then I have no choice but to terminate the interview and report back to Superintendent McKenna.' Stowing notebook, papers and pens in her bag with shaking hands, Janet rose. 'I trust you will ensure your client abides by the restrictions on her conduct and communications,' she added. 'I also trust you will remind her she is liable to arrest should she choose to breach those conditions.'

<h1 style="text-align:center">4</h1>

'Damn it!' Janet thumped the steering wheel. '*Damn it!*'

'Stop over-reacting,' Ellen said. She looked back at the bungalow, where the light from the room they had just vacated glowed warmly behind closed curtains, dimly illuminating the ice-rimed shrubs and hedges of the little suburban garden. 'Pawsley's an embittered, frustrated old dyke panting to get her hands inside Lewis's undies and, living in hope, she'll dance to whatever tune Lewis plays. Right now, her "little girl in distress" routine is plucking at the old bat's heart-strings.'

'And very successfully,' Janet commented, firing the engine.

'Then again,' Ellen added, 'it could be her only tune. In my opinion, Lewis reached the limits of her emotional and intellectual development about twenty years ago, and she's spent the time since perfecting the art of manipulation. When Mother kicked the bucket, probably out of utter desperation, Pawsley became the poodle.' She yanked down the seat-belt. 'They're both seething with sexual frustration, and I thought the atmosphere was very girls' boarding-school. Didn't you?'

'It was something,' Janet agreed, 'and rather suffocating, but all that aside, they've presented us with a serious problem. Dugdale's obviously been shooting off his mouth.'

'Don't fall into Pawsley's trap. She *wants* us to drop on him like a ton of bricks, but she probably got her information from Hinchcliffe.' Massaging her cold hands in front of the warm-air vents, Ellen added: 'The legal profession survives on internal networks and tittle-tattle. These solicitors will be in touch constantly, updating, querying, planning strategies, while, in total ignorance, Dugdale and co. think only *their* interests are calling the shots. Believe me, I know.'

'I'm sure you do.' Driving along the poorly lit road, Janet several times felt the rear wheels lose grip on patches of black ice.

'What's your impression of Lewis?' asked Ellen. 'As a police officer?'

'My impression of her as a person, which will entirely determine how she functions professionally, is that she's weak, indecisive, lacking in insight, influenced by emotion and passing thoughts, and has poor reasoning.' Reaching the High Street, she turned left. 'And because she herself hasn't a clue what she's doing or why she's doing it, she creates confusion in others. Quite frankly, she's the last person I'd have in charge of area child protection.'

'She's very taken with her own hunches.' Gazing through the window at empty pavements, darkened shops, and garishly lit pubs, outside which ugly-looking men circled and taunted bare-legged women in tiny skirts, Ellen shivered. 'God! This is one depressing town.'

'It's no different from a lot of other towns, although I do find the moors rather sinister. But that's inevitable, I suppose, being so near the old haunts of Myra Hindley and Ian Brady.'

'And if they'd lived somewhere else, perhaps they wouldn't have turned out quite so bad. Your perspectives and behaviour depend on your environment.'

66

'Human pain and misery are much the same everywhere.' Seeing the Junction Inn ahead, Janet prepared to turn.

'But pain and misery are usually the outcome of what people do, not the reason,' Ellen commented. 'After all, you didn't embark on last year's holiday romance with a life-threatening upshot in mind, did you?'

The car jerked as Janet's hands tightened on the wheel, her knuckles gleaming white.

'Hard though it may be,' Ellen went on, 'it's time to put it behind you. We're all liable to lapses of one kind or another.' She smiled gently. 'After all, I was five months pregnant on my wedding day.'

'But your child lived.'

'And yours didn't, because an ectopic pregnancy is completely unsurvivable. It was no one's fault.'

'I thought of having an abortion,' Janet admitted, 'and when the decision was made for me, it seemed like God's judgement.' She fumbled in the open cigarette pack on the dashboard, clicking her lighter three times before it flared. 'I became my own child's tomb.'

'Don't be so Gothic,' Ellen said. 'What d'you think made Lewis what she is? Whenever push comes to shove, I'll bet she collapses with relief on the indoctrination of a lifetime, where the authority and infallibility of the Church, and of God's representatives on earth, otherwise known as Father this, that or the other, rule her head and her heart. She's irrational and irresolute because unquestioning obedience was drummed into her from birth. She wouldn't even dare a reasonable doubt, let alone active heresy, for fear of eternal hell-fire. And don't say,' she added, as Janet almost rammed the wall of the Bull's car-park, 'that your religion's any different.

67

You're completely indoctrinated with guilt over matters of the flesh.'

'It's one way of keeping the beast under control.'

'Oh, for heaven's sake!' Ellen was exasperated. 'That's complete drivel, especially from a woman of your intelligence!'

Janet stared through the windscreen, with tears in her eyes.

'I'm willing to offer a shoulder to cry on,' Ellen went on, 'but only up to a point. You've already had more than adequate support from your colleagues, and it's time you took yourself in hand. Career-wise, McKenna's given you a plum job by bringing you into this investigation, but if *I* come to the conclusion you're not functioning on all cylinders, believe me, Janet, you'll be back in North Wales so fast your feet won't touch the ground. *And* you'll be facing a compulsory medical and psychological evaluation.' She opened the car door, shivering in the blast of freezing air. 'You're not a child, and you've got to take responsibility for yourself. And you can start by eating properly. Just remember, I'll be watching you.'

5

Taking the first batch of laundry from the washing machine, Julie Broadbent wondered if she worked the graveyard shift more often than the other staff at the Willows because she lived in, or because this was yet another imposition she allowed the world to thrust upon her. She opened the door of a tumble drier, to find clumps of fluff stuck to the inside and, biting her lip with annoyance because she also seemed to be the only person ever to carry out the irritating little chore, she detached the filter, pulled off the blanket-like layer, replaced the filter, loaded the machine, and put another batch of soiled sheets in the washer. Every night the same four or five residents would wet the bed and, at times of particular stress, many more followed suit, as if punishing the staff. Summer and winter, the laundry stank of urine, because the machines had to be used when cheap off-peak electricity was available, and Julie had lost count of the spring and summer nights spent loading and unloading washers and driers, folding and smoothing sheets, pillowcases, quilt covers, and mountains of clothing, while the rest of the world was free to chase its dreams.

The machines busy for the next forty-five minutes, she went to the kitchen to make a drink, and found herself donning rubber gloves to scour greasy sinks and work tops while the kettle boiled. The Willows employed cooks and cleaners, but like the fluff in the driers, the grease in the kitchen was left for her attention. Sprinkling scouring powder, rubbing surfaces, wringing out cloths in steaming water, she stared absent-mindedly through the big window over the sink, watching lights pop off one after another in the raw brick houses which now overran the decimated grounds. In her childhood, the Willows had been surrounded by acres of terraced lawns, formal flowerbeds, and trees, all a source of heart-twisting envy to one from a damp-infested two-up and two-down with a backyard barely long enough for the clothes-line, and a front door flush with the pavement. She would kneel for hours on end at her bedroom window, her fingers prodding relentlessly into the rotten wood of the frame, and dream of being a real daughter of that imposing hillside house.

As she hung the dishcloths to air over the edges of the sinks, Julie remembered that horrible afternoon when reality had punctured her eleven-year-old's dreams like a rusty nail popping a pretty balloon. She had been exploring a new way home from school to avoid the tedium of an endlessly repeated journey and, about to cross the road by the old grammar school building, she heard the clatter of horses' hooves behind her. Dramatic, heroic scenes of rescue flashed through her mind at the speed of light, but then Beryl Kay rounded the corner, tensely astride the pretty dapple-grey horse for which her grandfather had just paid £7000. The animal pulled at the bit, saliva dripping from its mouth as it tried to release the stranglehold, while Beryl, indoctrinated with the belief that animals must be controlled if they were not to run amok, reined back so hard that the bit drew blood, streaking the saliva with red.

At the time, Beryl was eighteen, and had her own car as well as the horse. Julie could not know, because she could not differentiate between those luxuries, that Beryl infinitely preferred the mindlessly obedient car to a horse, which required a level of empathy and communication completely beyond her ken. All Julie could do was judge the incongruity and utter unfairness of a beautiful animal at the mercy of this sullen-faced girl whose eyes were dulled by constantly looking only inwards upon herself. While her gaze followed Beryl and her heart kept pace with the beat of the hooves, her mind assessed the unbridgeable differences and rammed the knowledge down her throat like a purgative. In that instant, Julie was near overwhelmed by the need to rush into the road, to startle the horse into throwing Beryl or to be trampled under the dancing hooves; but to make a defining gesture and create a memorable moment. As it was, she simply hung against the wall until Beryl went out of sight.

To Beryl's grandfather, the horse symbolised the achievements spawned by his own early envies, so she was obliged to perform her role in his scheme of things, and whether she liked or loathed the animal was not the point. When she sulked around the paddock in the grounds of the old parsonage, he saw the incongruity in a different light, and feared that while his money might give her the proverbial leg up and keep her astride her patch of the world, he could not buy her breeding, for all he could buy her a thoroughbred horse. The blood which filled her veins was sluggish with commonness, and her voice and manners spoke only of vulgar money.

Julie no longer envied Beryl, whose eyes grew duller each year, and, having realised the dream of living at the Willows, albeit by strange default, she knew that too was far from enviable. It had nothing to do with the ravaged acres of once forbidden gardens, the Formica tables and plastic chairs strewn across the parquet floor of the dining-room, the rickety chip-board furniture in the bedrooms, the cheap flowered cretonne at the windows, or the smells of urine in the laundry, but was simply her response to a building constructed, like Beryl's life, for its own sake, and without reference to the shape of its occupants.

While her teabag brewed in its mug, Julie leaned on the work-top, a cold draught touching her ankles. A north-easterly wind, yet to reach full strength, whined around the gable ends, and she fancied there was already the smell of snow in the air. Tea in hand, she went into the hall, to listen for a few moments at the bottom of the huge carved staircase, but heard only the noises which belonged to the house itself, and the wind thumping in the chimney behind the blocked-off fireplace. Two other members of staff were in the house with her, sleeping-in on call, as the jargon went, while she was on waking duty. Satisfied her charges were quiet for the present, she unlocked the office, switched on the overhead light, sat behind the desk, and opened the log book. Cyril Bennett, the manager of the Willows, had left no instructions for her and, for once, the residents had passed an uneventful day. Their individual files disclosed neither novelty nor urgency and, the regular trips to the laundry excepted, she would be hard pressed to fill the hours until the day shift arrived at seven. No one would know, or mind, if she went to the flat in the old attic nursery, which had been her home for the last five years, but she would not settle if she did. Readying herself for the night shift, she had slept most of the afternoon, dreaming a confusing jumble of images and impressions, which made sense in sleep but none when she woke to the summons of the telephone beside her bed. She knew from the colour of the sky that darkness had not long since come and, listening to the voice on the other end of the line, she wondered if the man who, she was told, insisted on seeing her on Wednesday, might be the same man she had seen earlier today, trying to escape from Trisha's house.

But whether he were or not, it made no difference. She would keep her own counsel, for even if he believed her, whatever she might say would come too late. Staring unseeingly at the candy-striped curtains that Mrs Bennett believed might bring some colour to the dismal room, her thoughts jumped once more on to the mental treadmill they were condemned to trudge, getting nowhere because there was nowhere to go. It was her own vision of hell, without an exit, so she put up her hands and gripped fistfuls of hair, tugging until the pain turned to pleasure.

As a child, she was beset by the fears that haunt all children who think beyond the immediate. She feared hunger, homelessness, her mother dead, her mother taken away, herself dragged screaming from her mother's arms, but nothing prepared her for what she would bring upon herself, simply by breaking the unconscious habit of a lifetime. In Trisha Smith she recognised the shape of a fellow being, and cast aside innate caution to share her thoughts and her secrets. In so doing, she brought about Trisha's death, while her own, infinitely smaller punishment was to have Trisha's friendship replaced by mortal terror, which had now kept her company through 825 days. And Julie remembered, all those long nights since she had first realised, as she was climbing into bed, that she might be about to spend her last night on earth, a notion that scuttled through her mind like a spider invading a house each time she laid her head on the pillow.

Until Smith left, Trisha's life was not worth living, but afterwards she would tell Julie of the small excitements and little pleasures which were, unbeknown, only lighting her path towards the flames that would consume her. Julie was on her way to Trisha's house when she first saw the smoke rising from the copse. Knowing the billowing grey mass told of more than a fire in the sitting-room hearth, she ran towards the derelict mill, terrified that Smith, who loved destruction, had been seduced into some violent extravagance. She went through the gap where the mill gates once stood, and into the yard, stumbling among the strewn rubbish and broken bricks, crunching over shattered glass, towards the short-cut to the house. When the front of the house came into view, she stopped dead in her tracks. Later, she thought of the fire as an orgy, flames alighting on objects and each other with consuming passion, but then she thought only of Trisha. By the time she saw him, careening out of the lane in a small blue car, she was in the telephone kiosk, panting out a frantic message to the emergency services, and praying that Trisha, if she had not escaped, was already dead.

To this day, she did not know if Trisha's killer had seen her. He went about his usual business without a sign of the extra burden on his soul. But, Julie admitted to herself, so too did she, for life forced such accommodations on guilty and innocent alike. She stopped tugging her hair, and began to count the strands she had torn from her scalp.

I

COMING OUT

Our chief reporter, Gaynor Holbrook, has an exclusive interview with Piers Stanton Smith, whose conviction for the murder of his first wife, Trisha, was recently quashed on appeal.

Piers Stanton Smith and myself sit in matching wing chairs in the study of his home. It is a tasteful, book-lined retreat with fine antique furniture. Firelight plays on the chiselled bones of his face, emphasising his brilliant blue eyes. Smoking incessantly in nervous little puffs, he wears an open-necked silk shirt, an Aran cardigan, designer jeans, Gucci loafers, and a Rolex watch. Bitter memories haunt his eyes as he describes the terror of going to prison for a crime he did not commit.

Throwing his cigarette in the fire, he runs his fingers through his fair curly hair. He is finding it hard to believe in his freedom. 'I'm terrified it was just a dream,' he says. He fears being taken back to prison, and now has a counsellor. But nothing can change public opinion about Trisha's death. Beaten senseless by her killer, she suffocated in her blazing house. He says her family will always be after his blood. 'I'm like a dog with a tin can tied to its tail.' He is afraid the police will also hound him. 'I'll get the blame when the officers who put me away get prosecuted

75

themselves.' He regards Superintendent McKenna, who is investigating the actions of Haughton police, as a 'saviour'. 'I hope he comes to see me soon,' he adds.

He has never denied that he was occasionally violent towards Trisha during their marriage. Without that history, people would have been less inclined to believe he killed her. But he denies being a vicious bully. Explaining the build-up of pressures and tensions which led to their rows, he talks of the pain and frustration which led him to lash out. 'Trisha never understood me, and I know her sister Linda just fed into her fantasies about me. Trisha started the rows every time, knowing exactly how they'd end. She did it on purpose to make me feel like a monster.'

Shuddering, he reaches for another cigarette. 'I didn't say much at the trial, because everybody had enough grief, but Trisha was incredibly screwed-up, and she projected it all on me. She couldn't be nasty enough. She called me a work-shy parasite because I couldn't get a job. Then I bought myself a teddy bear. I never had one when I was little. It was comforting, so I carried it around sometimes. She said I looked as camp and silly as Sebastian Flyte in the *Brideshead Revisited* film, so I threw the bear on the fire to shut her up.' He looks at me steadily, his eyes opaque. 'She tried to destroy me, and that's why the violence erupted. I felt I was in the thick of a battle, and the only thing on my mind was getting out alive.'

Trisha's divorce petition referred to an horrendous attack after she had been in hospital. 'It wasn't like she said,' he insists. 'I never kicked her. She started bleeding because she'd come out of hospital too soon, and wouldn't take it easy. I was thunderstruck when I saw what she'd written.'

During the marriage, he became a Roman Catholic convert, and that led to further problems. 'Religious convictions are the most deeply personal things, but Trisha was forever sneering.

When Father Brett tried to talk to her about what me becoming a Catholic meant for us, she wouldn't even let him in the house. She accused me of putting up another false front, like when I changed my name. Thank God Father Brett stopped her from poisoning my faith the way she'd poisoned everything else that mattered.'

When he was sixteen, he discarded the name 'Peter Smith'. His new name was an extension of the childhood fantasy life which allowed him to survive the brutal reality. His marriage to Trisha at the young age of twenty-one was another part of the fantasy. She was several years his senior, like Beryl. 'I hoped for a new history by giving myself a new identity,' he tells me. 'But the real challenge is to make something of little Peter Smith from the council flats.'

At the trial, it was claimed that little Peter Smith watched his teacher Joyce Colclough burn to death in her crashed car. When I broach the matter, his body jerks into the foetal position, arms locked around his head. 'Only you know what happened that day,' I add.

Slowly, he exposes his face. 'Mrs Colclough was kind to me. Before we moved to the council flat, she used to take me home from school. We lived well out of Sheffield, in a dreadful hovel near a stream. The floors were just tiles on top of mud, and every time it rained, the mud soaked through the mats. I had to wear wellingtons indoors.' There is a long, sad silence. 'I don't remember what happened. Maybe a rabbit ran into the road, or a cat. She cried out and swerved, and we hit the tree. There was an awful noise, then nothing. When I tried to move, I couldn't feel my legs, and I think I passed out. I remember being outside the car, trying to open her door. Then I smelled petrol, and at the same moment there was a sort of whooshing noise, and my legs started to burn. I ran up to the road, praying for somebody to come, but nobody did.'

His physical scars amounted to slight burns, a

few scratches and a bruised head. But the mental trauma of the accident was pernicious. It was almost too shocking to talk about, like his squalid childhood. After he left home at sixteen, he never saw his mother again, and burned the few photographs he had. But memories of her are ingrained in his mind like the dirt and nicotine stains ingrained in her skin.

'Her real name was Hilda,' he says. 'But she liked being called Bunty. That's probably how I got the idea of changing my name.' He takes another cigarette from a slim gold case chased on both sides, then puts it back. 'All I know about my father is that he took up with her, stayed around long enough to father me, joined the army, went AWOL, got run over by a train, and had both his legs cut off.'

I ask myself how one innocent person can be pursued by so much tragedy. He continues talking, his moods shifting unexpectedly in a way I begin to find quite disturbing. Some of the things he says are striking. Bunty was 'his only point of reference', because there was no extended family. He recalls grinding poverty, filth, rats, head-lice and bedbugs. His childhood memories are like the 'mess dogs make of a bin bag'. As he succumbs to the temptation inside the golden cigarette case, he tells me about the 'uncles' Bunty entertained. The shame she never felt is another tin can tied to his tail. Trisha knew all about that childhood. It was something else she used as a weapon after twisting it into a horrible new shape.

Suddenly he says: 'In a way, it's Bunty's fault Mrs Colclough died.' His glance flicks over me, like fingers. 'I used to walk the three miles back from school to keep out of her way as long as possible. Mrs Colclough found out what I was doing, and made me have lifts in her car.'

I remember what was said at the trial about that accident.

'Forensic examination of the car yielded no clues,' Counsel for the Prosecution commented. 'And at the scene, there were only the marks

some forty feet away where she skidded off the road before plunging down an embankment and into the tree.'

'Joyce was the most careful driver,' Henry Colclough insisted. 'I think he pulled the steering wheel. I know he did something!' Wringing his hands, he added: 'I saw him when the police drove me there, and there was a light in his eyes as if the flames were still blazing in front of him. And I know he hated Joyce. She told me about the trouble she was having with him at school, and all because she was trying to help!'

'None the less, Mr Colclough, that's a far cry from suggesting he precipitated your wife's accident.'

'He'd threatened her. And she took it seriously. He said if she didn't leave him alone, he'd make sure she had to.'

But as good teachers have always done, Joyce Colclough was simply trying to help a poor, inadequate mother.

Bunty claimed benefits, never declaring her casual jobs. Swindling the system landed her in prison. 'First the social security people

came knocking on the door,' he says. 'Then the police turned up.' He was sent to a children's home run by nuns. 'It was like going to heaven. I prayed they'd keep her locked up for ever.'

He paints vivid pictures of his dead mother. One of Bunty's jobs in the black economy was sweeping up in a knife and fork factory. 'She'd come back with her shoes and trouser hems silvery with swarf.' She also worked nights in a chip shop. 'Then the whole house stank of stale fat.' Her unwashed hair hung like weeds round her face, and smeared grease on the chair backs.

After the trial, I visited the corporation block where he lived as a child. It is still notoriously deprived. I saw another generation of under-class children playing in squalor. They had runny eyes and noses, and sneezed a lot. Somebody told me it is an allergy to cockroaches.

Bunty occasionally hit her son. Most of the time, she paid him little attention. 'After I spent those few blessed months with the nuns,' he explains, 'I saw my foul little world with different eyes. It wasn't from spite that people called Bunty a "dirty slut". Even in that dump, she marked us out, and I got bullied for it. The other kids chucked stones at me, like I was a mangy dog, so I started going on the attack first. That's why I could be violent to Trisha. I was sensitised by experience.'

He talks at some length of the insights counselling has provided. Uppermost in his mind was the deep need to escape his circumstances before they destroyed him. Books were his first escape. He quotes a telling remark by Rousseau. 'When society treats someone as ugly, they *become* ugly.' Shockingly, he saw himself as others must. It was the spur to leave Bunty. He rented a bedsit and worked as an office boy for a while. After he got a job with an advertising agency, he was sent to Haughton to help with Kay's spring campaign. Trisha was one of their salesgirls.

'Would to God I could put back the clock!' He looks inward, eyes darkened. 'I came out of the marriage with the clothes on my back and a few books. I didn't want any reminders. But I can't forget!' Anguished, he talks of the vain hope he had cherished of a reconciliation. And of the way Trisha's own hidden instability resurrected his childhood terrors. While he feared his own violence towards her, he was growing increasingly afraid of hers. More and more often, she threatened him with kitchen knives and fire-irons.

Such violence is often a projection of unresolved feelings towards others who have caused harm. When I ask him about the sexual problems in their marriage, he is clearly very uncomfortable. Trying to avoid a direct answer, he blames his own low self-esteem for affecting intimate relationships. But he admits that he began to see a pattern in Trisha's behaviour. She would deliberately pro-voke a row as a ploy to avoid sex. Taking a deep breath, he says: 'I realised she hated anything to do with sex, so I challenged her.' Trisha eventually admitted that she had suffered years of sexual abuse at the hands of a male relative. 'She wouldn't say who, but there weren't many to choose from. Linda could've been another victim. Even if she wasn't, she must have known. She and Trisha were closer than twins.'

He explains why he did not unburden himself of this terrible knowledge at his trial. 'I couldn't bring myself to cause her family more pain.' Trisha's abuser *must* be a potential suspect for her

murder. But he fears the police will not see it that way. 'They still think Beryl might have done it. Because she'd have been paying Trisha's alimony until I got a job.'

That seems a very unlikely motive for murder. Money is the least of his new wife's problems. There is pride, of course, and resentment. But is she that kind of person? We shall find out tomorrow. The self-effacing Beryl Stanton Smith has agreed to set the record straight exclusively for our readers.

2

A thick tweed coat over her clean overall, short brown suede boots with tassels and cleated soles on her feet, and the furry brown hat from Debenham's keeping her head and ears warm, Rene slithered more than once on icy patches as she made her way gingerly along Church Street at half past seven in the morning, every so often grabbing with woolly-gloved fingers at a doorknob for support. The wind was cutting, still threatening rather than strong enough for snow, but bitter all the same. Looking at the sky, where dawn was breaking over Bleak Moor to the east, she saw no prospect of sunshine to lift the chill from the day.

She yawned, but from cold rather than tiredness. Early rising was the habit of her lifetime, part and parcel of the well-ordered existence she had fashioned too long ago to recollect. Keeping busy was another part of that life, and she had been quite overjoyed by the prospect of taking care of the policemen from North Wales, for she controlled her world, and the people in it, with domestic order, food, and ritualised routines designed to keep anarchy at arm's length. She regarded domestic skills as instantly redeployable in innumerable settings, and since the dye and print mill on the corner by Trisha's place closed ten years ago, where she had been in charge of quality control, Rene had successfully and profitably charred and cooked for most of the strangers who holidayed in the many village cottages now given over to tourism. In the process, she also made a whole new batch of friends, some of whom lived abroad, and she often thought the postman must be quite envious when he pushed postcards from Paris and crinkly airmail letters from Australia and America and even Hawaii through her letter-box.

As she progressed along the street, the railings intruding on her peripheral vision like shafts of black light, she noted absent-mindedly which housewives were not scrubbing their doorsteps and polishing their letter-boxes properly, and shook her head. Pausing for breath, she watched the rooks clattering in the trees, making that dreadful noise of theirs even before first light was properly over the horizon. Whatever time of the year, that sound obliterated all other bird-song, and she could not imagine how the people who lived with it day in and day out could bear it. When she was a child, the local guns came every so often to cull the rooks before the nesting season, and would line up, spaniels and retrievers to heel, alongside the railings, which were blacker then, with gold paint on the finials. She remembered as if it were yesterday the sharp crack as the guns went off, the noise ricocheting off the church walls, then the sound of the rooks crashing like stones through the trees, snapping twigs as they went, and the thud as they landed on the graves below. Sometimes their wings were torn off during that plummeting to earth, and hung off branches like broken black fans, and always there was a shower of spiky black feathers settling to earth for a long time afterwards, and the smells of blood and gunsmoke draped in the air. Unconsciously chewing the inside of her cheek, because her new teeth had not yet made themselves at home in her mouth, her thoughts returned involuntarily to the newspaper she had read over breakfast and, for all the iciness of the day, her blood threatened to come to the boil once more.

On her way home last night, she had called in at the newsagent's and arranged to have that particular paper delivered for the rest of the week. While McKenna and the others were out seeing Barry Dugdale yesterday afternoon, she had read the newspapers left in an untidy pile on the dining-room table, wondering who this Gaynor Holbrook thought she was. This morning, reading the latest batch of lies, Rene could hardly believe her eyes, and she almost choked on her scrambled egg and toast. She had washed the dishes, put the parlour gas fire on low to keep the room warm, and checked the central heating thermostat, still mulling over the article. More than once, she had to make sure her eyes had not deceived her, but there it was, in black and white for all the world to see. She considered contacting Linda, but decided to bide her time, even though her mind seethed with the pictures Gaynor Holbrook evoked. Thinking sourly that if God had chiselled Smith's features, he must have used a very blunt tool, she set off again, her mind's eye filled with the photograph which accompanied the article. Smith's face was brutally coarse, hard as a granite outcrop on Bleak Moor, his eyes stone cold, his lips thin, and she decided then that, like the rooks, he should be shot for the vermin he was.

The backs of the Church Street houses had little sun even at the height of summer, and always smelled of damp earth. Had she not showered the alleyway cobbles and the garden path with salt last night, they would be like an ice rink. Compelled to glance at the camera above her head, she latched the back gate and walked crabwise to the back door, wondering if her bug-eyed image was being watched inside the house. Still wary of falling and perhaps being cut off from the excitement of life with a broken leg or hip, she grabbed the door handle. The kitchen should have been dark and empty, awaiting her attentions, but it was warm and brightly lit, smelling of breakfast. McKenna had eaten, and was washing his dishes, while Jack, the newspaper she had already read propped against the milk jug, was spooning cornflakes into his mouth, a little drop of milk trickling down his chin.

Wiping away the milk with a napkin, he smiled at her. 'I was expecting to see snow by now.'

'It'll come,' she muttered.

'How are you today?' McKenna too had a smile for her. 'Your shepherd's pie was lovely, by the way.'

'Glad you liked it,' Rene said. She took off her coat, and went to the hall, where she put the coat on a hook, then removed the hat, and fluffed out her hair. She would change her boots for house shoes later, when her feet and the house were warmer.

Tea towel in hand, McKenna came to the kitchen door. 'Is something wrong?' Advancing into the hall, he added: 'Please don't think we're trying to make you redundant. I'm programmed to clear up after myself, and Mr Tuttle's just programmed to find food. We had breakfast early because I have to be in Manchester for nine.'

'Oh.' She stared at the floor.

'So, if you were thinking . . .' McKenna began, then saw tears shimmering in her eyes. 'What is it, Rene? What's wrong?'

'Have you seen the paper?' she demanded, fists clenched. '*Have* you?'

He leaned against the wall, running the tea towel through his hands. 'Yes.'

'It's not true! That woman's writing horrible lies!'

'If she is, it's only because Smith's telling them.'

'What d'you mean? *If*? Nobody touched Trisha. I'd know. And Linda, well, she'd've killed anybody if they so much as tried to lay a finger on her.' Rene paused, breathing noisily. 'And she'd've done the same if anyone laid a hand on Trisha, too. She's got a real fighting spirit, that one.'

'Unfortunately, we can never be sure whether or not a girl's been interfered with,' he said. 'Even if they're asked, they often hide the truth, out of shame, or guilt, or fear.'

'Trisha was pure as the driven snow when she married that monster,' Rene insisted.

'How d'you know?'

'How d'you think?' Rene said impatiently. 'Off the doctors and nurses, of course. When she had the operation.'

McKenna coaxed her back to the kitchen, and made her sit at the table. 'Which operation d'you mean? We only know about one, and that was after she married.'

Sitting opposite Jack, who was forking egg and bacon into his mouth while he listened, Rene turned her teacup round and round in the saucer. 'I don't like saying this in front of men. It doesn't seem right.'

'Not to be coarse,' Jack said gently, 'but it won't be anything we haven't heard before. We develop hides like rhinos in this job.'

She nodded. 'My hubby used to say much the same.' Picking up the cup, she held it to her lips, then put it back in the saucer after taking only a sip. 'Trisha's periods started when she was fifteen, and she had trouble right from the start. Dorothy worried herself sick about it. The poor kid got the most awful cramps and she'd bleed like a stuck pig for days on end. They lost count of the time she missed off school. On top of that, it was ever so embarrassing, because after the first few times they all knew why she was away.'

'And?' McKenna asked.

'Well, she went back and forth to the doctors, but they weren't much use. She was tired and run down all the time, and looked as pale as a little ghost.' She picked up the cup again, and took another sip. 'The doctors were all for putting her on the pill, but Dorothy wouldn't hear of it, so they gave her vitamin pills and iron.'

'Did that help?' Jack asked.

'She got a bit of colour back in her cheeks, but she was still laid up every month. Dorothy told me she was going to *make* the doctors do something, then things settled down of their own accord.' Rene began to twist her wedding band round and round her finger. 'But her troubles came back, about a year before she got married, and she had to have an operation. She had what they call a D&C. A scrape. She had fibroids in the womb. There was no end of improvement afterwards, although they did say she'd probably have to have it done again. And she did.' She

86

stopped turning her ring, and put her hands flat on the table. 'The sister at the hospital told her she'd be a lot better if she was leading a normal life, and it wasn't good for a young woman of twenty-five to be a virgin. Apparently, the nuns have a lot of problems because of that.'

'I see,' McKenna said.

'So, the hospital could prove what that woman wrote is a lie, couldn't they?' Rene asked.

He nodded. 'Unfortunately, because Trisha's dead, the matter can't be pursued. I'm afraid people can say what they like about the dead, true or not.'

'What about Linda?' she demanded. 'She's not dead, and that woman's saying she was molested.'

'It's libel,' Jack commented, pushing aside his empty plate and reaching for the toast. 'It's defamatory to say a woman's been raped or sexually abused when she hasn't. It damages her reputation.'

'Does it really?' Rene's eyes gleamed in the kitchen light. 'Can Linda go to a solicitor?'

'She can indeed.' Jack nodded. 'But we're not supposed to comment or offer any advice, so do me a favour, and forget you heard it from me.' After a moment's thought, he added: 'And, given the implications about the identity of this alleged abuser, Linda's father should see a solicitor as well.'

Rene began to stack used crockery, then stood up and made for the sink. 'What would you like for your meal tonight?' she asked. 'I could get a nice cut of meat from the butcher, because it comes in fresh today. Do the ladies eat meat?'

'Ellen will eat anything,' Jack said. 'She's like me.'

'The other lass doesn't look as if she eats at all. She's very smart, but I swear, if she stood side on against those railings, she'd disappear before your very eyes.'

Like Rene, Craig Newton liked his life tidy. Reared on Haughton's oldest council estate, he had seen too many other lives go out of control for want of a little forethought ever to risk the same. To that end, he surprised parents, teachers, neighbours, and peers by making decisions for the future long before the need arose, and by never deviating. Working with wheels was the first major plan, because he fell in love with them even before he fully understood their function, and he trained as a motor mechanic as soon as he left school.

At twenty-two, he fell in love for the second time, at a friend's wedding, when twenty-year-old Linda Jarvis smiled shyly at him from under the brim of a pretty hat, and a year later he walked down the aisle of All Saints church with his virginal bride. His wise moves on the chessboard of life matured him, although he never forgot that pride usually comes to grief. Their first son was born six years ago, and their second eighteen months later, exactly ten months after Craig's promotion to chief mechanic.

This morning, knowing it would be wrong to disrupt the boys' routines, Craig called his boss to say he would be late, then made up lunch boxes, zipped the boys into their padded jackets, and put them in the car for the ten-minute drive to school. Linda would usually do all those things, but since the newspaper had been stuffed through the letter-box over an hour before, she had slumped at the kitchen table, surrounded by breakfast debris. She was still there when he returned.

Rolling up the sleeves of his quilted plaid work shirt, he began clearing up. 'As soon as I've done here,' he said decisively, 'I'm ringing our solicitor.'

'But he's coming tomorrow,' Linda pointed out. 'When those coppers interview me.'

'I hope you're not fretting about that,' Craig said. 'It stands to reason they might think Barry fitted up that bastard, for old times' sake, if nothing else, but we know he didn't. Mind you,' he added, trying to persuade Linda's pink rubber gloves on to his huge hands, 'nobody round here'd lose any sleep if he had.' Unyielding gloves put aside, he plunged his naked flesh into almost scalding dishwater, cringing as the heat bit. 'What's more important, Lin, is what that bastard's saying about you and Trisha in the paper.' He wrung out the dishcloth, as he might wring Smith's neck, given the opportunity. 'We'll sue him,' he added. 'As well as that bloody paper.'

Behind him, he heard the scrape of chair legs on the floor, then Linda's arms crept around his waist, and she leaned her head against his back. 'I'll finish the dishes,' she said. 'You make another pot of tea.'

He turned, soap suds up to his elbows, and kissed her forehead. 'We're not letting scum like him mess up our lives again. He's done enough damage already.'

Sighing, she moved away. 'I'd better call Dad. Somebody's bound to say something to him.' She bit her lip. 'God knows how he'll feel.'

'He'll be bloody seething, like us, but he knows there isn't a word of truth in it.'

'*We* might know,' she said impatiently, 'but what about the rest of the town? How could he!' Her face flushed with rage. 'The shit! The sodding, bloody shit! Why did he have to say something so awful?'

'Because he's a bloody shit, like you said, and he wants a good horse-whipping,' Craig replied. 'But we can't give him what he deserves, so we'll have to make sure he gets his come-uppance some other way.' He picked up the tea towel. 'When I've had a word with the solicitor, we'll go to your dad's.'

But for once, decisions were taken out of his hands. He and Linda were chatting over mugs of fresh, strong tea when the telephone chirruped in the hall. Both leaped from their chairs, but long-legged Craig reached it first, Linda hanging on to his arm as he listened.

Like Rene, like Linda and Craig, and so many others in the town or with an interest in the matter, Fred Jarvis had ordered Tuesday's edition of Gaynor Holbrook's newspaper. As he read the article beside the photograph of his erstwhile son-in-law, he thought what a pity it was that Trisha *had* never stuck a bread knife in the bastard's guts. But then a sudden pain jabbed him in the chest, then in the shoulders, then in the back, then all the way down his left arm. Breath trapped in his chest, he began to gasp, doubled up with pain and fear. His right arm was like lead as he reached out for the telephone and knocked over his third cup of tea since waking, watching it topple almost in slow motion. The liquid was soaking into the carpet when at last he managed to pull the receiver from its hook, and slowly punch the number nine button three times.

He was still alive when the ambulance arrived, still alive when the next-door neighbour, roused by the siren's banshee wail, rushed into his house, and still alive when he was stretchered through the hospital doors. But Linda knew only what the panicky neighbour had gabbled into the telephone and, not knowing if her father were alive or dead, she sat mutely beside Craig as their car raced through Haughton's busy streets, horn honking.

The sky above Haughton and the moors was a dense, grey pall, still resisting the gusting north-easterly, which cut like glass splinters when it hit bare flesh. On his way out of town, McKenna stopped at the large garage at the lower end of High Street, where Craig should have been at work. He wasted ten minutes searching the racks which covered a whole wall, without finding what Rene had impressed upon him as a necessity, then he went to the counter, to be told that in view of the weather forecast everyone had already sold out of snow chains.

Traffic hedged him in back and front as he retraced yesterday's journey under Dent Viaduct, over which a toy-like train rumbled towards Dentfield and the station buildings crammed into one of Dark Moor's deep gullies. Rene had told him the moor was so named because even the brilliance of a summer's dawn was extinguished as soon as the light touched the earth. Glancing upwards as he reached the junction by the abandoned dye and print mill, McKenna saw for the first time how the enormous shadows thrown by the moor and the viaduct seemed to come together above the shattered roof of Trisha's house.

Today, he turned left instead of right, passing drab terraced houses, small shops, hairdressing salons, ram-shackle garages, and two more mills, now producing compressed-air tools and recycled paper, before joining a new four-lane carriageway. Breasting a long, very steep hill, where ancient stone buildings stood cheek by jowl with the twentieth century, he accelerated as the road ran seamlessly into the motorway. The horizon to his left was broken by Hattersley's multi-storey apartment blocks, built in the 1960s to house Manchester's slum population before the city's old heart was ripped out. Somewhere beyond the brow of the hill, he realised, was the terrace of four brick houses called Wardle Brook Avenue, where, in September 1964, Myra Hindley's grandmother carried in horror, along with her pets and chattels and granddaughter, when she moved into number sixteen. In the dangerous imagination of the young woman with bleached hair and cruel eyes, Hattersley's tower blocks looked like Manhattan, as she no doubt said to the thin young man with empty eyes and his own imagination, who slept, as protocol dictated, on the put-u-up in the lounge, although rarely alone. As the horizon changed once more, the tower blocks falling behind, McKenna wondered if number sixteen were still standing, and who might live there now, for Granny Hindley must be long dead.

The twenty-odd-mile journey to Manchester's outskirts took no longer than the two-mile stop-start to the city centre, where he followed traffic around Piccadilly Gardens before finding the street where Frances Pawsley plied her trade. Her offices were on the tenth floor of a tall, glass-faced 1970s structure, commanding a wonderful view of the city's skyline, but the original interior decor now had the slightly seedy air of something past its prime.

Corseted still in tweeds, she sat behind her large desk, at an angle to the floor-length window. McKenna sat opposite, looking down on the area where an IRA bomb had created as much devastation as the city planners, only in a much shorter time.

She followed his gaze, her own eyes bright with malice. 'That's what your ancestor died for,' she commented. 'Are you proud of what he spawned? What's the tally of death in Ireland's so-called fight for independence, I wonder?'

'I've no idea, Miss Pawsley.' McKenna's face was stiff, his voice curt.

'Really?' Ostentatiously, she arched her thick, greying eyebrows. 'Well, there are certainly more innocent citizens lying dead and maimed than there are terrorists. We should take a leaf out of the American book, and bomb the Irish Republic.'

'That's an appalling suggestion!'

'Why? You fight fire with fire. Jumping into political bed with terrorists might be fashionable at the moment, but believe me, it'll end in rivers of grief and blood. Your sort of terrorism's bred in the bone through generations.'

'Miss Pawsley, I'm here to discuss *your* conduct. You must save your thoughts on Ireland for more sympathetic ears.'

'Oh, come now, Superintendent!' Frances needled. 'You can't pretend your past's irrelevant.' She leaned her elbows on the desk, jacket straining at the seams. 'That journalist dragged your integrity right through the dirt, not to mention how her articles will affect your investigation.'

'Unlike you, Holbrook is not in a position to have an effect. I want to know how you found out what passed between Dugdale and myself, without any prevarication about lawyer's privilege.'

'But it *is* privileged.'

'As Dugdale is not your client, rules of privilege do not apply, but in any case, I do not believe he spoke to you or to Sergeant Lewis. I think Hinchcliffe discussed the interview with you, without Dugdale's knowledge, and you saw an opportunity to compromise my investigation.' He paused, watching her florid face and narrowed eyes. 'The legal profession is notorious for gossiping like housewives over the garden fence, and there would normally be nothing unusual or necessarily problematic in Hinchcliffe's tale-bearing, but your disclosing that information in front of Wendy Lewis is a different issue altogether. It amounts to an attempt to pervert the course of justice, which, as you know, is a criminal offence attracting a custodial sentence.'

'Hinchcliffe's entitled to talk to me, and I to him,' she said imperiously. 'You'd have to prove intent.'

'Oh, come now, Miss Pawsley. Have you forgotten your law? That responsibility lies with the Crown. I'm obliged only to arrest and charge you.'

'You wouldn't dare!' Her face darkened to a beetroot purple. When there was no response, save for a slight shrug, she snarled: 'People say you're a ruthless bastard. Did you know that?'

He nodded. 'And at times, people like me are necessary to any organisation.'

'Don't you care?' A wheedling note crept into her voice. 'I can't believe you don't have *feelings*.'

'I don't harbour the sort of feelings you're suggesting, Miss Pawsley. They would interfere with the proper discharge of my responsibilities, moral and otherwise.' He rose, and picked up his briefcase. 'As a matter of urgency, you must ensure that Sergeant Lewis has alternative representation, and for the duration of my inquiries further contact between you is forbidden. I'm sure you'll agree that you've placed her in a thoroughly invidious position.' Looking down at her, and feeling not one iota of compassion, he added: 'And I suggest you arrange your own legal representation with similar urgency. I shall make a decision about your future by the end of the week.'

5

Four years earlier, Colin Bowden had uprooted himself from his Warwickshire home ground to resettle, with little success to date, in the foreign soil of his fiancée's territory. He met Vicky Lane, who was a courier for a Manchester travel agency, on a package holiday to Greece. She noticed him at the airport as she welcomed aboard the passengers, and rarely let him out of her sight for the next two weeks. He drank little, his manners were impeccable, and he treated her like a lady, much to her chagrin as the heat of a Grecian summer and the urgency of the holiday wore on. Their relationship progressed in fits and starts, punctuated by long separations when his time off clashed with her latest trip abroad. Eventually, she issued an ultimatum and, ignoring his own vague disquiet as well as his mother's meaningful silence, he applied for a transfer from Warwick Police and presented Vicky with an engagement ring.

His first two years in Haughton were spent miserably in a grim boarding-house, then he moved to a furnished flat in a converted chapel behind the High Street. Waiting for his interrogators to arrive, he realised how claustrophobic was the enforced idleness of his suspension, as if the walls of the flat were closing about him. He roamed back and forth to the window, glancing once or twice at Vicky's postcard from Marbella, which was propped on the wooden shelf above the electric fire, and starting to curl with the heat.

'Oh, do sit down!' Anna Singh snapped. 'You're getting on my nerves! You're so tense you'll drop yourself in it as soon as you open your mouth.'

'There's nothing to drop myself in,' Colin told her, but sat down obediently.

Irritably, she flicked through the documents spread out on the glass-topped coffee table, her coal-black hair swinging forward to hide her dusky cheeks. She was quite exotic, he thought, even dressed in lawyer's grey, with big, dark, black-lashed eyes to match the hair, and pouting, thickish lips glistening with ruby lipstick. Heavy gold rings stretched the lobes of her ears, and a bracelet of thick gold links clinked repeatedly on the edge of the table. Occasionally, she looked at him, pursing those ruby lips, and he decided that she was really very beautiful. The fact that he instinctively, and thoroughly, disliked and distrusted her had nothing to do with race.

'You've got to be careful,' she said. 'Do you understand? McKenna's in a different league from the officers you've come across before. He's quite ruthless, and doesn't in the least mind making very big waves, or care who gets swamped by them.' She paused, frowning at him. 'I shouldn't really tell you this, but he's threatened one of my colleagues.'

'With what?' Colin asked. 'What for?'

'Even though you've all got separate representation, it's vital that we solicitors keep abreast of developments. What affects one of you affects all of you.' She shuffled the papers together. 'McKenna found out Dugdale's solicitor had talked to Sergeant Lewis's solicitor, and started throwing his weight around, although why he should be bothered about what we say to each other is beyond me.'

'I imagine that depends on what's been said,' Colin commented. 'And when, and to whom.'

She turned her head quickly. 'You're not going to be difficult, are you? You must let me guide you in the right direction.'

'I'm not an imbecile.'

'You're out of your depth,' Anna said sharply. 'This

was the first big case you worked with Dugdale, and you've no idea what sort of stunts he might have pulled in the past to get results. Being a detective inspector at his age is quite unusual.'

'No, it isn't,' Colin contradicted. 'He's thirty-five. Warwick had several younger than him.'

'This isn't Warwick,' she said impatiently. 'This force is bigger, more diverse, and has entirely different concerns and policing requirements. What bothers me about Dugdale is his local connections.'

'Why? They're more use than hindrance.'

'Provided they're not exploited or abused.'

'In other words, you believe Dugdale fitted up Smith, don't you?' Colin demanded. 'Well, he didn't, and I'm not going to say he did, to please you or anyone else.'

6

News of Fred Jarvis's heart attack, and its cause, swept through Haughton the way fire ravaged the moorlands during a hot dry spell, when sunlight, catching a splinter of glass, could set the land alight. Rene heard a whisper in the butcher's, as she was buying meat for dinner, then fretted her way in and out of the bakery and the greengrocery in search of greater detail. When none was forthcoming, laden with shopping she panted back up the hill to Church Street, dumped the bags on the kitchen counter, and telephoned one of her cronies who worked at the hospital.

She was still in a lather when Linda rang. Her voice was soggy, Rene thought, as if it were drenched in tears.

'They think he'll pull through,' Linda told her. 'It

97

wasn't a very bad attack, and he got to hospital fast. It was the shock, you know.'

'I'm not surprised,' Rene said. 'I've never heard the like, I really haven't. You and your Craig must be out of your minds. Where are the little ones?'

'Craig took them to school, but he's going for them at dinner-time so they can come and see Dad.'

'If you want anything, lass, you let me know. I'll be along later to see Fred.'

'I'll tell him.'

'He's conscious, then?'

'Sort of,' Linda replied. 'Enough to say he's going to rip off Smith's head, and shit down his neck.'

'He didn't! Fred doesn't use language like that.'

'He does now,' Linda asserted. 'I thought I was hearing things myself, at first, till he said it again.'

'I never! Well, he can get in the queue when he's better.' Rene smiled grimly. 'And by the way, Linda, you don't have to put up with what that woman wrote about you.'

'Craig was going to phone our solicitor when we heard about Dad.'

'Yes, well don't drag your feet. I got it from a horse's mouth it's libel to say a woman's been raped or molested. So mind that newspaper gets told you know, before they print any more lies about you and Trisha.'

7

Every community, small or large, has its quota of elderly women, who, dropped by the mainstream of life, can only watch the run of the tides as they themselves drift with the undercurrents. Sheffield, where Gaynor Holbrook's Tuesday offering about a

98

one-time son of the city was avidly read by many a pair of old eyes, was no exception. Her forays into the realms of investigative journalism went over the heads of some readers, and drew jeers of derision from others, but when Ida Sheridan finished reading the long screeds of small print for the third time, in case her eyes had deceived her twice before, utter amazement was her only reaction.

Leaving the newspaper open at the double-page spread, she stuffed it into a Tesco carrier bag, went to the lobby of her tiny one-bedroomed maisonette, pulled a quilted fawn jacket from its hook, wrapped a plaid scarf around her ears, checked her pocket for keys, purse, and handkerchief, and opened the front door to the first-floor walkway. The wind hit her in the face the way her husband used to do, trying to knock her to the ground, so she bowed her head automatically, chin tucked into her chest. Making her way along concrete scoured almost white by the wind, plastic carrier clutched under her arm, she decided the wind was no less a relentless demon than her husband.

Head down, she struggled past six windows identical to her own, where metal grilles obscured daylight, and condensation glued uniformly dingy net curtains to the glass behind. Some of the grilles were deformed, wickedly sharp edges poking out to tear at clothes and unwary flesh, the windows shattered and covered over with what she always thought looked like sheets of mashed wood shavings. Shaking her head at the badness in the world, taken in with every breath by the children and addicts who wreaked the havoc in their scavenging for anything of worth, she passed six stout doors, some already dented by the violence of steel-capped boots, their little panels of glass also barricaded, then leaned against the frame of the seventh, gloved finger on the doorbell, while the wind went on battering her about the head and body. Feet shuffled towards the door, a small shadow darkened the frosted panel, dead bolts clanked, and when the door opened hot air whooshed into her face.

'Let me in.' Squeezing past, Ida headed for the big electric fire, rubbing her hands. 'It's cold enough to freeze the what'sits off a brass monkey.'

'You should've stayed indoors, then.' Closing the door, the other woman drifted towards her like a wisp of smoke.

'Wanted to show you this, didn't I?' Ida pulled the newspaper from its wrapping. 'You'll *have* to do something this time. It's gone too far. It's slander.' The heat began to sear the back of her legs, and she moved. 'I reckon they owe you enough to keep that fire going day and night for the rest of your natural.'

8

Susan Dugdale was not, like Craig, habitually decisive, nor was she, like Wendy Lewis, cowed by commitments, for until yesterday, accepting Dugdale's marriage proposal was the only important decision she had ever had to make. She barely reacted to his suspension from duty, knowing that when Smith was freed they would be caught up in the backlash. She trusted her husband, but trusted more the simple faith that truth would prevail. The revelation of his relationship with Julie Broadbent came like an explosion, destroying all her certainty. Now, with hours of questions and arguments and a sleepless night behind her, she could still only focus on this secret history of her husband's and the power it wielded over the present. She told him she was going to her parents, to think things through, but while she hurriedly filled the suitcases last used for their Florida holiday, she lied to the children, telling them that Gran was not very well.

Dugdale did not contradict her. As she packed luggage and children into her own car, he shivered on the doorstep, his face as bleak as the moor behind him. 'The kids'll miss school,' he said dully, silently begging God to make her change her mind.

'They'll catch up soon enough when I've got something sorted.'

'Sorted?' A horrible leaden feeling settled in the pit of his stomach. 'Like what?'

'We'll see.'

'What about the neighbours?' His voice was hoarse with desperation.

'What about them?' She couldn't care less, he thought. 'Tell them my mother's ill, not that it's any business of theirs.'

The children waved as she drove away, but long after the car disappeared from view, Dugdale remained where he was, hoping against hope that she was simply making a gesture, looking down the road until his eyes glazed over for the blue car which was not coming back. Chilled to the marrow, he eventually went indoors, thinking vaguely that perhaps he should tell McKenna the truth before he heard of Susan's desertion from other mouths.

9

The living-room of Colin's flat was airless and over-crowded and, squashed next to Anna Singh on the narrow sofa, the solicitor's pin-stripe-clad thigh pressing hers, Janet felt extremely uncomfortable. Ellen had her back to the door and her machines rigged up on an uncared-for drop-leaf table, wires and cables snaking over the side and across luridly patterned carpet to the wall sockets, while Jack and Colin Bowden sat on unmatched upright chairs to each side of the electric fire. Two of the fire's four bars were switched off, but the heat still burned Janet's cheeks and dried her throat and, as Anna Singh outlined her concerns to Jack in a rather whiny voice, she assessed the room's cramped spaces, cheap fittings, low ceiling, and poor proportions. She looked through the window, at dingy brick and millstone grit walls, dark slabbed roofs, and in the far distance the rise of endless moor, and thought how miserable were both the colours and pro-portions of everything in this bleak place. Whenever she saw a meeting of the moors, she searched for the glimmer of sea between the folds, and felt strange, and even anxious, because there was none to be seen.

Jack had begun the interview. 'I understand you'd worked with Inspector Dugdale on several burglaries and assaults before he specifically asked for you to be assigned to investigating Trisha Smith's death.'

Colin nodded. 'Yes, sir.' Avoiding Anna's meaningful stare, he added: 'I felt very honoured to be included in the murder team. I had a high regard for Mr Dugdale. I still have.'

'How much time did you spend with him? We know you and Sergeant Lewis did some interviews together.'

'I attended all the interviews with Smith, and I also attended the crime scene and autopsy.'

'Was information shared between you all on a regular basis?'

'Yes, sir. And with the station superintendent.'

'Did you have personal contact with Super-intendent Ryman at HQ?'

'No, sir. Mr Dugdale briefed him regularly.'

'Was this your first murder investigation?'

'No, sir. I'd worked on the murder of a barman in Warwick. That got complicated too, when we uncovered a drug connection.'

'Did you have adequate supervision on that case?'

'I think so.'

'Do you feel you were adequately supervised on the Smith case?'

'Yes.'

'Do you have reservations about the investigation?'

'Inspector Tuttle! Please!' Anna intervened. 'Of *course* Sergeant Bowden has reservations *now*. A man was wrongly convicted.'

'I'm sure he understands that I'm not interested in hindsight,' Jack replied. 'I want to know what he thought at the time.'

'I didn't have reservations at the time, sir,' Colin replied. 'And I don't now, despite what's happened. In my opinion, on the evidence available to us, to Crown Prosecutions, *and* a jury, Smith's conviction was the only possible outcome.'

'That evidence was entirely circumstantial,' Jack commented.

'That isn't at all unusual,' Colin countered.

'Can you elaborate on the enquiries made about Trisha's adverts in the lonely hearts columns?'

'There's not much to say. We worked like beavers, and came up with nothing, because any replies Trisha had went up in flames with her and the house.'

'Why are you going over old ground?' Anna demanded. 'Are you trying to catch out one or other of our clients in conflicting stories?' Without giving anyone time to respond, she added: 'Linda Newton gave the police a photograph of her sister, copies of which then went to every newspaper and TV station in Britain, and were taken around every pub, club, hotel, shop and restaurant within a seventy-five-mile radius.' She glared at Jack. 'But you already know all this. And if you've no idea how to proceed on this particular issue now that Smith's release has technically reopened the investigation into Trisha Smith's death, that is not my client's problem.'

'Linda Newton may know more than she revealed,' Jack pointed out.

'I don't agree, sir,' Colin said. 'She was desperate to have Trisha's killer found. She wouldn't have held back.'

'On the subject of "holding back",' Janet began, 'can we discuss Julie Broadbent?'

'Must I watch this investigation every step of the way?' Anna's voice was tart. 'My client outranks Constable Evans and, whether or not,' she said to Jack, 'she acts under your instructions, my client may object to being questioned by a lower ranking officer.'

'Then your client may do so,' Jack said tersely.

'I don't care *who* asks the bloody questions!' Colin rounded on his solicitor. 'You've got together with Hinchcliffe and that Pawsley woman to bugger things up, haven't you?'

As a flush discoloured her dusky cheeks, Jack added: 'Please understand, Miss Singh, that we shall have no hesitation in taking action against anyone who tries to impede or interfere with the investigation.'

'Please don't threaten me, Inspector. And it's "ms", not "miss".' Sulkily, she nodded to Janet. 'You may continue.'

'Sergeant Lewis told us she believed Broadbent was holding back,' Janet said. 'What was your opinion on the matter?'

'I never got round to making one,' he admitted. 'I was too fascinated by her to bother.' As Anna looked horror-struck, he continued: 'So I don't remember much about the Willows except trying to engineer excuses to go there. Sad to say, Wendy Lewis was always there, as well.'

'Why did Broadbent have that effect on you?' asked Jack. 'D'you think she set out to beguile you?'

'No, I don't. I doubt if she's any idea how she affects people.' He smiled. 'And she's nothing special to look at. She's not very tall, and quite thin, and she's got a slightly pointed face, and very pale skin, but there's something absolutely mesmerising about her. It must be in her eyes. They're fantastic.'

'What crass, sentimental drivel!' exclaimed Anna.

'It's the truth,' Colin insisted. 'And as far as the interviews at the Willows were concerned, I was only there to make up the numbers. Wendy Lewis didn't let me get a word in edgewise, because she wanted to show off her superior social-work knowledge. And although we managed to work together quite well,' he added, 'I don't very much like Wendy Lewis. She became extraordinarily condescending once she found out Julie wasn't qualified, and at times she was even downright spiteful, so if Julie clammed up, I'd say Wendy's to blame.'

'I can't allow this to continue,' Anna interrupted. 'You're deliberately encouraging my client to damaging indiscretions.'

'Sergeant Bowden has admitted only to noticing that a potential witness is attractive,' Jack responded. 'And as he was apparently no more than a bystander at the interviews, his feelings could not interfere with his conduct. In any case, police officers need to be aware of their feelings to prevent their interfering.'

'Exactly!' Colin said forcefully. 'If I was going to let

my feelings get the better of me, believe me, I'd have throttled Smith.'

Janet felt the stiffening in the flesh which pressed against her own and, glancing at the now silenced Anna, saw only the overripe mouth and the sweep of hair. Pleased by the solicitor's vexation, she said to Colin: 'Were you satisfied that the residents at the Willows had no pertinent information?'

'I'm not sure, to be honest. They're not all stupid. And some of them aren't incapable of *pretending* to be stupid.'

'Could we get to the point at issue?' Anna asked. 'I thought you wanted to discuss Father Barclay's alleged letter.'

'I intend to,' Janet told her, and received a toss of that deceptively lovely head in response. To Colin, she said: 'When did you first learn of the existence of that letter?'

'When we received the appeal papers.' He ran his fingers through his hair. 'Before then, Smith was history in our book, and put away where he belonged. Beryl moved heaven and earth to get an appeal, and, when we first heard it was on, we just assumed she'd chucked the right amount of money and influence in the right direction. Then the bomb dropped.'

'As you know,' Jack said, 'it's been suggested that Inspector Dugdale wilfully suppressed the evidence of Father Barclay's letter. I must put that allegation to you, and ask if you have any relevant knowledge.'

'No, I don't,' Colin asserted. 'I've only got my instincts to rely on, but I don't believe Mr Dugdale ever received the letter.'

'Unfortunately, instincts can mislead,' Jack pointed out. 'After all, everyone got it wrong about Smith. Bearing that in mind, you have the opportunity to change or amend any statement, including that last comment. Like other organisations, police close ranks at times of crisis, or when under threat. If you feel unable to be completely frank for fear of breaking rank, this is the time to say.'

'I've nothing to add, sir, and I don't want to alter anything.'

'Not even with regard to your infatuation with Julie Broadbent?'

'No, sir, and it wasn't an "infatuation". I just thought she was lovely. There's nothing wrong with that, is there?'

10

When first convicted, Piers Stanton Smith, as he insisted on being called, spent three weeks in Salford's Strangeways Prison awaiting allocation before being transferred, handcuffed and caged, to his new domicile at Longmoor. Imagining Frances Pawsley already rearming herself for their next skirmish, McKenna followed in his tracks.

As the car flashed through a high-sided underpass to join the northbound motorway, he glimpsed a cat lying as if asleep below the wall, and was about to flatten the brake, compelled to attempt rescue, when he realised the dusty-looking animal must be dead, struck by some anonymous vehicle and thrown accidentally into that position. Grief for the poor creature further bleakened the rest of a joyless journey, through grey urban wastelands where the verges were littered with human detritus, the walls and ramparts of motorway and bridges defaced by graffiti, and a dirty wind created by thousands of vehicles tumbled litter and flattened weeds. Somewhere in that miserable landscape, he stopped at a service station for petrol, then went to the adjoining restaurant for a snack. The place was laid out like a cattle market, with slatted seats and rough tables imprisoned inside slatted pens, under a bare pitched roof from which dangled several enormous television sets with their sound turned down. He joined the queue being processed along the food counter towards the till, watching, like everyone else, the meaningless pictures flickering overhead.

11

Julie saw Trisha's killer again when she took out some of her charges for a mid-morning walk. The blue car which hurtled away from Trisha's immolation had been traded in within weeks for an anonymous white vehicle, and that, in turn, exchanged for the mulberry-coloured saloon speeding past her and the little crocodile of mental defectives as if they were non-existent. The car was heading towards Dark Moor and, as it disappeared around a bend, she had another heart-stopping thought to keep company with her older terrors. Had she been alone, she wondered, would the car still have raced away? For surely, the advent of the faceless police officers from another country had changed everything.

Thanking God for the unwitting protection of idiots, she herded them down the road towards the little café where Muriel Szabo spent her remaining years guarding her till and ruling with a rod of iron the girls who worked there on their way from school to marriage. Her now dead husband, who fled the Hungarian uprising to find himself in Haughton, had been known only by a self-conscious garble because no one ever learned to pronounce his Christian name.

And, despite occasionally sharing her bed with him before each of his seven children arrived, when Muriel, in the last weeks of pregnancy, was bellied like a cow in calf, even Julie's mother, Kathy, was defeated by the tongue-defying medley of consonants, and simply called him 'the Hungarian'.

Julie remembered his gravelly voice, his own enjoyment of the linguistic pitfalls which upended everyone's best efforts, and the small acts of kindness and consideration he offered whenever he saw her out with Kathy. He made the café opposite the old dye mill into a patch of home soil, beguiling the local palate with strange concoctions of stewed meat and vegetables, light-as-air pastries, and dark, chewy breads. To Julie, it had never lost that atmosphere, even though Muriel now served sandwiches of white sliced bread, cheese or beans or egg, or all three together, on toast, pots of tea with tea-leaves, instant coffee made with hot milk, jam-sponge or syrup-sponge pudding with runny yellow custard, and the home-made chocolate cake, fruit pie, crumbly scones, and nutmeg-dusted egg custard her four daughters supplied with precise regularity.

Muriel tolerated custom from the Willows because it stoked up the takings now the dye mill's regular trade was a thing of the past, but her sharp old eyes were always on the watch. She tolerated Julie, but never welcomed her. Her memory was too long, and as sharp as the eyes in her seamed face, and Julie often thought she probably knew all about the trade in another kind of sustenance that had passed between Kathy and the Hungarian.

I

McKenna parked in the visitors' car-park at Longmoor and headed for the gatehouse postern, looking up at the endless length of inwardly curving wall, the inner defence of a great snarl of barbed wire just visible above the top. He was admitted to a small chamber surrounded by bullet-proof glass, where he and his identification were rigorously scrutinised, before being escorted to the deputy governor's office via clanking keys and automatic steel doors. The doors opened with a sigh and closed behind him with a sucking of air and a sough like the wind, and he relished the thought that even Smith, for all his posturings and his arrogance, must have felt a stabbing, panic-inducing hopelessness as one after another of the impenetrable exits shut behind him, seemingly for many years.

Shaking hands with Noel Cooper, the deputy governor, he said: 'Thank you for seeing me at such short notice. Smith's time here is probably not relevant to my investigation, but I like to be thorough.'

'What happens if you turn up evidence pointing towards that poor woman's killer?' Cooper asked.

'We hand it over, and the investigation would be reopened.'

'Pity Smith can't be tried twice for the same offence, isn't it?' Cooper commented. 'Still, there'll be another opportunity to put him away, if our experience is any indication.'

'Don't you think he attracts a rather unreasonable level of condemnation?' McKenna suggested. 'Marital violence is a commonplace and, while it's unacceptable, there are usually reasons why it occurs.'

'And were we prejudiced before he even set foot in his cell?' asked Cooper. 'Even if we were, there was no gainsaying his impact. Misfortune followed him like it was his own shadow, but it always affected others, never him. He loves conflict, and he's exceedingly manipulative. He's got a bad aura, which is probably why his past is littered with violent deaths and tragedy. And I fully expect his future to be the same, if not worse. His confidence will be impregnable now.'

'Not one of your more popular inmates, then,' McKenna said, rather taken aback by Cooper's vehement dislike.

'You and I both know that tension virtually drips from the walls in a lifers' unit. We have to be constantly on the alert for inmate attacks, attacks on officers, and suicide attempts. Our mix is always volatile, but there was an almost universal sigh of relief when Smith went, and a marked reduction of tension in all quarters.' Doodling on his blotter, the deputy governor added: 'The only person who was sorry to see the back of him was one of our lady counsellors.' He gestured to a stack of files on the side of his desk. 'I've had permission to give you copy documentation relating to his residence, although I expect you're already awash in a sea of paper. Anyhow, I included her reports, as well as the psychologist's and a psychiatric evaluation carried out on his recommendation.'

'Anything useful in them?'

'I can give you a run-down of the counselling reports. In many ways they're just an extension of the rubbish that was in the paper today,' Cooper said. 'Same tune on a different violin.' He took the top file from the stack. 'I highlighted the relevant bits.' He handed over the documents, and sat back in his chair, gazing through the window.

His attention directed only to the blocks of words stressed in fluorescent yellow, McKenna leafed through the many pages of reports on

Piers Stanton Smith, Category B Life Prisoner (no minimum specified period)

Initially – extremely withdrawn – breakthrough interview – four months into sentence – probably – first opportunity to talk about himself – deepest fears – feelings

His childhood – dreadful – impact of being reared by – mother where – no counterbalancing influences – cannot be overstated – near revelation when – realised – person does not need to be conscious of emotion to experience its effects – discussed – grief – terror – shame – chronic anxiety

He said – felt like person with terminal illness – 'illness' himself – evidence of disturbingly negative self-image – the possibility of self-harm must be considered

He has – avid desire to learn – make up for inadequate general education – realise person within himself – motivation vacillates – prone to bouts of depression – I suggested anti-depressant therapy – very resistant – mother took pills

To say – obsessed with childhood – not – overstatement – children who live with fear, violence depravity absorb – even replicate behaviour in later life. It is not their fault – but must – grow towards acceptable levels of functioning

Initial settling-in period – extraordinarily difficult for life prisoners – moods appeared stabilise – periods of extreme despondency – wife's efforts to secure appeal – inclined to self-doubt – depressed emotions after her visits

He has spoken at length of first wife – horrified recognition – near clone of mother – possibility unconsciously drawn to similar women on 'devil you know' basis – despite admitting – became – terrorised by first wife's conduct – fantasised about her death – his liberation – adamant innocent of murder – maintains hope – evidence to clear

Of second wife – wholly uncritical sufficiently mature to meet his emotional needs – aware personalities involved in relationships hold potential – create harmony – discord – violence – calm – referred to philosophical 'third entity' – Beryl brings out best – Trisha brought out worst – violence offered Trisha – rooted in deep feelings of inadequacy – she – very immature personality – easily waylaid by transient emotions – his fear provoked panic attacks containing violence

Recommendations:

1 Work prison library – continue – additional responsibilities
2 A programme teaching literacy skills – other prisoners
3 Support Open University degree course
4 Formal psychological counselling – including Transactional Analysis – Cognitive Therapy

5 Continued oversight – recognition of circumstances where self-harm might occur. Self-harm – way – expressing externalising inner anguish – much still troubles this man – I see generalised suffering – morbid social phobia embracing most social contacts – inhibiting, generalised anxiety state characterised by disproportionate apprehension

'Her offerings are all pretty much the same,' Cooper said, when McKenna closed the file. 'But you should read the psychologist's reports, especially the one for annual review. He took against Smith with a vengeance, but only after Smith threatened him. Our anti-hero reverted to type when the psychologist challenged him about yet another death-by-fire he'd discovered. That little outburst cost Smith twenty-eight days' loss of privileges, and me an ear-bashing about "draconian and inappropriate sanctions" from ·the counsellor.'

'Did you have any contact with Beryl? I see she visited at every opportunity.'

'I had a lot of contact with Mrs Stanton Smith the second,' replied Cooper. 'And I also received letters of complaint from her on a regular basis. She wanted his sensitive and artistic soul shielded from the rough and tumble of prison life. So did the priest.' Frowning at his visitor, he added: 'Father Fauvel made nine visits here: I checked with the visitors' log before you came; so it beats me why he never mentioned the other priest's letter, at least once.'

'He didn't mention it at the trial, either. We intend to ask him to explain his lapses.'

'Well, I doubt if you'll get very far. He's too

smooth; one of those Teflon-coated individuals.'

'You mentioned a psychiatric evaluation,' McKenna reminded him. 'What was the opinion?'

'No specific or treatable mental illness. In other words, Smith's a sociopath. Have you met him yet?'

McKenna shook his head. 'And unless he features in our inquiries, I don't intend to do so.'

'You're a wise man.' Cooper smiled. 'By the way, d'you know when his mother died? The psychologist got a bee in his bonnet about the late Mrs Smith. He contacted the Registrar's office in Sheffield, but they had no record of her demise.'

'Sheffield police tried to find her before the trial, but found another old woman living at the last known address. She was called Sheridan, if I remember correctly. She showed them her pension book.'

'Didn't she know where Bunty Smith had gone?'

'Said she'd never heard of her. Mrs Smith could have moved elsewhere, of course, or even followed her son's example, and changed her name.'

'A dead end, then,' Cooper said.

'Not necessarily. The National Insurance Register in Newcastle should have a record of her death.'

On the road from Longmoor to the motorway, McKenna passed an ancient-looking wayside inn, and decided to treat himself to a hot pie and a tot or two of warming spirits. Feet up on the brass fender around the log fire in the pub snug, he took out the psychology report Cooper had recommended.

> 1 Following conviction and allocation, Smith was assessed on arrival and judged fit for non-segregation and work
>
> 2 Following referral for counselling, concerns were voiced about the possibility of

self-harm: in my opinion, based on Smith's presentation and the absence of precedent, a serious suicide attempt is remote. Although the usual supervision must obtain, I believe such behaviour would be purely attention-seeking, or, more probably, designed to escape the consequences of some mischief. Additionally, Smith is too self-centred and vain to wreak any significant damage upon his person

3   Prior to completion of this report, I have conducted seven separate interviews with Smith, observed him during recreation, association and work periods, and discussed his functioning with unit staff

4   Since his admission, there have been several unexplained incidents where other prisoners suffered injury, or appeared very fearful. No reasonable explanation has emerged, and unit staff are worried by the increase in random and unpleasant accidents, and the overall tightening of tension. Smith progressed through the internal hierarchy very swiftly and with considerable ease, and now occupies a position of power, which bespeaks a personality very different from the passive, damaged, timid, and often humble individual presented to officers and professional staff. In observing Smith with other prisoners, I note that even the most notoriously violent and confident studiously avoid irritating him: others defer to him, but in the manner of those hoping to appease a dangerous animal

5   During the first course of interviews, Smith was intent on discussing what he presented as a dreadful childhood and adolescence at the hands of an horrendous mother, sneering teachers, wicked neighbours and their evil offspring,

expertly weaving references to his allegedly savage past into every sentence. He presented himself as a victim of the world, and I had the distinct impression he expected me to be seduced into unquestioning and uncritical sympathy. That is not my role, and I explained to him that he was unlikely to make any psychological or personal progress without first examining his own input into these interpersonal relationships. He responded by becoming very angry very quickly, and this was not feigned: I reached a tentative conclusion at that point, which was only reinforced by subsequent contact, that if the self-image Smith wishes to present is criticised or threatened, he will fast resort to aggression

6 Attempts to provoke Smith to discuss the feelings and anxieties of others were invariably fruitless. He is profoundly self-absorbed, self-regarding and narcissistic, and has almost perfected the art of self-satisfaction, at whatever cost to others, clothing it with sickly, hypocritical affectations of humility when necessary. He is prone to abuse those weaker or less ruthless than himself, as is evident from the history of assaults on his first wife, and I suggest that obvious weakness in others is likely to make him even more vicious and exploitative. He is power-hungry and tyrannical and, like all tyrants, driven to extremes of outrageous behaviour if thwarted or challenged. Experience has taught him that people can be bullied and terrorised into meeting his needs and adapting to his ways of thinking. Some even conveniently die to appease or please him. Belief in that level of power is the victim of its own success

7 Discussions about his mother and his first

wife never advanced from first base, which was the basis Smith insisted on adopting, telling me he must be unconsciously drawn to such women through conditioning. The monstrous aspects of both women were embellished with each telling, and thus their responsibility for what happened to them at his hands grew apace. He suggested that the abuse of his first wife was a hangover of unsatisfied feelings towards his mother: in plain language, he would have been justified in punishing his mother, but battered his wife instead. He also claimed that having been reared with violence, it was inevitably absorbed into his own functioning, and went on to say that his change of name and 'rewritten' early biography were a means of escaping the depravity of his childhood, before that too became psychologically intrinsic. He admitted to periods of emotional disturbance, when the chains of the past threatened to pull him back, and said he felt terribly guilty about things he may have done during such times when he was not in control of himself. However, each admission of violence or cruelty was attached to blame for the victim, and all his conduct was thus projected. I lost count of the times he stated: 'it wasn't my fault', 'I couldn't help it', 'she made me do it': every person within his orbit, particularly the women, was unbelievably wanting, and provocative of their own misery

8 In later interviews, after Smith realised I would not enter into his games, he became surly and monosyllabic, and could present as exceedingly insolent. Violence occurred during the last interview, since when he has refused to see me. On that occasion I had obtained child

psychological and school reports, and particularly those from the period following the death of his teacher, when the school felt he was in need of trauma counselling. Starting with the teacher's death, I tried to get Smith to discuss the startling catalogue of deaths by fire in his history, and he refused. I then tried to discuss some comment made at the time by the educational psychologist, who had expressed fears about the implications of his seeming divorce from reality. This issue arose when it became clear that Smith's presentation of his home circumstances was untrue. The psychologist visited Mrs Smith, and found the home, although sparsely furnished, to be clean and tidy, as was Mrs Smith. She worked hard, and was herself on friendly terms with several neighbours, one of whom had previously looked after Smith in the period between his return from school and Mrs Smith's return from work. That arrangement ceased after the family's pet dog, a small mongrel, went missing one afternoon, to be found later that night impaled on a piece of railing stuck in the ground. While still alive, the dog had been doused in petrol and set alight. Two children from a tenement block which overlooked the area identified Smith as the culprit, but although the matter was reported to the police, no action ensued. Other children in the area disclosed their own fears to the police, stating that Smith bullied and hit them, and was always playing with matches. The issue of Smith's personal cleanliness was explored with his mother, who reluctantly disclosed that the child was wilfully dirty. He wet his bed, but would not wash himself, and refused to wash his hair or clean his teeth. If she tried to force him, he attacked her, biting and kicking and, on one occasion, thumped her so hard on the side of the head she passed out. Mrs Smith put forward the view that his behaviour had deteriorated even more since he spent several weeks in a children's home while she was in hospital, and she was of the opinion that he was hoping to engineer another admission. He had received toys and new clothes from the home, and since his return, demanded luxuries she could not afford. It was when I broached these matters with him that the violence erupted. His face suffused with rage, and he jumped to his feet and began to smash whatever was within reach. He then leaned over my desk, issued various threats, and stormed out of the room

9 At his trial, the issue of Smith's sexual orientation was raised, but I do not recall more than doubt and innuendo. In early interviews he was more than willing to discuss the extremely unsatisfactory sexual relationship which allegedly existed in his first marriage, citing his wife's traumatised response to childhood sexual abuse as the reason. Again, there appears to be no evidence that his wife was abused, and no other source to the claim apart from Smith. From another viewpoint, if the attack on his wife which apparently triggered her action for divorce was typical, it is hardly surprising she should reject a sexual relationship. Smith admitted to that attack (he had no option), but again resorted to rationalisation, presenting me with a textbook Freudian response, to the effect that he lashed out despite himself out of a deep-rooted fear of her capacity to emasculate him.

He also suggested that when she collapsed in front of him, he was terrified she might die and therefore abandon him, and again lashed out in fear, to rouse her. At this point he said he thought Transactional Analysis might well enable him to unravel his confusions. My suggestion that he kicked her in the genitals because it was the most humiliating and painful mode of attack he could devise upon a woman was met with outrage, then floods of tears. He even began to hit himself about the head, and to thump his chest, but there were no marks on his flesh. He is guileful in the extreme: he admits to these outrageous acts, then invites sympathy and compassion because he has been forced to suffer their pain. During this first year, he appears to have gleaned a quite considerable knowledge of psychology, and it is my view that it would be a serious error of judgement for the professionals involved with him to provide any more ammunition, or to pander to his preferred view of himself as world victim: he seems to have a remarkable ability to turn anything and everything to his own advantage. In that, he shows the unvarying characteristics of the true sociopath, for whom egotism and immediate self-gratification are the mainsprings of all action, and who persistently expects the world to adjust to his wants

10   Although I am loath to allow personal reactions to affect my assessments, I feel obliged to comment as Smith will be with us for a long time, and his interactions with other prisoners, and staff, therefore become significant. In observing him, I have noted that he takes every opportunity to approach women, and appears

able to ingratiate himself very quickly. He unashamedly exploits capacity for guilt wherever it is to be found, which is more likely to be with women than with men, but once the victim begins to understand the nature of that exploitation, and to resist, he becomes vicious. He also gravitates towards prisoners known to be homosexually inclined, and his own mannerisms at times suggest he is of similar bent, although my observations suggest that he deliberately exaggerates the standard affectations in such company. His emotional development, apparently arrested in infancy, his overweening vanity, and his total self-absorption are all typical of homosexuality, in itself possibly a symptom of arrested development, but my personal opinion tends towards another diagnosis. There is an unwholesomeness about him, admittedly more sensed than seen, which is focused on his attitudes towards the sexuality of others, involving prurience and disgust, and engendering a great unease in the observer. He attempts to 'seduce' others, literally as well as metaphorically: therefore, his potential to create serious problems for other prisoners, and possibly to compromise officers and professionals, should not be overlooked. I am of the opinion that he uses his sexuality as and when and how it might suit him, and it is therefore yet another dangerous tool at his disposal

11 Despite the clear deliberation in Smith's conduct, it is my view that he is profoundly and dangerously disturbed, and functions from bases of rationalisation which preclude his taking any responsibility for his actions or their

consequences, however dreadful for others, or from any comprehension of guilt. Blame is projected universally, which allows him to continue with his excesses of conduct without any remorse. Even if he is innocent of the murder of his wife, as he maintains, the casual fashion in which he admits to his violence towards her, which was probably worse than we know, is chilling, as are his endless justifications for his actions. He is cruel and greedy, and seems to enjoy the pain he causes others, because they 'deserve' it, and he uses his intelligence, which will always be limited by his lack of emotional empathy, to torture and taunt his victims. Although people like this are capable of destroying others without necessarily lifting a finger, as he has already come to enjoy the power he can acquire through physical violence, it is unlikely that he will lose that taste: on the contrary, its future satisfaction will demand greater and greater excesses. In this context, I feel justified in referring to new research into the 'serial-killer' phenomenon, which suggests such people often commence their career with sadistic attacks on animals

12 To my knowledge, Smith has so far received three psychiatric evaluations: for the defence pre-trial (to which we are not privy), for initial assessment, and for this upcoming review. Whilst inconclusive, the in-house evaluations concur in many respects with my own views. We can therefore read the evidence as pointing towards a serious personality disorder. Such disorders fall outside the definition of mental illness, and are generally regarded as untreatable either by medication or surgery. However, our

job is not to warehouse prisoners, but to rehabilitate, and we have an ongoing responsibility to the wider society with regard to any prisoner who may pose an indefinite risk. It is my view that Smith should receive further psychiatric evaluation in order to exclude specific mental illness – for example, schizophrenia – and in order to attempt a specific statement of need. In that way, his future management and therapeutic input may be designed to address those needs

2

Unable to match Rene's outrage at the news of Fred Jarvis's heart attack, Jack murmured the usual words of sympathy, hoping she would leave him alone.

'It's no good pretending it's not your business,' she nagged. 'Smith's *made* it your business. It's his fault it happened. He leaves a trail of misery wherever he sets foot, that one.'

'There's nothing we can do,' Jack said. 'It's up to Linda to deal with it.'

'Why can't you ring that damned reporter?'

'Because we'd be seriously overstepping the mark. We're walking on eggs as it is.'

Arms akimbo, she stood over him. 'Why?'

'Because we have to be completely impartial.' Ellen stood up, and took Rene's elbow. 'Let's make some tea. I know you're terribly upset. Linda's almost like one of your own, isn't she?'

Grudgingly, Rene allowed herself to be moved. 'And I feel for Fred like he's one of the family. By God!' she exploded. 'That Smith's got it coming to him!'

As soon as Rene was out of earshot, Janet said: 'She keeps uttering threats, and local feeling seems to be running higher by the hour. How d'you rate Smith's long-term chances?'

'Let's say I'm very glad I'm not in his Gucci loafers,' Jack replied. 'If he's any sense, he'll change his name again, go to another town, and start all over as a virgin, as the saying goes.'

'He can afford to.'

'He could afford to go to the ends of the earth, or at least, Beryl could afford to send him, but I expect he'll brazen it out here, because he reckons he's done nothing wrong. He doubtless sees himself as the victim of a lynch mob mentality that succeeded in corrupting the police.'

'We're not making much progress with Dugdale and the others, are we?' Janet asked.

'I'm not sure there's progress to be made, in the sense of breaking open a conspiracy.' Jack yawned, as the church clock struck the hour. 'My gut instinct, coupled with my professional judgement, inclines towards the view that Dugdale didn't receive the letter, and therefore there's nothing for us to pursue in that area. So, when Mr McKenna's had time to get to grips with the notion of a possibly corrupt priest, we'll go after Fauvel.' When Janet shivered as a draught from the window caught her back, he added: 'Rene's determined we'll have a blizzard before morning.'

'It's still too cold to snow.' She frowned at him across the desk. 'Assuming Fauvel lied about the letter, he must have realised what the consequences would be. Why should he want Smith behind bars?'

Jack shrugged. 'I've no idea. He's a completely unknown quantity at the moment.'

'Wendy Lewis thinks the sun's rays originate under his cassock.'

'You took against her with a vengeance, didn't you?'

'She's a simpering hypocrite,' Janet said. 'And more than happy to drop Dugdale in the mire if the alternative involves her in questioning the integrity of the wonderful Father Brett. What sort of name is Brett Fauvel, anyway?'

'Of the same ilk as Piers Stanton Smith in my book.' Jack grinned. 'Pretentious in the extreme, and cringingly artificial.'

3

Clamping a pen between his teeth as he picked up the receiver, the newsroom clerk at the London office of Gaynor Holbrook's paper tried to remember the last respite from the tyranny of telephones. 'Yeah?' he said, voice surly.

'I want to speak to that Holbrook woman.'

He heard harsh breaths and even harsher vowels straining in the woman's tones. 'D'you mean Gaynor?'

'That's her.'

'She's not here.'

'She works there, doesn't she?'

'When she's in London, but she's not here now.'

'Where is she, then?'

'Who wants to know?'

'I do!'

He imagined the words snapping between her teeth, and coming out broken. 'Why?'

'Because she's been writing a pack of lies, and it's going to cost her. That's why!'

He pulled the pen out of his mouth and scrabbled around amid the rubbish on the desk for a piece of paper. 'Who are you? What's your phone number?'

'You going to tell her?'

'That's the general idea.'

'You writing this down?'

'When you tell me what to write.'

'You tell her Mrs Sheridan's got a bone to pick with her, and it's a big one.'

'Right. Will she know who you are, or what it's about?'

'She will when she rings me, so mind you tell her to hurry up about it, or she'll be sorry.' She reeled off a telephone number. 'You got that?' She repeated the number, then hung up before he could answer.

'There!' Ida Sheridan sat down in a rush and stared at her friend, her face flushed, her eyes bright, and both the women in awe of her daring.

'D'you think she'll get in touch?'

'She will if she's any sense, and if she doesn't, why, I'll ring her boss.'

'Are we doing the right thing?' the other fretted, her pinched old face lined with worry.

'Yes!' Ida patted her scrawny arm. 'They can't be let to get away with it. It's criminal.'

'Shouldn't I go to a solicitor, or something?'

'You can't afford it.'

'Story of my life.' The other sighed.

4

'Much as we sympathise with Mrs Newton's position, I'm afraid we cannot involve ourselves,' McKenna said. 'This is essentially between Mrs Newton and the newspaper.'

'I'm not asking you to involve yourselves!' Linda's solicitor barked down the telephone. 'I'm asking you to postpone tomorrow's interview, in view of what happened to her father. She's distraught, and therefore in no fit state to withstand police interrogation, especially as she's nothing to answer for in the first place.'

'How is Mr Jarvis?'

'Rallying,' the other man admitted with reluctance.

'So I heard,' McKenna said. 'Did Mrs Newton ask you to approach me?'

'I act in her best interests.'

'But did she ask?'

'Not specifically.'

'If she does, please get in touch immediately. Otherwise, I'll expect to see you both at the appointed time tomorrow.'

'You were a bit hard on him,' Jack commented, when McKenna hung up.

'I've had a bellyful of these solicitors and their shenanigans. He's no doubt part of Pawsley's magic circle, doing his own bit to scupper our job.'

'The Federation called while you were out. Lewis refused to have another brief, so they want to know our intentions.'

'We proceed on the basis of her being un-represented, as that's apparently how she wants it.'

'You know it isn't,' Jack chided.

'I will *not* be manipulated! This is a blatant attempt to blackmail us into letting Pawsley back on the scene.'

'I know that, but we can't let Lewis be without a solicitor.'

'She's been offered an alternative, so it's her choice. She's a grown woman, not a child in need of protection. For heaven's sake, Jack! Wendy Lewis is two years *older* than you! Try that perspective.'

Sitting cross-legged on her sitting-room floor, her face almost scorched by the fire, Wendy snatched another tissue from the box beside her, and snivelled. The telephone was slippery with her tears. 'They can't do this! They can't take you away from me!'

'They'll try, dear,' Frances replied. Beyond her office window, the lights of the city sprang to life, piercing the winter twilight. Her left ear was ringing from Wendy's assaults, and she moved the receiver to her other hand. 'But we gels must stick together. Us against the world, eh?'

'I've told them I won't have anyone else!' Wendy exclaimed.

'Was that wise? You need somebody.'

'I need *you*!'

'Have they said they want to see you again?'

'No. Not yet, anyway.'

'They'll probably be back with the statement transcript for you to sign, but that's not a problem. Just make sure you read it carefully, and if there's anything you're not happy about, don't sign it. I've got a copy of the tape, remember.'

'When are you coming to see me?' whined Wendy. 'Tonight?'

'I don't think I ought, dear. McKenna told me to stay away, and I wouldn't put it past him to have you under surveillance.'

'He can't do that! You're my friend.'

'Of *course* I'm your friend!' Frances tried to summon a smile into her voice, but felt as wearied, had she known it, as a mother might by the incessant demands of a spoiled toddler. 'But McKenna's very powerful, so it wouldn't be sensible to cross him.'

'But you must do *something*!' Wendy insisted.

'Can't you talk to your police contacts?'

'I'll try, dear.'

'Can I ring later to find out?'

'I'll call you when there's something to report, but I think you should try for an early night. You must be quite worn out with stress.'

'I won't sleep a wink! And I'm sure I was awake most of last night.'

'All the more reason to try to make up for it tonight, then. I really must go, dear. Someone's been waiting to see me for the past half-hour.'

6

Sitting on coloured plastic chairs outside the cardiac care unit, with the end of Fred's bed just in view, Craig and Linda waited for the nurses to finish their half-hourly observations.

'Fred'll be alive and kicking at a hundred, and getting a telegram off the Queen,' Craig commented. 'I've never seen such a fighting spirit.'

'He's like that 'cos there's unfinished business.' She leaned her head against Craig's shoulder, and closed her eyes. 'I feel like I could sleep for ever.'

He put his arm around her. 'Stress does that to you. What say we go home? My mum said she'll keep the boys overnight, if we want.'

Comforted by the closeness of his big, strong body, she let her thoughts drift to the carefree days of marriage before the boys arrived, before she noticed her father looked as if he would follow her mother to an early grave, and especially, she remembered, before her poor dead sister dropped her guard and the pretence of a happy marriage. Linda grew up knowing about the viciousness hidden behind net curtains and pumiced doorsteps, because Rene and her like would purse their lips and frown over the sight of one housewife or the other with her right eye blacked that week instead of her left, but she never imagined such horrors might cross her own family's doorstep. They were too decent, too conscious of the scrutiny of others, and therefore too afraid of losing face by showing bruised flesh to the world and, from the deep and enveloping sense of safety which was the most potent memory of her early years, she knew that nothing other than honest, loving transactions had passed between her parents. Fred Jarvis grieved long and hard for his dead wife, but never with the sly face of guilt.

Linda stopped inventing convoluted reasons to explain the obvious, but mysterious, decline in her sister's well-being on a rain-washed summer day when she called unexpectedly at the house and, about to open the front door, heard Smith's hysterical ranting. She wavered on the doorstep, flinching when the crashing and shattering noises began. In the brief silence which followed, she found she was holding her breath, then there was another sound: a gurgling, hardly human cry, like an animal in mortal fear. She barged through the door and into the room where Trisha was later found burned to a crisp, to see Smith, eyes alight, a froth of spittle at each side of his mouth, gloating over the splinters and shards of his tantrum, while Trisha crouched against the wall, hands clutched to her bloody face.

'Get out, bitch!' Smith moved on Linda, fists raised.

Trisha launched herself at him, clawing his back. 'Leave her alone!'

He swatted her, drawing more blood, then pushed past Linda and ran upstairs. Within seconds, he ran back down, through the front door, and out into the lane, and even now, the memory of it made Linda's heart stop dead.

'Hey!' Craig kissed the top of her head, and squeezed her trembling shoulders. 'Fred's going to be fine. We'll bring the boys again later if he feels up to it.'

'He'd like that.' Joints aching, Linda rose, trying to banish the ghosts, at least for the time being. 'I'll ring Rene. She'll want to visit.'

'She won't be home yet.'

'I'm sure those coppers are human enough to pass on a message.'

'You don't have to see them tomorrow if you don't want.'

'I do want. Sooner the better, as far as I'm concerned.'

7

Rene knocked on the office door, walked in without invitation, laid a tray in the middle of Jack's desk, then retreated to the doorway, folded her arms, and looked down on the four souls around the room. Trying to evade the cold, which crept outwards from every corner, Ellen and Janet both huddled inside heavy sweaters.

'Decent of you to let me speak to Linda,' Rene said, to the room at large.

'Not at all.' McKenna smiled. 'How's her father?'

'Better than a body's any right to be, in the circumstances, and he wants to talk to you.'

'Why?' asked Jack.

'Why d'you think?' Rene sighed.

'Perhaps we should wait until he's a little stronger,' McKenna suggested.

'That won't be long, then,' Rene said. 'I'll tell him later, when I visit.' Unfolding her arms, she stuck her hands in her apron pockets, and fidgeted. 'I know you think I'm a gossip, but sometimes, things need to be said.'

'And?' McKenna asked.

'Well, there's been a lot of toing and froing today, what with people going to the hospital, and ringing to ask about Fred, and the like. He's always been respected, but people took a lot more interest in him after Trisha was killed, and now, with that Smith on the loose again and the newspaper rubbish and his heart attack, well, nobody's talking about anything else, are they?' She paused for breath. 'Linda said there's been a couple of reporters at the hospital, and Fred's next-door neighbour, the one who rang Linda this morning, had a man from the *Manchester Evening News* leaning on her doorbell.'

'I'm sure the hospital would get rid of the press if they're bothering people.'

'That's not what I mean,' Rene said. 'Linda can sort a few hacks. After all, they were crawling all over during the trial.'

'Then what's the problem?' asked Jack, making inroads on the tea tray.

'The town's thick with reporters, and some folk don't mind opening their gobs for a few five-pound notes or even just for the attention. Barry Dugdale's next-door neighbour's one of them, apparently.'

'I see,' McKenna said. 'And what's she been saying?'

'She heard Barry and Sue rowing last night till well past midnight, the kids didn't go to school this morning, then Sue drove off in her car with the kids and their toys, and a load of suitcases.'

'Who told you?' McKenna asked.

'Linda heard it off somebody else, and she said if Sue's left Barry it's another nail in Smith's coffin.'

8

Shivering on the doorstep, while the wind whipped around her and snapped at the hem of her jacket, Ellen looked into Dugdale's blank face and bloodshot eyes. 'D'you remember me? I'm Ellen Turner. I was here yesterday. Superintendent McKenna's asked me to make an unofficial visit. He'll decide later if a formal interview is necessary.'

Holding the door wider, Dugdale stood aside, then followed Ellen into the front room, his feet making trudging noises on the carpets. The room was almost as cold as the doorstep, the fire unlit, the big radiator under the window fighting a losing battle with the plummeting temperature.

'What is it?' His speech sounded as if he were drugged. He stood before the dead fire, trembling from head to foot.

'Shall we light the fire?' Ellen suggested.

'What?'

'The fire. It's freezing.'

'Oh.' Casting around as might a stranger, he knelt down slowly, moved aside part of the decorative front plate, and pushed the ignition button.

Crouching beside him, Ellen said: 'You have to turn on the gas first.' She twisted the knob, and the fire sprang to life. 'That's better, isn't it? May I sit down?'

'Sue usually lights the fire.' Dugdale still trembled. 'Where is she?'

'Gone to her mother's.'

'Why?'

He collapsed into an armchair, as if someone had

clouted the back of his knees, and drooped forward, hands dangling.

'Why has she gone, Mr Dugdale?'

'I'm supposed to say her mother's ill.'

'But she isn't?'

'Sue's left me.' Tears filled his eyes. 'And she's taken the children.'

'What happened?'

'I had to tell her about Julie.'

'I don't quite understand.'

'I *had* to. I'd told Superintendent McKenna.'

Wondering if she had missed some crucial disclosure the previous day, Ellen said: 'You said you and Julie went together years ago.'

'Yes.'

'Didn't your wife know?'

'No.'

'I see. Did she know about Linda?'

'Yes.'

'Did that bother her?'

'No.'

'So, what's the problem with Julie?'

He gazed unseeingly at the fire. 'I'm not sure. It all got terribly muddled up. I think it's because we slept together.' Pausing, working his mouth, he went on: 'Or, perhaps Sue thinks we're *still* sleeping together.' He stopped speaking yet again, then said: 'Or maybe, because I didn't tell her about Julie, but told her about Linda, she thinks there's something sinister there.'

'Has she any grounds to suspect you're being unfaithful?'

'No, and I'm not. I haven't been, ever.'

'Why didn't you tell her about Julie?'

He looked at her, face gaunt. 'Because I was ashamed.'

'Of what? Going with a girl who had a bad reputation?'

'Of helping to give her that reputation, and I'm not the only man in town with the same cause to be ashamed of himself.'

'You were very young, and behaved rather thoughtlessly, but at least, you accept that, where most wouldn't.'

His features twisted into a haggard smile. 'Julie was my first love, you know. She could break your heart with just a look.'

'Does your wife know that?'

'God, no! She reckons Julie's a dirty trollop.'

'Did she say that when you were rowing?'

'Yes, and I told her to be quiet. People think they can say what they like about Julie, and it's not right.'

'That's probably why your wife's angry. Women hear with their instincts, not their ears.'

'How did you know we'd been rowing?'

'Bush telegraph.'

'As in Rene Minshull and Linda?'

Ellen nodded. 'You need to know there's been a sudden upsurge of media interest in the Smith case, partly because of Gaynor Holbrook, and partly because Linda's dad had a mild heart attack this morning.'

He covered his face with his hands. 'Oh, God! I didn't know. How is he?'

'Recovering.'

'That's a blessing. They've already had more than enough tragedy.' He frowned. 'Who's Gaynor Holbrook?'

'She's writing about Smith for one of the popular national papers. You've not seen her articles?' When he shook his head, Ellen said: 'Well, yesterday, she did a résumé of the murder, trial and appeal, and suggested Superintendent McKenna's strings will be pulled by vested interest, and today she interviewed Smith. It's Beryl's turn tomorrow.' She watched him. 'If you read the articles, under no circumstances must you react to anything in them.'

'Why should I?'

Without responding, Ellen said: 'I'm surprised Hinchcliffe hasn't brought them to your attention. By the way, have you told him your wife's left?'

'No. Should I?'

'Yes, and be prepared for a lot of gossip and speculation. The media bandwagon's rolling, and they're waving cheque-books, so you might see some lurid headlines associating your wife's departure with our investigation.'

'They can write what they like as long as they leave Julie alone.'

'When did you last see her?'

'Two weeks before I got engaged, to say I was planning to get married.'

'Why didn't you tell us this yesterday? You rather played down the relationship.'

'I don't want Hinchcliffe knowing. He prattles like an old woman, and I wouldn't trust him as far as I could chuck him.'

'Isn't that rather unfortunate?'

'He's a necessary evil. He'll probably do what he's paid to do well enough, but the less he knows about my personal affairs, the better.'

'Unfortunately, in a situation like yours, you can't pick and choose what to disclose,' Ellen concluded. 'You'd better warn your wife about the media, in case they find out where she's gone.' She smiled. 'She might decide staying away isn't worth the potential scandal.'

'You think?' His eyes were almost dead. 'She's far more likely to decide to stay away for good.'

9

'What did you say?'

Gaynor's voice was hard enough to split stone when she was in one of her moods, the newsroom clerk thought, which was more often than not. Rubbing at a smear of ball-point ink on the telephone, he said: 'This woman wants to speak to you. She's called Mrs Something Sheridan, and she said it's urgent.'

'What the fuck does she want?'

'I don't know, Gaynor. She didn't say. She just left a number.'

'Where?'

'Where what?'

'Jesus! Where was she fucking calling *from*?'

'How should I know?'

'Give me the number.'

Obediently, he complied, then waited, while, at the other end of the line, she rustled papers.

'That's a Sheffield number,' she told him. 'Why should somebody in Sheffield want to speak to me?'

Rather than: 'How the fuck should I know?' he said: 'I've no idea, Gaynor. Where are you now?'

'Freezing off my butt in the back of fucking beyond!'

'Well, wherever you are, you'd better call her,' he said mildly. 'It sounded urgent.'

10

Completing her report on Dugdale, Ellen said: 'There's always such a mess when people's feelings and motives get exposed.'

'Only because they're a mess to begin with,' Jack commented.

'Be fair. We've stirred up a hornet's nest.'

'The nest was thoroughly agitated long before we arrived,' McKenna said, 'and we keep prodding until the last hornet comes sizzling out. I've brought forward Father Barclay's interview to this evening, around eight, and once we've heard what he has to say, we go after Fauvel.' To Jack, he added: 'I'd be grateful if you and Janet will examine statements for discrepancies, or anything that was overlooked first time around. I know much of what Smith told Holbrook isn't in the trial transcript, and that could be because he's making it up as he goes along, but we'll ask Linda Newton to clarify the issues relating to her sister which might impinge on Dugdale's conduct.'

'His statements are models of consistency,' Jack said, 'apart from the news about his relationships with Linda and Broadbent, but Lewis is a different matter. She seems to change her tune by the hour.'

'I must ask Barclay if he knows her.' McKenna scribbled in his notebook. 'Did you contact the National Insurance Register about Bunty Smith?'

Jack nodded. 'I also put queries on Hilda Smith and Bunty Smith through our computer, but nothing showed up, so the psychologist was probably right about her going to hospital, and not prison.'

Rene's dinner of roast lamb and vegetables, and apple tart with hot custard, all of which Janet, watched hawkishly by Ellen, consumed steadily, was almost over when Superintendent Ryman telephoned McKenna.

'Something happened today I feel you should know about,' Ryman began, his voice steely. 'A rather unpleasant incident, I may add. Mr and Mrs Stanton Smith drove into Haughton this afternoon, and in the chemist's, where Mr Stanton Smith tried to purchase some toiletries, the other customers very ostentatiously turned their backs on him. Some even went so far', he added, 'as to hold their coats over their faces, as if he had the plague!'

'Mr Stanton Smith has no one but himself to blame,' McKenna replied. 'If he wanted to keep a low profile, he should have refrained from spilling his guts all over the national press. People will react as they see fit, and apart from that, the father of the late Trisha Smith had a heart attack this morning, provoked by what the family claim are Smith's wicked lies. He's heaping insult on injury.'

'You've only got *their* word for that.'

'Apparently, there's independent evidence available to disprove what was published. However, I understand the family's dealing with that in their own way.'

'Are they? How?'

'By the usual means, I imagine.'

'A libel action? Have they got that kind of money?'

'I'm grateful for your information, Mr Ryman, but I won't discuss the issue further.'

'That's all very well, but it didn't end with the cold-shouldering,' Ryman added hurriedly. 'When they got back to the car, they found the tyres slashed.'

'That's for your local officers to deal with, although it might not be wise to construe the tyre-slashing as a personal attack.'

'What else could it be? Beryl Stanton Smith drives a cream Mercedes, with a personalised number-plate.'

McKenna had taken Rene to the hospital, and Janet and Ellen were washing up, when Colin Bowden arrived unexpectedly. Following Jack into the office, he pulled a chair close to the gas fire and, elbows on knees, stared at its white-hot heart.

'Shall I switch on the tape-recorder?' Jack asked.

Colin shrugged. 'It's up to you, sir, but this isn't about the investigation. It isn't your problem, either, but I don't know who else to talk to.'

'Ms Singh? The Federation?'

'I can't trust her. She's got some agenda of her own, and I don't think she's advising me properly, so I asked the Federation for another solicitor.'

'As is your right.'

'Is it? Anyway, she'd beaten me to it, and told them she'd want out if I continue resisting her advice.' Rubbing his hands to warm them, Colin added: 'I don't know what they said to her, but they virtually told me beggars can't be choosers, and I either toe her line or suffer the consequences. Bearing in mind what you said about breaking ranks, sir, I said I'd prefer the consequences.'

Jack sighed. 'That strikes me as being more of a knee-jerk reaction than a considered decision. Have you thought this through? You're obviously somewhat headstrong, and you might not appreciate her frames of reference. She's obliged to protect you from getting shafted, and she has to presume that we pose a very real threat to your future, and even, perhaps, to your freedom.'

'She's muddying the waters, sir, and putting the wrong construction on things. I *know* I didn't collude with Inspector Dugdale to suppress evidence, and I *know* I didn't help stitch up Smith, but she won't accept that. She's convinced I'm holding out on her.'

'Perhaps she's just convinced that *something* happened, whether you know it or not, and trying to protect you from others' mischief.'

'There was no mischief.'

'You're isolating yourself,' Jack said. 'Putting yourself right out on a limb. In a worst-case scenario,' he pointed out quietly, 'whether or not *you* did anything wrong, you face going down. You were too close to Dugdale for dirt not to rub off, so I suggest you think again before cutting your only lifeline.'

As he finished relating the gist of Colin's visit, Jack said: 'It's like that song Queen and Freddie Mercury used to belt out at the top of their voices.'

'I know.' McKenna nodded. '"Another one bites the dust", as in solicitors going down like ninepins. Joking apart, it's time we made our own representations to the Federation, so you can drop them a line while I'm out. Express our general concerns, advise them to get their solicitors back in line, and include Pawsley's admission about Hinchcliffe's gross indiscretion. That might alert them to the possibility of solicitor collusion.'

The bodywork of McKenna's car was cloudy with frost, the pavement sparkling with millions of microscopic crystals, and the trees in the churchyard, their branches whitened, looked like ghosts, and quivered just as mournfully in the wind.

'Rene's convinced we'll be under ten feet of snow before long,' he said, managing a wheelspin at the turn of the hill. 'D'you think she's exaggerating?'

'I doubt it,' Ellen replied. 'My grandparents' house in Yorkshire was buried roof deep at times. We should get snow chains for the cars, you know.'

'I tried, but everywhere's sold out in anticipation.'

I

Father Barclay stood at the parlour window of the small presbytery outside Buxton, looking through his spectral reflection to the steep lane down which his visitors must drive. So weary he could barely stand, and almost beside himself with the bone-deep pain which dogged him day and night, he once more pondered the early arrival of his own death. The wilful, strong-minded young man who was so convinced of his calling that nothing could stand in its way was now a forgotten stranger, and he could not even remember the energy, let alone the fiery spirit, which compelled him to holy orders. Now, that spirit was humbled and turned in upon itself, he thought, as he watched McKenna's car, headlights swinging wildly, bump over the humps and ruts of the lane. He began to move restlessly around the room, equilibrium and faith once more threatened by experience, by the close, cold brush of death's wings, and by his responsibility for releasing a sadist upon the world.

The decorations in this cheerless room must be pre-war, McKenna thought, the unyielding, hide-upholstered armchair in which he sat even older, and although the coals in the hearth burned bright, the chimney must cough when the wind turned, for the wallpaper above the mantel was discoloured by smoky stains.

While Ellen rigged up her machines, he studied the tall young man who sat in another ancient chair, and thought he saw the shadow of death still about him. Barclay's eyes burned holes in his parchment-like skin, and McKenna could almost see the blood pulsing through the matrix of veins on the beautiful hands folded in the priest's lap. He was not clad in the garb of his calling, as McKenna had expected, but in old corduroy trousers, a fisherman's rib sweater, and checked shirt. Firelight struck gold in his thick brown hair, and warmed his engaging features, but did nothing to dispel the shadow.

'Thank you for allowing us to record the interview,' McKenna said, 'although I must stress that you're not under caution.' He smiled and, receiving a smile in return, felt as if he had seen the sun break through cloud. 'Do you have any questions of your own?'

'None that I can think of, and none that man can answer anyway I'm afraid, pretentious though that may sound.' Despite the lingering smile, the priest's eyes were dark with weariness. 'If Father Fauvel saw me now, I think he'd be very contented. On my last day in Haughton he advised an unremitting search of soul and conscience. He thought I was perilously close to heresy.'

'Did he?' McKenna asked. 'What had you done to warrant such chastisement?'

'I questioned the humanity of His Holiness's last encyclical on birth control. I believe the Church has no right to promote uncontrolled fertility when half its flock is already starving. Unfortunately, we don't have the gifts of Our Lord when it comes to feeding the masses.'

'In another age you'd have sizzled at the stake for comments like that.'

'Priests who share my views would sizzle now, if some of the cardinals had their way. But the Church is more likely to founder through arrogance than by reassessing its position according to the time and place. What is acceptable in a country with state welfare is wholly inappropriate in the Third World, and even here, both spiritual and material poverty results from the compulsion people feel to have children they can't afford.' He stared thoughtfully at McKenna. 'We can only ever guess at the shape of God's Will. Doubt *must* inform our convictions. Apart from that, unquestioning faith tends to give others the wrong opportunities.' Impatiently, he ran his fingers through his hair. 'I'm sorry. I'm being very pompous. To be truthful, Father Fauvel and I were close to real conflict, and not only over theological issues. I found his conservative routines rather irksome, and he very much resented my criticism.'

'He probably saw it as a power struggle,' McKenna suggested. 'The Church is no less prone than other institutions to vices like ambition. But at least, in South America, you were *expected* to make a difference. Will you go back?'

'When my strength returns. It's a long time coming.'

'It's a wonder you're still alive,' McKenna said. 'You were very ill.'

'What sort of missionary work were you doing?' Ellen asked. 'Our documents don't say.'

'You've probably heard about the street children in South American cities,' Barclay replied. 'They're beggars, there are literally thousands of them, and they're looked upon as vermin. Every so often, the "social cleansing squads" execute a few dozen here and there. Our mission was taking children off the streets, and providing food and shelter.' The smile he offered was bleak. 'A far more worthwhile enterprise than getting Piers Stanton Smith out of prison. I wish I'd never come back.'

'Did you know him well?' McKenna asked.

'Only by sight. Converts were traditionally Father Fauvel's property.'

'I have to ask you this,' McKenna said. 'Are you absolutely sure you saw Smith in church on the afternoon Trisha died?'

'Absolutely.' Barclay nodded. 'He turned up not long after two o'clock, wanting Father Fauvel. I told him Father Fauvel was in Manchester for the afternoon, at a meeting, but he waited. He must have footled around for the best part of three hours. It's perfectly possible he was giving himself an alibi, but then, he also had a lot of time on his hands. I imagine he still has.'

'Who else was there?'

'The ladies who do the flowers and the cleaning, and I was in and out all the time. We were busy with preparations for Easter.'

'You went abroad at the beginning of April, and wrote to Father Fauvel early in September,' McKenna began. 'I appreciate that from your point of view, he was the more certain conduit, and in a position to ensure the letter served its purpose, but why didn't you lay greater emphasis on its importance?'

'I almost didn't write at all,' Barclay admitted. 'Smith and Haughton seemed terribly remote, but, more to the point, I knew there were other witnesses. My statement wasn't crucial.'

'But it was,' McKenna said. 'And you should have said as much in your covering note to Father Fauvel.'

'It wasn't his business.' Barclay was adamant. 'It was a matter for the police.'

146

'Did Smith say why he was anxious to see Father Fauvel?'

'No, but there's nothing sinister in that. As the most junior of the priests, I hardly figured in his scheme of things.'

'Did Trisha ever attend your church?'

'I don't know. I never met her.'

'Do you know her sister, Linda?'

'No.'

'What about Wendy Lewis?'

Barclay nodded. 'Of course. She's very devout, and she also, I suspect, has a crush on Father Fauvel, although in that, she's definitely not alone.'

'Really?'

'He's quite charming, and rather handsome, in that bland, old-fashioned way.' He smiled. 'A few years ago, two teenage girls virtually besieged the presbytery. They'd turn up in the morning before school, in the afternoon as soon as school was out, and be permanent fixtures nearly all weekend. When they took to peeking through the slits in the curtain nets he asked their parents to take them in hand.'

'Interesting.' Stifling a yawn, McKenna asked: 'D'you know Julie Broadbent?'

A strange expression crossed the priest's face. 'Yes, I know Julie. A very lovely woman.'

'Is she? We haven't met her yet.'

'No, but I'm sure you've heard plenty about her, most of it bad. Take my advice, and don't heed. She isn't what people say, and if she ever was, she's redeemed herself.'

'Like Mary Magdalene?' McKenna suggested.

'I hope that isn't mockery, Superintendent,' Barclay said, an edge in his voice. 'Julie's a good person. She has purity and charity, whereas she'd be quite entitled to bitterness and anger. She's been badly wounded.'

Seeing the expression on McKenna's face, he added impatiently: 'Not as Smith claims to be damaged! Julie was saddled with her mother's shame, and when she went somewhat awry, most people saw it as proof that immorality is inherited. Personally, I believe the accident is responsible for any lapses.'

McKenna frowned. 'What accident?'

'Has no one told you? When she was eleven, a pan of boiling fat spilled over her. She's very badly scarred, and I've often thought her so-called promiscuity was simply the outcome of an equally blistered self-image.'

2

Trying to redeem some control over his life, Dugdale waited until the late-evening television news was over, then telephoned his wife. 'How are the kids?'

'Fine,' Sue replied. 'Asleep, of course.'

'And your mother?'

'Fine.'

'And you?'

'OK.'

'The police came back,' he said. 'Not McKenna, but that Turner woman who's doing the admin.'

'Why?'

'Linda's dad had a heart attack this morning, for one thing.'

'Oh, no! That's awful! Is he dead?'

'No. They think he'll pull through.'

'I hope he does.' She fell silent, and he could hear her breathing. Then, she asked: 'Surely, she didn't come just to tell you that?'

'They wanted to warn me. Some woman's writing articles about Smith in one of the nationals, and the town's overrun with reporters again. They've heard about us.'

'What?' Sue drew in her breath sharply. 'Heard what? How could they?'

'People talk. I expect someone overheard the row last night, and saw you go off this morning with the kids.'

'Have *you* told anyone?'

'Only Turner, but I had no choice. She reckons I should tell Hinchcliffe, but I haven't. Not yet. Anyway,' he went on, 'you'd better be prepared. I can see the headline now: "Wife runs out on dodgy copper".'

'I hope you're not lying,' Sue said. 'You didn't come clean about that woman, did you?' When he failed to respond, she asked: 'Why didn't you? Why did you never tell me about her?'

'I don't know.'

'Are you still in love with her?'

'It's almost eighteen years ago!'

'I think you're trying to protect her, although I haven't a clue why you should.'

'Last night, you said I was trying to protect *myself*.'

'I've had time to think. *Are* you protecting her?'

'I don't want to cause her more grief. She's got nothing to do with this business, so I don't see why she should be dragged into it, but I couldn't keep quiet because McKenna already knew.'

'How d'you think he found out?'

'No idea, and there's no point asking him.'

'Ryman probably told him,' Sue suggested. 'He had his fingers in a lot of pies when he worked in Haughton. I expect he told McKenna about you and Linda as well.' After another silence, she said: 'Incidentally, what grief has that woman already had, apart from what she made for herself? You said you don't want to cause her *more* grief, or was that just a figure of speech?'

'No, it wasn't. D'you know something, Sue? You're turning into a jealous harpy. We flogged this to death last night.' He took a deep breath. 'If you can't accept you weren't the first woman in my life, there's nothing I can do, but I'd be grateful if you'd stop referring to Julie as "her", "she", or "that woman". She's as much right to her name as you have.'

'And what name is that? Tart? Trollop? Whore?'

'This is pointless! Maybe you should stay away!'

'Maybe I will!' she snapped, and dropped the receiver with a clatter.

3

Sitting bolt upright in her friend's fireside chair, with her nerves strung like piano wire, Ida had the telephone within hand's reach, but she kept nodding off, then snapping awake with a pounding heart, terrified that she might have missed the summons. She had dreamed of telling the doctor how, if she sat in a soft chair, or even a hard one, her eyes fell shut of their own accord in less than five minutes, as forceful with him as she had been on the telephone, and refusing to be fobbed off with platitudes about age and worn-out bodies, and yet another prescription for anti-depressants. The next time she returned to full consciousness, another twenty-five minutes had been lost.

'She won't ring now,' the other woman said. She had kept her own part in the vigil by padding back and forth to the kitchen to make cups of hot, sweet tea to fortify her friend. 'There's no point you hanging on.'

'Damn her eyes!' Ida scowled. 'She'll be sorry.' She struggled upright, her legs planted far apart. Her ankles were swollen with tiredness and fiery with the heat.

The other woman stood by the door, holding Ida's jacket and scarf.

'I'll be back in the morning,' Ida said, fighting with the jacket sleeve. 'As soon as I've done my shopping. We'll get that madam sorted, you see if we don't!'

'If you say so, Ida.'

'What d'you mean by that?' Eyes narrowed, Ida stared. 'I'm doing this for you. It's your problem. No skin off my nose either way.'

'I'm just not sure we're going about things the right way,' the other fretted.

'What other way is there? If there was another way, we wouldn't be doing this, would we?'

As the door closed behind her, she realised how ferocious the wind had become while she dozed by the fire, for when she turned to make her way to her own front door, the wind caught her in the back and pushed violently. She tottered along the walkway, scuttling past darkened windows, almost lifted off her feet, and slammed into the high iron railings which caged each level of the maisonettes. By the time she reached her own place, she felt as shaky and fragile as a leaf bowled in front of that wind.

4

'Jools? Jools! Are you coming down? Father Brett's going now.'

Seated in front of the silent television, Julie put her head in her hands, wondering for the thousandth time why her colleague made the long trek up several staircases to the attic flat to speak to her, instead of picking up one of the telephones. 'I'll be down in a minute.'

'Right. Don't be too long, will you?'

She heard the footsteps shuffling away and padding downstairs, the sound of doors opening and closing, of voices mumbling, then Fauvel's educated tones, so clear and sharp he could be outside her door. She began to shiver uncontrollably, teeth gritted, wanting to hit herself for being so stupid. Nevertheless, she listened like a hunted animal until his car crunched down the gravel drive.

'You've missed him,' her colleague said. 'You were ages, and you said you'd only be a minute.'

'There'll be another time,' Julie replied, leafing through the log book. 'Anything happened?'

'Since when? You've been around most of the day, even though you were on duty last night. Don't you need sleep like the rest of us?'

'Night shifts ruin my routines.'

'Well, for goodness sake get some sleep tonight, otherwise you'll be like a zombie tomorrow.' The other woman smiled. 'I saved you some supper. Make us a fresh pot of tea while I do the rounds. They should all be abed by now.'

Once again, Julie stared through the kitchen windows as she waited for the kettle to boil, watching lights pop off downstairs in the houses which sprawled over the once exclusive grounds of the Willows, while other lights clicked on in bedrooms and bathrooms. It was colder tonight, she thought, pulling her sleeves over her hands and knowing it would become even colder before there was that rush of warmer air which always preceded the snow. She had lived her whole life in this place, its seasons defining memories, events pinioned in her mind by the weather and the colours of the earth which formed their backdrop. Last week had seen the twelfth anniversary of her mother's death, then of her funeral, the earth where her grave was dug frozen two feet down. The first snows that year spiralled from a blackening sky as Fauvel, wreathed in incense and the earth's misty vapours, proceeded to the graveside. When he began to eulogise over the remains of a woman who suffered wholesale rejection by the Christian community during her lifetime, Julie was so enraged she had to bite her tongue. Briefly, her loss allowed the community to embrace her, but she had no idea what to do with their condolences, or whether to trust their warmth, so she thrust both away, and returned to the known wilderness she and her mother had always inhabited.

On the day she had asked her mother why she chose to be a prostitute, a spring sun shone with the first real warmth of the year.

'D'you really think it was a *choice*?' Kathy asked.

'You could've got a normal job.'

'Not when you were little. There was no one to look after you.'

'I wasn't always little.'

'It was too late by then.'

'No, it wasn't. You didn't try!'

'Nobody would *let* me try, Julie. Other people made me what I am, and wouldn't let me be anything else.' Kathy smiled with resignation. 'Especially the women. The men aren't so bad. They don't judge you the same way.'

'We could've moved,' Julie insisted. 'Gone to live somewhere else, where nobody knew.'

'Where? There was nowhere to go.'

On an earlier spring day, Julie had demanded to

know about her father. Kathy had been young, then, yet somehow seemed so old. The rain was falling, gurgling in the gutters and splashing under the wheels of the trucks and cars and buses, which roared incessantly along the road outside their house.

'He was my first boyfriend,' Kathy remembered wistfully. 'I was only seventeen when you were born.' She sighed. 'Your gran and grandad put me in the Willows when I said I was expecting. I was supposed to give you away, then go back to them as if nothing had happened.'

'I know. You've said before.'

'If I'd put you up for adoption,' Kathy mused, 'you'd have had the best of everything, like Beryl Kay. Are you angry with me because I didn't?'

'How can I be angry about something I'll never know about? And who wants to be like Beryl Kay?' Julie's voice was snappish. 'What was my dad like?'

'Sweet,' Kathy said. 'Gentle.'

'Then why didn't you marry him? Weren't you good enough for him?'

'I couldn't. He died.' He was a merchant seaman, and had died not from age or sickness, but by accident, drowned in the Bay of Naples, and in ignorance of the child he had fathered. 'You look like him.' Kathy ruffled the girl's hair. 'You've got his eyes.'

Julie had one faded photograph of that stranger, and she kept it, with other precious relics, in a locked wooden box on the chest in her bedroom. The key to the box hung on the fine silver chain she wore around her neck, even though it often chafed her scars.

Her colleague's footsteps thumped overhead, and her voice called cheerily as she checked each small dormitory. Julie scalded the pot, brewed the tea, took a film-wrapped plate of sandwiches from the refrigerator, and carried the tray to the office, trying to imagine how her mother had felt to be carrying a child. She had never been pregnant, and not, she thought wryly, for want of youthful trying, especially with Barry Dugdale. She had been fond of Barry, and of some of her other lovers, which was, she thought, too grand a name for any of them. The vow of chastity, which crept up on her after the event and without her knowing, proved so much easier to keep than the vow of silence, self-imposed in the bleak years before Barry warmed her frozen little heart.

'Jools? Jools!' Her colleagues voice held that low, intense tone people reserve for anxious moments in the near dead of night.

Julie went to the bottom of the staircase. 'What is it?'

The other woman leaned over the banister. 'Have you seen Debbie? Did she come downstairs? Only, she's not in her room, or the toilet.'

'Did she go up?'

'I can't remember. I thought she did, but I was seeing off Father Brett.'

'Look again,' Julie said. 'I'll check down here.'

The living-rooms and dining-room were empty of all but their perpetual institutional odour. Julie tried the bolt on the front door, and returned to the kitchen, switching on lights as she went through the building. The back door was locked, and the laundry contained only the usual heaps of soiled, stinking linen. Wondering where to look next, she heard a faint, strange noise, and followed it down the stone-flagged passage to the unused sculleries, while the sound grew as if the walls around her were moaning. She found Debbie sitting on the floor of a tiny room with an old stone sink, her back against the cracked tiles which covered the lower half of the wall, her bare feet scuffing backwards and forwards in the dust on the floor. She needed to be taken to the hairdresser soon, Julie thought, looking at the girl's unkempt gingery hair, and she had made a terrible mess of the best clothes obviously donned in honour of Fauvel's visit. Her blouse was undone, exposing a lacy white bra, and her new black shoes were flung into a corner.

'What on earth are you doing in here?' Julie knelt down, and began to button up the blouse, sniffing as a faint odour of stale tobacco drifted under her nose. 'You'll catch cold.'

Debbie giggled, her mouth slack, and slowly lifted her hands, then ran them over Julie's breasts. 'Soft,' she said. 'Nice.'

Wincing, Julie moved the kneading fingers. 'I've told you before not to do that, Debbie. Not to me, not to anyone else, and not to yourself.' Out of the corner of her eye, she glimpsed other footprints in the dust. 'How long have you been here? You're ice cold.'

'Don't talk,' Debbie said, clamping a hand over her own mouth.

'Of course you can talk!' Fatigue, and a total mind-numbing weariness, suddenly hit Julie. 'Don't be so silly.'

'Not allowed,' the girl insisted, mumbling through her fingers.

Julie's hands stilled themselves in mid-air. 'What did you say?' Her voice was a whisper.

Debbie pushed her feet against Julie's knees, almost toppling her, then lunged forward, and began beating Julie with a violence to match the swelling growl in her throat.

5

When she awoke that morning, Janet had been disorientated by strange noises and unfamiliar scents. Rolling over in a huge bed that smelled of lavender and old wood, she located the window, reassuringly half lit around its edges. When she pulled back the curtains, she realised that the screeching and squeaking paining her ears was coming from the inn sign fixed to a bracket on the outside wall, on which the white-faced Hereford bull looked all the more menacing for being so crudely painted. She squinted as the sign was dragged back and forth by the wind, noticing how the bull's eyes stared into hers from every direction.

In front of the pub, Church Street became a steep hill, bordered on one side by a row of medieval cottages, and by the graveyard on the other. From her room, Janet's view of the church was a deep perspective of geometric planes and lines within the tangle of bare trees, where the steeple towered over the loftiest branches, its weathervane luminous. Day and night, a faint reddish light glowed behind the chancel window.

Now, the curtains drawn on the night and a large towel enveloping her body, she sat on the edge of the bed, switched on the hair drier and let heat caress the back of her neck and her shoulders, wondering if she would ever again feel a man's hands do the same. Her short dark crop fell into place of its own accord, and, unplugging the hair drier, she unwrapped the towel, draped it over the radiator, and stood naked in front of the large oval mirror on the wardrobe door. Her ribs cast shadows through her skin, her pelvic girdle was a bony protuberance around a concave space, and her skin hung so thin on the bones that she looked like a half-starved old mare. Her feet and hands, she thought, might well belong to one of the churchyard rooks.

The proud red weal across her belly seemed to glisten. She touched it, holding her breath, wishing so desperately that her child were still inside her, instead of sluiced down a hospital drain, along with her vitality, her youth and the blood which poured from her, the doctors said, for hours on end. Then, sickened by the sight of herself, she pulled her pyjamas from the hook on the door. But she had to pass the mirror again to get to the bathroom to clean her teeth, and, compelled to look despite herself, stood there in her turquoise silk pyjamas, trying to imagine Julie Broadbent's pain when a pan of boiling fat tipped itself all over her.

I

THE POWER OF LOVE

Beryl Stanton Smith talks exclusively to our chief reporter, Gaynor Holbrook, about her marriage and her husband, Piers, whose life sentence for the murder of his first wife, Trisha, was recently quashed on appeal.

Beryl Stanton Smith is forty-one, seven years older than her husband. Her family home is a beautiful Regency house surrounded by matured grounds and swagged stone walls. As she ushers me to the drawing-room, I see the groundsman closing the high wooden gates.

She fiddles with a silver coffee pot on a silver tray, still very distressed by her young husband's imprisonment. During our talk, it becomes clear that the experience badly scarred both of them. The fact that the police who secured his conviction are under investigation is also acutely disturbing. Both fear the backlash.

Her hands shake as she pours our coffee, adding a dribble of cream and a little sugar to her own. Rather inconsequentially, she says she has put on weight, and is dieting. But she looks the same as she did at her husband's trial. She is small, slightly plump, brown-haired, green-eyed, almost homely. Clad in a suit which has seen many better days, there are no give-aways to her huge wealth. Her wedding band is simple. On her right hand, a jet-and-diamond mourning ring glints darkly with each movement. It belonged to her mother, who died only a week before Beryl's marriage. The old woman had bitterly opposed the relationship. 'But sick old people get strange ideas,' she explains. 'She'd even tried to get in touch with Trisha. I found some notes among her papers.'

Beryl is convinced she and Piers Stanton Smith were fated to come together. They married by special licence. Simply cohabiting while Beryl recovered from the shock of her mother's death was out of the question. His high moral standards would not permit it.

There was a chilling experience on the morning of that hurried wedding. The telephone rang about six o'clock. 'When I answered it,' she remembers, 'no one spoke, but I felt someone was there, *trying* to say something.' Common sense tells her it was a wrong number, not her mother calling from beyond the grave. But she still finds it ominous.

She offers to show me the house. The housekeeper and groundsman have a spacious flat on the top floor. Another husband-and-wife team come in daily. But the house is remarkably littered and untidy. I pick my way around stacks of books and overflowing boxes. 'Piers is completely redesigning the interior,' she says. 'He's already finished his study.' She looks at the mess at our feet. 'But he has to feel in the right mood. The tiniest thing can still throw him right off balance.'

The two huge bathrooms have wonderful Victorian brass showers. She thinks they will be ripped out. 'Piers says they're not very ecological.' We trail through six bedrooms, every one with a fine view of the moors. But the rooms are filled with clutter. Battered old furniture is humped against good Art Deco pieces, and I notice a rare Mackintosh cabinet dull with neglect. Fine china is thrown almost carelessly into crates, and almost every wall is covered with pictures. In a landing recess, I find a set of Lowry drawings.

Convinced her husband's fickle enthusiasm is still alive,

Beryl says: 'You won't recognise the house when Piers has finished. He's *terribly* artistic.' Close to tears, she adds that the brutality of prison was a particular tragedy for him.

Downstairs, she is about to bypass his study, then changes her mind. She raps gently on the door, and opens it a few inches. He is at his desk, cigarette in hand, staring into space over a pile of papers. When he turns, face in shadow, cigarette smoke curling like white mist, I sense the coldness. Beryl backs away without a word.

'He hates being disturbed when he's working.' She hurries me to the dining-room, then the breakfast room. She says he is 'writing', but knows nothing about it. 'It's a very private thing. I won't intrude.'

She claims to feel privileged to support him. She is angry when I suggest he seems like a spoiled child. '*You* might see an unequal relationship,' she asserts, 'but you couldn't be more wrong!' Once more, she regales me with details of his awful childhood and sluttish mother. She adds that Trisha made everything worse. His wrongful conviction for her murder was the last straw. 'Now, *society* owes a debt to Piers.' She never once doubted his innocence.

It is hard to make her focus her mind on her own unhappiness. While he was in prison, she felt imprisoned herself. Her monthly visits and their letters were the only glimmer of light. But that bleak period is still marring their relationship. 'A crisis can drive couples apart,' she tells me. 'Relationships are terribly fragile at the best of times. The smallest change can be fatal. We were faced with utterly cataclysmic changes. Piers and I must now renegotiate our whole life together.'

I try to probe deeper into her feelings. But she again talks about her husband, as if someone has yanked a chain. She starts to tell me about his barbaric treatment in prison. 'The prison staff are utterly emotionally illiterate!' Suddenly, she jumps to her feet. After rooting in a bureau, she hands me a clutch of letters.

'You *must* read them. Then you'll understand.'

She watches me tensely. His letters from prison are a catalogue of self-centred complaints that must have fed her own apprehension. Occasionally, he mentions happy moments from their marriage. But everything is coloured by dark despair, and frequent suicide threats.

'Those letters broke my heart,' she admits tearfully, telling me more about his misery. She still resists talking about herself. 'There's nothing to say. I'm completely defined by my marriage.' I manage to glean a few details about her early life. She is the only child of a rich family, and went to an exclusive boarding-school. At home, her grandfather doted on her. But the local girls resented her privileged lifestyle. She became somewhat withdrawn. 'I even began to feel guilty about having so much money!'

The years before her marriage to Piers Stanton Smith appear to be a wasteland. 'Happiness can be a long time coming.' She looks at her two rings – one for love, one for loss. Then she drops a bombshell. 'Actually, I've been married before. I was nineteen.' She is bitter. 'Because my husband was poor, Daddy said he must be a gold-digger. Every girl dreams of a white wedding, but he wouldn't pay. We had to get married in a register office.' After six months, her husband walked out. Her father had offered him a lot of money to leave. 'But I've never forgiven Daddy for destroying my illusions. We need illusions to be happy.'

Her eyes light up as Piers Stanton Smith comes in without warning. He glides over to sit on the arm of her chair. 'More of your armchair philosophy, darling?' he asks.

Beryl clings to him girlishly, prattling. Her self-consciousness is extravagant. Perhaps that is why he pulls a face behind her back. Then he rises, patting her arm. He leaves us, saying: 'Back to the grindstone!'

She continues to glow even though my questions become very pointed. She dismisses the criticism which followed her second marriage. 'I did not *buy* my husband!' She denies being exploited. 'People can say what they like,' she assures me. 'I don't care. They're probably just jealous of our togetherness.'

When I suggest her upbringing left her immature and vulnerable, she refuses to respond. But about her husband's tendency to marital violence, her answer is all worked out. She escorts me to my car. Her words are chosen with exaggerated care. 'He never denied being violent towards Trisha. But she asked for it. She often attacked *him*, quite viciously. Or she'd frighten him so much he couldn't help lashing out. He had to fight back to survive. Everybody thinks I'm living in a minefield. But as long as I don't give him cause to attack me, I have nothing to fear.' As I get into the car, she has the last word. 'Do I?'

2

Three floors up in her hutch under the cold Sheffield sky, Ida Sheridan decided, after much dithering, to use her own telephone. Sooner or later, she would redeem the cost and, hopefully, share otherwise in the good fortune she was guiding towards her friend.

She had passed most of the night in agitated wakefulness, alert for the twang of her letter-box, and when the delivery boy came she was already at the front door, dressing-gown swaddling her body while her ankles turned to ice in the draught. She snatched up the paper, riffled the pages anxiously, then leaned against the wall, still in the draught, reading the third instalment of Gaynor Holbrook's foray into the heart of the matter. As the hole the woman was digging for herself simply got deeper, Ida's smile grew broader.

'It's the likes of Beryl Kay that make men think they've got the *right* to batter their women,' Rene announced, edging aside Janet's newspaper to make room for a plate of bacon and tomatoes. 'Well, I hope she doesn't think her money'll protect her when the crunch comes, because it won't.'

'D'you know Beryl?' McKenna asked.

'Only by sight, but you can't miss people like her. The whole family set themselves up high, even though they were just shopkeepers.' Stacking cereal bowls in the sink, Rene added: 'Beryl's parents didn't do her any favours, you know. She's no notion of the real world, so she's fair game.' She turned on the hot-water tap. 'Folk rumoured for years that she got wed when she was barely out of school, but nobody knew for sure. I wonder why she's talking about it now?'

'Probably to broadcast her version of events in case her ex comes out of the woodwork,' Jack suggested.

'Probably,' agreed Rene, watching Ellen watch Janet eat, and wondering what else was going on under her nose.

'She's very stupid,' Ellen commented. 'I was quite sorry for her before I read this garbage, but in her own way, she's as nasty and insensitive as her husband.'

'You're not the only one to think like that,' Rene told her. 'If you look a bit further on in the paper, you'll find something about the tyres on her fancy car getting slashed yesterday.'

4

'Why aren't they here?' Fretfully, Linda paced the length of her combined sitting-and-dining-room.

'Sit down,' Craig ordered. 'You're wearing holes in the carpet.'

She stared at him, almost crackling with tension. 'Can they *really* think Barry and me fitted up that bastard?'

'We'll ask when they get here,' Craig said patiently. 'What did the hospital say when you rang?'

She flopped on the sofa, and began kneading the cushions. 'Dad slept like a baby, and he's had a good breakfast.'

'When can he come out?'

'I didn't ask. I'll do it later.'

'And don't forget to remind the police he wants to talk to them.'

5

Henry Colclough, the widowed husband of Smith's teacher, had sent a letter, penned rather waveringly in black ink on white paper.

Dear Superintendent McKenna

I don't know if you intend to see me – indeed, I can probably add little to what I said at the trial, except these few observations, which may or may not be useful to you.

Despite the lack of proof, and the boy's vehement protestations of innocence, I remain convinced that Smith somehow deliberately brought about Joyce's death: it is that conviction which stops me from letting go. The memory of her death will always be indelible, for I loved her deeply, but the manner of her death left an open wound. Perhaps your brief does not extend to investigating this distant past, and I know Smith will never admit the truth, but if you should find yourself able to offer some peace of mind, I shall go happier to my grave. I long ago abandoned hope of vengeance, but when Smith went to prison for killing his wife, I toasted justice, even if it was not specifically for Joyce. When I learned of his release, then read the sickening rubbish besmirching the papers, I confess I gave up hope of justice in this world, and can only pray that it awaits him in the next.

I should be happy to see you at any time, although, as I say, I have little to offer.

Yours very sincerely
Henry Colclough

6

Ida glared at her telephone, willing Gaynor's editor to ring, as promised, 'the moment Mr Davidson reaches the office'. When the instrument actually trilled, she was so shocked her heart missed several beats and skipped to her throat.

'Yes?' she croaked, swallowing hard.

'I'd like to speak to Mrs Sheridan. My name's Davidson.'

'And I'm Mrs Sheridan.' She inhaled deeply. 'Ida Sheridan.'

'And what can I do for you?'

'I rang yesterday, to speak to that Holbrook woman, but she never phoned back.'

'Ms Holbrook is on assignment in the north of England.'

'I know she is! That's what I'm talking about.'

'Is there a problem?'

'I'll say there is! Leastways, there is for *her*.'

'I see. Can you be more specific?'

'It's this rubbish she's writing about Smith and his mother.'

'Who?'

'Peter Smith, as was. He goes by a fancier name now.'

'Oh, *that* Smith. What about him?'

'He's a liar. He's told that Holbrook woman a pack of fairy stories, and now they're in the paper for all the world to see. It was bad enough at the trial.'

'That's a very serious allegation, Mrs Sheridan, but what proof have you got that we might have published inaccuracies?'

'They're not "inaccuracies",' Ida asserted, suddenly feeling on much firmer ground. 'They're out-and-out lies.'

'What are?'

'What Smith said about his mother.'

'I'm sorry, Mrs Sheridan, but there's only your word for that.' Davidson sounded smugly relieved. 'Mrs Smith is dead. The police searched for her exhaustively before Smith's trial.'

'You call that an exhaustive search, do you? They knocked on one door, then went away, and that was the end of it.'

'You can't know that.'

'Oh, yes I can!' Ida gloated. 'It was *my* door they knocked on. Bunty Smith lives seven doors down, and she never saw hide nor hair of them.'

7

Even with the toll of fatigue and anxiety evident in every gesture, Linda Newton was extraordinarily pretty and vivacious, McKenna thought, and remarkably self-possessed. She guided Ellen to the dining-table, her solicitor and himself to armchairs, then arranged herself beside Craig on the sofa. On a small table nearby were various family photographs in attractive pewter frames, some of Linda, Craig and the boys, others of Linda and her sister and father, and an old studio portrait of a rather beautiful woman, her face framed by a cloud of dark hair.

'May I?' McKenna asked, reaching for the photograph. 'Is this your mother?'

Linda took another from the group. 'And this is Trisha, when she was twenty-four.'

Before Smith withered her bloom, Trisha was as pretty as her sister, but with darker hair and more serious eyes. Linda's hair was a vivid russet-red, and her eyes sparkled like mountain water.

'And after she'd been with that bastard for a few months,' Linda added, 'she looked like an old hag.'

'Violence in an intimate relationship,' McKenna said, 'rapidly eclipses every other aspect of the relationship and the violent partner's personality, including memories of the decent times. So, may I suggest that even your former brother-in-law must have some redeeming features?'

'Not in our book!' Craig snapped. 'He told enough lies at the trial, but he's really got the bit between his teeth now, hasn't he?'

'Unfortunately,' the solicitor commented, 'Mr Smith can defame his first wife with impunity, but Mrs Newton's case is quite different.'

Linda bared her teeth. 'He's heading straight for a horrible fall, and so is that bloody reporter.'

'Did Holbrook ever approach you?' asked McKenna. 'To ask for comment, or a response to Smith's allegations?'

'No, so she's either very stupid, or so puffed up

with her own importance she can't think straight.'

'People get like that,' added Craig, 'when they're being bamboozled by a sly bastard like Smith.'

'I may want to pursue this further at a later date,' McKenna told Linda, 'but today, I intend to discuss your relationship with Detective Inspector Dugdale. Are you happy for your husband to remain?'

'Don't be silly!' Linda snapped. 'Barry's been our friend for years. We get on with Sue as well and, until you lot stuck your oar in, she was getting on famously with Barry.'

'I can't comment on that,' McKenna said.

'You can't split up marriages and walk away from what you've done,' she insisted. 'Sue knew all along about me and Barry, but she didn't know about him and Julie.'

'How d'you know?'

'She told me on Monday. I wanted to talk to Barry, about you coming, but she wouldn't let me. And,' she added impatiently, 'don't start going on about conspiracies! We don't think like that, even if you do.'

'In fairness to Dugdale,' McKenna pointed out, 'we must explore every possibility, one of which is that you and he conspired to saddle Smith with your sister's murder.'

'If only!' Linda wished. 'If we had, believe me, he'd *never* get out of prison!'

'How did they go about conspiring?' Craig demanded. 'What did they do? How did they fix him?'

Nonplussed, McKenna said: 'I can't discuss specifics.'

'Why not? If you think they did it, you must know how.'

'Smith's conviction rested entirely on circumstantial evidence, much of which was supplied by your wife.'

'And a lot came from elsewhere,' Craig countered, 'including Trisha's divorce petition.'

'From reviewing the prosecution's case, it's clear that the evidence against Smith was very tenuous,' McKenna said. '*So* tenuous, in fact, that the prosecution should not have been pursued.'

'That wasn't up to Barry,' Linda said.

'He put the case together, and he recommended prosecution.'

'Everything pointed to that bastard!' Linda exclaimed. '*Everything*!'

'But he was innocent,' McKenna replied.

'Was he?' Craig asked. 'Are you sure about that? Maybe Mrs Moneybags paid someone to batter Trisha and torch the house, while she gave herself an alibi at the dentist, and he got one off the priests.' His face hardened. 'But whatever *did* happen, I know Trisha would still be alive if it wasn't for him. Have you any idea what he's done to this family? When Trisha died, Linda cried so much her eyes nearly bled, and Fred looked like he'd drop dead in front of your very eyes.'

'We know little of Trisha herself,' McKenna said, 'but she clearly had an effect, and that determined how people reacted. While I'm not suggesting Dugdale framed Smith out of affection for her, it's possible that he was misled.'

'What about?' Linda asked. 'Everything came out during the divorce.' She paused, eyes downcast. 'Up to then, she'd hidden some of it, to protect me, like always. And she was so *ashamed*! About being beaten, and the way he humiliated her, the way he behaved, and the trouble he caused that came back on her.'

'What sort of trouble?'

'Sex and money,' Craig said. 'He looks like a bloody queer, he talks like one, and he flounces

170

around like one, but if anyone dared call him one, he'd get hysterical, and start a row. Then Trisha got dragged in, to "prove" he wasn't, and there'd be threats about solicitors and suing for slander. He'd cause such a ruckus nobody knew if they were coming or going, and it was nothing but a smoke-screen to take their minds off what started the rumours in the first place. People got so they couldn't trust their own eyes and ears, and because she didn't walk out on him, or chuck him out, they stopped trusting Trisha. One way or another, he saw off all her friends, 'cos they thought she was as bad as him.'

'When really, she was sweet, and good, and caring,' Linda said defensively. 'She always looked for the best in people, which is why she made excuses for him for so long.'

'Every step of the way,' Craig went on, 'he took advantage of her, and he was so cruel with it. He played on her sympathy, even when he'd given her a battering. He *blamed* her for it, like he blamed her for everything else. It was her fault they had no money, her fault he had no job, her fault everybody was nasty to him.' He leaned forward, hands clasped between his knees. 'He's wicked, and so clever he makes you doubt your own reason.'

'And what did he do to you?' asked McKenna, almost able to feel the other man's rage and pain.

Taken aback by the question, Craig looked to Linda. She stared hard at McKenna, and said: 'They used to come for supper on Saturdays, then, without a word, they suddenly stopped, and when I asked Trisha why, she got really edgy. She hardly spoke to me for months, and wouldn't even give Craig the time of day.'

'So, I went to see her at work,' Craig added. 'I figured he'd been making some kind of mischief, and

I was right. He'd told her I'd made a pass at him, and no way was he ever coming near me again.'

'And she couldn't come on her own, of course.' Linda resumed the story. 'She'd be betraying him if she did. He spoiled everything one way or another, spiting her friends, lying about us, just to have her beholden to him. We started going there, because I wasn't having my sister at his mercy like that, but we had to stop in the end because the boys got so upset. He knew we knew, and he knew we didn't believe a word of it, so he created these awful atmospheres, like just before a storm breaks.'

'And you'd be on the edge of your chair waiting for it.' Craig's face was grey. 'And he'd be staring, with those horrible eyes of his. It got so bad our older lad used to throw up when he thought we were going to that house.' He paused, face troubled. 'And whatever Lin says, I could see the evil doubt he'd put in her head every time I looked at her.'

'He didn't put *anything* in my head.' She reached out to stroke his neck. 'That bastard never made *me* think black was white, even if he convinced Trisha the batterings were all her fault. No matter what I said, she made excuses, until the day he kicked her.'

'When did you learn about that?' McKenna asked.

'The day after, like I said at the trial. She phoned, wanting me to go to the doctor's with her. She sounded so ill I asked Craig to take me there, and we found her sitting in a puddle of her own blood, on a heap of old towels on a kitchen chair. She was as white as a sheet, and shivering fit to fall apart, so we rushed her to hospital.'

'Trisha told them a cock-and-bull story about tripping on the stairs,' Craig said. 'She had to say something, because the kicking she got bloody near ruptured her innards.'

172

'And when did she tell you the truth?' McKenna asked.

'There and then,' Linda said, 'but she begged us not to say. We weren't brought up to wash mucky linen in public, and she still had a bit of pride, though God knows how. That bastard even made her feel dirty for wanting a normal marriage.'

'He told her he wasn't up to it,' added Craig.

'Up to what?' McKenna queried.

'He said he was impotent,' Linda snapped. 'Sodding liar! He blamed his mother's goings-on, and his miserable childhood. Trisha told him he could get counselling, or even medicine, so she got another battering.'

'Were these assaults ever reported to the local police?'

'I've told you, she blamed herself. Anyway, she was scared stiff of what he'd do to her.'

'She could have obtained an injunction,' Ellen said.

'She was too bloody *terrified*! If you've never been there, you can't know what it's like. She got so worn down she couldn't even work out how to get dressed in the morning.' Eyeing her visitors one by one, she added: 'But you know she was battered, from what the pathologist found when he cut up what was left of her.'

'Indeed, so.' McKenna nodded. 'No one denies the assaults took place. Tell me, did you ever seek advice on the issue from Dugdale, prior to Trisha's death?'

'No, but I wish I had,' Linda replied. 'She might have listened to him, instead of waiting till she was nearly kicked to death.'

Watching her, McKenna knew she would be hounded by guilt for the rest of her life, and her husband perhaps even more so. 'But you still blame yourself for not taking matters into your own hands.'

'We both do,' Craig told him. 'I should've given that monster a taste of his own medicine.'

'While Trisha was still living with him, there was little you could do without placing her in even greater jeopardy,' McKenna argued. 'And once she moved out, the danger diminished.'

'She came here from hospital,' Craig said. 'Fred couldn't have coped if that animal had come after her, and it was months before he'd get out of their house so she could go back.'

'That was when things really started coming out.' Linda took her husband's hand, squeezing his fingers. 'One thing after another. I could hardly believe what I was hearing at times.'

'I couldn't get my head round the way she'd kept it all bottled up for so long,' Craig added. 'But she said in her experience, trouble shared is trouble doubled, not halved.'

'Did Smith bother you?' McKenna asked.

'No, thank God!' Linda shivered. 'He makes my flesh crawl. When that poor old man talked about his wife burning to death in the car, I knew exactly what he meant. That bastard's got eyes like stones!'

'He smells bad, too,' Craig added. 'Sour, like a wild animal.'

'That's because he eats raw meat,' Linda told him. 'I know because I saw him one day when he was making his usual song and dance about doing a bit of cooking. I went to the kitchen for a glass of water, and copped him stuffing raw liver in his mouth. He said it was good for the blood.' For a moment, she stared wide-eyed into the past. 'I wanted to faint. I mean, you never knew from one minute to the next whether he'd throw a screaming rage, or be nice as pie, and he just smiled at me, but his mouth was all smeared with blood, and it was actually dripping off his teeth.'

Breaking that bloody strand of memory, but only to be enmeshed by another, McKenna said: 'Did he do a fair share of the housework?'

'Are you being funny?' Linda demanded. 'Apart from the odd bit of cooking, when he made the kitchen a pig tip and expected Trisha to clean up after him, he did damn all. He was too scared of getting his hands dirty, or breaking his fancy nails.' She turned to Craig. 'His nails are longer than mine, aren't they?'

As Craig nodded, McKenna, despite himself, glanced at Linda's nails: neat, pink ovals just reaching the tips of her fingers, and realised that she and her husband were as obsessed with Smith, if not more so, than Smith with himself. He listened without comment or question while, ashen-faced, they competed to recount the worst outrage, coming to see this obsession as the thriving child of their guilt. He heard that Smith used those unseemly nails to tear at Trisha's face, that he was afraid of honest labour, and forced her to hump coal from the yard in all weathers.

'And when Fred went to the house one day, he found her sifting ash for bits of clinker to put back on the fire,' Craig said. 'They were that poor.'

But such poverty, Linda asserted, was rooted in Smith's greed. 'He'd think nothing of spending twenty or thirty pounds on a bottle of aftershave, while Trisha had to buy her clothes in the charity shops.'

Before Craig discovered that his sister-in-law was living in abject terror, he had chastised Linda for lending her money, for paying for little luxuries, as well as replacing the things Smith destroyed in his rages. 'But you couldn't ever replace some things,' added Craig. 'Like that pretty flowering plant your mum had just before she died, and that photo of her that he smashed to smithereens.'

Linda brushed her hands across her eyes. 'It's water

under the bridge.' She sighed. 'Perhaps it's time to let her go.'

'How can we?' asked Craig. 'It's not finished with.'

'In your evidence at the trial,' McKenna said to Linda, trying to focus her attention, 'you hinted at unpleasant and destructive secrets between you and your sister.'

'No, I didn't.' She began to fidget. 'We didn't want Dad to know about the beatings because he'd have gone after that bastard with an axe. And we didn't tell him about the sex part of it because he'd have been mortified with shame for her.'

'The "sex part"?'

'The way he made her feel dirty for wanting what was normal.'

'You also implied that she may have colluded with the violence.'

'I didn't!' Linda was close to tears. 'That bastard's brief put words in my mouth. He pushed me into a corner, and wouldn't let me say more than "yes", or "no". I couldn't *explain*. I couldn't say how frightened she was.'

'Tell me about the advertisements for escorts?'

'Oh, God!' She put her hands over her face.

'Were they your idea?'

'Yes.' She told him how Trisha dreaded opening the post. 'There was always something for her to worry about, or more bills she couldn't pay. I wanted her to have something nice to look forward to, for a change.'

'Did you place the advertisements yourself?'

'Yes!'

'You never told me!' Craig was astounded.

'And who replied?' McKenna demanded.

'A couple of blokes.'

'Who? Where did they live?'

'One lived outside Manchester, the other near here.'

'Do you have their names? Their addresses?'

Reluctantly, Linda nodded.

'Speak for the tape, please, Mrs Newton.'

'I know who they are and where they live!'

'Did you share this information with Inspector Dugdale?'

'No.'

'Why not?'

'Because!'

'Because if you had,' McKenna said, his eyes as flinty as his voice, 'suspicion might well have fallen on someone other than your former brother-in-law.'

'Trisha never met them,' Linda insisted. 'She wouldn't even write back, or ring up.'

'You can't know that, Mrs Newton. You wilfully suppressed evidence vital to a murder investigation.'

8

'I'm not burdened with much of an imagination,' Ellen commented, 'but by the time Linda finished, I felt almost inside Trisha's skin. What really got to me wasn't Trisha's nightmares, but the ones she had during the day, when she was ironing, or cooking, or just watching TV. She'd suddenly start shuddering, apparently, and be fighting for her breath within seconds.'

'Smith haunts people.' McKenna rooted on his desk for cigarettes. 'He worms into their brains like a parasite, and they can't get rid of him.' Reaching for his lighter, he added: 'When she refers to him, Linda spits out the words as if they're choking her.'

'She's more likely to choke on her own mischief,' Jack said. 'What on earth possessed her to keep quiet about those letters?'

'She didn't want Dugdale's attention diverted.'

'Well, if *we* go after the poor saps who replied to Trisha's lonely hearts ads, we're technically reopening the murder investigation,' Jack pointed out. 'That's not our remit. Shouldn't you take advice from the chief constable first?'

'He'll be asked to arrange for the Haughton police to detain the local man, and to liaise with Manchester police about the other one. We'll sit in on the interviews.'

'Fair enough,' agreed Jack. 'Are you going to inform Hinchcliffe? Dugdale has a right to know about Linda's shenanigans.'

'So do Bowden and Lewis,' McKenna said, 'but as far as we know, they're currently unrepresented, and I'm not willing to offer information to one party and not to another.' He tapped the ash from his cigarette. 'So, while I'm out interviewing Broadbent, you can, on my behalf, warn the Federation that I regard the needless confusion about alternative representation for those two as an attempt to subvert my investigation.'

I

Between nine o'clock that morning, and eleven thirty, Wendy Lewis telephoned Frances Pawsley's office fourteen times and, on each occasion, was asked to hold the line, while the same few bars of Mozart's *Eine Kleine Nachtmusik* tinkled in her ears. When Frances remained 'not available', at eleven forty, and after emptying a pack of cigarettes newly opened when she woke, Wendy contacted the Federation, begging for their intervention. She argued for thirteen minutes, demanding representation by Frances or no one, but learned only that her options were reduced to zero. She smoked another cigarette, and once more telephoned Frances's office, now to be told that Frances was in court for the rest of the day, and had not left any message.

At twelve twenty-seven she threw the stub of another cigarette into the sitting-room grate, took an unopened bottle of gin from the sideboard, and walked along the corridor to the bathroom, where she slid open the door of the medicine chest and debated which of her mother's old pills to mix into a cocktail. Brown plastic pill bottles in one hand, tooth glass and bottle clutched in the other, she went to her bedroom, put bottles, glass and gin on her night table, picked up the telephone extension, and gave the minions in Frances's office a message which no one could ignore.

Smugly pleased to have discovered an option unconsidered by the Federation, she peered at faded chemist's labels, shook out pills from this bottle and that, topped up the glass with gin, and swirled the cloudy mess with a yellow biro. White grains and scummy colours stuck to the side of the glass, and, irritated, she watched undissolved powder quickly settle to the bottom. Giving the mixture one more vicious stir, she downed the draught in one swallow. It tasted quite vile, and left sticky powders coating her teeth, so she returned to the bathroom, scrabbling along the wall in case she was suddenly enfeebled by the drugs, rinsed her mouth with copious amounts of running water and, despite the dire warnings of her dead mother, also drank from the bathroom tap. Staggering back to the bedroom, she lay atop the quilt with her arms behind her head, watching the bedside clock tick through the minutes she had allowed for her message to reach Frances, and for Frances, panic-stricken, to respond.

At one twelve, she fell into unconsciousness without any awareness of the event, and her body began to chill by the minute.

2

Mineral water brimming in a lead crystal tumbler in one hand, mobile telephone in the other, Gaynor stood at the window of what was once a hunting lodge owned by the Duke of Norfolk, and was now an exclusive hotel. In the drive below, her own expensive car was parked with others of its kind.

'It's a try-on,' she assured her editor. 'Linda Newton can't do anything because she can't prove she *wasn't* molested.'

'We can't prove she was,' Davidson argued. 'You've only got that con's word.'

'She can't afford a libel trial.'

'The lawyers might offer no win, no fee.'

'For libel? They'd have to be out of their minds!'

'Newton's solicitor reckons they can prove the dead sister wasn't molested, either.'

'They can prove she was the Virgin Mary for all I care. She's dead, and you can't defame the dead.'

'But it'd add weight to Newton's claims.' Davidson paused. 'And what about this business with Smith's mother?'

'What about it? The coppers couldn't find her before the trial, and we had no cause to think she wasn't six feet under. We published in good faith.'

'You think of every angle, don't you?'

'That's what you pay me for. How are the sales figures?'

'They rocketed yesterday, and today's should be better still. You really whetted Joe Public's appetite.'

'More fool Joe Public.'

'What's the matter, Gaynor?' Davidson's voice had a spiteful edge. 'Is Mr Smith not quite what you thought?'

'He makes even *my* flesh crawl, so use your imagination. And his wife's an utter moron. While she thinks she's embroiled in the romance of the century, he's sneering behind her back.'

'Well, they've made their own bed. I take it you're going to Sheffield to see Bunty Smith?'

'Yeah, later.'

'Keep me informed. Have the police been after you again?'

'No. I've already said "sorry".' She watched two figures trudging along the crest of the moors, perhaps a farmer and his dog searching for stragglers among the lambing ewes, to bring them to lower ground before the suffocating snows began to fall. Both man and animal were little more than faint smudges against the sombre sky. 'And I hope you gave our lawyers a rocket. It's their job to vet copy for things that need to be checked, not mine. I just write the stuff.' Wandering over to the desk, she put down her glass and reached for a sheet of crested notepaper. 'What's Bunty Smith's address?'

'Seventy-seven Primrose Walk. Sheridan lives at seventy-one, and if the coppers could write their ones and sevens properly, there wouldn't have been a mistake in the first place.'

'The beastly Bunty could be overjoyed to get right of reply, you know. How much can I offer?'

'Not enough to make her think we've got a guilty conscience. I don't want that Sheridan harpy on our backs for hush money.'

Gaynor laughed. 'I'd worry more about being savaged by a dead sheep.'

'Never underestimate Joe Public,' Davidson counselled. 'We're not always the only ones with aces up our sleeves. And maybe giving Bunty Smith's address to the police would be a useful quid pro quo. After you've talked to her, of course.'

'Why should I?' she demanded. 'It's not my fault they were too lazy to look for her properly.'

3

'*Very* Dickensian,' Ellen said, looking up at the dour façade of the Willows as McKenna's car drew to a halt in the flagged courtyard. 'These Victorian mansions always seem to end up as institutions, but I suppose they're obsolete otherwise in this day and age.'

'So they're ideal for housing people who lack the sensibilities the rest of us enjoy, aren't they?' Janet asked acidly. 'Like mental defectives.'

' "People with learning difficulties" is the correct terminology.' Helping Ellen to unload her machines, McKenna saw the almost bitter light in Janet's eyes, but said no more, because there was nothing more to say. Tape-recorder in his arms, he followed her up the steps and into a hall of baronial proportions, where a massively carved staircase rose heavenwards, and the great leaded windows were inset with crests. A tall, very thin man wearing half-moon spectacles waited for them, snapping his heels on the parquet floor.

'I'm Cyril Bennett, the manager.' He frowned. 'Julie said you're investigating this alleged miscarriage of justice. Is she in some kind of trouble over it?'

'I can't comment,' McKenna replied.

'You see, if someone's under police investigation, we're supposed to suspend them pending the outcome.'

'Our business with Miss Broadbent is not connected with her work. She's one of a number of people we're interviewing.'

Bennett persisted. 'The police were in and out of here for weeks on end after that poor woman died, and I'd have thought anything Julie had to say was said at the time.'

'Our frames of reference are quite different.'

'Has the management committee given you permission to come here?'

'No,' McKenna said patiently. 'To be frank, we're not obliged to ask, but if you object to our seeing Miss Broadbent on the premises, we'll make other arrangements. And if anything *should* crop up relevant to Miss Broadbent's suitability as an employee, rest assured you'll be the first to know.'

4

Gaynor cruised twice past the tenement block which housed Primrose Walk on its middle level, Bluebell Way at ground level, and Daffodil Close up in the sky, before accelerating away towards a secure city centre car-park. She took a taxi back, extracting a receipt from the driver, then made her way up the filthy concrete staircase which linked the three levels of two-storey maisonettes. The walls were daubed with graffiti, some obscene, some merely inane, and stained with the urine of which the whole area stank. Poking out from the rubbish kicked into a corner at the turn of the stairs, she noticed a syringe and shreds of silver foil, and here and there on the surface of the walls, the pock-marked ulceration of concrete cancer. She reached Primrose Walk panting with the effort of holding her breath against the tide of smells.

The bitter wind swirling about her was dirty with stale exhaust fumes and city pollution, and she was briefly overwhelmed by the terrible thought that anyone, even herself, could end their days in a benighted slum such as this. Glancing as she walked at the plastic numbers screwed to the doors, she found number seventy-seven, and rapped sharply on the glass.

A fat old woman dragged open the door. 'Fancy someone your age getting puffed walking up a few stairs,' she observed, eyeing Gaynor up and down. 'Wasn't the lift working? It was yesterday.'

'Are you Bunty Smith?' Gaynor asked.

'Who wants to know?'

'I'm Gaynor Holbrook.'

'Are you really? You'd better come in, then.'

Following her into a meanly proportioned, meagrely furnished, and fuggily overheated shoe box of a room, Gaynor saw another old woman standing by a big electric fire, hopping from one foot to another.

'That there's Bunty Smith,' she was told. 'I'm Ida Sheridan, the one that phoned.'

Ignoring Ida then, and summoning an expansive smile, Gaynor rushed forward, hand outstretched. 'Mrs Smith! I'm delighted to meet you!'

'Are you?' A frail, claw-like hand brushed hers. 'Why's that?'

'I've heard so much about you, of course!'

Ida snorted. 'That's one way of putting it!' She circled Gaynor like a dog around a sheep, edging her towards a chair already pulled out from under the small table by the window. 'Sit down, *Ms* Holbrook, and get your purse and cheque-book out. We've got terms to talk, haven't we?'

5

Julie's flat, created out of the old attic nurseries at the rear of the house, consisted of a bedroom, a sitting-room, a tiny bathroom and WC, and a kitchenette, all with dormer windows, their protective bars still in place, that looked vertiginously on to the rear yard and what remained of the grounds. There was not a willow tree in sight, nor a member of staff, McKenna thought, watching a small group of outlandishly dressed residents hack their way with axes through a thicket of dead trees and shrubs. Two supermarket trolleys were parked on the yard's mossy flagstones, waiting to be filled with twigs and broken branches.

Turning to take his seat, he looked down on the back of Julie's head, and thought the back of her neck, with its translucent skin and tendrils of curly brown hair, was perhaps the most tender and lovely thing he had ever seen, inviting his protection, and even his caress.

'What happens to the wood they collect?' he asked her. She wore jeans and a sweater and, perched on an old-fashioned dining-chair, her arms loosely folded, stared gravely at him, evoking in him the ghost of Colin Bowden's brief enchantment, and what had, years before, beguiled Dugdale into a rashness he now had cause to regret.

'They make bundles of firewood. Several local shops have a regular order.'

'What about other work?' Ellen asked. 'Firewood's only seasonal.'

'The paper mill sends waste to be weighed and packed, and we occasionally get odd jobs from other factories,' Julie replied. 'Work's hard enough to come by for normal people, so we take what's offered.' Impatiently, she added: 'Can we start? I'm on duty later.'

'We should wait for your solicitor to arrive,' McKenna said.

'No one's coming.'

'You were advised to have representation,' he pointed out. 'This interview will be under caution.'

'I know.' Today, she thought, he resembled a clever fox, whereas when she saw him on Monday, trying to escape from the lane by Trisha's house, he looked like one pursued by the hounds of hell. The woman with the machinery was like a mouse, scrabbling in the skirting boards for electrical sockets instead of crumbs, and the other woman, painfully thin and gauntly dark, was, to Julie, simply kindred wounded.

'You're entitled to free legal representation in such circumstances,' McKenna added.

'I know. I don't want anyone.'

'Are you sure?'

'I'm quite sure! I only *work* with retarded people.' She fidgeted when he began the caution. 'I know the procedure. You've no doubt heard.'

'That's one of the issues I want to discuss,' McKenna said. 'It's possible that your previous experiences made you less than forthcoming during the investigation of Trisha Smith's death. It's been suggested you were "holding back".'

'Who said? Wendy Lewis?'

'I'm not at liberty to comment.'

'It must have been her. The man she brought with her never opened his mouth, but she was like a dog with a bone. She really upset some of the residents.'

'How?'

'She kept insisting they'd seen something. She put them under a lot of pressure.'

'Some of them may well have had relevant information.'

'They may,' Julie conceded, 'but you'd need someone with much better skills than Lewis to find out.'

'Point taken.'

'Has Cyril Bennett said anything to you?' she asked suddenly.

'Why d'you ask?' Her eyes were truly remarkable, he thought.

After a small silence, she said: 'Unless you intend to waste your time and mine, stop treating me like something that got on your shoe. Lewis looked so far down her nose at me she must have gone cross-eyed. Bennett's already muttering about suspension, and whatever you might think to the contrary, even somebody like me has rights.'

'No one's denying your rights, Miss Broadbent.'

'He just needs setting straight. He's not a bully, and

he's not unfair, but he's scared he'll be accused of taking risks with resident welfare, because that's how it looks when the police start cautioning the staff.'

'I've already told him this interview has no connection with your work, but that's the only assurance I can give at present,' McKenna said. 'I'm here to discuss Barry Dugdale.'

Her smile was incredibly sweet. 'You *are* wasting your time.'

'You were close once.'

'Almost twenty years ago. Did Ryman snitch on us?' When he failed to respond, she sighed. 'I know. You can't comment.'

'What was your relationship with Trisha Smith?' Janet asked.

'I knew her.'

Julie crossed her legs, easing the creased denim around her knee, while Janet, compelled to assess the length and symmetry of the legs, asked herself why someone of such mongrel ancestry should be blessed with such aristocratic proportions. Surreptitiously, she peered at the small areas of exposed flesh for signs of the blistering injury it had suffered, but saw nothing. 'How well did you know her?' she added.

'Like I know Linda. We all grew up in the same place, we all went to Haughton Comprehensive.'

'What was Trisha like?'

'Nice. Ordinary. She wanted peace and quiet.'

'She was hoping for a job here, wasn't she?'

'She'd have done well.'

'Does the management committee employ non-Catholics?' McKenna asked.

'Idiots come from both denominations, so staff persuasions have to show a balance.'

'I thought terms like "idiot" were forbidden,' he commented.

'Which euphemism d'you prefer?' Her eyes were challenging.

'I'm not going to be side-tracked into a discussion on semantics,' he said. 'You're evading the issue of your relationship with Dugdale.'

'We spent one summer together. We had a lovely spring and summer that particular year. I thought it would never end. Afterwards, we'd get together now and then.' She smiled, as if to herself. 'We went for walks in the park, mostly. There's a gorgeous rose garden, and a tiny pet cemetery.'

'And your relationship was sexual.'

'Among other things.'

'When did you last speak to him?'

'Apart from saying "hello" if we met in the street? A couple of weeks before he married Susan Harrop.'

'Did you have *any* contact during the murder investigation?'

'No.'

'D'you know Smith?' Ellen asked.

Julie nodded.

'How well?'

'Enough to know he's a shit. Why?'

'Is that based on your own experience?'

'He once told me I'd no right to sully the church with my disgusting presence.'

Ellen raised her eyebrows. 'What did you say?'

'Like any good Christian, I turned the other cheek. I'm very good at cheek-turning, as you might imagine.'

'Did Trisha ever tell you he was assaulting her?'

'She didn't need to. It was written all over her face. You could tell by the way she looked at him, or rather, *didn't* look at him. She was always afraid, always desperately trying to please, like a dog that knows another whipping's just around the corner.'

'And where were you on the afternoon of her death?' McKenna asked quietly.

'You're supposed to be finding out what happened with Smith, not who killed Trisha,' Julie replied. 'So I don't think you've got the right to ask me where I was that day.'

'You told Sergeant Lewis you were here, asleep.'

'You'll have to make do with that, then. Won't you?'

'Can you tell us about your accident?' Janet asked.

'What about it?' Julie's voice was as raw as her skin must feel.

'How did it happen?'

'A chip pan fell on me.'

'Chip pans don't *fall*,' Janet countered. 'Not without help. Who knocked it over?'

Again, Julie shrugged. 'It was an accident.'

'It happened at primary school, didn't it? Did you have counselling afterwards? And did you get compensation?'

'The church looked after me.'

'But did they pay damages?' Janet persisted. 'You were entitled, accident or not.'

'That's my business!' snapped Julie. 'And it's nothing to do with Trisha.'

'I think we've gone as far as we can for now,' McKenna intervened.

'Who told you?' Julie demanded, glaring at Janet.

'Father Barclay mentioned it to Superintendent McKenna,' Janet replied. 'Dugdale never said a word, although maybe he should have done.'

'He obviously thought he should respect my privacy,' Julie said. 'Unlike Ryman.'

'How has Superintendent Ryman compromised your privacy?' asked McKenna.

'Why don't you ask him?' Julie suggested, her mouth tight.

'They certainly leave you with the donkey work, don't they?' Rene remarked, putting a mug of coffee and a plate of fresh cream cakes by Jack's elbow. 'Mind you, a married man's better off having nothing to do with the likes of that Julie Broadbent.' Smiling a little to herself when he said no more than 'thank you', she added: 'By the way, Fred Jarvis is wondering when you're going to see him. He's well enough now.'

'I'm not sure when we'll have time,' Jack said. 'But tell him we'll do our best to fit him in as soon as possible.'

'He's not got anything new to say, you know. He just wants to let you know how he feels.'

'That's perfectly understandable,' Jack agreed.

'I mean,' Rene went on, 'there's been so much rubbish in the paper these last few days, Fred thinks he's a right to give his side of the story.'

Jack selected a luscious-looking chocolate éclair, oozing with cream. 'He must feel very bitter.'

'He's angry,' said Rene. 'I know that. He's livid, in fact, but I'm not sure he's actually bitter. He's not the sort to let a feeling like that get the better of him, because he knows he'd be the one to get eaten up by it.'

'Bitterness *is* corrosive,' Jack commented, swallowing the last airy mouthful of the éclair, and choosing a wedge of more substantial-looking jam-and-cream sponge to follow.

'Now Susan Dugdale's a different kettle of fish altogether,' Rene asserted, folding her arms. 'She's coming back, I hear, but I wouldn't give that marriage more than another couple of years. She's the jealous type, and she'll throw things in Barry's face every time he so much as looks sideways at her, even though what he did and who he did it with before they met is spilled milk, isn't it?'

'How d'you know she's coming back?'

'Linda heard. She's quite pally with her.'

Cream cake half-way to his mouth, Jack looked up at this latter-day Greek chorus-girl, once again on-stage to prod the action. 'When did you speak to Linda?'

'When I went home at dinner-time.'

'Did she discuss her interview with us?'

'Of course she did!' Rene's eyes snapped. 'You don't think you can stop people talking, do you?'

'You're not supposed to talk, Rene. You know that.'

'Don't get uppity with me! I just listen.' She was breathing heavily. 'And for what it's worth, I think Linda's been very stupid about those letters, even though I didn't say it to her.' She scratched her cheek fretfully. 'She's worried sick. She thinks she could go to prison. And she doesn't know *how* she's going to tell her dad.'

'I won't discuss it,' Jack insisted, returning to his cake and coffee.

'I don't expect you to!' Her voice stung. 'But you can do what I do, can't you, and listen?'

7

The old woman's jeering voice ringing in her ears, Gaynor ran down the squalid staircase from Primrose Walk, her fine leather boots slipping on the globs of spit and other vile stuff besmearing the concrete. Once at ground level, she stood under the defaced sign for Bluebell Way and used her mobile telephone to call up the number on the back of the taxi receipt, then hurried away from the tenement towards the shop on the street corner, where she waited, shivering, for the taxi to arrive. Half expecting to see Ida Sheridan panting along the road in pursuit, she wondered inconsequentially if Ida's alliance with a Sheridan was accidental or deliberate, and if the evil old bitch realised that her name was so alliterative.

<h1 style="text-align:center">8</h1>

The argument was still unresolved when Janet, Ellen and McKenna returned to the Church Street house. The cawing churchyard rooks were, he thought, no more raucous than the women's voices.

'I'm not challenging your authority,' Ellen said to him, 'but you know perfectly well that we can't request a comparison of Julie Broadbent's voice with the tape of the 999 call about the fire. That could only be done if the murder investigation was reopened. The fact that we now have her voice on tape is irrelevant, and anyway,' she added, draping her coat over the back of a chair, 'we've no cause to suspect she made the call. Nothing emerged from the interview.'

'Precisely!' McKenna snapped. 'Nothing at *all* emerged from the interview.'

'Maybe that's because she's not significant,' Jack suggested.

'Whether she is or not, she's got evasiveness down to a fine art.' McKenna lit a cigarette. 'So, whatever else her failings, Lewis was spot on over that.'

'Perhaps we could ask for a comparison of *all* the tapes so far,' Janet said. 'No one would be singled out that way, and it would just be part of the ongoing inquiry.'

'That would let us off the hook up to a point,' Ellen replied, 'but what do we do if her voice matches?'

'Notify the powers that be,' Jack said, bored with the discussion. 'Fred Jarvis wants to know when he's having his fifteen minutes of fame, and Rene told me Dugdale's getting his wife back, and that Linda's scared of being sent down.'

'With luck,' McKenna commented, 'fear might improve Linda's memory a bit more. She was extraordinarily stupid.'

'So Rene said,' Jack added. 'And the letter writers have already been detained, so we'd better sort out the interviews.'

'I want to see Ryman again,' McKenna said. 'His name keeps cropping up in the most unexpected places.'

'Don't forget we've arranged to meet Fauvel this evening,' Ellen reminded him.

'I won't.' Glancing through the notes Jack had made in the report book, he asked: 'Where's the fax from the National Insurance Register?'

'Here.' Jack extracted a sheet of paper from the stack on his desk. 'The city of Sheffield and its environs have no less than seventeen pensioners by the name of Hilda Smith, and without a maiden name or date of birth, we can't narrow them down. However, Sheffield police are willing to go door-knocking on our behalf.'

'Get them to do it, then. Has the Federation sorted itself out?'

'Singh's to continue representing Colin Bowden, much to his disgust, but they couldn't contact Lewis, so she stays out on a limb. Pawsley's apparently keeping her head down, but Hinchcliffe's been on to them, pressing for movement with Dugdale.'

'As things stand at the moment,' Ellen said, 'it's still Dugdale's word against Fauvel's.'

'It has been all along,' Janet commented rather waspishly.

I

'How did you get on with Smith's mother?' Davidson asked his star reporter. 'Is there much more mileage in this story? Maybe Smith's had his day. Readers like novelty, you know.'

'Come on!' Gaynor coaxed. 'I'm supposed to be finding out who stitched him up, and I can't do that if you pull me off the job. It's big,' she reminded him, 'and it can only get bigger.'

'Only if you can outmanoeuvre the police investigation. How d'you plan to do that?'

'There are always ways and means, and sources of information.' She fiddled with her pen. 'I think McKenna and his crew are simply looking for a scapegoat. When did you last hear of coppers shafting one of their own?'

'So, what's your angle?'

'I go after the priest.'

'No way!' Davidson was horrified by her suggestion. 'Exposing a queer-boy wife-basher is one thing. Putting a highly respected Roman Catholic priest in the spotlight is in a different league entirely.'

'I was very kind to Smith,' she protested.

'Only if you don't read between the lines,' Davidson commented. 'And when his wife's reread today's offering a few more times, she'll get a different message.'

'Nobody twisted their arms!' Gaynor snapped. 'They were begging for it.'

'Maybe they were, but this priest isn't. Have you got a death-wish, or something? What d'you think the police'll do to you if they find out?'

'They can't do anything,' Gaynor said. 'It's all public-interest and right-to-know stuff.'

'*What* exactly is "public interest and right-to-know"?'

'Which one of them's lying. Dugdale, or Fauvel. Because,' she added, with uncharacteristic patience, 'one of them succeeded in causing a miscarriage of justice, which is going to cost Joe Public a bloody fortune in compensation. Not to mention the lawyers' fees, and what McKenna's investigation will cost this police force. It all comes out of the taxpayers' pockets.'

Davidson was silent, mulling over her proposal, then he said: 'But Fauvel swore on oath that he handed the letter to Dugdale.'

'He may well have done,' she conceded, 'but d'you really think we'll be told if that's true? Then again, *he* might be lying.'

'Why should a priest lie?'

'Because he's a man!' she said, increasingly exasperated. 'And he's not exactly whiter than white. There was a lot of gossip a few years ago about him and a couple of teenage girls.'

'What sort of gossip?'

'What sort d'you think?'

'That still doesn't make him a liar,' Davidson said. 'I'll sleep on it, and I'll have to talk to our legal people in any case, so keep your head down till you hear from me. How *did* you get on with Smith's mother, by the way? I was expecting copy for tomorrow's paper.'

'Not very well, because Ida fucking Sheridan was directing the traffic.'

'Yes, but what does she want? And what's she got to say?'

'I don't know! As I said, Sheridan was sticking in her oar all the time.'

'Stop playing games, Gaynor,' Davidson instructed her. 'You're squirming like a fish on a hook. We let Smith bad-mouth his mother from here to hell. She must have *something* to say.'

'Sheridan says it'll cost us fifty grand for Bunty even to open her mouth, and at least twice as much for her to keep it shut.' The sounds of Davidson's mirth were like a red rag to a bull. 'It's not funny! You weren't there! And Sheridan's out of a fucking *nightmare*.'

'Met your match, have you? And don't start swearing at me. That kid in the newsroom complained to the union about your language. They told him it amounts to sexual harassment.' He continued chuckling. 'What did you offer?'

'Five grand.'

'And?'

'Sheridan told me to sod off, so I did.'

'Then I'll expect her to call again when she realises you're not waiting on her doorstep with another offer.'

'She can take a running jump for all I care,' Gaynor told him. 'And Bunty looks like she's got cancer, so I don't see her as a long-term problem. Not fifty grand's worth of a problem, anyway.'

2

Jack went first to Manchester, negotiating a road made treacherous by large tracts of black ice, to see the seventy-year-old widower who had responded to Trisha's advertisement. Then he returned to Haughton, and the second respondent.

The widower had, he disclosed to the police officers, hoped to find a kind, decent woman to share his modest wealth and comfortable home, and to care for him in his last years. Trisha's advertisement, a little dog-eared, was tucked in his wallet and, as he showed it to Jack, he said she sounded a really 'nice lady', and he was sorry she never replied.

'I expect she found somebody younger,' he added wistfully. 'I do so hope she's happy. I'm still looking, but what d'you expect, at my age?'

The second respondent was very much younger, and considerably wealthier, with kind eyes and a gentle manner. 'I'd never before replied to such an advert,' he admitted, 'because they seem to represent an admission of failure, but I used to read them every week. Indeed, to be honest, I looked forward to them. Hope springing eternal, as they say.'

'Why did you respond to this one?' asked Jack.

'She sounded different.'

'In what way?'

'After a while, you learn to read between the lines. You realise there's a sort of hidden code in certain words or phrases.' He smiled. 'And usually to do with sex or money. But this one was open, and honest and, I felt, completely genuine.' He paused. 'To be frank, when there was no reply after three weeks, I wrote again.'

'To where?'

'The newspaper box number, of course.'

'Did you get a response?'

'No. Why am I being interviewed, anyway? It was a long time ago. Has something happened to her?'

3

At eight minutes past seven, Wendy returned to some level of consciousness, roused by the bitter cold of her room, the near numbness in her legs, and the seeping wetness under her body. She struggled into a sitting position, tapping her fingers on the bed covers in search of the source of dampness, then the smell of urine reached her nostrils and she fell off the bed in horror, to crawl to the bathroom, sodden skirt slapping icily against her legs.

At the bathroom door, she began to vomit. Heaving and retching, she dragged herself through a trail of bile and slime to the lavatory pan, just in time to spew up what felt like her whole stomach. The pain was terrible, burning from her lips to the deepest reaches of her insides, and she cried and howled like a dying animal.

It was a long time before she could summon the strength to crawl to the telephone on the hall table, and dialling Frances's home number seemed to take an eternity. But there was no reply, and no message on the answering machine, so she called Father Brett's personal number, to be told by an automated female voice that the number was not responding but that a message could be left. Despairing, betrayed in her hour of greatest need by those closest, Wendy dialled the emergency services, and slumped against the wall, great splashes of vomit on her urine-sodden clothes, while she waited for the ambulance to wail to a halt outside the door.

She found it gratifying that the paramedics had to batter their way into the bungalow, and somehow fitting, like the siren which whooped overhead while she was rushed the short distance to hospital. As she was stretchered into the casualty department, like

Fred Jarvis the day before, one of the reporters on watch outside surged forward, peering at her face, tape-recorder at the ready. He recognised her instantly, which was even more gratifying. She could barely stop herself responding to the questions he threw out as he chased after her, but instead, she gasped dramatically, and rolled her eyes.

4

Subdued by the oppressive atmosphere between their parents, the Dugdale children had eaten their tea without any of the usual bickering and chattering, and escaped upstairs to play.

'They're confused,' Dugdale said. 'And I'm not surprised. I am, too.'

'You've let things go.' Susan fidgeted with the ornaments on the sitting-room mantelpiece. 'There's dust everywhere, as well as crumbs. Have you been eating in here?'

'Yes.'

'You know I don't like food in the sitting-room.'

'You weren't here.'

'Oh, that's typical, isn't it? Out of sight, out of mind!'

'Don't be so childish! I've got more to worry about than a few bloody crumbs!'

Tears welled in her eyes. 'And whose fault is that? McKenna was seen at the Willows this afternoon.'

For the first time in his marriage, Dugdale looked at his wife, and not only disliked what he saw, but could not forgive her for it. Then he felt again that pain for the girl who had trusted him with her scarred body, and taught him how it felt to be loved. 'Much as you'd like nothing better than to blame Julie, my suspension has nothing to do with her.' His own tears began to threaten. 'Priest or not, Brett Fauvel's a liar, and if you can't believe in me, then I think you should leave for good, because there's no future for us if there's no trust.' He turned his back on her, and made for the door. 'We'll sort out custody and maintenance later. You won't go short, so don't worry, and you can have the house if you want. It'll be far too big for me, anyway.'

5

Ida was long gone to her own home for supper and television when two uniformed policewomen, one barely out of her teens, rapped on the glass panel of Bunty's front door. She let them in, offered cups of this and that to take away the chill, then sat in her favourite chair, patiently waiting.

'Your real name's Hilda, isn't it?' the older one asked.

'That's right.'

'And you're Peter Smith's mother? The one who's just been let out of prison?'

Bunty nodded.

'Why didn't you come forward before?'

The young one was quite aggressive, Bunty thought. 'There's no need to be sharp! I haven't done nothing.'

'No one says you have,' the older one soothed, frowning at her companion. 'But obviously, we'd like to have been able to talk to you.'

'Why? I don't know nothing now, and I didn't then, so you'd be wasting your time. I told her that this afternoon.'

'Told who what?'

'That reporter. She offered me five thousand quid, only Ida says it's not half enough, considering how the paper's made me out to be so wicked.' She sighed. 'It's him that's wicked. He always was. I *knew* he'd do something really awful one day, and I wasn't wrong, was I? Couldn't leave the fire alone, from the time he could crawl, and look what happened to that poor teacher because of it.' She shuddered, her wasted body threatening to fall apart. 'Then that dog, even though he screamed the place down denying it, and when I wouldn't fall for his lies like usual, he punched me so hard I fell over. When folk asked about the bruises, I had to say I'd tripped over a cat.' She paused, taking short, rasping breaths. 'See? I was still lying for him, wasn't I? But I swore I wouldn't, ever again, so that's why I kept my head down when he killed his wife.' She looked up at the older policewoman, her eyes bleaker than the dark moors beyond her window. 'And God alone knows what's in store for that other woman. Stupid creature! Can't she see?'

6

Barely five minutes after leaving Church Street, McKenna turned into the presbytery drive, stopped the car, and lit a cigarette. 'As yet, we're not in a position to suspect Fauvel of suppressing Father Barclay's letter,' he told Janet and Ellen, 'but we can certainly demand a few more explanations. Let's hope we get them. Broadbent could have learned her evasiveness from him, along with the catechism.'

'Everyone's got an agenda we know nothing about,' Janet pointed out. 'Anyway, Broadbent might be the same with everybody, except the people she looks after. She's very withdrawn and isolated, which isn't surprising. She's been an outcast all her life. Dugdale seems to have been one of the few people to show her any kindness.'

'Fancy Smith having the gall to insult her like that!' Ellen commented. 'I'd have smacked him in the mouth.'

'You'd have cause,' McKenna said. 'Broadbent doesn't believe she has.' Thoughtfully, he knocked ash into the tray. 'Suppose her association with Dugdale isn't ancient history, as we've assumed? Susan Dugdale doesn't appear to believe it's all in the past, does she? Is Broadbent more important than we think?'

'How?' asked Ellen. 'Granted, she knew Trisha and Linda, and she's even fallen foul of Smith's nasty mouth, but she's lived here all her life. There must be hundreds like her, who know all of them, but it doesn't tie them in to Trisha's death or Smith's conviction.'

'Once you know about the accident, it hurts to look at her,' Janet said. 'Even though you can't see the scars.'

'It's probably worse to imagine them.' McKenna glanced at her, but her face was turned away. 'She didn't want to talk about it, did she? But, as you so rightly said, chip pans don't fall over by themselves, so negligence must have been a factor. If the injuries were as bad as Father Barclay intimated, she would have been entitled to substantial compensation.'

'Well, she can't have had any,' Ellen said. 'If the daughter of Haughton's most notorious prostitute suddenly came into a fortune, it would go down in folklore.'

'She hasn't even got a car,' Janet added. 'I asked her when we were on the way out. She says she's saving for her old age.'

After checking that the video-recorder had indeed recorded *Coronation Street*, and not switched itself off while he was out, Jack went into the front room of the Church Street house to summarise the interviews with the letter writers. The place was cold, even though the gas fire was full on, and he shivered in front of the computer screen, pecking at the keys like an old bird.

> 'Both respondents expressed considerable shock on being informed of Trisha Smith's death. Indeed, the older one appeared on the verge of collapse, although he was possibly reacting to being questioned about a murder.
>
> 'Neither respondent could give an alibi. Given the time lapse, a ready alibi would tend to *provoke* suspicion. Both have been bailed pending further investigation of their whereabouts on the day, and further investigation of any possible sightings with Trisha Smith, but it is my view that neither is a likely candidate as a suspect.'

As he waited for the printer to accept the file, he noticed a message from Ellen's children flashing on her computer screen. 'ET PHONE HOME,' it said, and he smiled to himself as the printer spewed out a copy of his summary. He put the single sheet on her desk underneath the tape-recordings of the interviews, then telephoned his own family.

'The weather's awful,' he told his wife. 'And the wind's straight out of Siberia. Everyone's predicting a blizzard before the week's out.'

'Are you likely to be home by then?'

'Not a chance. We're still chasing our own tails.'

'Something will break. It always does.'

'I wish!' Jack said.

'You sound very out of sorts.'

'I can't settle.'

'You never can when you're away from home. You said the house is quite comfortable, and I'm sure you're being well fed.'

'It is, and I am, but I can't sleep for that blasted church clock.'

'And *I* can't sleep because Michael McKenna's cats are rampaging around the house all night.'

Jack chuckled. 'They must be missing him.'

'I suppose. They're unsettled, like you.'

By the time he finished the call, there were two new messages logged on the call minder facility, one from Sheffield police to say that Hilda Smith, also known as Bunty, had been located and interviewed, and was apparently under pressure from a reporter called Gaynor Holbrook. The other was from a reporter with the *Manchester Evening News*, asking for comment on Wendy Lewis's attempted suicide.

He abandoned any notions of relaxing in front of the television, scribbled a message for McKenna, and left for the hospital. His car, its windscreen striated with ice, its bodywork cold enough to burn, started at the fifth attempt, engine whining piteously and coughing vapours. Above the sputtering, he could hear the branches of the churchyard trees cracking under the bite of frost.

'She downed a hell of a cocktail,' the casualty doctor told him. 'Diuretics, anti-inflammatories, a few sleeping pills, drugs her mother had to treat angina, topped off with the usual rubbish folk keep in the bathroom cabinet. She pissed herself, which serves her right, she was sick as a parrot, and she should have her backside kicked. I can't be doing with her sort. Would you believe she admitted she did it for the attention?'

'Whose attention?' asked Jack wearily.

'Some woman who won't talk to her, apparently. Is it a falling out between middle-aged lesbians? It's got all the hallmarks.'

'Has she asked for anyone?'

'Well, the parish priest sort of figured in the scheme, but only so that she could tell him what she'd done.'

'Can I see her?'

The doctor frowned. 'I'd rather you didn't. For all it's self-inflicted, she's not very well, and seeing her woman friend will be enough excitement for the time being.'

'Have you contacted her? The woman friend?'

'Yes, she's on her way. She lives in Manchester.'

Torn between anger and pity, Jack said: 'I'll wait until she arrives. She can't see Miss Lewis, so you'd better be ready for more hysterics.'

8

The Catholic presbytery was a large square building, fashioned from the ubiquitous millstone grit which so quickly weathered to drabness and, like the church it served, designed with fine proportions and embellished with classical features. Father Fauvel, in a swirl of black cassock, took his visitors into what McKenna could only think of as a drawing-room, and showed them to seats already pulled close to a roaring fire. On an antique table nearby were various glasses and tumblers, four crystal ashtrays, and a tantalus crowded with decanters. He gestured towards the drinks and, when McKenna refused, poured out for himself a large measure of whisky.

He was completely at ease and completely in control, Janet decided, wondering what it would take to puncture his confidence. He reminded her of her father, for while of a different persuasion, he wore the certainty of his own convictions as elegantly as his garb of office. When he sat down, completing the semicircle around the hearth, she saw the hems of black trousers, black silk socks, and fine leather shoes. The silver crucifix hanging from his waist dragged on the floor, turning and rolling each time he moved, and every so often he hitched it back into his lap, a little smile playing on his lips. He was slightly sun-tanned, even at this time of the year, and handsome, but in a characterless way, with crow's feet beginning to pull at his eyes, and little dewlaps marring the line of his jaw.

'I trust I won't be speaking out of turn, Superintendent,' he said to McKenna, 'if I say that your investigation really turns on whether Inspector Dugdale is telling the truth, or whether I am.' He smiled, quite fulsomely, the crow's feet wrinkling. 'I could, of course, swear on the Holy Book, but then, the *word* of a man of God should be sufficient, should it not?'

'I'm glad you appreciate the irony of the situation,' McKenna responded.

'I also appreciate the seriousness of it. Inspector Dugdale's whole future hangs in the balance.' The smile died, to be replaced by a more appropriate expression, and Janet was unable to rid herself of the idea that he was acting out a well-rehearsed scenario.

'For the record,' McKenna asked, 'would you provide brief details of your background?'

'Certainly.' Fauvel nodded. 'I was fifty last August,

and I came to this parish almost twenty-six years ago, shortly after being ordained. Apart from brief forays to other parts of the diocese, and a spell at the Vatican, I've been here ever since.' He smiled at each in turn. 'To be truthful, it took me a long time to settle. My family home is in Sussex, and I found the north literally another country.'

'I understand you graduated from Cambridge, with degrees in Classics and Theology. I'm surprised you didn't aspire to greater things than a simple northern parish.'

Fauvel seemed deeply amused. 'There's a lot to be said for knowing where you stand, Superintendent. As I told you, I've been to Rome, and suffice to say that Italy remains the country of Machiavelli and the Borgias, and the cardinals have never forgotten.' As he reached into the pocket of his cassock for cigarettes, and a gold lighter, his sleeve was pushed a little way up his arm, and Janet saw some livid scratches near his wrist. 'This parish is like any other, anywhere in the world, as I'm sure Father Barclay has now discovered. A priest's duty is to serve the needs of his flock, and I can do that as well here as elsewhere.'

'Your duties include supervising the instruction of converts. How well do you know Peter Smith?'

'He really does prefer to be called "Piers", you know. Persisting with his old name smacks a little of spite, don't you think? At best, it's rather uncharitable to keep reminding him of the past.'

'We've had no contact with him, so it's not at issue.'

'Whatever.' Fauvel shrugged, his mouth turning down sulkily, then flicked his lighter. 'Do smoke, if you wish. Are you sure you wouldn't like drinks?'

'Positive, thank you,' McKenna said. 'Please answer my question.'

'As I supervised his instruction into the faith, I'm

bound to have come to know him very well, and I must say I was impressed from the outset by the force of his commitment. But then, as an Anglican, he'd already suffered decades of anguish, trapped at the bottom of the abyss which the historical schism in the church has become, out of reach of the mysterious power of the true faith. You see,' Fauvel added, almost conspiratorially, 'once he realised that the Anglican church was born of the trickery, ambition, and sheer lust of the Boleyn woman, he was in outer darkness. In his opinion, losing her head was a very small punishment for the evil she unleashed upon the world.'

'What struck you about his personality?'

'His vulnerability, and his unhappiness. It bordered on despair.' Smoke drifted towards the ornate plaster ceiling. 'I hesitate to condemn anyone, but his first wife was destroying him as surely as if she were pouring acid down his throat.' Frowning, he added: 'She came to see me, you know. Just the once. She wanted my help. She said he was abusing her, and thought I had enough influence to stop him.'

'What did you do?'

'I counselled him, Superintendent. We had a very frank discussion, in which he admitted to being violent, and spoke of the terror of losing control of himself. And that, I'm afraid, is as much as I'm prepared to say.'

'By any account, Smith indulged in outrageous behaviour towards her.'

'So she said,' Fauvel commented. 'But I suggested to her that his behaviour was *always* outrageous, by one standard or another, simply because he had never learned any other kind of conduct.'

'You obviously feel bound to offer spiritual comfort,' McKenna said, 'but I'd suggest to you that spiritual comfort alone isn't much help. People need practical help, too.'

'Which I was unable to offer her. She was, in any case, very hostile towards the faith, and put every possible obstacle in the way of her husband's conversion.' Staring hard at his interrogator, the priest added: 'As you know, we would prefer to absorb both partners into the church. Where that is impossible, we always investigate the spouse's attitude towards morality, birth control and children, but she harangued him mercilessly about what she called "invasions of her own privacy". Naturally, Piers had disclosed to me, in absolute confidence, the sexual abuse she suffered and its effect on their marriage, but her response was to threaten him.'

'To me, it appears you rejected both her, and her very real fears and concerns.'

'Trisha Smith had no understanding of her husband's spiritual needs, probably because she was, like so many, a creature of the material world. On the other hand, Beryl's very real empathy is evident in the way Piers has matured, and grown emotionally, since they married, despite the tragic set-back of his imprisonment. Hopefully, when she feels strong enough, she too will convert.'

Changing the subject without any preliminaries, McKenna asked: 'Why didn't you raise the matter of Father Barclay's letter at Smith's trial?'

Little spots of colour on his cheeks, the priest said: 'I'm not sure I like your tone Superintendent. Why should I have mentioned the letter?' He leaned forward, elbows on knees, the crucifix dangling. 'I simply handed it to Inspector Dugdale, and thought no more of it. After all, how could I know it was so vital? Father Barclay said nothing in his covering note, except to ask me to hand the letter to Haughton police. He didn't even say what it was about. There was absolutely no indication that it concerned Piers.'

'He asked you to hand it to the officer in charge of Trisha Smith's murder investigation,' Ellen said. 'You had to know.'

'I beg your pardon?' Fauvel stared at her.

'Father Barclay told us,' she added. 'We have his statement.'

'I'm very sorry, my dear, but he did not.' Fauvel shook his head, then smiled. 'But I'm not accusing him of dishonesty. He's been so very ill he can't possibly be expected to remember. He no doubt *believes* that's what he wrote, but I assure you, he did not.'

'Why did you give it to Dugdale?' asked McKenna.

'He happened to be there, that's all, and he introduced himself,' Fauvel replied. 'I knew him slightly, in any case, as I know several of the town's more senior police officers. My work brings me into contact with them quite frequently.'

'But why didn't you pursue the matter?' McKenna persisted. 'Surely, you expected him to come back to you?'

'Why should I, when the letter was from Father Barclay?'

'Weren't you even curious?'

'No, Superintendent, I was not.' He sighed rather ostentatiously. 'And that, I must confess, was my mistake. I could have saved Piers, *and* Beryl, so much grief. But then, it's usually the sins of omission which do most harm.'

Angered by the priest's righteousness, McKenna said: 'I suggest that remorse would be more appropriate where *Trisha* Smith is concerned. She came to you for help, but you sent her back to the hell of her marriage, and to her death.'

'It was a hell for both of them,' Fauvel insisted. 'Her misery was no greater than his. And perhaps she was one of those women who unwittingly bring about their own destruction. Who can know?' Then, sighing once again, he added: 'You speak as if you believe Piers is guilty of her murder. Forgive my bluntness, but would you sacrifice the truth simply to exonerate a fellow officer? Are you being misled by delusions about the integrity of your particular institution? A year in Rome disabused *me* of such notions, and a lifetime of watching the antics of others has served only to prove that where man walks, corruption is his shadow. I know little of Inspector Dugdale, but he, like every solicitor, judge and law officer in the country, will be part of one of the many magic circles of influence and Masonic fellowships which connect and overlap.'

'Do you have actual *knowledge* of police corruption?' McKenna demanded.

'Of course not! I was simply broaching the possibilities.'

'I'm quite aware of those possibilities,' McKenna told him. 'And I strongly suggest you keep such thoughts to yourself, because airing them in public could lead me to think you're trying to subvert my investigation. Now,' he added, 'I understand you sit on the management committee of the Willows. Were you involved in Julie Broadbent's appointment?'

'Julie Broadbent?' A tic snagged the corner of Fauvel's mouth. 'Yes, I believe so.'

'Was the committee aware of her teenage delinquencies?'

Fauvel nodded stiffly.

'But those weren't considered a bar to her employment with very vulnerable people?' McKenna persisted.

'There were special circumstances.' Tossing the butt of his cigarette into the fire, the priest fumbled in the pack, and extracted another. 'But I fail to see her relevance to your investigation. Sergeant Lewis is another matter, of course. She's *very* relevant.'

'We have reason to be interested in Broadbent,' McKenna said. 'Were you in the parish when she was injured at school?'

'I was indeed.' Fauvel shook his head sadly. 'That was a *terrible* business. The nuns were distraught.'

'The *nuns* were distraught?' McKenna was astounded. 'And what about the child?'

'I was speaking relatively!' The priest flushed. 'Of course, the child was in a dreadful state.'

'Whose fault was it?' asked McKenna.

'Fault? It was an accident.'

'All incidents have antecedents, Father Fauvel,' Janet said quietly. 'Accidents are no exception. Who investigated the matter?'

'Apart from being unwarranted, an investigation would not have benefited the child. She was larking around in the kitchens, despite the nuns and the cook having told her several times to go away. She was very disobedient, and an investigation would no doubt have led the church to deny liability. As it was, we took it upon ourselves to make sure she had the best medical treatment, and intensive counselling. The fact that she failed to appreciate the first, or respond to the second, is, I'm sorry to say, only typical.'

'Surely the National Health Service paid for her treatment?' Janet suggested.

'Not all of it,' Fauvel said, clearly irritated by her persistence.

'Was the social services department involved? Serious child protection issues are their responsibility.'

'It wasn't such an issue,' Fauvel snapped. 'The child's background was well known to us, and the reason why we forgave much for which other children would be held to account. She was disobedient by nature, and dishonest. For a long time she blamed the nuns for what was clearly a prank gone wrong, but I think it was that which led us to the conclusion that she was, poor child, quite disturbed.'

'And more sinned against than sinning?' McKenna suggested.

'Indeed.'

'And was residual guilt the reason you let loose on the mentally handicapped a woman who is, as you say, naturally disobedient, dishonest, and disturbed?'

'I was referring to the child!'

'When did she undergo her metamorphosis?'

'Superintendent, I find your attitude bordering on the offensive.'

'Then I apologise,' McKenna said. 'None the less, my question requires an answer.'

Collecting himself, the priest forced a smile, attempting to disarm. 'You know, as well as I, the charity of our church. To an extent, the woman has redeemed the child, by acknowledging the error of her ways. She conducts her life with probity, and is, I'm told, able to offer an important service to those even less fortunate.' Once again gathering up the straying crucifix, he added: 'In the end, she chose not to follow her mother's example. Miss Broadbent Senior rejected our spiritual comfort because she found our strictures too demanding. She took the easy path, which, some would say, led her to damnation. The poor woman chose to depart this world without Viaticum.'

'Wendy Lewis's mother must have gone the same way.'

'Ah, yes.' Fauvel nodded. 'But I was, of course, able

to redeem her soul. None the less, Wendy's conscience remains deeply troubled. I trust, Superintendent, that you won't overlook the effect Mrs Lewis's tragically sudden death had on her daughter.'

'She said it didn't affect her work,' Ellen offered.

The priest pursed his lips. 'Wendy is very proud, and rightly so, of her professional diligence, but she would need a heart of stone *not* to be affected. But her diligence isn't in doubt, is it? And her conscience is not only troubled by her being unable to attend her mother's dying moments. She fears that Inspector Dugdale deliberately suppressed Father Barclay's letter, and her divided loyalties are tearing her apart.'

'When did she tell you that?' asked McKenna.

'Oh, right at the outset of this sorry business, Superintendent. When the documents for the appeal hearing came to light.'

'We were led to believe her change of heart occurred much later.'

'Were you?' Fauvel smiled, as if to imply he trod much firmer ground. 'Does it matter *when*? People are often not rational at the best of times, and it could be unfair to apply your own frames of reference to someone under the dreadful pressure Wendy has experienced.' He paused, gazing speculatively at his visitors. 'Little things like that – wrong impressions, unintentional errors – have a capacity to mislead out of all proportion. And I fear you were misled over Father Barclay's letter. I handed it to Inspector Dugdale because he was there, and for no other reason.'

9

Too tired to continue standing merely out of politeness, Jack took one of the chairs in the hospital waiting room and let Frances Pawsley, her eyes red from weeping, stride from the door to the window and back again, her leather brogues squeaking with each step.

'*Why* can't I see her?' she demanded. 'Surely, this changes everything?'

'Sergeant Lewis's retreat into hysteria changes nothing,' he countered. 'In fact, I'd say it's all the more reason for you *not* to see her.'

'But we're so close!' Tears coursed unchecked down her cheeks. 'She depends on me. She really does.'

'In my opinion, she uses you, and she's not above trying to get her own way by coercion. Why did she put herself in hospital, if not to twist everyone's arms?'

'You don't understand her!'

'Oh, I understand her only too well, Miss Pawsley.'

'Have you spoken to her?' She stopped in her tracks, looming over him, her own distress weeping from every pore.

'I have.' Jack nodded. 'And I can assure you, she's not in any physical danger, because she knew that at worst, the tablets she swallowed would just make her very sick.'

'I blame myself!' Frances kneaded her hands until the knuckles gleamed white. 'She rang I don't know how many times, but I wouldn't take her calls. Then she left this *awful* message while I was in court.'

'What message?'

'It doesn't matter.'

'It matters very much. Who took the message? What did she say?'

'One of the secretaries spoke to her. Wendy said if I wouldn't speak to her, I'd be responsible for whatever happened.'

'That's sheer emotional blackmail, and the kind of drivel Smith's been feeding that bloody reporter.'

'It's just her way. I'm the only one she can turn to, you see.'

As Jack looked up into her miserable, downcast face, any pity he had earlier felt for Wendy Lewis evaporated in the heat of his anger. 'Who can *you* turn to?'

'Eh?'

'Who's there when *you* need someone? Or are you content to let the Wendys of this world bleed you dry, because it makes you feel wanted?'

10

'I don't know what's wrong with everybody tonight,' Julie's colleague said, completing the shift hand-over. 'You could cut the atmosphere with a knife.'

'It's probably the weather,' Julie replied, closing the log book. 'High winds always upset them.'

'The wind's dropped.'

'There's snow on the way.'

'Maybe they're worried about you,' the other woman suggested. 'They saw the police here earlier, and asked Bennett.'

'What did he say?'

'Just that they had to talk to you about the fire.'

'No *wonder* they're fretting!'

'He couldn't say much else, could he? They're hardly likely to understand about Smith being let out of gaol, and all the rest of it.'

'Then he shouldn't have said anything!'

'That would've been even worse.' Hands deep in her overall pockets, she looked down at Julie. 'What *did* they want, anyway?'

'What d'you think?' Julie asked, her whole manner dismissive.

From the office window, she watched her colleague drive away, knowing the air between them would be fraught with chills for the next few days. Overhead, and interspersed with the creak of footsteps, the noise of gunfire and squealing tyres came faintly from the first-floor quarters where the staff on sleeping-in duty were watching television before going to bed. For several minutes Julie stared down the empty drive-way, lost in thought, while her mind's eye roamed again the awful environs of that blazing house.

11

Haughton police were clearly angered when McKenna insisted that Gaynor Holbrook was arrested and detained for concealing the whereabouts of Bunty Smith. Sheffield police, however, were more than willing to co-operate with his request for Bunty to be guarded overnight.

It was almost midnight when Ryman telephoned. McKenna, dozing in the chair, was galvanised to wakefulness.

'I realise it's late,' Ryman said, 'but things need to be sorted out.'

'What's the problem?' McKenna lit a cigarette.

'Where would you like me to start?' Ryman's voice was vinegary. 'Firstly, why weren't we told about Sergeant Lewis's suicide attempt? Secondly, why haven't we been advised about the problems over solicitor representation? Thirdly, how d'you think my officers feel to be ordered by your Inspector Tuttle to mount guard on Sergeant Lewis? And fourthly, although I very much doubt lastly, what am I supposed to do with this reporter? Her editor is threatening us with an action for false arrest.'

'I intended to come to see you in the morning,' McKenna said. 'To discuss these and other issues.'

'They can't wait until morning. You had no right to force the Haughton officers to keep one of their colleagues under virtual arrest.'

'Sergeant Lewis is not under anything of the sort,' McKenna replied, trying to keep the irritation from his voice. 'Inspector Tuttle was simply making sure the media can't get to her. One of the many reporters currently swarming around town saw her being taken into hospital, and very kindly rang here for a comment.'

'That doesn't explain why she's not being allowed to see anyone else. Inspector Tuttle sent her solicitor away, even though he knew Sergeant Lewis was desperate to see her.'

'I'll discuss this with you tomorrow.'

'What about this Holbrook woman? We hauled her in on Monday for a ticking off, so why has she been arrested now?'

'For concealing the whereabouts of a witness,' said McKenna.

'If you know she's done that,' Ryman countered, 'you must know where the witness is, so why couldn't you deal with *her* tomorrow? The hotel where she's staying doesn't take kindly to police raids in the middle of the night, and I don't like my officers being used inappropriately.'

'You're exaggerating somewhat, I think.'

'You could have waited.'

'These decisions are mine, Superintendent,' McKenna pointed out. 'You're under no obligation even to comment on what I do.'

'In other words, mind my own bloody business!'

*

Jack was rapt in slumber when McKenna quietly left the house to drive very slowly and very carefully into town, the ice on the road so thick it crunched under his wheels.

Haughton's main police station, purpose built at the turn of the century in a squat, neo-Norman style, was half-way up a steep side street near the town centre. The barred, opaque glass windows of the original cell block just peeked above ground level, their few dim lights casting geometrically divided shadows on the asphalt yard. When he identified himself at the desk, the hostility became almost palpable.

'It's a bit late to be interviewing a prisoner, isn't it, sir? She's not committed a murder, as far as we know.' The duty sergeant stared challengingly. 'And I can't spare an officer for the interview. We're short-handed.'

'I'm quite capable of dealing with her myself.'

'The duty solicitor's not available, either. I know, because I already tried to get in touch for somebody else.'

'Ms Holbrook may not require representation.'

'I can't allow regulations to be bent, sir. *We'd* be the one to suffer the come-backs.'

'Superintendent Ryman telephoned from head-quarters,' McKenna said. 'He's under pressure from Ms Holbrook's editor, who's talking of an action for false arrest.'

The other man whitened. 'We only obeyed your orders, sir.'

'Precisely. I'm not obliged to explain myself to you, and I don't expect obstruction.'

Some time in the recent past, the police station interior had received a major face-lift. The interview room where McKenna sat facing Gaynor Holbrook was painted a soothing pale green, carpeted in a darker green, and decently furnished.

'Arresting me like this is a bit over the top, isn't it?' she asked. 'People at the hotel must think I'm an Irish terrorist from the way the plods came bursting in. I half expected to find a noose around my neck.'

'You have only yourself to blame,' McKenna commented.

'Bunty Smith is hardly a key witness.'

'You're not in a position to assess her worth.'

'She's not worth anything to me.' Gaynor smiled rather spitefully. 'And she won't be worth much to you if you don't collar her soon. She looks like she could drop dead any minute. She's probably got cancer.' As he stared at her, her eyes narrowed. 'And yes, Superintendent McKenna, I'm as hard-faced as you think I am, if not more so. That's how I get people to open up to me. You'd be surprised what I know. And by the way, Smith is desperate to talk to you. He can't *begin* to understand why you haven't battered down the barricades Beryl put up.'

'I'm here only as a courtesy to the local police. There's no need for your editor to harass Superintendent Ryman. You are not a victim of false arrest, and will be charged appropriately in the morning.'

'Superintendent Ryman, eh?' Her eyes glinted. 'He's quite a mystery, isn't he?'

'Is he?'

'*I* would think so. Wouldn't you?'

'I hope you're wise enough to refrain from further concealment, or from making misleading allegations.'

'Ryman should figure in your investigation. He knew all the relevant people. Even Smith, probably.' She toyed with a glass of water, and he tried to decide whether she were only toying with him. There was real intelligence in her eyes, and in the clearly drawn features, which would have been attractive but for their knowingness. Despite the late hour and her precipitate removal from the hotel, her whole aspect was one of neatness and minimal inefficiency, her white-blonde hair hugging her well-shaped head like a helmet, her clothes tailored and pressed, and elegant. 'I sat through every minute of the trial,' she added. 'It was riveting stuff.'

'I've read the transcripts.'

'They won't give you the atmosphere, though.' She drank some water, then set the glass precisely within the ring of moisture already on the table. 'At the end, I was completely convinced of his guilt, and d'you know what? I haven't changed my mind. As I see things, Dugdale, Bowden and Lewis are the fall guys. How *is* Sergeant Lewis, by the way? I believe she tried to top herself.' She smiled at him again. 'And Dugdale's marriage is on the rocks. What's in store for Bowden, I wonder? You leave quite a trail of destruction, don't you?'

'If you've nothing useful to say, Ms Holbrook, we'll call a halt.'

'You're rather like Smith in that way,' she went on, as if he had not spoken. 'He strews misery like bad seed. Are *you* compensating for what was done to you?'

'Bad seed usually fails to germinate,' he said crushingly. 'And therefore to grow, so, although colourful, your analogies are inaccurate.'

She looked amused. 'No, I wouldn't like to be compared with that wife-beating shit, either. But, if you recall, he claims Trisha was equally handy with her fists. Like your ex-wife, I understand.'

'I beg your pardon?'

'You see, I'm asking myself if you're quite the right

person for this job. You could have your own agenda to prove Smith innocent, in the face of all the evidence, simply because you share the status of battered husband.' She sat back a little, stretching. 'I think you're too emotionally involved, and I think you've kept away from Smith deliberately, because your intellect tells you that once you've smelled him, as it were – and believe me, he smells very unpleasant – you couldn't sustain the fantasy of his innocence.' Crossing her legs, and smoothing her skirt, she added: 'Your divorce petition was very explicit, wasn't it? Did *you* ever feel like retaliating with your fists? Do your colleagues know how vicious your wife was, or do they still think you just abandoned her because you're a bastard?'

He wanted to hit her.

'As I said before,' she commented, almost exhilarated by his rage, 'you'd be surprised what I know. Nothing's a secret for long, and provided I don't publish, there can't be any come-back.' Her smile was extraordinarily sweet. 'So don't bother threatening me.'

I

The freelance reporter who witnessed Wendy Lewis's admission to hospital sold the story to the national daily competing directly with Gaynor's paper, and earned himself a fat fee. The photographer who caught the policewoman's tormented face in his camera's eye was equally well-rewarded.

Wendy Lewis, the forty-two-year-old detective under investigation in the Piers Stanton Smith miscarriage of justice case, was last night admitted to Haughton hospital suffering from an overdose. After receiving emergency treatment, her condition was said to be 'stable'.

Lewis is one of three detectives suspended from duty pending the outcome of a major investigation by an outside force, headed by Superintendent Michael McKenna. Tragedy is stalking the investigation: apart from Lewis's overdose, the father of

the woman Stanton Smith was cleared of killing had a heart attack on Tuesday, and Detective Inspector Barry Dugdale, who headed the original murder investigation, has been deserted by his wife. Neighbours are devastated, as the Dugdale marriage was, according to one, 'as solid as a rock. This is a tragedy, especially for their children.'

McKenna and his team are keeping completely tight-lipped about their activities and, until last night, Haughton police had no involvement. However, local officers were compelled by McKenna's deputy to place Lewis under virtual arrest in her hospital bed, where she is being kept incommunicado, even from her own solicitor. Very late last night, again under orders from McKenna's team, Haughton police also raided an exclusive hotel on the moors outside the town and arrested Gaynor Holbrook, a national daily staff reporter who this week wrote three searching articles about the Stanton Smith case. Holbrook is still in custody, despite a midnight visit from McKenna, and no details have been released about why she was arrested in such dramatic circumstances.

2

'And behind bars is the best place for her,' Rene commented, peering over Jack's shoulder at the newspaper. 'She *deserves* to be locked up, because if she hadn't written that rubbish about Trisha and Linda, Fred wouldn't be in hospital. He gave me this letter last night, by the way,' she added, carefully placing a blue Basildon Bond envelope near McKenna's elbow. 'He said he was letting the Mountain know why Mahomet wants it to visit.'

Despite his foul mood, McKenna managed to smile. 'How is he?'

'He can't wait to get home. They said he can come out tomorrow, provided he's not left alone for a while, so he'll be going to Linda's.' She pursed her mouth. 'Not that Linda hasn't got enough of her own worries.'

'Stop fishing, Rene,' Jack said. 'You know we won't discuss her.'

'You could set *her* mind at rest, though. People are beginning to think you're very hard-hearted, like it says in that paper you're reading, only I know you're not like that, deep down.'

'You know nothing of the sort,' Jack replied.

'You've got a nasty job to do, and you're treating people as fairly as you can,' she asserted. 'Even that Julie Broadbent, so I hear.'

'What d'you know about her accident?' McKenna asked.

'Accident?' Rene frowned. 'You mean when she was little? That was no accident. It was downright carelessness, and those nuns should've been taken to court for it.' She shook herself, as if to get rid of the memory. 'It was terrible! I wouldn't wish something like that on my worst enemy.'

'How did it happen?'

'I suppose she hasn't told you, not that you can blame her for not wanting to talk about it. Anyway, she keeps herself to herself these days. Pity she didn't before, isn't it?' Rubbing the small of her back as she sat down in the chair McKenna pulled out, she added: 'I don't know all that much about the accident, really. There's always been a big wall between the Catholics and the rest of us.'

'I'm sure the gossip managed to get over it,' Jack commented. 'It usually does.'

She smiled at him. 'You're sharper than you look, aren't you?' Adding two heaped spoonfuls of sugar to her tea, she said: 'Kathy Broadbent, Julie's mother, wasn't from these parts. Her parents put her in the home for unmarried mothers that the nuns used to run, and she was supposed to put Julie up for adoption, but she wouldn't. She stayed on in town, in a tiny rented flat near the station. The National Assistance paid the rent, I expect, and gave her something to live on.'

'Where was the unmarried mothers place?' asked Jack, lavishing butter and marmalade on the last piece of toast.

'At the Willows. Didn't you know?'

McKenna experienced a strange frisson, which seemed to shift the focus of his thoughts. There was something both tragic and fitting, he realised, in Julie's return to the place where she had come into the world unwanted, to care for others for whom the world had no use. 'When was it turned into a home for the handicapped?'

'Oh, years ago,' Rene replied. 'Girls aren't put away these days when they're expecting. There's no shame now to having a baby out of wedlock.'

'There is for some,' Jack said, thinking of Janet. 'What happened to her mother?'

'She died,' Rene told him. 'Ten, twelve years ago, it must be. She wasn't even forty.'

'What was wrong with her?'

'People said it was God's judgement because of the life she'd led, but not even that Father Brett could answer that one,' Rene commented sourly. 'She had cancer. She just wasted away before your eyes, then she died. Give Julie her due, she nursed her to the bitter end, and never a word of complaint.' She fell silent, biting her lip. 'I've often wondered if Julie's grandparents are still alive. They might not even know Kathy's dead.'

'You were going to tell us about the accident,' McKenna reminded her gently.

'Yes, well, it's a miracle there weren't others, the way those nuns treated the kiddies. Call themselves Christians!'

'Is this fact, or gossip?' Jack asked.

'Witnessed with my own eyes,' Rene snapped.

'What was?'

'I don't know if it's still the custom,' she said, 'because I'm too old to bother about some things, and I don't have call to go past the Catholic school very often, but there used to be an early Mass every morning at the church.' Making herself more comfortable, she picked up the teacup. 'The Catholic kiddies were supposed to go. Never mind the weather, never mind anything else, they had to get out of their beds at the crack of dawn to kneel in church for hours on end.'

'I remember,' McKenna commented ruefully.

'What happened to *you* if you didn't?' she asked.

'Happened? Nothing, although my mother would nag at times.'

'Folk must be more human where you come from, then. Round here,' she went on, 'the priests and the nuns kept tally on every kiddie, and if they hadn't been to early Mass, they'd get a real belting off the nuns as soon as they turned into the school gates.' She looked from one to the other. 'And I mean a belting. They had a thick leather strap, with a huge metal buckle on the end of it, and you should have seen those kiddies' legs afterwards. They drew blood.' She shuddered. 'The way they'd stand there, beady-eyed and waiting, they reminded me of the rooks in the churchyard, flapping their habits, and the strap in their claws.'

'Did anyone complain?'

'If they did, they were shut up, because *we* never heard anything.' She drained her tea, and began to make neat, segregated stacks of the used crockery. 'You might be thinking the town's divided because of religion, but it's not. It's divided because of the way we've seen the Catholics behave. The priests and the nuns don't answer to anyone. They've got too much power, which is why they got away with hushing up Julie's accident, and not paying a penny compensation.'

'We *did* hear,' McKenna said, 'that she was larking

about in the kitchen, and knocked over the pan herself.'

'Well, you heard wrong! The older girls were made to work in the kitchen, as well as doing the cleaning, when they should have been in lessons, and that day Julie was having to cook chips for school dinner. You've seen her,' she added. 'She's not very big now, and she was a tiny little mite then, barely able to reach one of the sinks, I'd imagine. But that didn't stop them making her manhandle a huge pan full of boiling fat, and that's how it happened. She dropped it, because it was too heavy for her, and the school and the church should've got into really serious trouble, but they didn't. And believe it or not,' she went on, getting up from her seat and beginning to clear the table, 'they *still* make the girls do the cooking and cleaning at the school. Let folk get away with something once, and they think they can get away with anything.'

Fred Jarvis's grasp of language was neither as firm nor as clearly educated as Henry Colclough's, but his letter was equally touching and, while using different words to speak of his own loss, conveyed the same sense of outrage.

> William Bagshawe Ward
> Haughton General Hospital
> Wednesday, 3 February

Dear Mr McKenna

I've asked Rene to give you this letter. She was a good friend to Dorothy, my dear late wife, and she's been the same to my girls and me since Dorothy died. I trust Rene, and so should you, even if you might think she speaks her mind too often.

She was very shocked, Linda said, when she

heard I'd said I'd get better so I could rip off that creature's neck and shit down his neck, because Rene's never heard me utter an oath in her life. Linda hadn't, either, until then, because I'd kept my sorrow to myself. But things have changed, now, and it's time to speak my own mind, although the threat and the foul language were just an old man's fury. Still, it made me feel a bit better, even if it'll be left to someone else to pay him back for the misery he caused my daughter.

Linda's finally told me everything, and I'm very cross with her. I understand she was only trying to protect me, but I've told her she was very, very stupid to keep quiet about those letters. She didn't do it out of spite, or anything like that. She's not quite sure now why she didn't tell Barry right at the beginning, but people do things they can't give reasons for, don't they? Especially when something dreadful's happened. Anyway, I hope you understand, not that I'm expecting you to let her off the hook. I can see how what she did makes things look even worse for Barry, though she can't, because she says he had nothing to do with it – I do believe that, Mr McKenna. Barry's a very decent young man, and an honest policeman, and even though he was genuinely upset about Trisha, he wouldn't ever do something dishonest just to put someone in prison, even if he hated the person.

You'll have heard a lot about some people in this, but probably not much about my dear dead girl. Linda's very precious, and she's all I've got left, but she was always the baby of the family, even when Dorothy was alive. She doesn't remember much about that time, because children of that age don't, do they? Somewhere along the line they forget, but Trisha was different. She remembered everything, and she was so like her mother in so many ways, where Linda's more like me – sharper, if you like, when Trisha was very kind and sweet, and always looking for the best in people. That's why that creature got away with hurting her for so long.

Mr McKenna, I expect you've known lots of people who've had their loved ones murdered, but I don't know anyone else in that situation, except Linda and me. And Rene. Don't forget her – she loved Trisha like her own, and that's why you'll have to forgive her if you think she's talking out of turn at any time.

In a way, it didn't matter at the time if anyone went to prison for killing Trisha, or not, because the only important thing was that she was dead, and she wasn't coming back. I think I would've felt the same if she'd been in an accident, because you're not supposed to outlive your children. When she went, she took all the memories we'd shared, not just of Dorothy, but of me and her and Linda together too, and I know it sounds dreadfully selfish, but I didn't feel there was anything left of my life worth bothering about – the real part of it was buried with her and her mother. Anyway, after a while, I got going again, because there was Linda, and her boys, and while they're not the same, they're still my blood, so to speak, and I found my heart could beat for them, when I'd thought it was all dead and shrivelled. You'll have to excuse me rambling on, Mr McKenna, but you might not have the time to come and see me, which I will understand, so I've been thinking about what I'd like to tell you.

I read in the paper, along with the terrible lies about my girls, that that creature is getting counselling – some poor sap to hold his filthy hands. We didn't have anything like that when Trisha was killed. The doctor offered, but we don't need to pay people to tell us what we already know. Losing a loved one hurts. It hurts so wickedly you think it'll kill you, and so much you pray it will, to stop the suffering. Time does heal, but it can't ever get rid of the scars, and in any case, you don't want it to – you might forget. Trisha's death is like a huge, horrible landmark in my memory, a wall going right across our lives. Her alive is one side of it, her dead is the other, and for a long time, I was stuck with my face against that wall, like everybody else who'd known her, including that creature, I suppose. Nothing else seemed as if it could ever matter so much and, until he was let out of prison, nothing did. Now, he's in clover, isn't he, and my dear girl's six feet under, but he's still not satisfied. He wants more attention, so he's making up these terrible stories about her. Rene can tell you they're not true, and how we can prove it, if she hasn't done already, and Linda can tell you herself.

You're a detective, and you might well be saying to yourself 'no smoke without fire', and you're a man, so you might also be asking 'what did Fred Jarvis do for sex after his wife died? Could it be true that his lovely daughter took her mother's place in his bed?' It could be, but it wasn't. Nobody could take my wife's place, which is why I never even thought of getting wed again. For a long time, I thought that part of life was buried with Dorothy, but the sap rises whether we like it or not, and once every two weeks, I'd get Rene to have the girls overnight – and she probably knows exactly why, though she's never said a word – while I had my 'date'. The lady would come to my house, through the back ginnel so nobody saw, and sometimes we'd just have a drink and a chat, because it was enough. Other times, there'd be more, and I've got sweet memories of the few years we had.

Mr McKenna, does anybody else need to know? The lady's long dead, another grave I put flowers on from time to time, but her girl's still alive, and trying to live a good life, even though she's had her own terrible troubles. We all know each other, but don't know that we do, if you see what I mean. Trisha was very friendly with the lady's daughter, and Linda likes her as well, but she might feel different if she knew about me and her mother. The lady in question, and she was a lady, whatever you might think about somebody who lives the way she did, was Kathy Broadbent, Julie's mother.

I hope we'll get to meet, but I've said what I really wanted to say, and I know you'll respect my confidences as much as you can, not that I'd want to let them get in the way of your job. For what it's worth, I've got my own doubts that the creature killed my Trisha, though I don't know who else could have done, unless it was somebody we don't know about. I don't have any doubts about Barry, but I'm not trying to influence you. I'm simply saying what I think about him and, apart from anything else, he always loved his work too much to make a mess of things. Did you know he wanted to be a policeman right from when he was a boy? You'd often see him on a Saturday afternoon, on the coat-tails of the bobbies on the beat on the High Street, and he got to be a bit of nuisance at times, because I remember his dad telling me how Inspector Ryman had been to the house telling them to find another way of keeping Barry occupied at the weekends. Mind you, Ryman was a miserable sort, too full of himself for a town like this, especially after he joined the Lodge. I'm sure he's much happier now he's sitting behind a desk giving orders.

Anyway, I'll see you if I see you, as they say, and best wishes with the job – it can't be easy.

Yours sincerely

Fred Jarvis

'What's he got to say?' Jack asked.

'Nothing very much,' McKenna replied, 'except that Ryman found Dugdale a pain in the rear, long before he joined up.' He folded the letter, replaced it in the blue envelope, and put that in his briefcase. 'I'm seeing Ryman this morning, so you'll have to sort out the other interviews with Janet. The two girls who were pestering Fauvel must be traced and interviewed, but Bunty Smith's your priority for now.'

'What about Holbrook?'

'She's to be charged with wasting police time, and bailed.'

'Is that all?' asked Jack. 'Bit of a damp squib after last night's dramatic arrest.'

'I want her on the loose, and I want her to think she's put one over on us, because I'm sure she's up to something, and I want to know what that is.' He smiled wolfishly. 'Then we can throw the book at her. Attempting to pervert the course of justice will hopefully be the least of it.'

'Obviously,' Jack said mildly, 'you've taken against her. Shall we interview Lewis, if she's well enough?'

'No. There are no assurances to give her, and she can't have Pawsley back, but you *can* tell the Federation to get her another solicitor.'

'And this newspaper report?'

'Ignore it. The media's out there, and until something new takes their attention they'll be watching us, and what they don't know they'll make up, as usual.'

'Father Barclay's a sweetheart,' Ellen said, as she put down the telephone. 'I could really go for him if I wasn't married.'

'You still couldn't have him,' Janet pointed out. 'He's taken a vow of chastity.'

'I think that's an awful waste. He'd make a lovely husband and father.'

'But is he a good source of information,' asked Jack irritably. 'Does he remember the names of the girls with a crush on Fauvel?'

Ellen nodded. 'It was obviously a significant event in parish life.'

'Why? It's not uncommon. Even you would be a priestly groupie, given the chance.'

'Julie could be another one pining with unrequited love for Fauvel,' Janet mused. 'And what Rene said about her being born at the Willows opens up all sorts of possibilities.'

'I don't see how,' Jack said. 'I can't see a single useful possibility about it, even by exercising my imagination.'

'I'd like to talk to her on my own,' Janet decided. 'D'you think Mr McKenna would mind?'

'You can ask him later,' Ellen said. 'We really should be on our way to see Bunty. Snow's definitely

236

forecast for today, and I don't fancy being marooned in a ten-foot drift on the road between here and Sheffield.'

'It's physically impossible for ten feet of snow to fall in a day,' Jack commented, gathering papers and notebooks.

'Not when it's blizzarding in a north-easterly gale,' Ellen argued. 'Listen to that wind howling outside. What d'you think it's like up on the moors?'

3

Their talons hooked around the wildly threshing branches, the rooks in the churchyard trees watched them leave, cawing throatily, then fluttered out of the trees to eddy around the steeple.

The road to Sheffield climbed to almost two thousand feet as it snaked across Bleak Moor, then ran straight for a few miles before plunging into the forestry plantations lining the shores of a massive reservoir. The landscape was white with frost, the waters at the edge of the reservoir sharded with ice that glittered and tumbled and pointed as the wind tore over the surface. Dark-grey cloud lay low and heavy on the moorland peaks, shredded wisps of paler grey filling crevices and snagging in the tree-tops.

In the back seat, Ellen stared through the car window, puzzled to find this land alien and alarming when she rejoiced in the bleak and unforgiving aspects of the Welsh mountains. 'I couldn't live round here,' she said. 'Everything's the wrong colour. I don't know how, but it is. Even the sheep look sort of dirty, although I suppose they could just be a different breed from our sheep.'

'It's more likely the Sheffield pollution,' suggested

Jack, as they emerged from a deep gulch in the hillside to see the city sprawling below, uniformly drab beneath the darkening sky.

He parked below the block where Bluebell Way, Primrose Walk and, right under the sky, Daffodil Close housed the city's elderly. 'Is it me, or is there something very wrong about putting old folk in a high-rise?'

'It's not really a high-rise,' Ellen said. '*Those* are high-rises.' She pointed to the other side of the valley, where multi-storey tower blocks and rampart-like structures destroyed both human and natural proportion.

A uniformed policewoman came to the door of seventy-seven. 'Can I leave now, sir?' she asked, when Jack introduced himself. 'I've been here since midnight, and Mrs Smith isn't best pleased about it.'

Another figure loomed behind her, a rotund shape with sharp dark eyes. 'Fancy thinking Bunty'd do a bunk,' Ida said in some disgust. 'What d'you take us for?'

'It was simply to protect Mrs Smith.' Jack tried to summon a smile.

'What from?'

'Reporters and suchlike.'

'Even *they* don't come knocking on folks' doors in the middle of the night,' Ida commented. 'It's the kids and the junkies do that, and where are the coppers then, I ask you? Nowhere!'

'Yes, well you never know.' Dismissing the policewoman, Jack put Ellen's machines on the table by the window, then searched the gloomy room in vain for Bunty Smith.

'She's in the toilet,' Ida told him. 'The cold gets on her kidneys, not to mention all this worry.'

'We heard she's not very well,' Ellen said with a

sympathetic smile, looking for electrical sockets in the skirtings.

'Who said that?' Ida's voice was sharp.

'I really couldn't say. We've talked to an awful lot of people.'

'Well, you can't have talked to many about Bunty, because nobody knows about her, except that snotty little bitch of a reporter.' Standing four-square in front of the fire, Ida demanded to know: 'What did she say? And don't plug those things in until we've finished with the electric kettle and turned the fire down a bit. You'll blow every fuse in the block.'

'I'll get the battery pack out of the car,' Jack mumbled, and disappeared.

Ida continued to glare at the two women and, when Bunty eventually emerged from the toilet and crept downstairs towards the kitchen, she called: 'I'll brew the tea. You come in here.'

Bunty looked almost as wispy as the torn moorland clouds, Janet thought, as the old woman drifted into the room, eyes averted from her visitors. Ellen took her hand, introduced herself and Janet, and said that Inspector Tuttle would be back in a moment.

'Oh, for God's sake!' Ida snapped. 'Stop treating her like she's a moron. We had enough of that off that bitch of a reporter.'

'If you can't stop interfering, Mrs Sheridan,' Ellen told her, 'you can go back to your own place.'

'Bunty wants me here!' Ida's face reddened.

'Then please keep quiet,' Ellen replied. 'She doesn't need a guard dog.'

'If you're going to squabble,' Bunty said suddenly, her voice croaking, 'you can all go away. I can't stand arguments.'

'That's right!' Ida agreed. 'She can't, 'cos she put up with too many off that son of hers.'

'And you can't make me talk if I don't want to,' Bunty added. 'I haven't done *nothing*!'

4

As she signed her release papers and took the bailee instruction sheet from the custody officer at Haughton police station, Gaynor doubted if McKenna would let her off with only this minor charge of wasting police time. She knew she had provoked him too far, and expected trouble. She checked the SIM card in her mobile telephone and, item by item, the contents of her confiscated Louis Vuitton bag, then signed another paper, retrieved her car keys, and strode out into the biting wind, determined to find something, if not to bargain with, to neutralise McKenna.

She was not to know that Davidson was so worried by the turn of events that he had instructed the newspaper's lawyers to write to Linda Newton offering an unreserved apology and, without prejudice, the sum of £10,000.

5

When McKenna was shown into the superintendent's office at Ravensdale police headquarters, Ryman rose to meet him, offering an uneasy smile, and a Masonic handshake. The handshake, to his chagrin, went unacknowledged.

'Do sit down, and let me apologise for the somewhat abrupt tone of our conversation last night,' he said. He was a tall, heavy-set man, with a thatch of almost pure white hair, and handled himself confidently. 'You must appreciate that we're very concerned about the welfare of Dugdale and his colleagues, and when we heard of Sergeant Lewis's overdose, it was a nasty shock.' He seated himself in a padded leather chair behind the desk. 'I, for one, never imagined she'd do anything like that. I thought she was made of sterner stuff.'

'It was purely an attention-seeking gesture,' McKenna replied. 'She was in no danger of killing herself, which she well knew.'

'Can we be sure about that, though?' He stroked his chin. 'She's in an extraordinarily stressful situation, after all.'

'All the more reason for the Federation to insist on her having solicitor representation.'

'I understand Miss Pawsley's a family friend of considerable long-standing,' Ryman said. 'Isn't there a way she could be allowed back on the scene? It would solve the problems.'

'She deliberately attempted to subvert my investigation, Mr Ryman, so no, there's no way I'm going to give her another opportunity.'

'I must say, Mr McKenna, I hadn't realised your investigation would be either as far-reaching or as – well, ruthless is the only word which springs to mind.'

'Is there any reason why you should? It doesn't concern you.'

'These are *my* officers!'

'They are officers of this force, like yourself,' McKenna pointed out.

Ryman surveyed him, eyebrows drawn together. 'Are you implying that *I'm* under investigation now? You've rather changed your tune since our meeting last week, haven't you? That was wholly amicable, as I recollect.'

'I have certain questions to put to you, on issues

which have arisen since. At present, they appear to be fairly general queries, but you will appreciate that I can give no assurances for the future.'

'Does the chief constable know about this?'

'He's been informed.'

Drumming his fingers on the desk, Ryman asked: 'Is this interview to be under caution?'

'I was hoping for your co-operation.'

'I see.'

'It's your decision, of course,' McKenna added, 'but you must accept that your reluctance to co-operate will be assessed accordingly.'

'All you're supposed to do is find out who framed Smith.'

'Firstly, Mr Ryman, I must be sure that Smith *was* framed.'

'Don't be ridiculous! He was in church when it happened. You surely can't gainsay a Roman Catholic priest, who knew nothing about it and had no involvement with any of the principals.'

'We're fairly sure Father Barclay has told the truth, but there are any number of other people involved in this matter who have not, or who are only telling half the truth.' Noticing an ashtray on the desk, McKenna lit a cigarette. 'Smith and Beryl could have arranged elaborate alibis, while a paid villain did the job for them. Beryl has a stake in this, as well as her husband.'

'I can see that,' agreed Ryman. 'But it doesn't solve the problem of Barclay's letter. Either Dugdale's a liar, or Father Brett is and, with the best will in the world, I can't see why Father Brett should lie.'

'Dugdale made regular reports to you throughout the murder investigation. How much *real* effort was put into checking the alibi Smith claimed to have?' When Ryman began to frown again, McKenna went on: 'I've read the statements Dugdale and his team took from various members of the congregation, but such documents only present half the picture. Why did no one see Smith at the church? Why did no one mention Father Barclay as a potential witness? He wasn't long gone at that time.'

'I don't know why! But I do know they were as thorough as they could be, and if you recall, when the women who were in the church that day were re-interviewed for the appeal hearing, not one of them could say that it was definitely that particular day when they saw Smith in church. Hardly any of them knew him, anyway, because he'd only recently finished his conversion, so he wasn't a regular.'

'And Father Barclay?'

'Out of sight, out of mind, probably. He was a very junior priest, anyway, and they're so used to priests coming for a few months, then going off again, he wouldn't have had time to make a mark.' Ryman paused, frowning. 'And I don't know why you're digging over this particular ground again. You know what lousy witnesses most people make, when they're willing to be witnesses at all, that is. I could go outside, chuck a brick through a shop window, and if you asked ten people what I looked like, you'd get ten very different descriptions, and even if I was standing right in front of them most of them wouldn't recognise me.'

'I'm aware of that,' McKenna conceded.

'And I suppose the next thing you'll ask is whether Dugdale told me he'd had the letter, and I told him to bin it?'

'Did he? Did you?'

'No, and no!' Ryman's irritation, and anxiety, were increasing.

'You've known Dugdale a long time, haven't you?'

'Since he took it into his head he wanted to be copper, and made a thorough nuisance of himself "learning the job". He was about twelve then. In the end, I had to tell his parents to warn him off.'

'Was that provoked by a particular incident?'

'At one time, we didn't bother locking the cars when they were parked in the yard, so we could make a quick get-away if the need arose. Dugdale, of course, cottoned on to this, so he'd slip into one when no one was looking, and curl up on the floor behind the front seats. God knows how many jaunts he had, before someone found him when they went to put a prisoner in the back.'

'Very enterprising,' McKenna commented. 'Was there any come-back for you?'

Ryman flushed. 'I was in charge of the station.'

'Of course.' McKenna nodded. 'Do you feel resentment towards him? Potentially, he has a hold over you, however small.'

'He wouldn't have got on so well if I had.'

'Surely progress or otherwise depends on merit?'

'Stop laying traps, Mr McKenna. I won't fall into them.'

'There are implications in that comment, you know, but we'll leave them aside for now.' Stubbing out his cigarette, McKenna said: 'Why did you feel the need to tell me about Dugdale's long ago associations with Julie Broadbent and Linda Newton?'

'I thought they might be relevant.'

'Why? What reasons do you have?'

'Where Newton's concerned, it's obvious, isn't it?'

'That implies you believe he either conspired with her to frame Smith, or framed Smith out of regard for her.'

'I've already told you I can't question Father Brett's integrity.'

'So where does Broadbent fit into that scene?'

'People were pretty scandalised when Dugdale took up with her. Getting involved with a girl like that says a lot about him. His judgement, and his disregard for convention, at the very least.'

'Come on!' McKenna chided. 'They were teenagers. I'm sure you, like the rest of us, at least kissed a few girls your mother would have turned her back on.'

'I have never consorted with a prostitute!' Ryman seethed. 'Or with the daughter of one, before you make any more smart remarks.'

'None of us can know what people do in their secret lives,' replied McKenna and, with Fred Jarvis's poignant disclosures in mind, added: 'Women like Kathy Broadbent often fulfil a genuine need. We have no right to condemn her out of hand.'

'So you're happy to fly in the face of two thousand years of Christian morality, are you?'

'On the subject of Christians,' McKenna remarked, 'Father Fauvel talked of magic circles around the police, the legal profession, and Freemasonry, implying that the truth was bound to remain locked inside. Might your loyalty to him be misplaced?'

'We all need someone to look up to in this world, and a priest is a more certain example than most,' Ryman argued. 'And he was probably just trying to tell you that Dugdale's corrupt, without actually saying so.'

'In your regard for a Papist, you're a most unusual Anglican,' McKenna said. 'And an even more unusual Mason, but that's irrelevant, I imagine. Tell me, what do you know about Broadbent's accident?'

'That it *was* an accident,' Ryman said flatly. 'And entirely her fault. In my opinion, she was lucky the Church didn't have her put away, instead of paying out thousands for plastic surgery.'

'Why should the Church pay for treatment that was freely available on the NHS?'

'They wanted her to have the best.'

'Which would be available on the NHS,' insisted McKenna. 'Do you know for a fact that the church actually paid out a penny? Or was all that a smoke-screen to hide the truth? According to some sources, her injuries were the result of criminal negligence.'

'She's still putting *that* story about, is she?' Ryman stared at him, eyes narrowed. 'You want to be very careful with her. She's cunning, manipulative, dishonest, and downright dangerous. And the kindest thing anyone could say is that life has brought her so much pain she wants to give others the benefits of her experience.'

'I didn't realise you knew her so well.'

'You know perfectly well her delinquencies came to our attention when she was younger and, to be frank, I shudder to think what she's up to these days. Like mother, like daughter, in my view.'

'She's doing an important job and trying to rebuild her life,' McKenna said.

'I wouldn't even let her work in a dog's home. Father Brett must have a hell of a lot of faith in human nature to risk giving her a job, but I expect he keeps an eye on her. He's no fool.'

'Mr Ryman, you are aware of the statutory responsibility for child protection that falls upon the police, aren't you?'

'Of course, I am!'

'Then why did you fail Broadbent? Why didn't you involve the social services department? Why did everyone deny the child a fighting chance?' McKenna stared at the other man's stony face. 'You never even cautioned Kathy Broadbent over her activities, let alone prosecuted. In fact, you *condoned* her life-style, and abdicated your responsibilities not only to her child, but to the community you were paid to serve.'

'What was I supposed to do? Prosecuting the woman would have brought shame on upstanding men, and destroyed families and marriages. And for what? D'you really think it would have made an ounce of difference?' His face was dark with anger. 'There's an old saying in these parts, Superintendent. You can't make a silk purse out of a sow's ear, and believe me, Julie Broadbent's more like a sow's backside. You can scrub off the filth, but she'll wallow again at the first opportunity.' He smiled then, quite savagely. 'Has it occurred to you that *she* might have killed Trisha Smith? No one knows where she was that day, and she can't *prove* she was in the Willows.'

'Please answer my question about Kathy Broadbent,' McKenna told him. 'Did you condone her activities because some of these "upstanding men" you talk about were police officers?'

'How *dare* you suggest that!' Ryman was white with rage.

'Or were they perhaps the town worthies who might be useful to your own advancement?' McKenna went on. 'There's nothing like a small town for back-scratching, is there?'

'Listen to me,' Ryman snarled, 'and listen good! We couldn't do anything to that woman because we never caught her at it. She didn't walk the streets, and she didn't solicit in public. Her reputation went by word of mouth.'

'And where did she carry out her trade? In her home, in front of her child?'

'If she did, no one ever told us.'

'She was a notorious prostitute,' McKenna reminded him, 'and her child was therefore at risk. You did nothing to protect that child, and even when she was so horribly injured, you *still* did nothing.'

'I've already told you the Church looked after *her*.' An unpleasant smile began to play about Ryman's mouth. 'And d'you know, none of this is any of your damned business! You're just muck-raking about things that have nothing to do with Smith or Dugdale, and you're overstepping the mark. Dangerously so, in fact. Maybe people should be told.'

'Then feel free to tell them.' McKenna rose, and picked up his briefcase. 'But don't forget that Trisha Smith may have died because she fell into a heap of other people's muck.'

I

The heat from Bunty's fire was making Jack very sleepy. Stifling another yawn, he asked: 'Why is your son telling such exaggerated untruths about his childhood?'

'Because he was born with lies on his tongue,' Ida replied.

'I suppose it puts him in a better light,' Bunty ventured, ignoring her friend. 'And he always had ideas above himself. He was never content with me, or what I could give him. He wanted more, and he thought he had a right to it, but heaven knows why.'

'And what he couldn't get honestly,' Ida added, 'he'd get another way.'

'How long have you two known each other?' asked Janet.

'Donkey's years!' Ida said. 'Since we both got jobs in one of the knife and fork factories after we left school. That was where Bunty met her husband.'

'You were married to your son's father?' Ellen's eyebrows shot up.

'Of course she was!' Ida snapped.

'What happened to him?'

'Well, he didn't run away from the army and get his legs cut off!' Ida barked.

'He took to the drink,' Bunty said.

'Why?'

249

The old women looked at each other, then shrugged.

'Because men do,' Bunty suggested. 'Women do, as well, these days.'

'Bunty threw him out. He was drinking the money she needed for rent, and baby food and suchlike.' Ida pursed her mouth. 'She should've thrown his offspring after him, and saved herself a lot of grief.'

'He wasn't a bad man,' Bunty said, defending her absent spouse. 'He was never nasty to me, and he was a good husband before the drink took him.'

'He must've had bad blood,' Ida countered, 'and it came out in his son.'

'Where's your husband now?' asked Jack.

'I don't know. He took to the hills thirty-three years ago, and that's the last I saw of him.'

'When did you last see your son?'

'When the nasty little thug was sixteen.' Once again, Ida responded. 'He disappeared one day, without a word, and it was just as well, if you ask me, 'cos Bunty was near the end of her tether with his evil goings-on.' She leaned forward, and tapped Jack's knee. 'You see, that's why I never said when the coppers came asking before. Bunty's never got on the wrong side of the law, so I reckoned it must be something to do with husband or son, and both of them'd done enough harm already.' She shook her head angrily. 'And now he's saying he was put in a children's home because Bunty was in prison, and that's another wicked lie. She had to go into hospital.'

'And when the police came calling,' Bunty added, 'it was months before then, maybe even a year.'

'What did they want?'

'There'd been an accident outside the old YMCA place on Division Street,' Ida said. 'A man got knocked down and killed by a car, and Bunty saw it all, so she had to be a witness in court.'

'It's not unusual for young children to confuse time, and connect unconnected events,' Ellen offered. 'Perhaps your son should have the benefit of the doubt over that.'

'Benefit of the doubt nothing!' Ida turned on her. 'He knows damn well Bunty was in hospital, because I used to get him from the home every Wednesday evening and every Sunday afternoon, and take him to see her.'

'What was the operation for?' Janet asked.

Ida looked at her friend, who simply nodded. 'She gets tired easily, and she's not had a decent night's sleep since that son of hers was let out of prison, because she's scared he'll find out where she is, and come causing her more grief, so that's why I'm doing most of the talking, in case you're wondering.' She folded her arms across her ample stomach, and took a deep breath. 'Bunty's mam and dad, *their* parents, cousins, aunties, uncles, and her big sister and little brother were wiped out by a German bomb in the war. They were all together having a party for Bunty's third birthday, and *he* knows all about it, so you can forget the fairy stories in the paper. Anyhow, Bunty was dragged out of the rubble by an air raid warden. She had her picture in the papers as far away as Newcastle and London, and the warden got a medal for saving her. Nobody expected her to pull through because she was broken up like a doll that'd been stamped on, but she did.'

'But I've always had a lot of trouble with my bones,' Bunty said.

'That's why she never grew very big,' Ida went on.

'She managed all right for years, but having a baby made things go wrong, because of the weight. She struggled on for a few years, then the doctors made her go to hospital to be screwed back together again.'

Bunty levered herself from her chair, went to the sideboard, and pulled a bulging, tattered envelope from the top drawer. 'Have a look in here,' she said, handing the envelope to Jack. Her fingers, he thought, were like broken claws. 'There's old newspaper stories about the air raid,' she added, 'and other bits and pieces, and letters from the doctors at the hospital.'

'It was like she started falling apart after *he* was born,' Ida added, embellishing the awfulness, while Jack moved to the table, spilled out the contents of the envelope, and began to read.

Ellen frowned. 'How d'you mean?'

'Oh, Ida, you don't half lay it on!' Bunty chided. She offered Ellen a surprisingly sweet smile. 'My pelvis got broken in the raid, and it was fastened together with screws and things. It all got pulled around when I was expecting, so it had to be repaired. That's all there was to it.'

'And how's your health now?'

'I manage,' Bunty replied. 'I could be worse, considering my age, and everything.'

'Do you remember the air raid?' Janet asked.

'I can't remember a thing, which I've always thought was a blessing. A friend of my mam's in the next street had a photo of her, so I know what *she* looked like, but there's nothing left to remind me about my dad, or the others, or my sister Betty, or little Eric. He was barely a year old.' Again she smiled, warming Janet. 'Sometimes, when I'm dozing by the fire, or even wandering round the shops, I'll get little pictures flashing through my mind, right out of the blue, and I have the loveliest dreams some nights, and I know they must be about my family, because they make me feel everything will be all right.'

'Some hopes!' Ida commented. 'And I don't know what went wrong, either,' she added, seeing the expression on Janet's face. 'How somebody like Bunty gave birth to him is beyond me.' She chewed her lips thoughtfully. 'Maybe they swapped him at the hospital.'

'Don't be silly,' Bunty said. 'I'd've known.'

'You did your best for him,' Ida insisted. 'You worked hard, you looked after him much better than a lot of mothers, and you wouldn't hear a word against him even after that teacher died.'

'Maybe I didn't love him enough,' Bunty said. 'Folk say you can't do for your children what wasn't done for you, and I can't remember having a real mam, so perhaps I never knew how to be one.'

2

'I've often thought,' Jack observed, fighting to steady the car against the onslaught of the wind, 'that we should listen to what ordinary people have to say instead of the claptrap psychologists put about, because in the end,' he added, swerving towards the verge as the wind suddenly voided itself, 'psychology amounts to nothing more than basic common sense. Bunty was spot on in my opinion with what she said about not knowing *how* to be a mother.' As the first flakes of snow spattered the windscreen, he switched on the wipers. 'Some experts believe Mary Bell's early influences were really to blame for the fact that she killed two little boys when she was only eleven herself.'

'Mary Bell's mother was a prostitute who offered sado-masochism as part of the service,' Ellen said. 'And she traded from home, so Mary would have seen a lot, and heard the rest of it. She might even have been forced to play her own part. That child was the product of ordinary human nastiness in bed with grim circumstance, so the comparison doesn't hold water.'

'It's the early influences that determine which aspects of a child's personality will flourish,' Jack insisted. 'And which won't. Mary Bell only learned about violence and depravity. On the other hand, from what we've seen of Bunty, the foster parents who reared her must have been decent people.'

'I expect they were,' Ellen conceded, 'but they probably couldn't offer the emotional warmth she'd have had with her birth family, so *she* couldn't show her own child the emotional empathy any child needs to be healthy and whole. And don't forget we've only heard her side of the story. It's bound to be subjective, if not as biased in its own way as what Smith says. We should really be looking for some middle ground.'

'Why?' Janet asked, watching the snow spiralling, and even flying upwards, as the wind drove into it. 'Maybe people like Smith just evolve through the genetics of evil. Even if they don't, he's had enough counselling to know exactly what his problems are and where they stem from, so he hasn't a single excuse for the way he behaves.'

The moors above Haughton were dusted with white by the time they reached Church Street. Snow splattered the railings, and drifted against walls and tree trunks and gravestones. The rooks still clung to the threshing trees and, as he was locking the car, Jack saw a nest wrenched from a crook in the branches. It fell to earth with a clatter and a splintering thud, and a bevy of birds erupted about the steeple, cawing anxiously.

McKenna was in the kitchen with Rene, gossiping while she prepared their lunch. Jack poured tea for himself from the pot warming on the cooker hob, and sat down. 'It's snowing hard up on the moors,' he said.

'There's a surprise!' Rene smiled, reaching for a carving knife to cut the haunch of roast ham on the counter. 'You'll have your wings clipped if you can't get any chains for the cars, and I hear there's not a set to be had for miles around.'

'Couldn't we borrow some?' he asked. 'There must be spares at the police station.'

'I thought you and them weren't on speaking terms,' she commented. 'Especially after last night.'

'Yes, but *you* must know someone there who doesn't think we're poisoning the town's life-blood.'

Her mouth twitched. 'I'm allowed to play now, am I?' The carving knife was held still, its tip glinting.

'I've an idea you've been directing the traffic from when we set foot here,' Jack told her.

Smiling to herself, she sliced through the smoky brown flesh. 'I expect I could find somebody to help out, as long as Mr McKenna doesn't mind me using the telephone.'

3

Returning from her enforced absence to the hotel, Gaynor expected a reception frostier than the outside day, and a discreet invitation to step into the manager's office, but she was admitted as if last night's extraordinary events had never happened.

Thinking that was probably because of the platinum sheen on her credit card, the size of her car, and the matching suite of Louis Vuitton luggage lodged in an alcove in her bedroom exactly as she had left it, she went down to lunch. Afterwards she was still hungry, for she had literally turned up her nose at the breakfast offered in the cells, so she ordered sandwiches and coffee from room service, then set about catching up on missed telephone calls and disappearing opportunities.

She called Davidson first, and he obviously expected her to be enraged by his attempted appeasement of Linda Newton.

'I had no choice, I'm afraid,' he told her, launching into self-justification.

She let him finish, then calmly said: 'It was always on the cards we'd drop ourselves in *something* and, from what I've heard since, Smith really led us up the garden path there.'

'Oh.' Davidson was surprised. 'I see.'

'And he probably did the same over his mother,' she added, 'so maybe you should write to her in a similar vein, but only offer five thousand. She wasn't quite misrepresented in the same way, and we could always argue that she should have made her existence known long ago.'

'This is getting very expensive, Gaynor, aside from your hotel bills.'

'I'm sure the paper's still well in profit.' She munched a sandwich filled with a delicious concoction of meats and relishes.

'At the moment, but that's no guarantee it'll last. This is a dog-eat-dog world, as you well know. By the way, your articles provoked several very venomous letters, mainly about the police. What have they done with you?'

'Charged me with wasting their time, and bailed me.' Fingers hovering over the plate, she selected another triangle of thin brown bread, oozing with cheeses. 'Trust me, it won't go any further.'

'Trusting you is getting a bit risky.'

'Nothing ventured, nothing gained!' Her voice sharpened. 'You've done better than you dared hope for up to now.'

'Maybe things really *have* run their course,' he suggested, harking back to yesterday's argument.

'They won't do that until McKenna and his geeks sod off back to Troglodyte-land.'

'What's he like?' Davidson asked.

'He's a copper, and all coppers are bastards.'

The hotel was two miles down a winding track off the road that trailed over the top of Dark Moor and, with snow chains in the boot, Gaynor set off towards Haughton, to visit Beryl and her husband. Before she left, she had sent one of her scouts to trawl the local estate agents, to find out who owned the house where Trisha Smith had burned to death. She was amazed that the police had never bothered, for while the information might not be of any significance, no one was in a position to judge unless it was brought to light. Mentally ticking off the many aspects of the murder investigation where it was now clear that Dugdale had been negligent, she turned on to the High Street and cruised towards the town centre traffic lights.

Snow flurries gusted down from Bleak Moor, sticking to the windscreen and gathering in small drifts here and there. She flicked the wipers, then as the lights changed, surged up the road towards Beryl's house beneath the long, undulating edge of the moor. Absent-mindedly asking herself why she regarded the house, its contents, the servants and the money as *only* Beryl's, she realised how little investment Smith made in his environment. He took from it to the point of draining its life-blood, and returned nothing.

The tall gates stood wide open and, parking outside the front door, she glimpsed Beryl's car, with its self-conscious number-plate and brand-new tyres, in the huge garage. The gardener-handyman, whom Smith insisted on calling a 'groundsman', was nowhere to be seen, but a wheelbarrow filled with various tools had been left in the middle of the drive.

She closed the car door quietly, and tiptoed over the gravel, her journalist's nose twitching like an animal's. The place was too quiet, overhung with an atmosphere darker than the sombre snow clouds above Bleak Moor and, as she stepped on to the wide semicircular doorstep, she held her breath. Unable to distinguish a word of the altercation inside, she put her finger to the bell.

At the third summons, the housekeeper opened the door, looked her over from head to foot, then said: 'I don't know how you dare show your face, after all the mischief you caused.'

'Excuse me?' Gaynor raised her eyebrows.

'Oh, don't come the innocent! You know what I'm on about.'

'You're forgetting your place, and I don't talk to servants. I want to see your mistress.'

'And aren't you a hoity-toity bitch?' The housekeeper stalked away, leaving the door open. As Gaynor shut it quietly behind her, Beryl emerged from the drawing-room.

'Oh, it's you.' Her face was puffy and her eyes red, and she held a balled-up handkerchief in her hand.

'We need to talk,' Gaynor said, advancing towards her.

Beryl retreated, almost stumbling into the door frame. 'It's really not a good time. Piers is quite upset.'

Determined that he would shortly be even more upset, Gaynor almost pushed her out of the way. Smith was lounging in a fireside chair, a cigarette dangling from his fingers. He stared at her unblinkingly, and she chilled from head to foot.

'I wish I'd never set eyes on you!' His mouth was a thin, vicious line. 'Peddling your false fucking sympathy! D'you know what you've done?' He sprang to his feet, and began to jig around the room. 'People spat at me in the shops, and slashed the tyres on the car. I'm afraid to go out, and it's all your *fault*!' A shrill, ranting note came into his voice. 'You're like a fucking vulture!'

'Piers!' Beryl's voice was a horrified whisper.

Ignoring his wife, he jabbed his finger in Gaynor's face. 'When I've finished with you, you'll wish you'd never been born!' His breath was foul.

'I wrote what you told me.' Gaynor tried to hold her voice steady, but her heart was pounding. 'Too bad you couldn't tell me the truth! You lied about your mother, you lied about Linda Newton, and you lied about Trisha. You've already cost me a night in the cells, not to mention my paper getting stung with a libel action.' Enraged, she stood up to him, trying to ignore the cruel mouth and dangerous eyes. 'You made a fool out of *me*!' She jabbed her own finger. 'And don't you *dare* threaten me! *You* caused all the trouble.'

'You bitch!' he shrieked, dancing like a dervish. 'You *whore*!'

'Piers, please!' Beryl sobbed. 'Please, oh, *please*, don't!'

'*Shut up!*'

Beryl snatched at his arm, but he wrenched away so

259

violently she stumbled against a chair. Then she too turned on Gaynor. 'Go away! Please. Just go *away*!' Her eyes were wild, her breath came in little panting sobs as if her airway were obstructed.

'I don't think I ought to do that,' Gaynor said. 'Left alone with him, you'll probably end up like your predecessor.'

Smith stopped his jigging as if turned to stone, and Gaynor braced herself for the attack. She dodged when he moved, but he simply brushed past, mouthing more obscenities. Flouncing from the room, he pounded up the stairs, slammed drawers and doors, pounded down again, and ran out through the front door, leaving it wide open.

4

McKenna turned right off the lower end of High Street, negotiated a grid of streets tunnel-like with the never-ending stone terraces, then made a left turn into a wide avenue. In the far distance, the station end of Dent Viaduct defined the horizon.

Cruising so slowly that the driver behind almost nudged the bumper, he looked at the numbers and names variously displayed on the gates, porches and front doors of the large mock-Tudor houses on either side. Finding the one he wanted, he stopped rather suddenly, earning a protesting blast from the other driver. 'I should have let you take the wheel,' he told Janet, rubbing his eyes. 'I'm tired.'

'I don't understand why you went out so late last night,' she said.

'I rather wish I hadn't.' He stared bleakly through the windscreen.

'Did something happen?' she ventured.

'You could say that. I think I've underestimated Holbrook.'

'She's been after you from the start, sir.' Janet spoke almost dismissively. '*She'd* say she spotlighted us to make sure we do the job properly, but I think she's just getting mileage for her stories. Sensational innuendo about police corruption always sells papers.'

'I wonder where she'll stop.'

'There isn't much more she *can* say.'

Half turning in the seat, he looked at her. 'She's very bright and completely hard-faced. Additionally, and as she freely admitted, she seems able to find out whatever she wants.'

'You're half inviting me to ask what she's discovered about you,' Janet replied. 'But I'm not sure you'd want me to know.'

'If she publishes, the world and his wife will know, and her inventive turn of mind would skew the facts to imply something quite divorced from the truth.' He sighed. 'Never mind. There must be worse things than being grist to Holbrook's mill, and at least, I'm not alone in that.'

Unsure what she would do with this un-characteristic intimacy if it continued, Janet merely said: 'She doesn't seem to know about Julie's involve-ment with Dugdale. And so far, she's left father-one-foot-on-the-ground-and-the-other-in-heaven Fauvel alone.'

'Give her time. She's already niggling about Ryman.' He opened the car door.

'He had scratches on his wrist,' Janet added, as they went towards the house.

'Who did?'

'Fauvel, and he glared at me when he saw I'd noticed.'

The girl who once harboured a passion for Father

Fauvel, and whose parents lived in the timbered and plastered house, was away at university. Her mother, startled to find two police officers on her doorstep, reddened with embarrassment when she heard the reason for their visit.

'Oh, dear! Fancy that silly episode coming back to haunt.' She offered a tentative smile. 'Brenda will be *mortified*!'

'Perhaps *you* could help us,' McKenna suggested. 'We might not need to bother her.'

'Well, it was all a to-do about nothing. I mean, they didn't *do* anything, except hang about the presbytery after school. Silly young things, weren't they?'

'Why were they doing that?'

She sighed. 'There was a film on TV about a priest in Australia who falls in love with this girl. It put all sorts of romantic nonsense in their heads.'

'*The Thorn Birds*,' Janet said.

'That's it! I suppose they got carried away because Father Brett looks so like the actor who played the priest that people teased him about it.'

'Did Brenda ever tell you what went on at the presbytery?' asked McKenna.

'I'm not sure what you mean.'

'Did she comment about something she might have seen or heard? Something out of the ordinary, or puzzling, perhaps.'

The woman frowned. 'Well, no. She couldn't see what wasn't there, could she?'

5

On the other side of town, on a run-down council estate a world away from mock-Tudor gentility, Jack and Ellen ran to earth the girl who had shared in

Brenda's puppy love but not her bright prospects. Unemployed and, like so many of her kind, almost unemployable, Pauline Flynn was at home, getting under her mother's feet.

'Turn that TV down! *Now!*' Mrs Flynn yelled, standing in the doorway of her uninspiring front room. 'I can't hear myself think, never mind talk.'

Reaching for the remote control, Pauline pointed it at the huge screen and crushed a button under her fingertip. 'There!' she announced, as silence invaded. 'So quit nagging!'

'There's police here with some questions, so mind that mouth of yours.'

'What about?' Alarmed, Pauline leaped to her feet, eyes wide.

'Not that waste of space you call a boyfriend,' Mrs Flynn snapped. 'More's the pity.' She turned to Jack. 'She's running with a bad crowd, but does she listen to me? Does she heck!' Still muttering, she shifted a pile of magazines and knitting from the settee to the floor, and invited them to sit down.

'It's about when you and Brenda were at school,' Ellen said. 'You know, when you were hanging round the presbytery after school.'

'Oh, no!' Pauline collapsed back in the chair, hands over her face. 'Not *that* again.' Her wavy dark hair rippled around her shoulders.

'I'm sorry if it embarrasses you,' Jack said.

Dropping her hands, Pauline looked up, tossing her hair. 'It makes me want to curl up and *die!*'

'Why?' asked Ellen.

'Because!' She flushed. 'And if my boyfriend knew, he'd kill himself laughing.'

'What's so awful about a teenage crush?'

'It's him, though, isn't it? Father Brett. He's so *creepy*.'

'Why?' Ellen frowned. 'Because he's old?'

'No,' Mrs Flynn said, 'because he's creepy. I stopped Pauline going to St Michael's. She comes with us to St Saviour's now. He only takes services there once a month, so he hasn't got the same clout.'

'Why did you do that, Mrs Flynn?' Jack's scalp prickled with anticipation.

'Can't keep his hands to himself, can he? Everybody knows, only some think it's different for someone like him. Well,' she added, 'I don't, so that's that.'

6

Gaynor's imagination transformed Smith into a mythical creature that could travel magically and invisibly through thin air, and all the way along the lane from the house she expected him to appear before her, those dreadful eyes boring into hers. Reaching the main road without incident, she rebuked herself for being so silly: he had probably just hidden in the shrubbery until she left. But had Beryl not been in the room, or the housekeeper somewhere about, she was convinced he would have savaged her like a mad dog, and that visceral terror washed through her once more.

She parked behind the town hall, shivering to dislodge the fancies that clung like incubi to her shoulders, then went into one of the High Street cafés, and sat well away from the window with a mug of extra-strong tea. Smith, she knew, would not forget, and forgiveness was not a word in his vocabulary. He would add her name to the list of those who had offended his obscenely perverted self-centredness, and when she remembered what happened to such people, she spilt most of her tea on the pink gingham cloth.

Chastened and frightened, and almost able to smell her own burning flesh, she thought of tapping the mercy that was said to inform McKenna's dealings with the world.

Before she unlocked the car, she looked into the back, in case Smith was hiding behind the seat. She switched on the radio, then turned it off, in no mood for chatter or music. She wanted to flee, but knew she had to stay until the last act of this drama was played out. 'There at the cutting edge,' she said to herself, following the hypnotic sway of the windscreen wipers. The sudden livid glare of brake lights from the car in front catapulted her back to wakefulness.

Snow was already piling up on the roofs, and sticking on the roads and pavements, but for all that, the High Street was still thronged with shoppers, some not even wearing overcoats. Driving stop-start in the stream of traffic, she glanced at the ghostly relics of advertisements once painted on the gable ends of houses and shops: the sinister-sounding 'Bile Beans'; the legend 'Spratts', decorated with flaking pictures of a dog and a cat; 'Maconochie's Pickles', and the ubiquitous 'Hovis'. Rounding the bend where the long rows of terraced houses and small shops petered out, Dent Viaduct filled the horizon, its east-facing pillars blasted with snow, the gantries and wires along the top like lines inked in the sky. Wondering how many souls had plummeted to their deaths from that enormous height, she thought what a grim place this was, its people dwarfed by these massive industrial relics, its buildings overshadowed by a wasteland of moors and bogs.

By the wrecked mill near the ruined house where Trisha Smith had died, she followed a mulberry-coloured saloon on to the road that led to Dark Moor, and the safety of her hotel. The snowy pavement was deserted except for a small hooded figure scurrying, head down, in the same direction. Lights were on behind house windows, and curtains drawn against the early twilight. The road was too narrow for Gaynor to overtake, so she cruised behind the other car, then cursed lewdly when it slewed into the kerb without indicating. The driver's door opened as she passed, and a man jumped out. In the rear-view mirror, she saw him stride to the pavement and virtually pounce on the hooded figure.

A few yards up the road, Gaynor stopped her own car, and squinted through the globs of snow on the back window. The man kept reaching out, while the woman – for Gaynor was sure it was a woman – continually backed away, slipping and sliding on the treacherous ground. When he grabbed her arm and began to drag her towards the car, Gaynor shoved the gear-stick into reverse, rear lights blazing. He saw her coming, released the woman, leaped back into his car, and drove off at high speed. His face was a blur as he passed, and when Gaynor peered at the registration plate all she saw was another blur.

The fur-trimmed hood of the woman's coat had fallen about her shoulders, exposing a pale, heart-shaped face, and soft curly hair. She shook herself like an animal, and was about to recommence her trudging when Gaynor called out: 'I saw what happened. Are you OK?'

Hands in pockets, the woman barely paused. 'Fine, thanks.'

'Well, you *look* pretty shaken,' Gaynor said. 'Can I give you a lift? Apart from anything else, the weather's vile.'

The woman stopped, and looked up and down the road. 'I suppose. Thanks.' She climbed in, the scent of icy moorland winds and damp wool about her clothes, then began to rub her arm.

'Did he hurt you?'

She shrugged. 'Not really.'

'From where I was sitting, it looked pretty nasty.' When there was no response, she added: 'A good thing I was there, isn't it?'

'I suppose,' the other repeated. Her face was turned away, denying Gaynor even the benefit of her expression.

'Who is he?'

'Oh, just somebody I used to know.'

'Well, *he* seems to think there's unfinished business.'

'You can stop just up there,' the woman said, pointing to a junction on the right.

'Will you be all right?' Gaynor asked. 'I'm not very happy about leaving you alone.' She sensed a genuine drama slipping out of her reach.

'I live nearby. I'll be OK.'

'Shouldn't you report it to the police?' Gaynor persisted, slowing the car. 'I saw it all. I could help.'

'There's no need.' She pulled up the hood, ready to get out. 'He's just someone I used to know.'

I

'At first,' Jack began, reporting to McKenna on the visit to Pauline Flynn, 'I thought we'd struck gold, but when we'd cut through the crap, it was all a lot of hot air.' Warming his flanks by the gas fire, he went on: 'Mother Flynn said Father Fauvel can't keep his hands to himself, but that was because of what Pauline claimed he'd done, which amounted to nothing more than a priestly stroke of her hair as she was taking Holy Communion.'

'She's got very pretty hair,' Ellen said. 'Dark brown, and long and wavy.'

'So, Fauvel was tempted, and forgot himself,' Jack commented. 'Then again, people often stroke kids on the head.'

'She wasn't a "kid".' Ellen sounded exasperated. 'She was fourteen.'

'Some priests do a lot of touching,' McKenna said. 'It's part of their ritual, but it means nothing.'

'Exactly.' Jack looked a trifle smug. 'Mother Flynn, and her offspring, both had to agree it meant nothing. Pauline and Brenda blew up everything out of all proportion, because of some silly adolescent thing. Pauline told Brenda that the hair-stroking was a sign of the undying love Fauvel could never declare. Brenda was beside herself with jealousy, and had a tantrum, and that's when the trouble started.'

'What "trouble"?' McKenna demanded.

'Mountains out of mole hills,' Jack said, stifling a yawn. 'Initially, Mother Flynn told us *she'd* put the brakes on Pauline's attendance at St Michael's, but that wasn't true. The Flynns live in St Saviour's parish, but Pauline started going to St Michael's because Brenda was already smitten with Fauvel. They made such a nuisance of themselves the bishop wrote to tell Mother Flynn that Pauline had to attend St Saviour's. He wrote to Brenda's parents, as well.'

'Which Brenda's mother conveniently forgot to tell us,' McKenna said.

2

Noses pressed to the glass of the dining-room window, hands clasped together, the Dugdales' two young children watched the snow building into drifts in the corners of the window-sill. The garden was blanketed with white, and the distant moors gleamed beneath a dark sky. Standing by the door, seeing how they clung together for protection in case another row erupted between their parents, Susan hurt for them, and was enraged.

'Damn that McKenna and his bloody investigation!' she muttered. 'And damn that evil Broadbent witch!'

The children glanced round. She smiled stiffly, and they turned away again. She wanted to gather them in her arms, and weep into their soft hair, because she felt almost mortally wounded, and they were all she had left.

Dugdale had gone to the supermarket where Kay's shop once lorded it over the High Street. Usually, they went together, making an outing of a chore.

Sometimes, Linda and Craig and their two boys would be pushing a trolley down the same aisles, all dressed in matching leather bomber jackets and smart jeans. She liked Craig, and the boys were sweet. Linda could be spiky at times, but for all that, and her being a part of Dugdale's past, she posed no threat.

'When Daddy gets back,' she said, clinging to hope, 'we could all wrap up and play in the snow.'

They kept their backs turned. 'He won't want to.'

'Of course he will! He'll help you build a snowman, like he did last year.'

'It was different then,' her son replied.

3

During the afternoon, when a tearful and self-pitying Wendy Lewis faced the psychiatric interrogation imposed on all would-be suicides, she unleashed a deluge of complaint against McKenna and his pitilessness. Afterwards, she lay in bed feeling quite satisfied that once the proper authorities learned the reason for her misery, her tormentor would be neutralised.

She watched the snow through the tall sash windows that lined each side of the ward, then began to fret about her unheated bungalow falling prey to frozen pipes and disaster. Frances would have taken all those worries off her shoulders, she thought forlornly, and again cursed McKenna.

Two nurses squeaked into the ward, one pushing a steel hot cupboard on big castors, the other behind a steel trolley filled with clinking crockery, and knives, forks and spoons stuck into steel canisters. Wendy was third in line for tea, and when the nurses arrived by her bed she whined and dithered.

'Haven't you got anything else?' she demanded. 'I'm not sure what I should have. I've still got awful stomach ache.'

'It's your own fault,' one nurse commented tartly.

'You've no right to speak to me like that!'

'D'you want tea, or not? Other folk are waiting, and they're *really* poorly.'

'I'm really poorly,' Wendy moaned. 'I'm sick!'

'In the head,' the other nurse whispered, smirking at her colleague.

'I'll report you!' snapped Wendy. 'You see if I don't!'

'Please yourself,' the first said airily. 'But you'd better have your tea first, because you won't get anything else before breakfast except a couple of biscuits, and if you're going to report us, you'll want to keep up your strength, won't you?'

Wendy eventually chose poached fish and steamed vegetables, with sponge pudding and custard to follow. Taking tiny mouthfuls, she chewed each one to a mush, as her mother had said was necessary to avoid the evils of chronic indigestion. She could feel the food slithering into her empty stomach and sliding into the voids created firstly by the terrifying vomiting of the night before, then by the assault with stomach pumps she suffered at the hospital. Her guts were as raw as if she had been flayed from the inside out.

She left sufficient fish and vegetables on the plate to point to continuing frailty, but savoured every spoonful of the pudding and custard, not only for its taste, but for the comforting memories it evoked. She washed down the meal with mineral water, climbed gingerly from the high bed and put her feet on the cold linoleum floor. Her slippers were in the bedside locker, along with the few personal items brought during the night by one of her old colleagues. Frances would have known exactly what to bring, she thought resentfully, and while Father Brett would do whatever she asked, it was hardly appropriate to ask a man to rummage through her cupboards and drawers for toiletries and underclothes.

Once out of the warm bed, she began to feel nauseous. She sat on the side to steady herself, then reached for the hospital-issue towelling dressing-gown, pulled it around her shoulders, took slippers and purse from the locker, and stood up.

The young constable on watch just outside the ward was a stranger. With a huge jolt, Wendy realised that change had taken place since she was suspended, that familiar points of reference in her work world would have disappeared, and that the space she imagined people waited for her to reoccupy was already filled by someone else. She was as bygone as history.

'Sergeant Lewis?' The young man rose. 'Where are you going?'

'To the phone.'

'I'm sorry, Sergeant, but you're not allowed to make any calls at the moment.' He smiled sympathetically. 'But if you tell me who you want to speak to, I'll see if I can do it for you.'

'Who says I can't phone?' Her chest felt crushingly tight.

'Superintendent McKenna left instructions.'

'He can't do this!'

'Well, I'm sorry, like I said, but we're under orders. Who did you want to call?'

'Father Brett,' she whispered.

He pulled a small notebook from his shirt pocket. 'Yes,' he said, looking down the list of names. 'I'm allowed to call him. You go back to bed, and I'll let you know what he says.'

'I want him here!' she whined. 'He's got to come. Tell him I *need* him!'

4

Shortly after eight o'clock, Ellen obeyed the instruction that appeared daily on her computer screen, and telephoned home. Her husband had been in London since Tuesday, prosecuting a libel case at the High Court, and the housekeeper said the children were again calling themselves 'orphans'.

The eldest 'orphan', a strapping sixteen-year-old, compounded his working mother's chronic guilt by telling her that the youngest, his twelve-year-old sister, had fallen out yet again with her best friend, and had been crying in her room since arriving home from school. The middle child, a calm, intelligent boy of fourteen with his mother's liking for exactitude, added that his sister's histrionics had been interrupted by eating, and by *Top of the Pops*. For thirty minutes, Ellen chatted to them on the various telephone extensions, feeling the absence of each in turn. Hoping that the fast-falling snow would not cut off her weekend exit from this grim place, she said goodbye to them, then telephoned her husband.

She was tired, and her feet had not been warm since she arrived in Haughton. The nightly communications over, she returned to the investigation analysis begun when the others went out. McKenna had sent Jack to see how the back-together Dugdales were faring, and had himself gone to visit Wendy Lewis at the hospital. Now in a position to see the gaping holes in the fabric of Dugdale's investigation, Ellen had little patience with him, and even less with Wendy Lewis and her self-inflicted miseries. Colin Bowden had sought McKenna's permission to visit his parents in Warwick, and Ellen hoped the distance between him and Dugdale might provoke Bowden to question his adolescent hero-worship of the other officer. On balance, she doubted that it would, because such mindless loyalty was usually the glue that held police officers together.

Janet was visiting Julie Broadbent. McKenna had been reluctant to let her go.

'Ryman clearly thinks our interest in the Broadbents is superfluous and irrelevant,' he had told her.

'All the more reason to pursue it, then, in my opinion,' Jack commented. 'We're not here to dance to Ryman's tune, are we?'

'No, but he could still be right.'

'She might be more forthcoming if I was on my own,' Janet suggested.

'If you're hoping for a woman-to-woman chat, you're wasting your time,' McKenna told her. 'She's at least ten steps ahead of you, walking wounded or not.'

For her analysis, Ellen had drawn on the thousands of pages derived from old and new witness statements, the trial transcript, the appeal transcript, the copy reports acquired from the prison, and forensic and scientific reports, but its most significant aspect was its brevity. As a pointer to the way forward it was almost useless, for it stated little other than the obvious. She mulled over the printout, picked up a red pen, and ringed the few paragraphs that warranted further thought.

The historical associations between Ryman and

other principals may be significant. He pointedly disclosed Dugdale's liaisons with Newton and Broadbent, and is clearly hostile to Broadbent. He resents criticism about his *laissez-faire* attitude towards her mother's activities. He may fear being sidelined into early retirement because of poor performance and, as the senior supervising officer, he may also fear being scapegoated for Smith's wrongful conviction.

Gaynor Holbrook withheld information about Smith's mother. She may be aware of relationships or other significant factors so far eluding, or hidden from, this investigation, and should therefore be formally interviewed.

One issue properly belonging to a re-investigation of the murder should be pursued by this investigation in the interests of clarification. Father Fauvel was not in Haughton on the afternoon Trisha Smith died, and his whereabouts should be formally established, commencing with his own statement.

When the telephone rang, Ellen thought one of her colleagues was calling in to report being stuck in a snow-drift, but she answered instead to Ryman's peremptory voice.

'I'm sorry, Mr Ryman,' she said. 'Mr McKenna's out. This is Ellen Turner. Can I help?'

'When will he be back?'

'I really can't say. It's snowing hard, so he could be delayed.'

'Can you get in touch with him?'

'If necessary.'

'I've had a call from Haughton police. Beryl Stanton Smith's just reported her husband missing since mid-afternoon.'

'In what circumstances?'

'She said he went out, and hasn't returned. As he doesn't drive, she can't think where he's gone.'

'Are you treating him as a missing person? Have you authorised a search?'

'No, I haven't,' Ryman snapped. 'I'm not having officers risking life and limb without good cause. I've sent someone to interview her. She's threatening to inform the media.'

5

All the way into town, Janet drove in the wake of a huge yellow gritting lorry, the chains on her tyres grinding through hard-packed, dirty snow. More snow poured from the sky, settling like fluffy cotton-wool on every surface. The tracks of human and animal feet criss-crossed the pavements, leading up to garden gates and doorsteps, and the imprints of birds' claws were scattered here and there as a bird fluttered to earth, then took flight once more.

The Willows was lit up like a Christmas tree, with brilliant white security lamps fixed to the gable corners. Several figures laboured on the wide steps below the door, shovelling snow into heaps and scouring ice from the stone with the backs of the blades, while Julie, dressed in a pale-coloured duffel coat with a fur-trimmed hood, strewed salt in their wake. When Janet's car rounded the bend in the drive, as one they ceased working to stare at her. With their squat shadows and goggling eyes, she thought they looked like a gang of gnomes.

'Can we talk?' she asked Julie.

'Why?' Julie responded, as the small audience gathered about her.

'Loose ends,' replied Janet, for want of something to say.

'I didn't know there were any.' Her eyes seemed to look right through Janet. 'Where's the rest of the posse? The woman with the machines, and your boss.'

'I just wanted a chat,' Janet said. The cold bit through her clothes, and she shivered.

'I suppose.' Julie sighed. 'But you'll have to wait till we've finished. You'd better go inside.'

Through the glass-panelled inner doors, Janet watched the group advance down the steps, the scrape of shovel on stone ringing in her ears. Julie emptied the salt bin, turned it upside down and shook it, then suddenly disappeared, along with the others. Five minutes later, she came through an inside door at the back of the hall, her right arm in the grip of a stocky, red-haired girl with slight bruises and a gingery down around her slack mouth.

'Are you on duty?' Janet asked.

'Not officially.'

'Then could we go to your flat? This isn't very private.'

Disentangling the girl, Julie said: 'Get your supper, Debbie. I'll see you later.'

Debbie's mouth turned down sulkily. Glaring, she advanced, pushing her face within inches of Janet's. She breathed heavily and noisily, and she smelled strongly of talcum powder.

'Debbie!' Julie's voice sharpened.

'All right!' The slippers on her feet slapping loosely on the floor, Debbie went, still glaring at Janet over her shoulder.

'How did she get the bruises?' Janet asked.

'She's epileptic,' Julie said curtly, and began to mount the staircase without a backward glance. 'And the anti-convulsants we feed her make the moustache grow. We can't wax it off too often because her skin's very delicate.'

'I see.' Hard on her heels, Janet asked: 'Had any more problems with your boss?'

'No.'

'I expect he'll be relieved when this is all over.'

'I expect so.'

On the first landing, Janet stopped to look up at the crested window. 'Who built this house?' she asked, trying to decipher the Latin motto on a banner under the quartered shield. 'Was it local nobility?'

'No. It was the man who owned the brickworks. He got the contract to supply the bricks for the viaduct, which is why you can see it from nearly every room in the place. He must have gloated every time he passed a window.'

'Don't you find it oppressive?'

'I don't notice it. If you see something every day of your life, it stops being a spectacle, even when it's more than a million bricks stuck together.' Reaching the top of the second staircase, she went along a wide panelled corridor, then turned through the arched opening on to the nursery stairs.

'The Victorians definitely liked their children out of sight,' commented Janet. 'D'you know which room you were born in?'

Putting her key in the Yale lock, Julie said: 'No.'

The flat was warm and, with the curtains closed, very snug. There were wall lights shaded with pinkish parchment, a colourful rug on the beige carpet, and jewel-coloured velvet cushions on the sofa. A vase of pale-yellow chrysanthemums had been added to the window-sill since Janet's last visit, and a sewing machine, a length of pretty lingerie fabric trapped under its foot, stood on the small table.

'Have a seat,' Julie invited, shaking off the

snowflakes which clung to her coat. She placed it carefully on a hanger, then hooked the hanger on the back of the door, stroking the garment into shape as a baby might stroke its comfort blanket.

The sofa was very comfortable. Janet's eyes suddenly felt like lead weights, and she yawned.

'The snow makes you sleepy.' Julie sat in the same chair she had occupied the day before. 'People don't realise. They go up on the moors to look at the scenery, and get so tired they can't even stay upright. It's usually city people, though. The locals have got more sense.'

'We get tourists dressed in trainers and shorts stranded up mountains,' Janet said. 'The helicopters from the RAF base on Anglesey have to bring them down.'

'I went to Anglesey once, with my mother. On holiday.'

'Whereabouts?'

'A place called Church Bay. We went out of season, before there were any leaves on the trees. There was a little church, tiny whitewashed cottages, sand dunes, hummocks, rocks, gorse bushes, wild rabbits, hundreds of sheep and lambs, lots of sand, and the sea.' She gazed into space. 'The sea was wonderful. My bedroom window looked out on it, and I sat there for hours every night, watching the moon and the waves and the wind. During the day, I sat on the rocks, or right at the edge of the sand with my toes actually in the water. I got very wet twice before I realised the tide came in. But I was only seven, and it was the first time I'd seen the sea.' As Janet fidgeted with her cigarettes and lighter, Julie reached behind her for an ashtray. 'I don't mind if you smoke. I quite like the smell. My mother smoked.'

'Rene Minshull said she died of cancer.' Janet lit her

cigarette. 'And she gave us another version of how you had your accident. Or rather, why.' When Julie remained silent, she added: 'She said it was sheer negligence.'

'It happened. Things do.'

'You could have sued.'

Julie's response was oblique. 'My mother said she couldn't have a proper job because other people decide what we're allowed to be. She had to be a whore.' She looked up at her interrogator, eyes penetrating. 'I was a whore's child. So, we took what was offered. It was better than nothing.'

'How many operations did you have?'

She shrugged. 'Eight? Nine? Skin grafting takes time, especially on children. My arm muscles and one of my breasts almost disappeared.' Seeing the expression Janet was unable to hide, she added: 'It only hurts where the nerves weren't destroyed.' She went quiet, then said: 'Father Fauvel said my flesh was seared to cleanse my soul.'

Janet felt her scalp crawl. 'What a terrible thing to say!'

'That's how priests and nuns think. It's their job,' she argued. 'Father Fauvel wanted me to enter the novitiate, but when I told Mother Superior, she shrieked in my face like a demon. She said I'd always be the wicked, sinful child of a wicked, sinful woman.' Once again, her eyes bored into Janet's. 'But I don't think you came for a history lesson, did you? You're like Wendy Lewis. You want to open me up like a can of sardines and rummage around till you find what looks like my bones. D'you think there's something more to dig up about Barry and me?'

'His wife walked out when she found out about you. Did you know?'

'How could I? I don't speak to them.'

Stubbing out her cigarette, Janet said: 'You speak to Linda Newton, and somebody said you knew Trisha "very well".'

'Did they?' Julie's face was unreadable. 'I'd talk to Trisha if we bumped into each other. Sometimes, she'd be in Muriel's café down the road. Muriel doesn't mind having the residents in, and once in a while they enjoy doing what normal people do.' She struggled to her feet, looking like a broken doll. 'You've had your smoke, so you'd better be on your way. It's snowing hard. You don't want to get stuck in a drift.'

'That's hardly likely. It's only five miles, and most of it through town.'

'The village is higher. It gets cut off first.' She pulled down Janet's coat, and held it out.

'*Why* won't you talk to us?' Janet demanded.

'What's there to say?'

Thwarted, as McKenna had foretold, Janet rose. 'You should have a pet,' she said, donning her coat. 'A cat, perhaps.'

'Animals die.' Julie opened the door, and stood aside.

6

Gaynor sat in front of her bedroom window, bewitched by the view. The snow played tricks with her eyes, creating light out of the dark, transforming the landscape into a white desert. Where there had been bracken-rusty moorland, cut by drystone walling into self-contained territories, there was now an expanse of vivid, icy whiteness here, a trench of deep blue shadow there, and all of it seeming to shift as she watched, like the rise and fall of a breathing body.

One of her many scouts had called earlier with the name of the owners of Trisha's house. At eight forty her mobile rang again, and she learned that Beryl Stanton Smith had just received a visit from two police officers in a marked car.

The telephone barely had time to connect before Beryl answered, her voice harsh and breathy. 'Piers? Is that you?'

'It's Gaynor. Is something wrong?' she asked innocently.

'You!' Beryl gasped. 'It's all your fault!'

'Don't hang up!' Gaynor said hurriedly. 'Tell me what's happened.'

'Piers hasn't come back!' Beryl was crying. 'I'm out of my mind with worry.'

'Have you told the police?'

'They won't look for him! They say he's not really missing, but he *is*!' She gulped. 'He could be lost on the moors, lying in a snow-drift.'

'Have you called the hospital? In case he had an accident?'

'The police did.' Quiet for a moment, except for the sobbing, Beryl asked: 'Didn't you see him on the road after you left?'

'No.' Gaynor stared into the night, praying that Smith was already dead under its weight. 'Could he be with friends?'

'I don't know. I don't know who he knows.'

I'll bet you don't, Gaynor thought. 'He might've gone to Sheffield to see his mother.'

'Don't be ridiculous! He thought she was dead till you came this afternoon, shouting about being deceived.'

'That's not quite right, is it, Beryl? He knew she was alive all along.'

'He didn't! I won't talk about him like this.' She

breathed noisily. 'It's your fault! You frightened him, flinging all his worst memories back in his face like that.'

'I flung the truth in his face,' Gaynor said. 'That's why he's run off, and if you've any sense, you'll count yourself lucky he's gone, and be praying he doesn't come back. And as for being frightened,' she went on, before Beryl could interrupt, 'believe me, I was bloody *terrified*! He's psychotic.'

'Oh, you wicked woman!' Beryl raged. 'You wicked, *evil* harridan! I'll report you, you see if I don't. I won't let you get away with what you've done to Piers. I won't!'

Beryl ranted venomously, like her husband and, almost stunned by the ferocity she had unleashed, Gaynor cut the connection and left Beryl screaming at thin air. With juddering fingers she punched out another number, and when she learned that McKenna was out, she felt sick with fear.

'Is it urgent?' asked Ellen.

'It's about Smith. He's gone missing.'

'We know.'

'I went to see him this afternoon, to say I was hacked off about being led up the garden path about his mother, among other things, and he went *berserk*!' She paused. 'If Beryl hadn't been there, he'd have gone for me. Anyway, that's why he's gone.'

'Did he threaten you?'

'Verbally, yes.'

'And are you afraid he'll come to the hotel?'

'What?' Gaynor almost vomited her terror. 'Oh, God! I hadn't thought of that.'

'Then why did you call?'

'Because there's a bloody psychopath on the loose! Suppose he goes after his mother?'

'I'll see that she's not at risk,' Ellen assured her.

'Thank you for calling.'

'Just a minute!' Gaynor all but shouted. 'I know who owns the house where Trisha lived.' She read out the names from her notebook.

'Superintendent McKenna already knows,' Ellen told her, 'but I'll tell him you passed on your information. Was there anything else?' Her chilly politeness was cutting.

'And I saw something rather strange earlier,' Gaynor rushed on. 'It might mean nothing, but it was rather disturbing.' She related the drama of the man and the woman on the deserted, snowy street. 'I've no idea who either of them is, but I can give you a description of the woman and the car.'

7

Only a few of the residents were still awake at the Willows, watching television upstairs, when Fauvel arrived. His car wheels cut deep tracks in the still falling snow, which had already obliterated Janet's trail.

Julie's colleague ran to open the front door. 'Father Brett! We didn't expect to see you so late.' She smiled, then blushed. 'Not that you're not most welcome any time, of course.'

'I've been sick visiting at the hospital.' Fauvel handed her his cloak, and scuffed his feet on the doormat. 'I see somebody's been hard at work outside.'

'Jools did it earlier, with some of the residents.' She glanced outside. 'Thank goodness she put down the salt! The snow won't stick quite so much, will it?'

'You'll still need another work party in the morning, I'm afraid.' Fauvel offered the charming smile which many thought lit up the world around him. 'Snow's snow, and there's plenty more on the way.'

'Come into the sitting-room,' she urged, her hand on his arm. 'I'll make a hot drink.'

'Is Julie on duty?'

'No, but she's still around. Then again, she nearly always is. I'm sure she lives for her work.' She switched on the electric fire in the sitting-room, then went to the kitchen, where Julie, rubber gloves on her hands, was washing the supper dishes.

'Leave those for now, Jools. Father Brett's just arrived. Talk to him while I make a drink.'

Julie's whole body stiffened. 'What does he want?'

'Nothing special, I imagine. Mind you, he *did* ask if you're on duty. Still, he *always* wants to see you, doesn't he?' She nudged her arm. 'Lucky you, eh?'

Slowly, Julie peeled off the gloves, and placed them on the counter. When she reached the sitting-room, she found him standing by the uncurtained window, hands behind his back. Light flickered across the top of the viaduct as a train made its way to Dentfield station. She watched her reflection advance towards him, and his reflected eyes meeting hers.

'What a little work-horse you are!' His voice was soft. 'Shovelling snow, scattering salt, on duty night and day. You must be exhausted.' He bared his teeth. 'All the more reason to accept a lift when it's offered, don't you think?'

'Not when *you're* offering. I had a lift, anyway, from that woman who scared you off.'

'No one "scared me off".' He frowned. 'You shouldn't take lifts from strangers.'

'I've told you, it was a woman.'

'And you think that makes you safe?' He turned towards her, black cassock swirling, the crucifix glinting in its folds. 'That's how Myra Hindley duped her victims.'

'Don't be ridiculous! I'm not a child.' She stared at him. 'Why are you here? What d'you want?'

'What I ever want,' he said quietly. 'To be with you.'

She flinched when he stroked her cheek, and when he twined his fingers in her hair, she wrenched herself away.

He looked at the strands of golden-brown hair in his hands. 'I've hurt you!' he whispered, tears glittering in his eyes.

'No, you haven't!'

He closed in on her, his body hard against hers, backing her into the panelled wall, and as she prayed for the miracle of a witness stark against the snow, he once more wrapped her hair about his fingers, pulling with a savage intensity.

8

'Freaky!' Jack commented. 'Fancy Holbrook trying to help *us*. She must be hoping to redeem herself.'

'She's scared witless,' Ellen said. 'And so she should be. Serve her right if she finds Smith hovering outside her bedroom window like a vampire.'

'He's more likely to be outside his mother's front door, with a pickaxe.' McKenna's voice was sharp. 'Sheffield police *do* understand that Bunty could be in real danger?'

Ellen nodded. 'I told them to put a guard on Ida as well. Better safe than sorry.'

'That's about it for tonight, then.' Jack yawned. 'And with luck, Smith won't resurface until the snow thaws.'

'The world won't be quite so conveniently rid of

him,' McKenna said. 'He'll be holed up somewhere safe and snug.'

'While Beryl goes mad with worry,' added Janet.

'That's no doubt his intention. How did you fare with Julie?'

'As you said, sir, she's at least ten steps ahead.'

'And I could've stayed indoors, for all the good trudging up to Dugdale's place did,' Jack said. 'I had to leave the car at the bottom of the hill, then hike through knee-deep snow for about a quarter of a mile. After the first few yards, all I wanted to do was fall over and go to sleep.' He yawned again, and his jaw cracked. 'And metaphorically speaking, it was like an icebox inside the house. The atmosphere between Dugdale and his wife was cold enough to crack.'

'How was Wendy Lewis, sir?' Janet asked.

'Intent on sending me on a guilt-trip, once Fauvel left,' McKenna replied. 'When I arrived, he was engaged in hand-holding, hair-stroking, and promising to make sure her bungalow doesn't collapse under the snow, or get flooded out by burst pipes.' Lighting a cigarette, he added: 'Lewis reckons my putting a guard outside the ward is tantamount to placing her under arrest, particularly in the eyes of press and public, who don't understand the nuances. She says she's being pilloried for telling the truth, and she intends to consult the Federation with a view to taking legal action against me.'

'She hasn't told the truth,' Jack said irritably. 'She's given us an opinion, of sorts, which is different from other opinions she's had.'

'And that's the best we'll get from her. She won't even *consider* the possibility that Fauvel could be lying. In her eyes, he can do no wrong, and by the time he's done with looking after her bungalow, I expect she'll willingly self-immolate for him.'

'Don't!' Ellen shuddered. 'I'm already having nightmares about Trisha and Julie.'

'According to Julie, it only hurts where the burns don't go deep enough to destroy the nerves, and she should know,' Janet commented. 'She seems to know an awful lot about pain.'

'Ryman said much the same,' McKenna said, 'although not with any compassion.'

'Fauvel's short on that as well,' Janet added. 'He told   Julie her flesh was burned to cleanse her soul.' Idly, she picked up Ellen's report on Gaynor's telephone call and, coming to the description of the woman under attack in the snowy street, caught her breath. 'Julie's got a coat just like the one this woman was wearing. She had it on tonight.'

'Really?' Looking over her shoulder, McKenna said: 'It might be worth asking her where she was this afternoon.'

'You're clutching at straws,' Jack told him. 'There must be dozens of coats like that in Haughton alone.'

'Straws are all we have,' McKenna replied. 'Bring Holbrook in tomorrow to make a full statement. And I'm going to see Ryman again.' He glanced outside. 'That's if we're not roof-deep in snow by morning.'

9

Estelle Ryman was proud of her home, her husband, and Shelley, her undergraduate daughter and, until this week, believed that the hard work and the necessary deceptions put into creating the family would always, like a charm, ward off misfortune. Like Susan Dugdale, she had married a young police officer in whose high hopes she could believe. For her the hopes were realised, whereas Susan's were now only fit for the scrap heap.

When her husband was promoted, they had bought a smart detached house with an enormous garden on the outskirts of Ravensdale. Now, she wandered around the sitting-room, moving ornaments, primping cushions, tweaking the folds in the deep-green velvet curtains as she passed the window. He was sitting in one of the chintz-covered chairs which so nicely toned with the carpet and curtains, gazing vacantly at the hearth, his head resting on his right arm, his face so pale he looked like his own ghost. He had hardly moved since the last telephone call, and anger suddenly flared in her, bringing another of those terrifying flushes which heated her whole body to boiling point and threatened to blow off the top of her head. Since that damned McKenna came with his shadowy band of interfering foreigners, the telephone had rung incessantly and, every time, her husband rushed to answer. He hardly dared to fall asleep in bed in case another summons came, but there was never any relief when he finished speaking, or, as was more usual, simply listening, to whoever called. He was like a man possessed by demons, but she flatly refused even to *think* that Dugdale suppressed Smith's alibi evidence on her husband's instructions. The consequences of that possibility were, as yet, only a meaningless scribble on every wall which loomed before her.

'You could have gone to the Lodge meeting after all,' she said, twitching the curtains together after peeking outside. 'The snow isn't too bad.' Her laugh tinkled bravely. 'This must be the first one you've ever missed. Wild horses wouldn't usually keep you away, never mind a few inches of snow.'

There was no response.

'Are you ready for supper?' She clutched at normality, while another hot flush suffused her body. 'What would you like? I got fresh salad earlier, there's some ham, and there's cheese, of course, if you think it won't keep you awake, or I could hard-boil a couple of eggs.'

'Anything,' Ryman muttered. 'You decide.'

Terrible questions seethed with the overheated blood inside her head. 'Are you all right? Only, you've seemed awfully out of sorts all week. Are you sickening for something, d'you think? There's a lot of flu about.'

'I'm all right.' His tone was dismissive.

'I'll do supper, then.'

The kitchen was her absolute pride and joy. She decided to make egg mayonnaise, and was reaching for the saucepan she used only to boil eggs when the scribble on the walls began ominously and irrevocably to resolve itself. If he lost his job because of some stupidity, she would lose not only her wonderful kitchen, but her entire home.

10

When Julie's colleague bumped open the sitting-room door with a tray of hot drinks and biscuits, Fauvel was beside the fire. For some unaccountable reason, Julie was on the window seat. Her face was very pale, and she was trembling.

The other woman wrinkled her nose at the smell of burning dust that always came off the fire, set the tray on a side table, and handed out mugs of hot chocolate. Fauvel's hands were warm as he took his, but Julie's were icy cold.

She was about to tell Julie to move when Debbie

plodded into the room. 'Saw the car,' she mumbled, glaring at Fauvel. 'Heard you.'

'Yes, dear,' Julie's colleague said. 'Father Brett's just having a hot drink. You get to bed.'

'No.' The girl lumbered forward, and said to Fauvel: 'Heard you. Heard Julie.'

Fauvel put his drink very carefully on the edge of the hearth. Debbie's shadow almost enveloped him. 'We were just chatting,' he said.

'Liar!' Debbie's fist shot out and caught him hard on the shoulder. He fell backwards, staring up at her, ashen-faced with shock.

'*Debbie!*' Julie's colleague launched herself at the girl, pinioning her arms behind her. 'Help me!' she yelled at the immobile Julie. 'Help me!'

Debbie shook her off as easily as a dog might shake water off its coat, then giggled.

'You wicked girl!' Julie's colleague shouted, trying to push Debbie to the door. 'You've hurt Father Brett!'

Still giggling, Debbie said: 'Made him happy.' She shambled over to Julie, lifted her from the seat, and all but dragged her from the room.

I I

Estelle ran water over the eggs in the pan, and walked with extreme care towards the cooker. The pan jittered as she put it on the hob, the eggs rattled, and water splashed out over the pristine enamel. 'Oh, God!' she prayed, fumbling with the ignition switch. 'Don't let him lose his job. Please!' Blue flame was licking around the pan and making bubbles rise in the water when she realised that her husband might not only lose his job, but go to prison.

Then the telephone rang once more. Her body jerked violently and her hands flew up, just missing the pan handle. The telephone bell stopped on the second ring.

Little sound carried through the walls of this well-built house. She had to creep into the hall to know that he was still talking. But again, he was merely listening. She crept back to the kitchen, and very, very carefully, lifted the extension from its mount.

'– but seeing as it's Miss Ryman, sir, I didn't think you'd mind us putting her through on this line, even though it's getting late. The snow must've cut off the phones somewhere. She's been trying for hours. Oh, and I told her we couldn't do anything about the call being recorded, but she said it doesn't matter.'

Estelle's heart fluttered with the unexpected pleasure of speaking to a daughter who only remembered her parents' existence when she wanted something, then with anxiety. She was about to announce herself when a stranger's voice came on the line.

'Mr Ryman? Is that you?' The ugly inflections Estelle had made sure Shelley never aped thickened this woman's voice like sludge. 'You know who this is, don't you?'

'Oh, God!' Her husband gasped.

'You've got to do something. You've got to stop him.'

In the silence beyond the stark demands, his breath rasped in Estelle's ears. Then he moaned: 'Stop tormenting me! Leave me alone!'

'I'm not tormenting you. I'm begging you to help, like I did before.'

'You were lying!' Estelle sensed the doubt in his voice.

'I was telling the truth, and you knew it. You've

292

always known.' The woman paused, while Estelle held her breath until her chest hurt. 'He's doing it to one of the girls here.'

'I don't *believe* you!'

'And he tried to drag me into his car today. He *said* he was offering a lift, but he's lying. He'll kill me when he gets the chance.' Behind the melodramatic statement, Estelle sensed desperation.

'Don't be ridiculous! Why should he?'

'Because you've already let him get away with murder.' Her words were inexorable.

'What d'you mean?' Estelle marvelled at the inadequacy of his response.

'I saw him at Trisha Smith's house the day she died.'

'You can't have done!'

'I *did*. I don't know how you can sleep easy in your bed.' There was another rasping silence, before she said: 'You've got no shame, and no decency. If you don't do something this time, I will.'

'Are you blackmailing me?'

Even though her voice was muddy with tears, the woman actually laughed. How could she, Estelle thought? 'I don't go in for blackmail. I'm not like you.'

For a few seconds, Estelle listened to the void on the line, then heard the snap as her husband replaced his receiver. Eventually, she put down the extension, then turned to watch the eggs, by now bobbing in the boiling water. Mechanically, she reached for the egg-timer, turned it upside down, opened the bread bin, took out a fresh tin loaf, slid open the cutlery drawer, reached for a bread knife, then fell to her knees, fingers slipping over the smooth, rounded edge of the counter, the knife clattering to the floor.

12

Being near Fauvel made Julie's skin crawl, where it was loose enough. On those parts of her body not much less disfigured by multiple grafts than by bone-deep burns, her skin was so tight that the smallest unconsidered movement could almost tear her apart. None the less, after she had settled the near-hysterical Debbie in her room, she returned eventually to the sitting-room, where her colleague fussed over the priest, still apologising endlessly.

'I can't think *what* came over her,' the woman bleated tearfully, repeating herself once again as she placed a snifter of brandy by his side. 'I really can't! Oh, I'm so awfully sorry! It must have been dreadful for you.'

Fauvel held up his hands, his face pinched. 'Please! There's no need to upset yourself. As I said, she didn't hurt me.'

'But the *shock*!' the woman breathed. She bit her lip anxiously. 'Maybe she's getting ready for a fit. She *can* get out of hand before a fit.' She gazed at Julie. 'What d'you think, Jools?'

'She's not due for at least a month,' Julie replied, going back to the window seat. 'Her fits are like clockwork.'

'Perhaps she's overtired, then. She *was* out in the snow rather a long time.'

'Debbie's as strong as an ox,' Julie said, staring at Fauvel. 'Isn't she?' she asked him.

'Oh, Jools! What a nasty thing to say!'

Fauvel twitched his lips into a semblance of amusement. 'She can certainly pack a punch, but never mind. We'll forget it ever happened.' He lit a cigarette.

'We can't do that,' Julie went on. 'Everything has to

be reported. I've already put a note in the log book.'
She continued to stare at him. 'Mr Bennett will want
to investigate.'

The cigarette trembled in Fauvel's hand. 'I said to
forget it.'

'It's too late now,' Julie told him.

'Jools!' the other woman exclaimed, alarmed by the
tension between them. 'You shouldn't have written
anything! It's up to Father Brett what happens.' She
smiled at the priest. 'Don't worry, Father. I'll cross it
out right away.'

13

The clatter from the kitchen failed to register in
Ryman's brain, and only when he smelled the stench
of burning eggs did he move from the reproduction
Hepplewhite chair beside the telephone.

For mysterious reasons of her own, Estelle was
kneeling on the kitchen floor, while the eggs burned
black. They exploded at the very moment he noticed
them. He turned off the gas and cast around for the
oven gloves, so that he could douse the pan in the
kitchen sink without searing his hands. His horror of
being burned far surpassed the wholly rational dread
of any normal man. The ways in which heat could
shear the flesh from his bones dwelled at the back of
his mind, and would erupt like a flash-over at the
least relevant trigger. School history lessons about
martyrdom at the stake, or the enemy melted under
cauldrons of boiling oil, or even King Edward's dis-
embowelment by red-hot poker, had left him cold.
Now, if he came across words such as 'burn', or
'fire', he envisaged himself embraced by flames, and
had felt Trisha Smith's incineration as if it were his

own. He did not even read the reports, let alone get near enough to the investigation to smell the fumes or feel the lingering heat, and cared not in the least whom Dugdale sent to prison as long as the matter was done with. And all, he thought, because a fourteen-year-old girl, desperate to show the measure of her own pain, had torn off her jumper, exposing a grubby white vest and her shrivelled flesh. Knowing how, if not why, she had come by the burns, he stared with almost clinical detachment, admiring the plastic surgeons for doing what they could. Then, realising how easily one of her type might wilfully misinterpret his stare, he had snapped: 'Cover yourself up. This minute!' She dragged the discarded jumper over her head, obscuring her face, and it was then that the horror almost blew him away like a flame-thrower, for her body was so puzzlingly lop-sided because only one swelling nipple peaked the grubby vest, instead of two. Because of her, because of that, all he had worked for was now as ashes in his throat.

When the cold water hit the wreckage in the pan, it hissed like a nest of angry vipers, throwing up great clouds of dirty steam. Estelle was still on the floor, her new pleated skirt fanned around her, the lacy edge of an underskirt snagged around her heels. For a few moments he stood over her, arms hanging by his sides, then bent down to lift the hair which had fallen over her face.

She had once had such pretty hair, he thought, smoothing the pepper-and-salt strands, but age had stolen its colour and sleekness. But she was still a good-looking woman, firm-featured and with only a slightly sagging jawline, and one any man should be proud to call his wife. She dressed well, and in keeping with her age and station, and even if the clothes were larger each passing year, she was not fat, but firmly rounded, and even stately.

'What is it? Aren't you well?' He patted her hair. 'Have you had one of your flushes?'

With unexpected suddenness she raised her arm and knocked his hand away, then began to crawl across the floor, tearing the underskirt hem.

He followed, his progress as slow and halting as hers. 'Estelle! What on earth's wrong?'

Reaching blindly for the edge of the sink, where the ruined pan still steamed and sizzled, she dragged herself upright. The backs of her legs were reddened with pressure, the skirt pleats creased, the torn lace hanging in shreds. Once on her feet, she leaned against the sink while she caught her breath, then, slowly, turned to face him. 'You've been lying to me,' she said accusingly.

'No! I haven't.'

'You have! You've been lying, and covering up, and we're going to lose everything!'

He advanced, trying to smile. 'It's not what you think, dear. There's nothing to worry about.'

Her eyes blazed with a strange light. 'Stop treating me like a fool! I heard that woman on the phone.' She began to move willy-nilly around the kitchen. 'You've been jumping like a cat on hot bricks every time the bloody thing rang. Were you *expecting* her to call?' She stopped by the sink. 'Who is she? What does she want? What does she *know*?'

'I can't say,' he muttered.

'Oh, but you can!' Red-hot sweat gushed from every pore in her body, and her eyeballs steamed over. Control at last evaporating, she reached blindly for the still scorching pan, yelping as it burned her hand, and went for him.

14

Fauvel escaped from the Willows only after Julie's
colleague had spent a further half-hour reiterating her
apologies, her worries about repercussions from
Debbie's behaviour, and her assurances that all
references to it would be expunged from the home's
records. As she showed him to the door, neither of
them saw Debbie, who was crouching on the landing,
her hands locked around the carved balusters.

The woman watched Fauvel drive away, then went
to the office to keep her promise. Julie had
disappeared after that strange, tense exchange, and
was probably in the laundry or the kitchen, giving in
to her compulsion to wash and clean.

The log book entry filled more than half a page. She
read it over, wondering if it could be doctored into
something trivial. Then she realised that she could
simply pull out the whole sheet, and remove its
corresponding half from further on in the book. She had
almost completed the enterprise when Julie walked in.

'Your shift finished ages ago,' Julie said. 'You
should be on your way home instead of messing with
things you don't understand.'

'I promised Father Brett. He doesn't want anyone
to know.' She looked up at Julie's angry face. 'I don't
know what got into you, I really don't. You were
horrible to him!'

'It's more a case of what got into Debbie.'

'Oh, don't be silly! Debbie's got an IQ of seventy-
five at best, *and* she's epileptic. There's no rhyme or
reason in *anything* she does. And,' she added, her own
anger rising, 'that's why Father Brett doesn't want her
blamed for it. He *understands* she's not responsible.'
With great deliberation, she put the two sheets of
paper through the shredder, while Julie watched every

movement. 'And I hope you'll refrain from snitching to Bennett. What he doesn't know won't hurt, as you've said yourself in the past.'

'That depends on what he's not being told.'

'You're just plain bloody-minded when you want to be!'

'Debbie might tell him herself.'

'Not after I've sorted her tomorrow she won't.' Checking that there were no tell-tale shreds of paper stuck between the folds, she closed the book. 'And don't go writing in her file as soon as my back's turned, either,' she warned. Then her face clouded once again. 'Oh, I can't get over it! I really can't! He comes for a chat and nightcap, and *that* happens.'

'You spent long enough talking to him afterwards.'

'I could hardly send him away on a night like this while he was so upset, could I? But a fat lot *you* care! Father Brett thinks the world of you, and you go treating him like dirt!'

Once again, Julie watched through the office window as her colleague drove away, the car slithering across the snow with vapours puffing from the exhaust. Then it disappeared around the bend in the drive, and Julie watched the snow fall relentlessly from a black sky.

15

Ryman was still on his feet, swaying as he held his hand to his wounded forehead. Estelle's hysteria at first gave way to fear, but now the anger was returning, assaulting her in equal measure. Surprised to find the blackened pan still in her hand, she put in on the counter, picked up a cloth and began methodically cleaning her sooty fingers.

'You fool!' Ryman snarled. 'How am I going to explain *this*?'

'Like you covered up whatever that woman was on about! You did a bloody good job there, if what I heard is anything to go by. And don't call me a fool! *You're* the fool!' she shouted, pushing him in the chest. 'Who is she?' she demanded. 'What did you do?' She stared at him assessingly. 'Or is it more a case of what you *didn't* do?'

'It's none of your damned business!'

'I'm making it my business.' Her voice was flinty. 'Either you tell me now, and we'll try to sort it out, or I'll tell the chief constable about tonight's mysterious tape-recorded conversation, and let *him* sort it out.'

Almost vacantly, he stared at her, his mouth slightly agape. 'The tapes are monitored.'

'You mean people listen in on every call?'

'No. They're checked daily.'

'I see.' She pursed her mouth. 'That's a bit of a bugger, isn't it?'

16

When the telephone rang well after eleven, Jack was sound asleep, and McKenna was engrossed in a highly erotic thriller on television. Cursing, he searched for the video remote control.

The caller was an Inspector Venables of Manchester police. 'We've got your Mr Piers Stanton Smith in custody, sir,' he said. 'I hesitated about phoning so late, but I thought you'd want to know.'

'Not to worry,' replied McKenna. 'Smith is a thorn in the side of many.'

Venables laughed. 'You know, we've been following his recent career more avidly than any TV soap, although that's not why he's in the cells. We picked him up with a cart-load of the like-minded in one of the gay clubs, flirting with a bunch of very young boys, who'll be interviewed as soon as social services arrive. Mind you,' he went on, 'I expect most of them will be in care. We've two got fourteen-year-olds from a local children's home coming up on attempted murder charges next month, would you believe. One of them decoyed a well-known head-master out of this same club on the promise of a fumble in a nearby alleyway, where the other boy ambushed him with a baseball bat.'

'D'you keep the place under surveillance?'

'Off and on. Tonight's raid was planned some time ago.'

'Are you sure you had grounds to arrest Smith?' asked McKenna. 'You can do without accusations of police harassment.'

'Oh, we're certain to be accused of *that*,' Venables said. 'We always are. His solicitor's here already, spitting feathers.'

'But Smith *could* have gone to the club in all innocence,' McKenna persisted. 'Did he seem out of place? Was it unfamiliar territory for him?'

'When we got there, the barman was calling him over for his drinks,' Venables said. 'By name. Then again, I dare say every queer this side of the Pennines knows Smith. How a faggot like him cons women into marrying him is beyond me.' He paused. 'I shan't say unless my arm gets twisted, but we've got him on video as well. He spent the early part of the evening cruising nearby public lavatories, then went arm in arm into the club with a very butch piece in head-to-foot black leather.'

'Sounds good enough.' Peering at the video-recorder to make sure it was working, McKenna added: 'Have you rung his wife yet? She reported him missing to the local police.'

'His solicitor called her,' Venables said. 'She rang us, and she was in a right state, but all she said was: "Tell him I'm on my way, and I love him." She didn't even bother to ask why he'd been arrested.'

'Don't be surprised if she doesn't arrive. The roads out of Haughton are probably blocked by now.'

Like Beryl, Smith's solicitor had happily rushed out into the snow on his client's behalf. At twenty past midnight, heedless of the hour, he called McKenna.

'My name is Andrew Lyons. I am Mr Stanton Smith's solicitor.' The voice was sharp. 'You should be here, Superintendent. My client is waiting to speak to you.'

'About what?'

'My client has some crucial information about the death of his first wife, and needs to speak to you as a matter of urgency.'

'Was Inspector Venables informed of this?'

'After he called you, we assumed you were on your way. My client has no intention of discussing such confidential matters with anyone except yourself.'

'In other words,' McKenna commented, 'nothing was said to Venables.' Without waiting for a response, he asked: 'Why haven't you or your client approached me already with this information?'

'My client expected the courtesy of a visit from you at the outset of your investigation. But you chose, most studiously, and for reasons of your own, to ignore him.'

'If he *has* significant information, you had an obligation to inform me.'

'The way Inspector Dugdale and his officers wilfully framed my client is *very* significant.'

'Please don't prejudge the outcome of my investigation.'

'To my mind, the "outcome" is staring you in the face,' Lyons said smugly.

'And to my mind, Mr Lyons, you're trying to create a diversion,' McKenna told him. 'If your client has *genuine* information about his first wife's death or Dugdale's investigation, you must approach me through the proper channels. I have no intention of interfering with the activities of Manchester police, as you seem to wish.'

Lyons finally set out his own agenda. 'This is nothing short of police persecution. My client has not committed any offence, and they have no right to detain him.'

'In the circumstances, they had every right. He isn't the only one in custody.'

'They had him under surveillance,' Lyons snapped. 'In my view, the raid on the club was a mere ploy, part of a deliberate stratagem conceived to neutralise an innocent man who is, unfortunately for him, in a position to bring down a number of corrupt officers. I fully intend to raise a formal complaint,' he went on, gathering momentum, 'and that will include a complaint about *your* attitude, Superintendent. Harassment like this could drive my client to suicide, not to mention what the media will make of his detention.'

'As your client deliberately put himself in the media spotlight, he'll have to take the rough with the smooth,' McKenna told him. 'He should have kept his head down, instead of causing people a great deal of bother. His wife reported him missing, you know, and by all accounts, she was worried sick. She didn't know he was cavorting around Manchester.'

'You fail to appreciate my client's fragility!' Lyons

303

was clearly seething. 'He left the house in considerable distress because he was being terrorised by a reporter.'

'The reporter tells a different version,' McKenna pointed out. 'She claims she challenged your client about being wilfully misled, and found herself on the receiving end of a violent tantrum. However,' he added, 'I see no point in further prolonging this conversation. I can offer no assistance.'

'You could insist on my client's being treated like a human being! The police have confiscated all his personal possessions.'

'You know full well that's normal procedure.'

'But how often do such possessions include a solid gold Asprey lighter, a lizard-skin wallet, hundreds of pounds in cash, platinum credit cards, and a Rolex watch?'

'As you know what was confiscated, you know what should be returned. I have nothing more to say, Mr Lyons.'

I

With gleefully salacious detail, every tabloid in the country reported on Smith's arrest 'when police raided a sleazy gay club in Manchester's red light district', and even the broadsheets thought it worthy of mention. It was only Gaynor's paper that could not offer its readers more titillation: marooned in the snow-bound depths of Dark Moor, and let down by her scouts on the ground, she had been inactivated.

2

Janet awoke to an eerie silence, the creaking inn sign stilled by a great swatch of snow draped across the bull's face. Twinkling icicles hung from the eaves above her window, and every stark branch and twig of the churchyard trees was defined with a white flourish, while the white blanket about the steeple gleamed almost blue. Massed snow obliterated the contours of every object and building, creating an alternative architecture and topography, and she thought the smoke of newly lit fires rising from the cottage chimneys resembled the strokes of an artist's pencil on colour-washed paper. Watching the verminous rooks fluttering about the roofs, slipping and sliding as they clawed for a toehold on the treacherous slopes, she suddenly pitied them.

'I hope we won't be stuck here all weekend,' Ellen said over breakfast. 'My kids are complaining about being abandoned.' She smiled ruefully. 'As usual!'

'The Manchester road's "passable with care", according to the radio,' Janet told her. 'I was listening while I got dressed.' She poured hot milk on her Readybrek. 'The Sheffield and Buxton roads are blocked solid, though. If Mr McKenna wants to get to Ravensdale, he'll have to go via Stockport, providing the roads in the south of the county aren't impassable.'

'I'm not sure he should go, anyway,' Ellen commented. 'He only wants to rattle Ryman's cage again, and we're not here to rattle cages.'

'Ryman's being extremely hostile,' Janet pointed out. 'There must be a reason. You think he was negligent, don't you?'

Ellen nodded. 'But not necessarily deliberately. His track record here as inspector leaves a lot to be desired, and he might simply have been promoted beyond his capabilities. It happens a lot.'

3

Grumbling and yawning, Jack staggered from the house at eight fifteen to collect Rene, and the tremor as he slammed the front door behind him loosened a huge raft of snow above the eaves. Huddled by the gas fire in the office, chilled to the marrow, McKenna heard the roar as it crashed to the pavement and tumbled into the road.

Venables telephoned a few minutes later. 'We've had trouble with Smith,' he reported.

'Who hasn't?' McKenna asked sourly.

'We had to call out a doctor in the early hours. Lyons insisted.'

'Lyons insisted I rush to Manchester to intervene over Smith's arrest, but I declined.'

'Yes, well that's what caused the trouble,' Venables said. 'Smith went up the wall when he heard you wouldn't be coming.' He paused for some time. 'Look sir, I'm not trying to elbow into your own investigation, but it does look as if what's transpired between you and Smith might be important. We've been barred from questioning him until he's talked to you.'

'*Nothing* has transpired between Smith and myself,' McKenna told him. 'I've kept well away from him, much to his annoyance.' He searched for his cigarettes and lighter. 'Lyons tried to persuade me last night that Smith has crucial information, firstly about Trisha Smith's murder, then about my current investigation. I said if that was the case, he must approach me through the proper channels, but I doubt if he will. Lyons seems to be the perfect foil for his client's duplicity.' Lighting his cigarette, he asked: 'Who stopped you from questioning Smith?'

'My superintendent, on the assumption we'd be trespassing into your territory. We're not entirely sure where your remit begins and ends, and by the time Lyons was done with relating the reasons for Smith's outburst, it seemed best to put things on hold until we knew the score. My superintendent was planning to call you as soon as he comes on duty.'

'My remit is to find out if Haughton police deliberately suppressed evidence.' McKenna coughed. 'In that context, Smith is irrelevant to my activities.'

'Well, sir, you're clearly not irrelevant to *him*. I'll read you what Lyons had to say.' Papers rustled, then Venables added: 'I'm quoting from the document he gave my superintendent last night. "Only Superintendent McKenna can put a stop to this widespread police conspiracy designed to persecute and neutralise my client. My client's wife is waiting to see him, but my client is too distraught to face her. She will not understand why my client was in Manchester unless Superintendent McKenna explains it to her. She will have no choice but to believe the distortions presented by the police, and will therefore spurn my client. In such circumstances, he would undoubtedly kill himself. My client came close to suicide on innumerable occasions while in prison: it was only his wife's loyalty which kept him alive. My client has recently disclosed that he was the victim of repeated gang-rapes during that time. He was then singled out by one prisoner who offered protection in return for sex. Like many others in such horrific circumstances, my client found himself tricked into feeling secure by permitting what he abhorred. My client regards these unnatural feelings as an incurable illness, and thus yesterday yielded to the compulsion to seek security after being terrorised by a reporter named Gaynor Holbrook. Mrs Stanton Smith was unable to protect him: she is both sexually and emotionally inadequate. In view of his own marital difficulties, Superintendent McKenna will have every sympathy with the misery my client endured at the hands of his first wife, and is under an obligation to safeguard my client's present marriage and emotional welfare. Superintendent McKenna also has an explicit responsibility to ensure that no further harm comes to my client as a result of this current investigation, and to ensure that my client does not give in to his negative desires to seek revenge for the many betrayals he has suffered." And that's it, sir, but you'll appreciate how it presents Smith as an active element of your investigation. I'll fax you a copy right away.'

When Jack inched his car along Church Street, with Rene in the passenger seat, he was amazed to see McKenna out on the pavement, ferociously shovelling away the snow which had avalanched off the roof. A tight-lipped McKenna merely told him to stay indoors, and read the fax from Manchester police that was on his desk. To a background of thudding and scraping, Jack obeyed.

When McKenna eventually came inside, his face pink with exertion, Jack said: 'We could probably get Lyons for attempting to pervert the course of justice, you know. I've never come across such twaddle. You're not Smith's social worker, you're not his counsellor, and you're not the "saviour" he talked about to Holbrook, and the only reason he wants you to sort Beryl is because you've got so much clout she'll believe anything you say. I know Smith knows the world is full of gullible fools who are bound, by the law of averages, to fall in his path sooner or later, but he can't be daft enough to think you're one of them.' He glanced again at the fax, then looked up at McKenna, who was standing by the fire, rubbing hands that were blue with cold. 'And why is Lyons bringing *your* marriage into it? How is that relevant?'

'It isn't,' McKenna said curtly. 'It's simply none-too-subtle emotional blackmail.' He took his cigarettes from the mantelshelf. 'Anyway, I've had more than enough of Smith for one day.' As soon as he lit the cigarette, he had a coughing fit.

'Your lungs don't seem to like this climate,' Jack commented. 'The tar inside them probably froze solid while you were outside.'

'Oh, be quiet! If you hadn't slammed the door and

brought down the snow I wouldn't have needed to clear it up!'

4

The snow which seethed across the Pennines from the North Sea had left only a dusting of powdery white in the Midlands, and when Colin Bowden looked from the bedroom window of his parents' Warwick home he fancied the town was coated with sugar icing. Shadows were sharp on the ground, and between the gables and roofs in his line of sight, the cloudless sky promised a beautiful day. He could not remember when sunshine last broke through the sombre cloud over Haughton's moors and, when Vicky had telephoned last night from Marbella, he had tried to explain why he needed to escape.

Because he was not where she expected him to be, she was irritable and annoyed, called him a fool for letting himself be caught up in Dugdale's mischief, and snappily said he should resign immediately from the force and sue for constructive dismissal. While she nagged into a telephone hundreds of miles away, he imagined the rest of his life at the mercy of that voice, and of the personality driving it like the engine of a car, and for the first time noticed the clanking and knocking. When it occurred to him that he could not simply take her to Craig Newton's garage for retuning, he laughed.

'Are you actually *laughing*, Colin?' she demanded. 'Well, really! That's the last thing *you* should be doing!'

'You laugh, or you cry,' he replied, incapable of communicating with her.

'You're absolutely *pathetic*! They're riding

roughshod right over you, and you're letting them.'

'I can't do anything until the investigation's over.'

'I've *told* you what to do.'

'Being in the police isn't the same as other jobs.'

'We'll see about that,' she threatened. 'I'm back on Wednesday, so you can tell that McKenna to expect me.'

'That won't work, Vicky.'

She nagged on, but he could only concentrate on the cold lurch in his innards triggered by the prospect of her return. Cutting across her, he said: 'I might not be in Haughton when you get back. Unless I'm told otherwise, I'm staying here until McKenna's finished.' He disconnected then, feeling as if he had sawn through a shackle, and when she called again almost immediately, his mother told her he had just gone out with his father.

5

Like Haughton's other children, apart from those marooned in isolated outlying farms, the Dugdale children went to school on Friday morning, baptising their new wellingtons in the snow. When she returned from the school run, Susan took off her own old wellingtons by the kitchen door, and padded through to the living-room in her socks.

'I saw Craig at the school,' she said, warming her legs against the radiator. 'Fred's coming out of hospital today. He's staying with them, of course, for the time being. Could we call round later to see him?'

'I don't know.' Dugdale frowned. 'I'll have to ask McKenna, but don't be surprised if he says not.'

Perversely, Susan kept her buttocks pressed against the radiator, even though the heat was smarting through jeans and longjohns. 'Why must all normal human contact be suspended?' she asked. 'Especially with people we've known for ever.'

'You know why.'

'I could go, surely?' she insisted. 'Without getting permission first.'

'Not really.' His voice was quite dull, she thought. 'Linda might say something to you, then you'd repeat it to me.'

'What could Linda say that I haven't already heard?'

'You know what I mean.'

'I don't, as a matter of fact.' Susan moved at last, and sat at the table opposite her husband.

He sighed. 'McKenna still doesn't know if Linda and I fitted up Smith.' He rose, as if unable to be close to her. 'D'you want a coffee?' he asked, making for the kitchen.

While he filled the kettle, and clinked spoons and mugs, she asked herself when, and how, the tiny rift between them had opened into this terrifying chasm. And all of them were teetering on the edge, she thought, including the children.

Tongue between his teeth to keep his hands steady, he returned with two brimming mugs and a tin of shortbread stuck under his arm. Despite her misery, Susan smiled. 'How does sticking your tongue between your teeth stop you spilling things?'

'I've no idea,' he said, setting the mugs on small coasters, 'but it works. Try it yourself.'

'Perhaps I will.' His invitation, and her response, seemed to linger between them, perhaps the first small signs of rescue. 'Tell me,' she went on, opening the tin and selecting a crumbly wedge, 'd'you still think Smith killed Trisha?'

'Much as I'd like to,' he replied, almost brushing

her fingers with his as he chose his own biscuit, 'I can't ignore the facts, and Father Barclay's alibi is one almighty fact.'

'OK.' Susan bit into the shortbread, catching the crumbs in her hand. 'So, if he didn't, who did?'

'I wish I knew!'

'Well, if the lonely hearts guys are non-starters, who else *could* it be?' As he shook his head, she prodded his arm. 'Think! Who might want her dead?'

He let his arm stay in reach of her fingers, and said: 'I keep coming back to Smith and Beryl. Trisha hadn't offended anyone else. She hadn't actually offended *them*, but, twisted buggers that they are, they don't see it like that. From Smith's point of view, the whole *world* offends him, and Beryl's too stupid, or too besotted, or both, not to go along with every crazy idea that comes into his ugly head.'

'You hate the pair of them, and it's blinding you. You *want* it to be them, and you can't get past it.' Instead of moving her hand, she put the biscuit on the table, making a spatter of crumbs over which she would usually rush for the mini vacuum cleaner, then picked up the coffee. 'But suppose she knew something about someone else which was so awful they killed her to keep it a secret.'

'But what? And who?' He swallowed the last of his own biscuit. 'There wasn't even a whisper about anything like that.'

'There wouldn't be if it was such a secret. In any case, Trisha was awfully good at keeping her mouth shut. She kept quiet about that bastard Smith for long enough.' She put down her coffee, and reached into the biscuit tin just as he did the same. This time, their fingers touched, and scrabbled together among the wedges and squares and rounds. '*What* could someone be desperate to hide? *Who* might have

313

horrible skeletons in the cupboard? You should do a "what could ruin who" exercise.'

'"Whom",' he corrected her. 'Not "who".'

'Are you sure?' She grinned. 'Who cares?' She extracted a round biscuit dusted with caster sugar. 'Get back to the point. Who did Trisha know, even slightly, who could be harbouring dangerous secrets? Who was in her circle of acquaintances, however remotely?'

He stared at her, a curious light in his eyes. 'Julie.'

Her hand jerked away from his arm as if stung, and she flushed.

'You started this, Sue. If you don't want to carry on because Julie's cropped up, then say so. Don't insult her again.' As she stared back at him, her face mask-like, he added: 'And quite frankly, I shouldn't think Julie's got any secrets left, never mind ones like that.'

6

True to her threat, Wendy complained about the two nurses who goaded and humiliated her Thursday tea-time, and was decidedly gratified to receive a visit soon after breakfast from the nursing manager, a stout, anxious, grey-haired woman who reminded her quite forcibly, and even poignantly, of Frances. But Frances was miles away, and obviously intended to stay there, whereas this other woman was here, so Wendy let loose the pent-up tide of stress, anger, loneliness, misery, fear, and outraged self-centredness which had carried her to this nadir in her life.

Patiently, the other woman let the maelstrom of words eddy around her, more than sympathising with her nurses' uncharacteristic loss of compassion.

'Will they be suspended and disciplined?' Wendy

demanded. 'They certainly ought to be. I'm in this mess for doing nothing. If I spoke to a civilian like they spoke to me, I'd be dismissed.'

'Naturally, I'll deal with it,' the other woman consoled. 'But if it comes to a disciplinary hearing, you'd have to give evidence.' She frowned. 'I'm not at all sure you'll be up to anything like that for quite some time.'

'What d'you mean?'

'Well, you saw the psychiatrist yesterday, and he *is* rather worried. He's *bound* to be, in the circumstances. You *did* deliberately overdose, and even if you didn't *quite* mean to kill yourself, you knew you'd make yourself very ill indeed.' She offered the bland, sympathetic smile she often used to sugar the nastiest pill. 'Mightn't it be best for *me* to deal with them? You know, give them the rounds of my office, and make them apologise? There's enough hanging over your head without you having to fret about somebody else's disciplinary hearing, and it would get very nasty once the union got involved.' She rose, puffing with effort, and smoothed down the navy-blue suit which failed to fit her in any meaningful sense. 'Anyway, dear, *you* know how it feels to be on the sharp end of the management stick, and I'm sure you wouldn't want to put anyone else through that kind of misery, would you?'

7

Fascinated by the blue light reflecting off the snow and colour-washing the whole room, Janet stared through the window instead of attending to the thankless routine of the papers on her desk. She saw the canary-yellow car with smoked glass windows cruise slowly past towards the Bull, then, a few minutes later, return, even more slowly. She could not see the driver, nor hear the engine die nor the door click shut, and snow muffled the driver's footsteps on the pavement, so when the doorbell pealed, she flinched. The security monitor showed the bug-eyed face of a stranger.

There was an exchange of words, Rene's rather gruff tones punctuated by a more high-pitched voice with the alien inflections of Estuary English. McKenna's head jerked up, a little spot of colour staining each pale cheek. He removed his glasses, dropped them on the desk, and went to the door, to find Gaynor in the narrow hall, dressed for the weather in leather jeans, suede walking boots, and a beautiful khaki jacket lined with pale fur. Her skin was like marble.

'I need to talk to you,' she said. Gone was the arrogant challenge of Wednesday night, and she looked almost desperate.

Without a word, he ushered her to the back room, followed her in, and shut the door. 'There is nothing I want to say to you. Now, or at any other time.'

'Please! Hear me out.' The plea was echoed in her eyes. 'It's about Smith.'

'Do you have something new to tell me?' When, mutely, she shook her head, he added: 'Are you on a fishing expedition? I see your paper failed to report on his arrest last night.'

Momentarily, the old challenge flickered in her look, but she merely said: 'I didn't know about it, and I don't want to know. Whatever he's done, it'll be bad. He's evil, and I'm afraid of him.'

'Arguably, you woke the monster.'

She shivered. 'It's been awake since he first drew

breath. He could barely keep his fists to himself yesterday.'

'Really? He sees things rather differently. He claims you terrified him so much he panicked, as a result of which he later found himself in a very disturbing situation.'

'I beg your pardon?'

'Your behaviour overwhelmed him with unbearable memories,' McKenna told her. 'Consequently, beside himself, he ran away from you, and into even deeper trouble. The frying pan into the fire, as it were.'

'He's blaming *me*?' She was astounded and appalled.

McKenna nodded, her genuine distress unwholesomely pleasurable.

'Where is he?' she demanded.

'I've no idea.'

'Of course you have! You *must* know!'

'I wouldn't tell you, in any case.'

'He'll come after me.' She stared at him, eyes pleading. 'I'm afraid!'

'Are you? Then, perhaps you should go back where you belong.' He paused assessingly. 'However, as you must remain available, you can't leave the country.'

'Available for what?'

'For whatever criminal charges may be put to you.'

'I've *been* charged. With wasting police time.'

'Only where Bunty Smith is concerned. The issue of contempt in your articles is still being examined and, of course, there's the matter of your admitted access to confidential court records.'

'I don't believe this!' Her fear was being challenged by anger. 'You can't abuse your power to pay me back over a personal matter.'

'It's only personal insofar as the documents you

saw, and discussed with Smith, if not others, related to my divorce. Inevitably, your admission begs the question of what other confidential documents and records you've seen, and doubtless copied. Make no mistake, Ms Holbrook, you went too far, and you'll answer for it, as will the contacts you must have in various places.'

'You can't do this! You *can't*!'

'We'll see, shall we?' He opened the door, and gestured for her to leave. 'Your editor can expect a search warrant to be executed on his offices in the near future, and your own premises will suffer the same fate, as will your electronic facilities.' As she brushed past, he added: 'Please make sure you remain in Haughton until you've given a statement about the incident you witnessed yesterday. My officers will contact you later.'

Stiff-legged, Gaynor walked to the front door, desperately turning over ways and means of protecting her priceless data. Sure he knew what was racing through her mind, she turned, the old antagonism lighting her eyes. 'You might have won this little battle, Superintendent, but the war's still on, and when the local flatfoots find Beryl burned to a crisp in the debris of her posh house, or otherwise very dead, don't forget I warned you, because I shan't.'

8

Craig had been called out at daybreak, to haul a stranded motorist out of a suffocating drift on the moorland pass above Beryl's house and, on his way back to town with the breakdown truck, he went home for a proper breakfast. By the back door, he kicked loose snow off his steel-capped, cleat-soled work boots, then went into the kitchen, where Linda was at the table, various newspapers spread before her. Her shoulders were shaking violently, and a strange noise came from her throat.

'Lin?' Craig covered the distance from the door in two huge strides, leaving giant snow-packed prints on the floor. Even as he leaned over, pushing her hair back from her face, the snow began to melt into puddles. 'Lin! What's wrong?'

Tears streamed unchecked from her eyes, but she was beside herself with mirth, not misery. 'He's been arrested! He's back inside. Well, he was last night. It's in the paper.' She scrabbled among the scattered sheets. 'It's in *all* the papers, except the one that bloody woman writes for.'

'What did he do?'

Gloatingly, she quoted: '"Piers Stanton Smith, whose conviction for the murder of his first wife was recently quashed by the Court of Appeal, was arrested during a late-night police raid on a notorious homosexual club in Manchester. A number of other men were also arrested, and it is understood that the police took several young boys into protective custody. Mr Smith is being held at a city police station. His solicitor, Andrew Lyons, arrived shortly after midnight, and within the hour his second wife Beryl, the daughter of a wealthy shop owner, drove up in her cream Mercedes, despite having to make a twenty-five-mile journey from the snow-bound town of Haughton."' She stabbed the paragraph. 'So, start praying!'

'What for?' asked Craig, rummaging among the reams of newsprint.

'For him to get AIDS, or something even worse, if he hasn't already,' Linda said. 'I want him crucified for what he did to Trisha, and then,' she added savagely, 'I hope he burns in hell for the rest of time.'

9

'Beryl?' The man's voice was soft, and familiar, the hand on her hair comforting. She saw the gleaming silver crucifix, and looked up, her face ravaged.

'Oh, Father Brett!' Her voice was hoarse with hours of weeping. 'They won't let him go!'

He sat beside her on the padded bench in the police station foyer, gathering his robes around him. 'Have you been here all night?' When she nodded, blinking, he said: 'You must be exhausted.'

'I'm so *worried*.' She gnawed her mouth. 'Piers must be absolutely frantic! They've shut him up in a cell again!'

'What happened?' He took the hand lying limply in her lap.

'That horrible reporter came to the house, saying he'd lied to her. She shouted at him, and he just couldn't cope.' Beryl choked back another sob. 'He ran away, and didn't come back. I waited and waited, then I took the car out, but I couldn't find him anywhere. When it started snowing so hard, I rang the police, but they wouldn't do anything.' She turned slowly, as if her bones were filled with lead, and looked into his eyes. 'Then Piers's solicitor rang about eleven, but he wouldn't tell me what was happening. I still don't know!'

Fauvel squeezed her fingers. 'It's not very pleasant news, Beryl, and unfortunately, the papers have got hold of it.' Her fingers trembled, then her whole body began to shudder. 'Piers was in a gay club here in the city when the police raided.'

'It's a lie!'

'It's not, I'm sorry to say.'

'Then it's a mistake!'

'How could it be?'

'Someone must have deceived him into going there.' Beryl was adamant. 'He'd never go to a place like that on his own!'

'Have you talked to the police? Or the solicitor?'

She shook her head. 'No.' Her hair was lank, her clothes in shoddy disarray and, hunched as she was beside him, her head poked tortoise-like from her body.

'Would you like me to see what I can find out?'

'Oh, please!' she whispered. 'Please do, and make them let him go.'

10

McKenna's humour was not improved when Ellen suggested he should refrain from contacting Ryman until there were grounds for an interview under caution. 'And irrespective of what I put in my report, you'll only be on a fishing expedition,' she added. 'Ryman's hardly likely to *volunteer* an admission of negligence, and I imagine he's far too wily to be trapped into one.'

'The chief constable needs to know Ryman's in the frame,' McKenna argued.

'The telephones are still working,' Ellen pointed out.

'So why don't we use them to let Longmoor Prison know about the alleged rapes on Smith?' Jack said, trying to defuse a discussion that McKenna was fast turning into an argument. 'I know it's not our business, but they might be glad of the warning.

Smith's solicitor is doubtless preparing to sue as we speak.'

'I'm not sure that's a good idea, either,' Ellen told him. 'We're so widely accountable we must be able to justify everything we do and say, and doing the odd favour and reacting to gut instinct won't be regarded as acceptable professional conduct by the Home Office, the Police Complaints Authority, or anyone else with a finger in this particular pie, even if the end might eventually vindicate the means. You *know* we're walking on eggs. Let's try not to break too many.'

'Perhaps we should pack up and go home now, then,' Janet remarked, as she put down the telephone. 'Fauvel's housekeeper says he's out, so that leaves us twiddling our thumbs until he comes back. That is, of course, if we're still allowed to speak to *him*.'

Venables telephoned again as McKenna was about to leave for the Willows. 'Smith can certainly pull them in,' he said. 'His wife's been cluttering up a bench all night, weeping and wailing and gnashing her teeth, Mr-five-hundred-quid-an-hour Lyons turned up again at the crack of dawn, and now there's a transvestite demanding to see me.'

'I beg your pardon?' McKenna unconsciously echoed Gaynor Holbrook.

'Sorry!' Venables apologised. 'Bad joke. I'm so bloody tired I don't even know what day it is. This priest turned up, in full regalia, wanting to know when Smith can be clutched back to the wifely bosom. The owner of the bosom called him about an hour ago, I'm told.'

'Father Fauvel,' said McKenna. 'So that's why he's not at home. We wanted to talk to him again.'

'Did you? Why?'

'It's a long story. What are you doing with Smith?'

'Sod all, and that's not another bad joke.' Venables sighed. 'We've finally finished interviewing the kids, and every single one of them says nobody so much as laid a finger on them, let alone plied them with alcohol or lewd suggestions. So, Smith and the rest of his faggoty friends are free to bugger off. Until the next time, that is, because there's sure to be one.' He paused, then added: 'Maybe they really can't help themselves. Who knows?'

I I

From her vantage point behind the glass-panelled inner doors, Julie watched McKenna's arrival, while the residents gathered into amorphous groups to do the same. She thought he made a wide berth of the shadow they cast upon the snow, and wondered if he too felt the weight of their presence. As he mounted the steps, his tall, thin body drooped with weariness – the mark of prey rather than hunter – but even as she imagined him on the run, she knew he might still have her in his sights, for she expected such transformations. Although she sensed none of the threat those odd, sullen creatures in the snow might present, being what he was he guarded his feelings and intentions, and her instinct to bolt for cover reasserted itself.

'That policewoman came last night, and now you're here. Who's coming next?' she asked. 'D'you think you'll wear me down?'

'That suggests you're hiding something.' His voice was quite gentle, and he spoke well for a policeman, without a trace of the accent she remembered from her childhood holiday.

323

Turning her back on the gaping residents, she took him to the office. Silence was the better armour, but evasion always provided some refuge. 'I don't know what you're talking about.'

'Where were you yesterday about five o'clock?'

'How should I know? Here, probably.'

'Did you go out in the afternoon?'

She shrugged. 'I can't remember. What am I supposed to have done?'

'A woman who could fit your description was involved in an incident.'

'What sort of incident?'

'She was apparently attacked in the street.'

'Who by?'

'A man jumped out on her out of a dark-red car.'

'Poor bitch,' Julie commented. 'Was she hurt?'

'We don't know. She hasn't come forward.'

'Why d'you think it was me? Do I look like I've been jumped out on?'

She looked simply exhausted, he thought, knowing he could watch her eyes for ever. 'She wore a rather unusual coat, apparently identical to the one DC Evans saw last night.'

Something flickered in her eyes, like shadows cast by candle-light. 'I bought that from a catalogue. I expect lots of other women bought one as well.'

'The person who witnessed the incident gave the woman a lift, and dropped her by the drive to this house.'

She said nothing.

'We'll get to the bottom of it, eventually,' he added. 'The witness is sure she could identify the victim.'

'Best of luck, then. Is there anything else?'

She was almost invincible, he thought. 'Did your mother teach you to distrust the world?'

'No, she lived in hope. She didn't learn from experience. Maybe she was a bit slow.'

'What was she like?'

'Not much common sense and easily intimidated.' She folded her arms, and stared at him. 'What does it matter? Why don't you just go away? You're like a dog with some old bones, but you won't find any meat on them.'

'I'll go away when *I'm* sure there's no meat on the bones,' McKenna said. 'The remedy's in your own hands.'

'So I can make everything come right by talking to you, can I?' She looked through him. 'Don't be funny!'

'That's not what I meant.'

'It wasn't, was it?' Once again, she stared at him. 'What you *meant* was you'll hound me until I break down.' Her eyes gleamed. 'Well, sorry, but it won't work. My mother let people browbeat her for years on end, and I swore I'd never do the same. She was so scared of her parents she wouldn't even let me tell them she was dying.'

'You know your grandparents?' he asked.

'Yes.' She nodded. 'They live in Buxton, in the house where my mother was born. They run a bed and breakfast. I go there for my holidays.'

'Well, at least you have family to turn to.'

'No, I haven't. They've no idea who I am.' She smiled, sweetly and disarmingly. 'Shared blood doesn't give off a smell, you know. And I've no desire to tell them, because, nice old couple that they are, they're still the same people who had my mother locked up here when I was on the way, then convinced themselves and everyone else she was dead.' She paused, regarding him. 'There's fear in their hearts, I suppose, and it's already turned them into monsters once. Best let sleeping dogs lie.'

Her capacity to keep secrets took his breath away.

'Most people would want revenge,' he argued.

'Why should I? They don't mean anything to me.' After another, much longer, pause, she added: 'I don't belong to them.'

'What about the misery they brought on you and your mother?'

'Don't you learn about God's will in Wales? I'm not saying I believe in it, but other people do, or so they tell you.'

'You'll be telling me next that God's will murdered Trisha Smith.'

'I can't help you with your investigation.'

'You know everyone involved, and believe me, they all have an opinion about you.'

'So what? I don't know who fixed Smith.'

'Whoever fixed Smith probably killed Trisha, and you know that as well as I do, but, like your grandparents, you'll convince yourself that black is white if it suits.'

Even that jibe failed to hit a mark. She merely looked at him, her face inscrutable.

'Suppose Trisha's killer comes after you?' he asked.

'I won't be going out today. I'm working later.' She smiled wryly. 'And I expect you'll be here again tomorrow. Or Sunday, or Monday.'

'I might be back before tomorrow.' He tried to goad her. 'I'm on my way to see Neville Ryman.'

12

For the third time, Estelle dabbed her eyes with one of her husband's large handkerchiefs. 'Oh, I'm sorry. I can't stop myself bursting into tears. It must be the shock.'

There were three assistant chief constables in

Ryman's force, and the one who sat opposite Estelle felt quite out of his depth. Making sympathetic noises, he offered her a fresh cup of tea.

'Oh, yes please,' she said gratefully. 'It always helps, doesn't it?'

Excusing himself, he left the room, although she was sure he had only to pick up one of the four telephones on his desk to obtain anything he might conceivably want. She gazed through the window, considering the best way to proceed along the ground she was so carefully preparing. The office was very gloomy, she thought, and must be just as dark on a bright summer's day, for a great overhang of limestone cliff almost touched the glass. What snow had fallen lay in pockets between the tufts of lank, dead grass that hung off the grey rock like hair off the scalp of a corpse.

'It'll be here in no time,' he announced, returning to his seat.

She rewarded him with a wan smile. 'You're really very kind.'

'Not at all.' He blushed slightly. 'Are you sure you wouldn't rather talk to a lady officer?'

'Oh, no!' That was the last thing she wanted. 'Neville said I should ask for you. He said you'd understand.' She laid the tiniest stress on the last word, but kept her eyes downcast. Under her relentless pressure, which continued through a makeshift, micro-waved supper, outside the bathroom door while her husband showered, and then in their bedroom, where she refused to switch off the light until he acceded, Ryman had eventually named the man in whose office she now sat: a fellow Mason, as senior in the arcane Lodge hierarchy as he was in the force.

'I understand in a way, Mrs Ryman, but I'm not

quite sure what I can do. Let's wait until Neville's well enough to return to duty, shall we?'

'But that'll be too late!' She squeezed more tears. 'The doctor said he's got to rest for at least a week.'

'What exactly happened?'

'Such a *silly* thing! He was setting off for his Lodge meeting, and when he stepped outside the front door, his feet just shot from under him. There was ice on the step, you see. He gave his head a really nasty bang.'

'Not nice at all.' He grimaced in sympathy.

She gazed at him, her eyes moist. 'If Neville wasn't poorly, he'd have seen you himself, of course, but this isn't something he could talk about over the telephone.' Sighing deeply, she went on: 'Usually, it wouldn't matter if *everyone* listened in to Shelley's call, because she just gossips about college, and shopping, and holidays. But this – well, it's *awful*!' She balled up the handkerchief. 'Hearing it ourselves was bad enough, but to think of others knowing – well! Neville's *distraught*.' She reached for the teacup, deliberately catching the edge of the saucer. 'When something like this happens to a young girl with everything to look forward to, you can't think straight.' Ideas gathering momentum, she added plaintively: 'We hurt for her, we really do, but what can we do? It's such a desperately personal tragedy.' She dabbed her eyes again, and sniffed. 'If Shelley thought other people might get to know, I shudder to think what she'd do!'

'No one would breathe a word, Mrs Ryman. Everything's absolutely confidential.'

'Oh, yes, I know!' Estelle spoke in a rush, afraid she had overstepped her own mark. 'I wasn't implying anything dishonourable. We just can't bear the thought of people knowing, that's all.' She put the cup in the saucer with a clatter, and choked back a sob. 'I *knew* something was wrong when she rang so late. Can you imagine how we felt when she told us? She'd just found out the man she *adores* is already married. And as if *that* weren't bad enough,' she wailed, 'she's pregnant! He's walked out on her, and now she's talking about an abortion.'

'You and Neville have my deepest sympathy. Shelley, too, of course.'

'Thank you!' Her voice was little more than a whisper.

He drummed his fingers on the desk top. 'What time did the call come in?'

She dropped her eyes, to hide her triumph. 'It was ten twenty-six exactly when our phone rang.' She smiled shyly. 'I know, you see, because I'd just started timing eggs for supper.'

'So Shelley would have rung here a minute or two earlier.'

'Probably,' Estelle agreed, success within her grasp. 'I could listen to that section of the tape, tell you when the call finishes, then it can be erased. I can't tell you how grateful we are!'

'It's not *quite* so simple,' he replied. 'Calls come in at all hours of the day and night, and *every* call, county-wide, is routed through our control room. Needless to say, we have several tapes running simultaneously, but not to worry,' he added, seeing the utter horror on her face. 'I'll authorise a superintendent to find your daughter's call, then clear that section of the tape.'

I

At ten forty that morning, the men arrested at the gay club were released. One by one, they came through the security door from the cell block into the foyer, some scuttling quietly away, others promising reprisal against fascist, homophobic police. Fauvel watched them. It was his habit to watch people, in search of souls deserving salvation, but this was a procession of the damned, he thought, beholding a shamelessness of biblical proportions.

Every time the door was unlocked, Beryl started from her seat, only to fall back with a sigh. Fear and tension emanated from her like heat, and when eventually the door opened on her husband she rose with a little cry, her arms jerking, ready to embrace. He came towards them hesitantly, met Fauvel's eye briefly, and deliberately averted his gaze from hers.

'Piers! Oh, Piers!' she whispered, longing, relief, and fear in her voice. Fauvel stood beside her with his hand on her shoulder, and he felt her body quake. Smith advanced, still refusing to look at her, like a child beaten for a crime he had not committed.

'He looks so pale,' she said to herself, 'so dreadfully *tired*.' She reached for his hand, but he made fists of both, and took a step back. She noticed then the dark-grey mohair overcoat draped casually around his shoulders, and the bespoke suit beneath, and realised that he must have changed his clothes when he rushed upstairs after the row with Gaynor. In her long torment yesterday, she had imagined him straying perilously through a blizzard clad in house clothes and indoor shoes, and she looked him over, puzzled and disturbed by the unexpected deliberation of his appearance. Anger began to constrain the welter of her emotions. 'He put me through hell,' she told herself, 'without a second thought.'

His own thoughts on similar lines, Fauvel merely said: 'We'd better get back. Beryl's exhausted. She's been here all night.'

'And I'm absolutely devastated!' Smith snapped. 'It was horrible!' He shivered, ostentatiously drawing the coat together. 'I had to have the doctor brought in!' He made for the outer door with short, quick strides, the coat-tails flying out behind him.

Beryl shambled after him. 'Why?' she asked. 'Why were you in that dreadful place?'

He tossed his head. 'I can't talk about it!' As he swept through the door, he was momentarily blinded by the flash of a camera. 'Oh, *God*!' Frantically searching for her car, he shielded his face with the coat as cameras flashed one after the other.

Beryl cried out, and had Fauvel not snatched her arm to lead her to his own car, would have rushed at the photographers who jostled even the priest, while yelling out obscenities to their quarry. Fauvel pushed Beryl and Smith into the back seat and drove off as fast as he dared. Cameras flashing, voices baying, the photographers ran after him, like jackals after food on the hoof.

Arms tightly folded across his chest, right leg crossed over the left, right foot kicking thin air, Smith sat as far from Beryl as the space in Fauvel's car allowed.

Whenever she tried to bridge the distance, he flinched further away.

'Piers, please!' she begged, her hand flapping uselessly. 'Why won't you talk to me?'

'Leave me alone!'

Fauvel drove fast along the slushy road, wanting to be rid of both of them. The rear mirror gave him only a partial view of Smith's face, but enough to show the hard light in his marbly eyes and the sullen, vicious downturn to his mouth. Chameleon-like in her husband's aura, Beryl had reverted to type, a feeble supplicant at the altar of his massive self-absorption, the doubt and confusion that briefly troubled her completely obfuscated by the smoke-screens he puffed up to cover his tracks.

The gates to the house stood wide open, as Beryl had left them when she careered through last night. Fresh snow almost filled the deep gouges cut by her wheels, and lay thick on the doorstep.

Fauvel switched off the engine. 'I can only come in for a little while.'

Smith threw open the car door and rushed into the house without a word. Beryl struggled out like a weary old woman and followed, with Fauvel beside her. The row was audible before they crossed the threshold. Carelessly tramping snow on to the carpet, Beryl scurried into the hall to find her housekeeper and gardener in wait, suitcases by their feet. In the shadows behind them, Smith breathed heavily, his face chalk-white and his eyes terrifying.

'What is it?' Her glance flicked fearfully to her servants, her husband, and back to her servants. 'What's the matter?'

'We're leaving, madam,' the housekeeper announced firmly.

'Leaving?' Beryl tittered. 'Don't be silly! You live here.'

'We've stood by you till now, but after yesterday's dreadful goings-on, and what's in the papers today – well!'

'But you can't!' Beryl was almost frantic. 'You can't just walk out!'

'We're ashamed to be here,' the gardener said. 'God knows what folk think of us, staying in this place with *him*!'

'Then get out!' Smith hissed. 'Go on! Get out!'

'In our own good time!' The gardener turned. 'You've brought shame on this house, you have.' He tensed as Smith moved forward. 'Don't you threaten me! You treated my wife like dirt on your fancy shoes, and you treat your own even worse. You're nothing but a filthy sponger!'

'And what are you?' Smith's voice was venomous. 'A servant! A jobbing bloody gardener! A fucking *nothing*!'

Quivering with rage, the housekeeper retorted: 'He's not afraid of honest work, and he's never knocked me about, like you did to poor Trisha Jarvis.' She turned to Beryl. 'We cared for this house like it was our own, and you let him make a pigsty of it. And what for, eh? He made a mess, then left it. Story of his life, isn't it?'

'We'll sort it out.' Beryl clutched the false hope. 'Stay, and we'll do it together.'

'If they stay, I go.' Smith glided silkily from the shadows. 'It's your choice, Beryl.'

'Don't do this to me!' she moaned. 'Don't make me choose. *Please* don't!'

'Don't fret yourself, madam,' the gardener said. 'We're not spending another night under the same roof as *that* bloody tart!' He glared at Smith. 'Most of the town thinks you killed Trisha, me included, and my blood runs cold when I think what you'll do to Miss Beryl. You've already battered her once that we know.'

2

Fauvel was so rigid with tension that he could barely handle the car in the few miles between Beryl's house and the presbytery. Never before, he thought, had he witnessed such outrageous vulgarity. Beryl wept and keened and begged, the housekeeper and gardener bellowed their resentments, while the cause of it all rampaged through the house, screaming, and thumping, and banging, before falling so eerily quiet that silence dropped upon the others like a pall. As Beryl's emotions see-sawed crazily, her desperate pleas to her servants turned like cornered rats, and she began to screech in their faces almost as savagely as her husband had done. White-faced, the servants dumped their baggage in the snow while the gardener brought his own car from the garage, then drove away without a backward glance.

'Good riddance!' Beryl shouted, her face sodden with tears. Calling out, she hauled herself up the stairs, while Fauvel, shocked and disturbed, waited in the hall. Eventually, he noticed the front door was still wide open, and closed it quietly.

At first, only Beryl's voice drifted down from above, then he heard Smith's. 'It wasn't my fault,' he whined. 'It was that Holbrook bitch, then those two. I'm *glad* they've gone. They've made my life hell, taunting me, sneering at me. I even caught her spitting in my food, but I didn't know how to tell you.' The wretched litany moaned on. 'And last night's not like you think.' But, witlessly, Beryl failed to ask how else it could be. Still consoling him, she led her woebegone husband downstairs. As he glanced at Fauvel, his expression belied his demeanour.

'You'll stay, won't you?' Beryl asked. 'Piers needs you.'

'I'm sorry.' The words almost stuck in Fauvel's throat. 'I must get back to the presbytery.'

'But Piers *needs* you!'

'I'm sorry.' Repeating himself, Fauvel wondered if Beryl had enough sense to fear being alone with her husband. 'I'll try to come back later.' He made his escape, as careless for her safety as he had been for her predecessor's.

Turning into the presbytery drive, he found a strange car in his parking space. His own housekeeper accosted him by the door, to say the police were waiting in the sitting-room. He knew the small, bird-like woman who dragged about her electronic machines like young children, but the large, dark-haired man who rose to greet him was a stranger.

'Good morning,' Jack said. 'I'm Inspector Tuttle, Superintendent McKenna's colleague. He's asked me to conduct a further interview.'

'At the very least, I would have expected the courtesy of being forewarned,' Fauvel replied. 'I'm afraid it's not convenient.'

'I'm afraid it *must* be convenient, Father Fauvel,' Jack insisted.

'Why?' Watching Ellen from the corner of his eyes, Fauvel thought she stared like a hungry bird. 'I told Superintendent McKenna everything I know.'

'You'll appreciate,' Ellen began, 'that an investigation such as ours inevitably proceeds on a day-to-day basis, responding to information as it arises.' She wondered what had ruffled the priest's composure. He looked anxious, and even hunted. 'We must cover every possible eventuality.'

'So?' Fauvel was curt.

'We'd like to discuss the afternoon Trisha Smith died,' replied Jack, sitting down again. 'And your whereabouts.'

Out of options, Fauvel arranged himself on the settee, the hem of his cassock brushing the floor, the silver crucifix turning in his fingers. '*My* whereabouts?' He sighed. 'If only I had stayed in Haughton on that day, Piers would never have gone to prison.' He stroked the crucifix with his thumb. 'My unwitting contribution to his conviction will haunt my conscience until the day I die.'

'How is he, by the way?' Ellen asked. 'We understand you've seen him this morning.'

The priest reddened under his tan. 'Am I under surveillance?'

'Of course not!' Jack smiled. 'Manchester police rang to let us know he was being released, and they said you were there. With Beryl.'

'I see.' Fauvel nodded stiffly. 'I brought them back. Beryl was in no state to drive.'

'And?' Jack prompted, sensing his tension.

'There was a scene with the housekeeper and her husband. They've left.'

'Why?'

'I think you should discuss that with Beryl. I dislike gossip.'

'But you witnessed it,' Ellen said, 'so it's hardly gossip.'

'I will not discuss their private affairs!' Taking a deep breath, he tried to smile. 'I *do* apologise! I'm afraid I have a lot of business to attend to, and I'm already well behind schedule.'

'And the sooner we discuss the afternoon Trisha

was killed,' Jack said, 'the sooner you can get on with it. Now then, Father Barclay *thought* you'd gone to a meeting in Manchester, but he wasn't sure. Can you remember? D'you keep a diary, for instance?'

'It's almost three years ago.'

'Yes, but it's one of those days you're not likely to forget,' Jack pointed out. 'Where were you?'

'Where Father Barclay thought I was.'

'Was it a private meeting?' Jack persisted. 'Were you on diocesan business? Where was the meeting held?'

Fauvel stared at him. 'Why do you want to know?'

'We're drawing up a map, as it were, of where everyone was at the time. Your name is only one on a long list.'

'I see.' Fauvel's fist clutched the crucifix so tightly it bit into his flesh. 'I suppose there's no harm in telling you. I went to see a solicitor.'

'On your own behalf?' Jack asked.

'As a matter of fact, no.' Fauvel relaxed, and smiled. 'It was a highly confidential issue involving a parishioner.'

'And who was the solicitor?'

'I'm sorry, Inspector, but I must take advice from my bishop before I say another word.'

3

After leaving the Willows, McKenna had driven into Haughton, and sat in a café for almost an hour, trying to work out a way to proceed. Ellen's advice rankled, but he suspected the mildest criticism would today have felt like a whip on bare flesh. The instinct she deplored had already taken him to the Willows, and now urged him towards Ravensdale and Neville

Ryman, but only, he thought, because instinct was all he had to follow.

To get to Ravensdale, he had to make a wide detour around the whole High Peak area, but once in the lowlands, he found the roads cleared, with dirt-splattered snow banked along the verges. Ravensdale's streets were awash with slush and, when he walked from the car-park to the police headquarters building, the breeze on his face was quite balmy.

Ryman, he was told, had had a nasty fall on some ice last night, and was at home. Plans thwarted, McKenna returned to his car, then decided that visiting Ryman to wish him a quick recovery would be a civilised gesture. And had he adopted a less confrontational approach at the outset, he realised, he might have made more progress: Ryman believing himself an ally was more use to his investigation than Ryman alerted by hostility.

He parked on the road outside Ryman's house, then decided to ignore more of Ellen's advice, and telephoned Cooper at Longmoor Prison. A silver Volvo estate car suddenly roared up, slewed through the gate without indicating, and skidded to a halt in front of the garage. A large, grey-haired woman, dressed in a grey wool jacket and pleated skirt, almost fell out and, slipping and sliding in the snow, rushed into the house, not even bothering to shut the driver's door.

'I don't believe it,' Cooper was saying. 'I'll look into it, of course, but I'm sure it's another fairy story.' He paused. 'Now, if you were saying the boot was on the other foot, that'd be a different matter. Smith as a rapist I can take on board with no difficulty whatsoever.'

'Anyone pining for him?' McKenna watched to see if the woman emerged from the house.

'I already told you,' Cooper replied. 'Everyone was overjoyed to see the back of him.' He paused again, for so long that McKenna thought the connection had fallen prey to the vagaries of mobile networks. Then he said: 'About four months after Smith arrived here, a youngster doing life for arson killed himself. He'd spent a lot of time with Smith, which we put down to a natural empathy between fire raisers. The autopsy showed violent penetration, but our investigations got nowhere. However, that's not to say we'll come up against the same wall of silence now Smith's out of the way.'

'Are you sure about that? It opens up the prospect of having him back.'

'But not here,' Cooper asserted. 'Not here.'

Estelle Ryman, for it must be she, McKenna realised, did not come back out to secure the car. He waited another ten minutes, smoked a cigarette, thought about her suddenly incapacitated husband, then locked his own car and walked up the drive. Large lawns on either side were edged with round, marbled chunks of rock and bordered with shrubs, all under a soft carpet of melting snow. A robin with a brilliant red breast swayed on the twigs of a laurel bush, its teetering and feather-shaking sending tiny showers to the ground.

The late-Victorian house was double-fronted, bay-windowed, tastefully embellished here and there with stained and leaded glass, and carved barge boards projected over the eaves and framed an imposing porch. The front steps were brushed clean and dusted with grit. He rang the bell, looking around at a pleasant prospect of similar houses lining a wide avenue and, in the distance, a line of trees on the crest of a hill in sharp relief against the sky. He thought he could just discern a glimmer of sunshine trying to break through.

The door was opened by the grey-haired woman, still in her outdoor clothes. Smiling, he said: 'I'd like to see Mr Ryman. And by the way, your car's open.'

'You can't!' Her eyes darted hither and thither, and her curt words snapped in the air, disturbing the robin, which fluttered away. 'He's not well.'

'So I believe, but I would like to speak to him.'

'Who are you?' Estelle demanded, suddenly focusing on his face.

'Superintendent McKenna.'

'*You*!' Breath explosively expelled, mouth working, she advanced. 'Get out! Leave us alone!'

'Mrs Ryman!'

'Go *away*!' Hands splayed, she stretched out both arms, and shoved him violently in the chest, her whole considerable weight behind the assault. He stumbled backwards, slipped off the side of the steps and, reaching for the window-sill, tried to stop himself from falling. '*Get away from this house!*' Arms flailing, she caught him a glancing blow to the side of his head, and knocked him completely off balance. He collapsed in the heap of soft snow beneath the window, while her arms and fists battered his head and shoulders. Then the attack ceased as suddenly as it began. He knelt there, his clothing soaked, and simply waited, as he would when his former wife erupted into violence. Estelle's feet in their grey suede shoes trampled the hem of his coat, and pinned him to the ground. They looked enormous, and her legs were like tree trunks. He expected her to bludgeon him with those feet, but she merely stood over him, breathing heavily, then shuffled backwards, dragging his coat with her. Out of the corner of his eye, he saw her reach for one of

340

the chunks of marbled rock, her large hand clasping and lifting as if it were a pebble.

4

Summoned back to Church Street to make her statement, Gaynor let her canary-yellow car crunch to a halt against the kerb. Behind the smoked-glass windows, she shook her hair into place and applied fresh lipstick, before stepping out into the cold and, with a flick of her gloved wrist, remotely activating locks and car alarm.

'Do sit down, Ms Holbrook,' Jack invited, as Rene brought her to the office. 'Would you like tea? Coffee?'

'Coffee, please,' Gaynor replied, wary of the welcome.

'Superintendent McKenna's out,' added Jack. 'Mrs Turner and myself will take your statement.'

She relaxed, but only a little. 'Will it take long? I have to get back to London.' And an editor almost incandescent with rage, she reminded herself. 'As you may know, Mr McKenna's asked for search warrants to be executed on my office, and my flat.'

'So I understand.' Jack nodded. 'It's not an unusual procedure when a journalist might be in possession of sensitive material.'

'It's an outrage,' Gaynor asserted. 'A gross invasion of privacy.'

'But can investigative journalists claim the same rights to privacy as members of the public?' Jack queried. 'Access to other people's secrets is your meat and drink – otherwise, you couldn't do your job – so the occasional official backlash is surely an occupational hazard.'

Ignoring his remark, she said: 'Doing something about Smith would be more to the point, don't you think? *Before* he gets rid of another wife.' She glanced at him. 'I've never been so scared as I was yesterday.'

'But no offence was committed, was it?' Jack said.

'That's a matter of opinion.'

'Well,' Jack said brightly, 'you could always write about it, couldn't you? It would make quite a story.'

5

In the few moments it took for Estelle's fingers to gouge out the rock, McKenna felt that a lifetime passed. He could not rise, for her feet on his coat skewered him to the ground. He could not roll out of her reach, for the brickwork under the bay window was bare inches from his face. If he stretched out his hand to grasp her ankle and pull her foot from under her, she might smash her own head on the coping. He had the option of attacking her to save himself, or of letting her do whatever she was capable of doing with a rock in her hand, a victim under her feet, and her control long gone.

Even as he flexed his ice-cold fingers and thought of toppling her, he knew that if he let his hand snake across that small distance, he himself would cross a chasm, to join the likes of Smith. He desperately wanted to stay where he was, yet, equally desperately, wanted to stay alive and, as she raised her arm, the rock and her hand moving out of his line of sight, he flexed his fingers for the last time.

There was a flurry of noise and a rush of air, then a blow in the middle of his back, which sent him sprawling face down. Her feet scrabbled, one grey shoe tangled up in the cloth of his coat, and he heard guttural breaths, rending fabric, and a crunching thud, before silence fell. She backed away, feet, legs, skirt hem, torn jacket, and her whole body coming into view. She stood in the middle of the drive, the rock still in her hand, watching from her own vantage point as first one drop of blood, then another, and another, splashed from somewhere above him, making dark craters in the snow. He rolled over and looked up, just as Ryman, a dark hole in the side of his head, fell to the ground.

A neighbour must have called for help. Estelle began to scream as she reached the gate, and went on screaming as she ran down the road, drawing people from their houses, and McKenna thought he could still hear her terror even above the wailing sirens of the ambulance and police cars which seemed to arrive even before he could get to his knees and crawl towards Ryman. As the paramedics gently edged him away from the stricken man, he heard a faint crash, when Estelle saw her hand was slimy with her husband's blood and flung the rock through someone's window.

Even after she discarded the stone, her bloody fingers left a trail as red as the feathers on the robin's breast in the snow on the pavement. She was cornered by three patrol cars where the pleasant suburban avenue, now beginning to swarm with the curious and the fearful, joined a main thoroughfare. The screams had dwindled as she ran, her breath conserved for flight, and it was a silent and breathless Estelle who faced the six officers now cautiously emerging from their cars. The sirens were silent too, the flashing roof lights stilled, and the two policewomen who approached her did not expect to need their long batons. Calmly, the shorter woman said: 'Shall we get in the car, Mrs Ryman? You look all in. Your jacket's torn. Did you know? Your shoes look very wet too.'

Estelle jerked her head to look at her shoes. The grey suede was horribly stained, and the fancy tassel on the left vamp was torn off, like three of her jacket buttons. The pleated skirt hung like a crumpled rag. She clenched her bloody hands into fists, enraged by the disgrace of public dishevelment, glared at the policewoman, and lunged, fists up level with her chin and working like pile drivers. Roaring as she came, she knocked her aside with astonishing violence.

I

McKenna had first met the force's chief constable at the briefing meeting ten days before. Then, he had been tense and rather defensive. Now, he was numbed with shock.

'It took four men to hold Estelle down in the end, and two of them got knocked about before the handcuffs were on. The lass she barged into had her arm broken, while Neville's fighting for his life.'

McKenna shivered uncontrollably. 'Because he saved mine.'

'It's not your fault. No one could've foreseen this, even if we'd put two and two together after she was here earlier.'

'She was here?' McKenna tried to light a cigarette. 'Why?'

'Something about a telephone call last night from her daughter. It had to be routed through the control room, so it was recorded, and Estelle wanted the tape wiped. She said it was very personal. She knew the exact time, give or take a couple of minutes, because she'd just begun timing eggs on the boil.'

McKenna coughed raspingly as smoke bit into his raw throat. 'It's absolutely imperative that the call isn't erased.'

'We haven't even found the right tape yet.' The chief constable regarded McKenna's pallid face and shuddering body. 'You should've gone to hospital yourself, at least for a check-up.'

'I'm more concerned with the tape.'

'So am I, now.' He stared bleakly at McKenna. 'God alone knows what's on it.'

2

Unlike the bored token guard outside the ward where Wendy Lewis fretted self-pityingly, the guards outside and inside Estelle's private hospital room were alert and, to the utter dismay of the medical staff, armed with batons and CS gas. Clad in a hospital-issue flannel gown, she was flat on her back in a high bed, snoring loudly, top lip drawn back in a snarl, and injected with enough sedative to fell a horse.

In another wing, her husband was flat on his back on an operating table, while a team of surgeons assessed the bloody, trench-like depression in his left temple and fought like demons to keep him alive. Lazarus-like, he was resuscitated three times before the surgeons nodded to each other, glanced at the clock on the wall, and finally downed tools.

3

In a small cubicle off the operations room, the chief constable and McKenna listened to the telephone call on which Estelle had eavesdropped and, as soon as McKenna heard the words: 'Mr Ryman? Is that you?' he knew it had provoked her collapse into madness, although he did not know why. A whole history lay between Ryman and the woman who first implored him, and then seemed to menace, with reminders of apathy and arrogance. McKenna listened to the end, removed his headset and, rubbing his temples, watched one emotion after another consume the other man's composure.

'No wonder she wanted it wiped!' The chief constable was horrified. 'Who is the woman? And what in God's name was she on about?'

'She's called Julie Broadbent,' McKenna said. 'She once walked out with Barry Dugdale, and that liaison was the first thing Ryman told me about.'

4

After McKenna left, Julie went to bed, and was still there well after lunch, the curtains closed, the duvet half over her face, the telephone bell switched off, and the bedroom door locked. She wanted to make a hole, and crawl into it, but for now, this was the next best thing.

Restlessly, she turned this way and that, lying on her stomach with her face buried in the pillow, then on her back, staring at the ceiling. She rolled on to her left side, and watched the bright red digits of her bedside clock until her eyes glazed and closed, and she fell into a fathomless sleep. A shaft of pale sunlight broke through the tiny gap between the top of the curtains and began to inch around the room, sliding across the bed like a finger. She woke briefly when it stroked her face, then slept on.

5

McKenna called Jack from Ravensdale police headquarters, and told him to detain Julie for

347

questioning. 'I haven't time to go into detail, but she telephoned Ryman last night. Now he's dead and his wife's gone off her head.'

'What did Julie say to him?'

'Nothing that makes much sense, although she was apparently the victim of yesterday's street attack. She said the man wants to kill her, possibly because she saw him at Trisha's house the day she died.'

'Then it would be more to the point to detain Fauvel,' Jack told him. 'Holbrook's been in to make her statement, and she said the man was driving a mulberry-coloured car. I've just seen Fauvel's car at the presbytery, and it's the same colour. You wouldn't have noticed before, because this is the first time anyone's seen it in daylight. I'll get back there right away. Janet can go to the Willows.'

McKenna's new knowledge created a terrible urgency, but driving as fast as he dared on roads treacherous with icy slush, he feared that death, its business over in Ravensdale, was already well on its way to Haughton, and too far ahead to be overtaken. Every traffic light was against him, every junction bottle-necked with other vehicles, and every time he tried again to call Jack, he found the connection cut by a sweep of moorland, the limestone cliffs of a ravine, or an interminable density of road-side trees. Stomach churning with tension, he eventually reached Haughton's outskirts, his destination marked out by the monolithic shape of Dent Viaduct drawing its own line across the horizon, its south end pointing towards the way he had come, its north almost overhanging the gabled roof of the Willows.

Fauvel's housekeeper finished the ironing, and took the laundry upstairs. She stacked the bedding and towels in the walk-in airing cupboard on the landing, then went to his bedroom and, although she had been in this rather grand presbytery for almost a year, she still tugged absent-mindedly at the locked drawer in the big mahogany chest when she was putting away his clothes.

Tuesdays and Fridays were laundry days, Mondays and Thursdays for cleaning, and on Wednesdays she went to the supermarket. On Saturdays she always found a reason to go into town, because she loved Haughton's weekend busyness, the full-to-bursting shops, the ritual tea and cakes in one of the High Street cafés, and the gossip. And wouldn't she have a tale to tell tomorrow, she thought, about that Lewis woman and her godless behaviour. The two girls who came in on Thursdays to do the presbytery's heavy cleaning would by now be up to their elbows in the filth of the policewoman's bungalow, and she would go later to inspect the cleaning, collect the things on the list the woman gave to Father Brett, and take them over to the hospital. As a devout Catholic, she would also hand over a piece of her mind with the knickers and bras and toiletries, because it was a terrible sin to try to take your own life, and she did not for one moment expect that Father Brett had chastised the woman. He was too kind-hearted to upset a soul in torment, even if it was deserved. She sighed, because he was too kind-hearted for his own good, in her opinion. He had rushed off to Manchester very early that morning on another mission of mercy, and now he was out again, chasing his own tail trying to catch up with himself, despite being bothered by the police when he should have been having his lunch in peace. And he needed a rest, she thought, because he had not been himself these past weeks.

She finished putting away his clothes, then plumped his pillows, although he made his own bed every day. He even did some of his own washing, too, which was amazing. She was in the bathroom scouring the sink when the doorbell jangled. Before she was half-way downstairs, the caller was banging at the door, and when she opened it she encountered the rather frightening police inspector who had been earlier.

'Where is he?' Jack demanded curtly. 'His car's not here. Where's he gone?'

She pressed her hand to her breast. 'I don't know.'

'You must have some idea. Think, woman!'

'Mind your tone!' she bridled. 'There's no need for rudeness. Father Brett had a bite to eat after you left, then went out as usual, about the parish business.'

'I'm sorry,' Jack said, 'but I've got to find him.' He frowned at her. 'Did he have any phone calls?'

'I didn't hear it ring.' She shook her head. 'But there might have been some messages from this morning. I only answer the presbytery phone. Father Brett's got his own number.'

'Show me.' Jack took her arm and almost dragged her along the hall.

Heart pounding, she opened the study door, and pointed to the machine. He closed the door in her face, then began punching buttons to rewind the tape. When he played it back he realised Fauvel had pre-empted him: all but a few words of the first message were obliterated, and Jack only learned that some time in the hours before he died, Neville Ryman had called.

7

At the Willows, the residents were out in the snow, trudging in circles, wandering in aimless squiggles, or standing like smaller monoliths under the viaduct's hard shadow. They looked hardly human, McKenna thought, slewing to a halt. The bird-like man he had seen at the end of the lane by Trisha's house flapped gauntly around the car, then seemed to fly away when he opened the door and, looking for his footprints in the snow, McKenna fancied he saw only the marks of a large bird's claws, scratches in the white carpet that glistened in the sunshine. Janet's car was parked by the steps, beside a glossy mulberry-coloured saloon.

He ran up the steps, face stinging, battered body complaining, and came up hard against the massive door. He hammered on the panels, bruising his hands, leaned on the bell-push, hammered again, then almost fell to his knees when the door opened. Janet gazed down at him, her face as white and glistening as the snow, then moved aside like a sleep-walker to let him see what lay on the parquet floor behind her. It looked like a monstrous rook that had crashed to earth and, as he watched, it began to drag its shattered body towards him, half-open eyes weeping tears of blood.

Janet muttered 'ambulance' and 'priest' before she tottered away to the office. Stupefied, McKenna waited, while the body inched onwards. He should have offered his own small comfort to the dying man, but by the time he could bring the words to mind, it was too late, and so, like Kathy Broadbent, Fauvel went without sustenance on his last journey.

I

Long before it would be extinguished at sea level, the sun had already dropped below the high horizons around Haughton, and where the frail afternoon sunshine had thawed the surface snow the bitter touch of twilight hardened the landscape with a glassy luminescence. Under a pellucid sky glinting frostily with stars, Gaynor drove slowly across Dark Moor, tyre chains biting deep into the tangle of frozen ruts left by other traffic. The outside temperature display on the dashboard flicked to minus nine degrees at the moment her mobile began to bleep. Seeing Davidson's personal number come up, she was tempted to ignore the summons, but as ever, curiosity bested her.

'If you've packed, unpack,' he said. 'And if you're already on the road, turn around.'

'Why?' Her voice was sullen. 'Not two hours ago, you were ordering me out of town before I cause any more mischief. Anyway,' she added spitefully, 'haven't I got to be on hand when McKenna's stooges raid your office?'

'Things have changed.' She heard the rustle of papers. 'There was a fatal attack in Ravensdale earlier on, and now there's an update on the wire services naming the victim as fifty-one-year-old Neville Ryman, police superintendent as was.'

'So?' Gaynor sniffed.

'So his wife's in custody. She bashed a hole in his head, with a rock intended for McKenna. Ryman shoved him out of the way.'

'Are you sure?'

'Eyewitness account given by a neighbour to a local hack.'

'How could the neighbour possibly identify McKenna?'

'She was helped by a very aggrieved local copper, after Mrs Ryman had gone berserk and attacked four of his mates.'

'I see.' Gaynor drew into the verge, the car's nearside wing hard by an overhanging drystone wall capped with icy blue snow. 'What have Ravensdale police got to say?'

'I've no idea because I haven't contacted them. I thought you'd like that pleasure. And a comment from McKenna would be pertinent, don't you think? In the public interest, of course.'

Ravensdale police headquarters batted her back and forth like a ping-pong ball from one close-mouthed officer to another before the force's press officer finally came on the line to tell her that a statement would be released in due course.

'Do me a favour!' She all but sneered. 'We know Superintendent Ryman's dead, and we know his wife's in custody. It was either a straightforward domestic, or something to do with the Stanton Smith case. You can't keep people in the dark for ever, especially about an investigation like McKenna's.'

'Nobody's being kept in the dark! The media were fully briefed at the outset, Ms Holbrook, you included. And you all know better than to expect a blow-by-blow account of an investigation such as McKenna's.'

'From where I'm standing,' Gaynor replied smugly, 'which, of course, is alongside the general public, his investigation is fast becoming an unmitigated disaster. Dugdale's marriage is history, Trisha Smith's father had a heart attack, Wendy Lewis tried to top herself, and now Ryman's dead. You can't *seriously* think we'll just stand by patiently waiting for some anodyne police statement?'

'Ms Holbrook, before you indulge in any more rash comment, or further transgress the bounds of legitimate journalistic inquiry, *I* seriously think you should consider your own position. You've already made yourself extremely vulnerable.'

Gaynor smiled to herself. 'Haven't I just?' she agreed. 'But, you know, I can't help wondering if that's only because McKenna and accountability inhabit different planets.'

'I'm not prepared to discuss this matter any further. As I said, we will issue a statement in due course.'

'Well, when you do, you won't neglect to explain why McKenna was at the Ryman house, will you?' She heard a sharp intake of breath. 'And why Mrs Ryman intended to kill *him*, rather than her husband?' She disconnected before he could respond and punched her fist in the air.

McKenna had gone to ground. She rang the Church Street house and Haughton police station, her heart thumping with trepidation in case he actually responded, but failed to locate him at either place. Pondering her next move, she gunned the motor and set off. Once over the crest of the moor, with Haughton below her in the deep-blue shadow of the valley trough, she could see the strobing lights of emergency vehicles somewhere on the hill where Dent viaduct bisected her view. Half skidding around the bend near where yesterday she had dropped her mysterious passenger, she expected to come upon a pile-up, but all she saw was a press of people on the pavement, stamping their feet and rubbing their hands. Their breath rose above them like smoke.

Nosing the car to a halt on the opposite side of the road, Gaynor crossed over, and began to nudge her way through the crowd. 'What's happened?' she asked a small fat woman in a padded jacket who was craning to see past those in front. 'Who lives there?' she added, peering through a phalanx of bare trees to the large house beyond and a forecourt littered with vehicles.

'The retards,' the woman responded, without even turning. Like an overfed rodent, she sniffed the air, wrinkling her nose.

'The who?' Gaynor was puzzled.

'The mental defectives,' the man beside her said. He wore an old greatcoat, with a flat cap rammed on his head, and the pulsating reflections of the lights turned his features into fluid forms.

'But what's happened?' Gaynor asked again.

'Something,' the man offered, nodding to himself. 'There's police there, and ambulances.'

'There's no fire engines, though, so they can't've set themselves on fire,' the woman said. 'It's not like it was when that woman was killed. You couldn't move for fire engines then.'

'And the bishop didn't come that time, either,' the man added.

Trying to elbow her way into a body of arcane knowledge as she had edged into the crowd, Gaynor said: 'I don't understand why the bishop should be here.'

'He isn't now,' the woman told her. 'He went off with one of them foreign coppers.'

'But why should he come at all?'

The woman turned to stare at Gaynor, and stated the obvious. 'You're not local, are you?' Looking her over, she pursed her lips while she counted the cost of the beautiful fur-lined jacket, then turned sharply away as a windowless transit van with 'Haughton Cleaning Co. Ltd' on its blue-panelled sides came up the road. When the van turned into the driveway, there was a collective tensing of shoulders and a hissing breath from the crowd.

'There's a mess, then,' the man said, with grim pleasure, watching the van come to a stop in the forecourt and discharge a cargo of three men in matching blue overalls.

'A mess?' Gaynor echoed.

'Blood,' the woman said, her eyes gleaming. 'Maybe brains as well. Them cleaning people only get called in when there's a mess nobody else'll touch.'

Opening the van's rear doors, the overalled men extracted plastic crates and industrial cleaners, then carried them into the building. Within minutes, a stretcher party brought out a sheeted body and bumped it into the back of a waiting ambulance. Slamming doors, the ambulance drivers backed away, turned, and came slowly down the drive, siren silent, lights stilled. The crowd watched greedily, then eyes swivelled back to the house as soon as the ambulance was out of sight.

Figures began to hurry back and forth from the house to the other waiting vehicles, but Gaynor's view was frustratingly segmented by the trees and the bobbing heads. She pushed forward, her nose assaulted by a medley of smells, her gloved hands impatiently tapping obstructive shoulders and backs, and reached the front of the crowd to find herself all but entangled in a low, thorny hedge. She kicked her way through, heedless of the damage to her leather jeans, and crunched over the carpet of crackling frozen leaves beneath the trees until she had a clear view of the forecourt. Moments later, other brave souls followed, their warm breath lifting the hair at the back of her head.

The front door of the house was wide open. In the shadowy interior, Gaynor could just discern movement, then people started to come out into the growing dusk, creeping down the steps arm in arm for support. A faller sat in the snow gaping vacantly around for assistance, to be hauled upright by others hurrying efficiently from the house. Before long, they were all shut up in cars and a small minibus, and ready to leave, and as soon as they were out of the way, two uniformed policewomen emerged, struggling with an overweight red-haired girl who slumped between them, weeping and howling. Followed by a tall thin man with half-moon spectacles, and a woman carrying a physician's bag, they climbed into one of the police cars, and sped away. Gaynor herself gasped, like the watching crowd, when the next to emerge was her erstwhile passenger, once again dressed in the fur-trimmed duffel coat and now flanked by an emaciated young woman with short dark hair and a ghastly pallor.

'Well!' someone behind Gaynor breathed. 'Wouldn't you know *she'd* have something to do with it?'

There was a murmur of assent.

'Why?' Gaynor asked, turning towards the speaker. 'Who is she?'

'Kathy Broadbent's bastard.'

'Who's Kathy Broadbent?' Frowning, Gaynor looked at the jumble of faces and hard eyes.

'Don't you know *anything*?' The voice snapped at

her, as brittle as the air, then the speaker looked past her, concentrating on the drama beyond.

Gaynor turned in time to see the two women being driven away in another marked police car, then, like her companions, she waited for something else to happen. One of the overalled cleaners came out to collect yet another crate from the back of the van, then there was a hiatus. She could see shadows flitting back and forth inside the building, and lights went on behind various windows, and as quickly went off again. As the air turned colder by the minute, the crowd became restive, but no one left. Someone pointed to a mulberry-coloured car now partly visible behind the cleaners' van, and said: 'That's Father Fauvel's car.' Someone else replied: 'Well, it would be, wouldn't it?' Gaynor peered at it, wondering if it were the same car she had seen yesterday, and if Father Fauvel were therefore the man whose attack on the duffel-coated woman she had intercepted, then felt her heart skip a beat when McKenna materialised at the top of the steps. He glanced at the gaping faces, walked to one of the cars, and drove quickly away. Pushing willy-nilly through the crowd, Gaynor ran to her own car and, speeding recklessly down the treacherous road, caught up with him by the derelict mill.

2

The housekeeper was in the kitchen, watched over by two middle-aged nuns from the convent down the road, and the sounds of her grief swelled through the presbytery like the surge of a tide. Standing over Jack while he bagged and labelled the tape from Fauvel's answering machine, the bishop remarked: 'She's Irish, you know. They do like to celebrate a death, don't they?'

'So I believe,' Jack said, wishing the man would go about his own business and leave him to do his. 'Don't you think you should see if she's all right? She seems to have thought a lot of Father Fauvel.'

'We all did,' the bishop mourned. 'This is the most *terrible* tragedy. I can't think what the parish will do without him.' He sat down rather suddenly in the swivel chair beside the desk. 'The nuns will take care of the housekeeper,' he added. 'They're very good at such times.' He clasped his hands, frowning up at Jack. 'Why are you taking that tape?'

'It's evidence.'

'Evidence of what?'

'I'm sorry, Your Grace, I can't discuss it.' Jack placed the bag to one side, then began to search the desk, while the bishop displayed his growing anxiety with a succession of facial contortions and white-knuckle hand clasps.

Finding nothing of apparent significance, Jack closed the desk drawers, picked up the bag and his briefcase, then said: 'This room will be sealed for the time being, along with Father Fauvel's bedroom, after I've had a look around.'

The bishop leaped to his feet, scurrying after Jack. 'Why?'

Once in the hall, Jack nodded to the scene-of-crime officer waiting for him to finish, then began to mount the stairs, the bishop hard on his heels. 'All sudden or unexplained death has to be investigated, Your Grace,' he said. 'The information is then presented to the coroner and an inquest.'

'Father Fauvel's death was indisputably nothing other than a dreadful accident.'

'Reaching that judgement is beyond our remit, I'm

afraid.' He walked along the close-carpeted corridor towards the room that the near-hysterical housekeeper had identified as Fauvel's, and opened the door.

The bishop jumped in front of him, barring the way. 'Why are *you* doing this?' he demanded. 'If it must *be* done, this is a task for the local police.'

Jack edged past. 'Please excuse me.'

'You haven't answered my question,' the bishop nagged, as Jack opened the double doors of a beautifully carved mahogany wardrobe.

'Father Fauvel was already included in Superintendent McKenna's investigation,' Jack replied, 'so the chief constable asked him to investigate the death.' He finished examining the wardrobe's contents, searched the bedside cabinet, tipped up the neatly made bed, then turned his attention to an antique oak coffer against the opposite wall. 'In any case,' he added, 'it's better that we do it. Some conflict of interest might arise with the local police.' The coffer was filled with vestments and robes of office. One richly embroidered chasuble was a work of art in its own right.

The bishop stood in front of the large mahogany chest of drawers that matched the wardrobe. 'How could there possibly be a conflict of interest?'

'I'm simply outlining what we must bear in mind. Our investigation of Smith's conviction is nowhere near complete and, until it is, we have to consider every possibility, however unlikely.' Closing the lid of the coffer, Jack made for the chest. 'May I?' he asked, reaching for the top drawers.

The bishop sidled away, but stayed so close that Jack could smell the incense about his garments. The top drawers yielded underclothing, socks, handkerchiefs, scarves, rolled-up leather belts, and a pair of embroidered braces. The others were filled with shirts and sweaters and cardigans, and everything was pristine and meticulously folded. The bottom drawer was locked. Jack rooted for a key in the carved boxes on the top of the chest, but found only cuff-links, various foreign coins, a penknife, two silver lapel pins shaped into crosses, and some old-fashioned collar studs. Hoping he would not damage the lovely wood, he opened the penknife and knelt down, sliding the blade between drawer and carcass.

'No!' The bishop clamped his thin, strong fingers around Jack's arm. 'Leave it be!'

'Your Grace!'

'I said leave it! Let the man rest in peace.'

Sitting back on his haunches, Jack looked up, to see utter anguish on the bishop's face. 'Your Grace, you appear to be obstructing me. Please, let me finish.' Gently, he removed the clasping fingers, feeling the other man's tension almost as an entity, then returned to the locked drawer, prying with the tip of the blade until he felt it catch. After several false moves, the lock snicked down, with only a slight dent on the edge of the drawer to show for the assault.

Hands over his face, the bishop turned away, breathing noisily. Emptying the drawer, Jack put the contents one by one on top of the bed, surveyed them with growing horror, then said: 'Clearly, Your Grace, *you* already had some idea of what I might find. Perhaps you would enlighten *me*.'

The bishop's face was as white as the bedsheets. 'I asked you not to do this! I *begged* you!'

Jack held up a jointed stick. 'This is a flail, isn't it?' He put it back, and picked up a leather whip with its end cut into knotted strips. 'And what's this? A cat-o'-nine-tails?' The tails were black with dried blood, like the thongs of the scourge with an intricately bound handle. Another whip had silver wires strung through its lash, and the twigs of a birch clicked against each other like dead bones. The bishop stared at the floor, in silence, while Jack unfolded the jacket-like garments of dingy coloured cloth, and opened them out to expose the coarse hair linings. One of them had a mesh of fine wire stitched into its fabric, and every garment was blotched with old blood-stains. 'Are you going to explain?' Jack asked. 'Or must we draw our own conclusions?'

'Father Fauvel was an adherent of the doctrine of pain,' the bishop muttered, his voice barely audible. 'He believed that mortification of the flesh strips away pride and cleanses the soul, and thus, brings one nearer to God.' He cleared his throat. 'It was his personal and private agony, and once again, I beg you to let it remain that way. It can have no possible connection with his death.'

'How long have you known about it?'

'I can say no more.'

'Your Grace, we can only respect privacy and confidences to a limited extent. How long have you known? How did you come to find out?' The bishop shook his head, his lips tightly closed. 'I have to know,' Jack went on. 'There may well be implications, and while we have every reverence for the sanctity of the confessional, we are driven by wider considerations.'

The bishop signalled his response by leaving the room. Jack heard his footsteps pad along the corridor and down the stairs, then a click as the front door closed. He waited until the scene-of-crime officer had finished sealing Fauvel's study, then called him upstairs. Together, they catalogued the abominable artefacts of the priest's rapacious and pitiable quest for pain, then sealed them inside evidence bags.

Gowned and masked, McKenna sat on a stool in Haughton hospital's basement mortuary, wondering what Gaynor Holbrook was doing. She had followed him in her gaudy yellow car all the way to the hospital, then called out to him across the car-park as he entered the building. He had ignored her, but expected to find her waiting like nemesis as soon as he tried to leave, for Ravensdale police had called while he was still at the Willows to say that she knew about Ryman's death, Estelle's arrest, and his own role in that piece of theatre. Before long, he thought, she would also know about Fauvel, if she did not already.

Extracted from his body bag, Fauvel lay on the slab, his robes sticky with blood. While the camera flashed repeatedly, and an assistant took off the priest's shoes and socks, the pathologist removed and bagged the blood-smeared chain and cross before unfastening the long row of jet buttons down the front of the robe. The dog-collar, crimson and sodden now instead of white and stiff, came next, and the bloody black shirt and the beautifully tailored trousers, then all activity ceased for a moment as the small group of the living considered what death had put on show.

Fauvel's feet were free of hard skin and corns, his toenails neatly trimmed and his tanned legs long, strong, and beautifully formed. His pelvis, upper body and arms were completely encased in a blood-soaked canvas carapace buckled diagonally to the shoulder like a Russian shirt. To the constant flash of the camera, and systematically recording his activity into the microphone above him, the pathologist unclipped the buckles and pulled away the fabric, exposing a welter of blood and wounds, through which, here and there, the stark white ends of shattered ribs and splintered sternum poked through. He stripped the body, examined it back and front, then turned his attention to the head. McKenna looked on, thinking only that there was now nothing left of the handsome face to which Brenda and Pauline once dedicated their loving fantasies.

4

Haughton's own police officers were exiled from the station's small complex of interview rooms and holding cells around which McKenna's team, and a support unit hurriedly drawn from Ravensdale headquarters, had dispersed some of the staff and residents removed from the Willows. Ryman's death was now common knowledge, and by nightfall news of Fauvel's had inevitably leaked through internal networks. Reporters jostled each other in the foyer, waiting for an official announcement, while others took their mobile telephones outside into the bitter night, and tried without success to extract comment on the day's dramas from the chief constable's office, the bishop's office, from Dugdale and Wendy Lewis and Colin Bowden, and from Smith himself. As deadlines drew nearer frustrations increased, and when McKenna eventually arrived, Fauvel's autopsy completed, he was mobbed. Gaynor was in the forefront, her tape-recorder thrust in his face.

Speaking softly so that the baying horde would be forced into silence to hear him, McKenna said: 'I can confirm that Father Fauvel died this afternoon. The coroner has been informed and a post-mortem is being carried out.'

'Is it true that he fell down the stairs at the Willows?'

'Until witness statements are available, we cannot confirm the circumstances of his death.'

'Is there a connection between his death and your investigation into Smith's wrongful conviction?'

'I am not in a position to comment at present.'

'Why aren't the local police investigating his death?'

'The chief constable is preparing a statement which should answer your queries.'

'Was it suicide?'

'I have already given you all the information I can at present.'

'What about Superintendent Ryman's death?' Gaynor asked. 'You can tell us about *that*.'

'The chief constable's statement will, as I said, answer your queries.'

'But you were there when it happened.' She moved closer, like a predator, eyes gleaming, breath pluming. 'How did you get those scratches and bruises? Did Mrs Ryman attack *you* as well?'

A hush settled on the group, which was now augmented by a clutch of uniformed police officers waiting on the steps to quell disorder.

'I have no comment.'

'Oh, really?' She was almost jeering. '"No comment" won't do, Superintendent. Tragedy's following you around like a lover, and the public has a right to know what's going on.'

'And when I'm ready I'll tell them,' he said, 'but you won't
be my mouthpiece. The public has a right to the truth, and we all know how positively frugal you are with *that* commodity.' He turned his back on the tittering media crowd, and as he walked up the steps the group of police officers parted like a biblical sea.

*

McKenna took over one of the interview rooms as a temporary office, and sat there chain-smoking, and thinking, as he looked at the papers accumulating before him, that he was stockpiling ammunition before re-engaging in battle with Julie. On top of the heap was the transcript of her call to Ryman, next the catalogue of Jack's finds in the locked drawer at the presbytery. Then there was Bennett's statement, and Janet's. She had reached the Willows some ten minutes after Fauvel swept through the door and told Bennett in passing that he must see Julie. He ran up the stairs towards her flat and met Debbie in the corridor.

For the most part, Debbie's interview had been an exercise in non-verbal communication. Flanked by Bennett and a solicitor, with the doctor and a policewoman in the background, she squirmed and giggled and sobbed in turn, and when McKenna tried to concentrate her mind on the circumstances of Fauvel's death, she giggled again.

'Made him happy,' she said, beaming. 'Made him happy yesterday,' she added.

'Tell me what happened,' McKenna persisted. 'What happened when you saw Father Fauvel going towards Julie's flat?'

She scowled ferociously. 'Told him to sod off. Julie asleep.'

'And?' McKenna prompted.

'Julie tired. Been up all night,' she reported, sniffling tears. 'Poor Julie!'

Fauvel had tried to push Debbie out of the way, and when she stood her ground, he grew violent. Jumping suddenly from her seat, she pantomimed for her audience how she drove him back to the head of the staircase. She blundered around the room, lunging and punching at thin air, the grotesque gingery fuzz

366

on her upper lip twitching and stretching like a caterpillar as she mouthed her rage. Then she clapped both hands over her mouth, her eyes almost starting from their sockets, as she relived the moment when she shoved him hard against the banister and watched him overbalance.

Julie had been put in one of the cells, and for more than two hours, she had sat on the bunk with her back pressed to the wall, writing. The skin around her eyes was bruised with weariness.

Every fifteen minutes, the custody officer pulled down the hatch in the door to check on her. On the third visit, he brought more paper and a newly sharpened pencil, on the fifth a mug of tea, and on the seventh another new pencil. Ten minutes after the ninth visit he unlocked the door and, in silence, escorted her to an interview room.

McKenna rose to his feet when she entered. The other policeman, large and swarthy-looking, whom she had seen earlier at the Willows, was already standing. He held out a chair for her, then walked to the other side of the table and sat down. McKenna stood beside him, looking at her. On the table, the large black tape-recorder was ready, its jaws open.

'I don't want to sound fanciful, Miss Broadbent,' McKenna began, 'but death has twice quite literally rolled at my feet today. This interview will be under caution, and I strongly advise you to make use of the solicitor who is already here.'

'I don't want a solicitor.' Julie put her sheaf of paper on the table. 'And don't bother asking me again like you did the other day.'

McKenna sat down and began the ritual of interview, labelling tapes and closing the jaws of the recorder before introducing himself. Jack recorded his own presence, then Julie identified herself as 'Julie Margaret Broadbent, age thirty-four, care assistant at the Willows'.

As McKenna recited the caution, she began to fidget. 'Where's Debbie?' she demanded.

'Elsewhere in the station,' McKenna replied.

'Why? What have you done with her?'

'That's no concern of yours.'

She clutched the edge of the table, and leaned forward, eyes blazing. 'What have you *done* with her?'

McKenna thought he could almost feel the heat from those wonderful eyes. 'She is being dealt with appropriately, and I understand the doctor is still with her. That's all I'm prepared to say.' Watching her, he folded his arms. 'Except that she has to live with Father Fauvel's death on her conscience, as Estelle Ryman has to live with her husband's death on hers. I don't know why these dreadful things happened, but I think you do. Your wretched evasiveness contributed greatly to this trail of destruction, and may have actually caused it. You were clearly the victim of yesterday's street attack, and if you'd talked to me this morning, instead of playing games, none of this would have happened.'

'You think?'

'Why did you telephone Ryman last night?' As her eyes flickered, he added: 'And don't bother to deny it. I've heard the recording of your call. Estelle Ryman listened in last night, and that's probably why her husband's dead. She went berserk and battered his skull with a rock, and if he hadn't pushed me out of the way at the last moment, I'd be on a mortuary slab instead of him.'

'You've a lot to be thankful for, then.'

'Before he died, Ryman left a message on Father

Fauvel's answering machine,' McKenna went on. 'I suspect that's why Father Fauvel rushed to the Willows to see you.'

'I wouldn't know. I was asleep in my flat, and you've got witnesses. Janet Evans had to wake me up.'

'There were witnesses *this* time, but there weren't when Trisha Smith died.' He paused, close to exhaustion with the interminable fencing. 'We *know* you lied about being at the Willows all that afternoon because you told Ryman you'd seen someone driving away from the blazing house. Who was it?' he demanded. When she remained silent, he added: 'Whoever it was, you wilfully concealed that knowledge from Dugdale's investigation, and helped to convict a probably innocent man.'

'Don't expect me to shed any tears for Smith. He'll get thousands for the few months he spent inside, so I did him a favour.'

'Doesn't this trail of death cause you any remorse?'

'It's what Father Fauvel wanted. He begged me often enough.'

'Begged you for what?' As he asked the question, McKenna knew the answer. Debbie's bizarre comment returned unbidden to his memory.

'To kill him. He wanted to experience the ultimate pain.' She gazed at him with those haunting eyes. 'Well, now he has done, so everything's as it should be.' Then she pushed the sheaf of paper towards him. 'It's all written down here.'

'Talk to me!' He put his hand over hers and, in the instant before she wrenched it away, something like fire shot up his arm.

'We know,' Jack said quietly, breathing in the tension between them. 'I broke open a drawer in Father Fauvel's bedroom and found his whips and sticks and hair shirts.'

369

What little colour there was drained from Julie's face, leaving her corpse-like.

'The bishop was with me,' Jack added. 'He said Father Fauvel was an adherent of the doctrine of pain.' He glanced at McKenna, then at Julie. 'Perhaps you could explain what he meant? As I'm not a Roman Catholic, I don't understand much about your religion. At the moment, all I can see is a series of unholy alliances that led to tragedy, and Father Fauvel's infatuation with pain is perhaps the worst of them.'

'Ryman said much the same. He said our religion is mysterious, and things happen in our church that don't happen elsewhere.'

'When did he say that?' asked Jack.

'Twenty years ago,' she replied, staring through him. Then she focused on him. 'I went to him because he had the power to stop Father Fauvel, but he wouldn't. At first, he thought I was complaining about sexual abuse, but I told him Father Fauvel had never laid a finger on me. He wasn't interested in my body. He only wanted my pain.' She paused, her eyes bleak. 'In the end, I showed Ryman some of my wounds, to *make* him understand, and he nearly fainted. Then he started shouting. He said everybody knew I was evil and dishonest, and if I so much as breathed a word to anyone else, he'd have me put away where I belonged along with my slut of a mother.'

'And that's why you accused him of blackmail, isn't it?' When she nodded stiffly, Jack said gently: 'Tell me how the accident happened.'

'You know.'

'We only know the older girls had to help in the school kitchen.'

She shrugged. 'That's how it happened. The chip

pan got too hot and started smoking. Cook made me move it off the burner, and I dropped it because it was so heavy.' She rubbed an invisible mark on the edge of the table. 'The bishop went to see my mother the same day, and when I came out of hospital I had a home tutor, and counselling from Father Fauvel. He was quite young then, about the same age as Father Barclay. He hadn't been in Haughton very long.'

'And?' Jack coaxed.

'He said he'd be like my own father, and I believed him. I had nothing to measure him by, you see. He was very kind and he was never shocked because I was so angry about being maimed. He said *anyone* would be angry, but when I understood that God had given me the pain for a purpose I'd stop being angry and be grateful. He'd show me pictures of saints having their flesh mortified, and said I was privileged by what had happened to me. What mattered was getting closer to God, and I had a head start when the chip pan fell on me.' She paused, furiously rubbing again at the non-existent mark. 'He gloried in my pain. I think he actually worshipped it. I loathed it and cursed it and despised my disfigured body. I didn't want to be like a saint. I just wanted to be like a normal girl, but I never could be. The accident made freaks of both of us, and but for me, his life might have taken another turning.'

'Why but for you? What did *you* do?'

'I let him put himself at my mercy,' Julie said. 'Four weeks after my twelfth birthday he told me he'd worn a hair shirt every hour of the day and night since he was sixteen, because he wanted pain. Then he showed me the things you found in his bedroom, and begged me to beat him until the blood flowed, and I did what he wanted because I understood how pain can become the only thing that matters.'

Overwhelmed by the nature of the world she evoked, Jack felt his scalp crawl. He swallowed, not daring to look at McKenna, who seemed almost to have ceased breathing. 'What made you approach Ryman?' he asked, for want of something to say.

'Father Fauvel wanted me to beat him to death.'

'Why?'

'So he could find peace.' She stopped rubbing the table edge, and clasped her hands in her lap. Her face was grey and beaded with sweat, as if she were in the throes of a fever. 'By then, he wasn't the only one with devils in his soul. He'd given me a terrible taste for cruelty. He'd kneel at my feet like I was the Angel of Death, begging me to go that little bit further, and the excitement of it made the blood pound in my ears.'

Willing her to talk of conscience and terror, Jack asked: 'What stopped you?'

'I couldn't bear the thought of the future without him.'

Dumbfounded, his imagination groped along the boundaries of the two worlds she had occupied: the banal limits of her everyday life, and the perilously seductive realm of their shared pain. As he was about to ask her when she realised those worlds were hurtling towards each other on a collision course, McKenna suddenly reached for the sheaf of paper, and began to read.

For a while, Julie watched them both, then said: 'When I abandoned Father Fauvel, I knew he'd have to find someone to take my place. That's why I betrayed him to Ryman.' Anger, or anguish, twisted her face. 'I knew Ryman would snitch, so I told Father Fauvel myself, but it didn't make the slightest difference, and when I started sleeping around, *that* didn't make any difference, either. Apart from the year he was in Rome, he never gave me a moment's peace. He said he needed me so much nothing else mattered.' She fell silent, and once again started rubbing the table. 'When he suddenly *stopped* hounding me, it was like having a pillow pulled off my face.'

While one part of Jack's mind persistently questioned why she would talk to him but not to McKenna, another told him to have a care that there was not worse lying in wait once he had finished dragging her through the bloody entrails of the past. 'When was that?'

'Fourteen years ago.'

She had, he thought, parcelled her life into segments, each tied up by a singular event. 'What happened then?'

'One of the novices at the convent had a total breakdown. She was literally carted off screaming, and nobody could understand why.' Eyes dark, she stared at him. 'But I could. When I challenged Father Fauvel, he said it was my fault for deserting him.'

'That was a wicked thing to say.' Jack spoke against the rustle of paper, and McKenna's hacking cough as he lit a cigarette.

'It was a wicked thing to *do*,' Julie corrected him. 'I thought what happened between us was *because* of us, not because he was wicked. After that, I saw how dangerous he really was.' She paused. 'And I knew it would happen again sooner or later. All I could do was watch him, but he seemed to be getting more and more desperate, and it got to be a terrible strain.'

'So you told Trisha Smith,' McKenna said suddenly. 'When she said she couldn't understand why people assumed priests were better men than most because they were just as prone to human failings and dark secrets as the rest of humankind. She'd crossed Fauvel during Smith's conversion, and knew he'd get his revenge by blocking her employment at the Willows.'

'And I wish to God I'd kept my mouth shut!' Julie snapped.

'So you say in your statement.' Paraphrasing what she had written, McKenna went on. 'Around two thirty on the day she died, she rang you to say Fauvel was due at her house in an hour. You immediately dressed and left the Willows by the servants' staircase that goes straight from the old nursery, which is now your flat, to the kitchen. You saw the smoke, ran down the road, saw the blazing house, and ran back to the telephone kiosk to call the fire brigade. Then you saw Fauvel driving away from the house.' He paused, gazing at her speculatively. 'Has it ever occurred to you that Fauvel thought Trisha intended to blackmail him?'

'She intended to *stop* him!' Julie's voice rasped. 'She was a good person. She thought she could make a difference.' She put her hands to her head and grasped fistfuls of hair. 'If only she'd known!'

'And if only you'd got there in time to tell her she'd written *and* signed her own death warrant,' McKenna added mercilessly, as she began to rock back and forth in the chair.

Appalled by the atmosphere between them, Jack could almost see Julie teetering on the brink of an abyss, and McKenna's hand reaching out to give the final push. In desperation, he asked her: '*Why* didn't you tell Dugdale? He wouldn't have called you a liar.'

After a few moments Julie sat still, but her hands were still snarled in her hair Her knuckles gleamed white. 'He'd have told Ryman, Ryman would have told Father Fauvel, and Barry could've ended up like Trisha. Even if he didn't, Ryman would've ruined him one way or another. He had too much to lose.'

'Dugdale could have gone to Ryman's superiors.'

'He'd still be repeating what I'd told him. And what does *my* word count for? Who'd believe *me* rather than Ryman and Father Fauvel? Everything I say or do is weighed against the reputation of a lifetime.' She untangled her hands and began to pick out the strands of hair from between her fingers. Her face was lined with pain. 'Whoever told you about Barry and me wanted to be sure you got the picture right. When he went out with me, people called him a whore's dog.'

'And last night,' Jack said, 'after Ryman refused to help, what were you planning to do?'

'What d'you think?' she replied. 'It was the only way out.'

Without warning, McKenna snapped off the tape-recorder. Squaring off the pages of her statement, he said to Jack: 'Would you arrange for Miss Broadbent to be taken back to the Willows?'

'Now?' Jack frowned. 'Have we finished?'

McKenna's tone warned against argument. 'Any loose ends can be picked up at a later date.' Still fiddling with the statement, he waited until the door closed behind his deputy, then rounded on Julie. 'Why didn't you tell *me*?' he demanded. 'I'm not another Ryman.'

'You're not, are you? You're more like Father Fauvel. You've hounded me the same way. You must have known I had something you want.'

5

Like the presbytery housekeeper, Janet seemed to draw on a bottomless well of grief and shock. Tears streaming from her bloodshot eyes, she stumbled around the back room of the Church Street house, her voice hoarse with weeping and her hands beating her forehead. Ellen sat quietly at the table, waiting for the frenzy to exhaust itself.

Jack closed the door on them and went to the office, where McKenna was hunched over the fire, his flesh livid with bruises, and a cigarette drooping from his fingers. Jack sat down and watched him, unable to think of anything other than pain, then began to leaf through Julie's statement, thinking how the long dashes she used to punctuate her text stitched together the words into a patchwork of her life. What she had told him earlier, what McKenna had paraphrased, was there, as tersely and bleakly written as the scenes that preceded Fauvel's death. And as a record of almost a quarter of a century of physical and mental torture, he realised, it amounted to very little but more of the relentless same.

Father Fauvel started haunting me again after Trisha died—maybe he just needed to be near me—maybe he knew I'd seen him. He kept begging me to go back to him—I played along because I thought that was the way to keep other people safe.

After he'd been at the Willows last Tuesday I found Debbie in the old sculleries—her clothes were in a mess—there were scuff marks on the floor and I could smell cigarette smoke. She started hitting me—she hits people sometimes but this was different—she was saying what he used to say to me—she repeats what she hears but makes it sound like her own words. I talked to her on Wednesday and yesterday—she said she and Father Fauvel had a "special secret game"—she acted it out for me. She said hitting Father Fauvel "made him happy" and if he was dead he'd be "as happy as an angel in heaven".

Yesterday afternoon he offered me a lift because of the snow—he only got angry because I refused. When he came to the Willows last night Debbie hit him in front of me and a colleague. I asked Ryman to help because of Debbie—but he called me a liar like last time. Then I said Father Fauvel would kill me because I'd seen him driving away from Trisha's place— he still didn't believe me.

I put a note in the log book about Debbie but my colleague tore it out—Father Fauvel wanted the incident forgotten—he said Debbie wasn't responsible for her actions.

As Jack put the statement with the hundreds of other documents amassed during the past week, the noise of Janet's keening intruded into his consciousness. With an empty feeling in the pit of his stomach, he said: 'This is probably the first time she's cried since she lost the baby. It'll do her good, even if it won't stop her having nightmares about Fauvel.'

'She said he fell so suddenly it was over before she knew what was happening.'

'But it wasn't for you, was it?'

McKenna stared at the tip of his cigarette. 'In the absence of a priest, I could have offered him spiritual comfort, but I didn't. Still, I'm sure the bishop will find a recipe to redeem his soul.'

'He'll have his work cut out,' Jack said caustically. 'It might be customary to condemn the sin while forgiving the sinner, but how often, and for how long, do you forgive the same sinner for repeating the same sin?'

'For as long as it's necessary, even if the sinner should know better.'

377

'But how many sinners are we talking about?' Jack began to swivel his chair back and forth. 'The bishop knew all about Fauvel's secret passions, but how come? Did Fauvel confess to him? Did he tell him about Julie? Even if he didn't, why didn't the bishop *do* something? He must have realised what a menace Fauvel could become. And how many others would Fauvel have confessed to over the years? When he went to Rome, he could have bared his soul to the Pope for all *we* know. Just where does the buck stop in your church?' He was becoming angry. 'Those people deliberately let Julie carry that dreadful burden all by herself. Nobody needed to break the seal of the confessional to put a stop to it. A nod and a wink in the right direction would have been enough. There are magic circles everywhere, as Fauvel told us himself.' He paused, his face drawn. 'And now she'll have to stand up in public and tell the world how she spent years beating the shit out of freaky Father Wonderful Fauvel.'

'Flagellation isn't uncommon, you know.' McKenna ground his cigarette to shreds in the ashtray. 'It's seen as a way of sublimating the sexual instinct, as well as a punishment for it. When I was an altar boy, I once found a mail-order catalogue for hair shirts and other instruments of torture on the vestry floor. It must have dropped out of the priest's pocket.' He rose and went to the desk. 'But what priests do to themselves and by themselves is an entirely different matter. I have no intention of making Broadbent say anything to anyone. We've got her statement and, along with all the others and my report, it will go to the Police Complaints Authority. I think we can safely conclude that Fauvel had grounds to suppress Father Barclay's evidence. We can therefore exonerate Dugdale of corruption. And that's as much as the world needs to know.'

'If Estelle Ryman goes to trial, things will *have* to come out.'

'We'll cross that bridge when we come to it.' McKenna reached for another cigarette. 'If we do. But in the meantime, we'll formally interview the bishop, and point out to him how he knowingly abdicated his responsibilities. Broadbent isn't the only one in need of protection. Debbie's just as likely to suffer from mob prejudice if word gets out, so the bishop has a part to play in keeping her where she belongs, and out of Broadmoor or Rampton.'

'Quid pro quo,' Jack commented sarcastically. 'Yet again.'

'You bargain with what you have,' McKenna replied.

6

When Julie returned to the Willows, the house was echoingly empty, but she knew that as soon as the residents came back, the routine threads of life would fast slacken the taut patterns woven that afternoon. All that was left to be seen of Fauvel's death was a drying patch on the parquet floor of the hall: by tomorrow, and with a smear of polish, that too would be a memory. On the staircase there were no new tell-tale signs amid the old scratches and wounds that scarred nearly every inch of the once-proud wood, not even on the banister rail over which Debbie had pushed him.

Walking quietly along the corridor, she climbed the nursery stairs to her flat, switched on lights and the electric fire, and went into the tiny kitchen to make a sandwich and a pot of tea. Pushing aside the sewing machine to make room – the pretty fabric was still trapped under its foot – she set the tea tray on the small table under the uncurtained window.

Outside, the earth was frozen, the trees fast in the ground, and already frost was braiding intricate patterns on the window-panes. She reached out to touch the icy ridges, and went rigid when a door slammed somewhere in the building. Listening tensely, she waited for other sounds of human occupation, telling herself it was too soon for Fauvel's ghost to be abroad. He would come later, and more stealthily, when his flawed and beautiful body was cold in the ground, and the time between now and his return would be as much an echoing void as the empty house. She had grown from child to woman closer to him than to her own shadow, and would go from now to her death with his ghost in her heart. He had loved her as much as he loved pain, and even if they were one and the same in his own heart, there had been that brief time in the long solitude of her life when she was able to love in return, before the love became the devil in her soul that whipped her towards all the other tawdry times when she sought out others to make her feel the same. Barry Dugdale was the only one among them for whom her scorched flesh held no terror, and for the first time in her life, she wondered if he too had truly loved her. Gazing blindly through the window, still listening for the sound of footfalls outside her door, she knew that even if he had it was too late now for both of them. They would never be more than prisoners of the question.

The inquest on Fauvel was held in the gloomy, old-fashioned room where the coroner's court sat in Haughton, and began on a fine spring morning when the silver-birch trees beyond the windows dappled room and occupants with ever-moving shadows. After evidence of identification, Dr Wilfred Spenser, the pathologist who had examined Trisha's charred remains, agreed that the priest's multiple fractures and fatal head injuries were consistent with his having fallen from some height. Evidence relating to how that fall had occurred was taken from those staff at the Willows who were present, from Janet Evans, and from Debbie, who explained with great difficulty how and why she had prevented her favourite member of staff from having her much-needed sleep disturbed. Debbie's further comment about making Father Fauvel happy as an angel in heaven simply drew a sympathetic but distant nod from the coroner, who, within less than two hours, delivered a verdict of misadventure.

The inquest drew a fairly large audience of still-grieving parishioners, but could not compete with the lure of the funeral, when streams of black-clad mourners flowed along the town's snow-covered streets to engulf St Michael's church in a flood of grief. Father Barclay had not been among them, nor had Julie. She disappeared from Haughton two weeks later, without even placing a posy of flowers on Fauvel's grave. Very few people knew where she had gone, and Dugdale was not one of them.

After the inquest, McKenna stood on the courtroom steps, chatting to Cyril Bennett.

'Thank God *that's* over,' Bennett said. 'It' seems to have been hanging over us for months.'

'My investigation had to be completed before the inquest could be reconvened,' McKenna told him. 'But it's done with now.'

Bennett regarded him thoughtfully. 'Will you be saying any more than what's already been in the papers? Reading between the lines, it looked as if Father Brett deliberately hid Father Barclay's letter, and that doesn't make much sense.'

'My job was to find out if *Dugdale* hid the letter. In the end, all we could do was balance the probabilities.'

Bennett smiled to take away any offence from his words. 'I reckon you know more than you're telling. You don't strike me as one of those policemen who'll say black's white just to get a colleague off the hook. Anyway, Dugdale's not off the hook, is he? I heard he's not allowed to do more than push a pen and answer the phone, and he has to get permission to do *that*. Still,' he added, 'I know you can't discuss the details.'

'But I accept that people would like to know what they are,' McKenna said. 'Tell me, how's Debbie?'

'She's getting on all right, but she misses Julie terribly. We *all* miss Julie, but not for the right reasons, in some cases. She did more work than a lot of the others put together, and she was straight.'

'What have you done with the woman who doctored the log book?'

'I went through the proper procedures and insisted the management committee sacked her. If she'd left things alone, I'd have done something about the incident as soon as I went on duty and, for all we know, Father Brett might still be alive.' He frowned, scraping the toe of his shoe on the edge of the step. 'It's the butterfly beating its wings in Borneo and causing an earthquake in South America syndrome, isn't it? Cause and effect.'

'It happens. All the time, I'm afraid. Have you heard from Julie?'

'No. Have you?'

'There's no reason why I should,' McKenna replied. 'I've had a letter from Father Barclay, though. He's setting up a new mission, about two hundred miles south of Bogota.'

'He's a *nice* young man,' Bennett said feelingly. 'I wish he'd stayed here. He'd have made a wonderful parish priest, but never mind, eh? I dare say there's far more of God's work to do where he is, don't you?' Pushing his hands in his pockets, he began to walk down the steps. 'I wish Julie hadn't just upped sticks and gone the way she did. She needs to be with people who understand what she's been through, because Father Brett's death must have been a terrible blow for her. They were so close.' He sighed. 'You know, he always seemed to be carrying some awful burden, and I reckon Julie was the only one who could give him respite. His eyes would light up when she came into the room. It was very moving.'

The only parking space McKenna could find on Church Street was two doors up from the old police house where they had lodged in February. The surveillance cameras were still bolted to the walls, and the grilles still fixed over the windows, but there were no signs of life about the place. The churchyard trees, now a sea of green leaves, whispered in the soft wind coming off Bleak Moor, and as Jack slammed the passenger door the rooks erupted, croaking their raucous song. Janet emerged from the back of the car and shut the door with a quiet click.

Single file, they walked along the narrow pavement, with McKenna leading the way. Janet stepped on his shadow at every pace, half expecting him to be pulled backwards by her weight. Behind her, Jack dawdled, hands stuffed in his pocket. As they passed the Bull Inn, the sign creaked in the breeze, the bull's face glaringly white in the sunshine.

Rene's front door was wide open, and before the gate was latched behind her visitors she was out on the step to welcome them. Shielding her eyes from the sun, she peered at Janet. 'Well, my goodness!' she exclaimed. 'I hardly recognised you. You *do* look well.'

Janet smiled. 'So do you.'

'*And* you've grown your hair. It looks ever so pretty.' She surveyed Jack and McKenna from head to foot, said: 'And you two look just the same,' then took them into the house, along the hall, and out through the back door to a suntrap of a patio. Her garden was a riot of colour, sheltered from the weather and prying eyes by banks of shrubs and a hawthorn hedge dripping with creamy blossoms. 'It's a pity Mrs Turner couldn't be here as well,' she added, 'but I expect she's very busy.'

'She wasn't required at the inquest,' McKenna told her. 'So she couldn't come.'

'And I suppose *you* had to get permission off the powers-that-be to have your lunch here, didn't you?' Rene asked. 'Well, never mind. Sit yourselves down while I bring out the food. I did plenty, seeing as Mr Tuttle was expected.'

Jack's eyes gleamed as savouries, salads, sandwiches and cakes appeared. Rene smiled at him. 'Quite like old times, isn't it? Apart from the weather, of course.'

'I don't know how you put up with snow like that, year after year.' Making inroads on several dishes at once, Jack added: 'But to see the place now, you'd think it had never happened.'

'It's always the same,' Rene said. 'Once it thaws, it's just a memory.'

'I thought it was quite beautiful,' Janet commented, selecting her own food. 'But it must have been a nightmare for the farmers. I expect they lost a lot of sheep and lambs.'

'Well, not really.' Rene set four teacups in four saucers. 'When there's bad weather on the way, the whole village helps with bringing the animals off the high moors. We've always done it, the able-bodied ones, that is.' She picked up the teapot. 'Same with the haymaking, even though machines do most of the donkey work these days.'

'I used to go haymaking,' McKenna offered, biting into a chicken sandwich. 'With a pitchfork.'

'I remember.' Rene smiled. 'You'd be out all day turning the hay to dry, then awake all night praying it wouldn't rain on it.'

'I've never done anything like that,' Janet said. 'My father celebrates Harvest Thanksgiving at the chapel, but I've never gone into the mountains to look for lost sheep.' She grinned. 'Mind you, I've met a few that went missing from *his* flock.'

'*We've* got plenty of *that* sort,' Rene told her. 'And so have the Catholics. Then again, who hasn't?' She pushed the sandwich plate within McKenna's reach, and jostled the conversation along the way she wanted it to go. 'In her own way, even though I've no time for the woman, you could call Beryl Kay a lost sheep.'

'Really?' Jack wiped his fingers on a napkin. 'Why's that?'

'Well, after the servants walked out on her she couldn't get a soul to go near the place. Folk said she can lie in the bed she made for herself, and they won't lift a finger to help.'

'I can't say I'm surprised,' Jack said.

'You can't but help feel a *bit* sorry for her, though.' Absently, Rene chewed the side of her mouth. 'My daughter has call to pass her place now and then when she's visiting the farms that way, and she's seen the mess. There's filth painted on the walls, the garden's a pig tip, the gate's in splinters, and even some of the windows got smashed. The hooligans were running riot for nights on end.'

'The local coppers should've sorted them out, then,' Jack commented.

'They did,' Rene said, 'but they couldn't stop the whispering and pointing and jeering every time Beryl showed her face in town, could they?'

'She could put a stop to that herself.' Heaping his plate with salad and sausage rolls, Jack said: 'All she needs to do is show Smith the door.'

'Folk reckon she's scared of him.' Picking up a long knife, Rene cut a fresh cream sponge into large wedges. 'According to the housekeeper, Smith wasn't the only one telling lies to that madam of a reporter. Beryl was, too. She'd already had a beating off him before that reporter even turned up.'

'Why doesn't *that* surprise me, either?' Jack wondered. 'What happened?'

'There was a row about the credit card bills Smith was running up, and he ended up going wild. He chucked the telephone through the window, then hit Beryl. The housekeeper said she had a real shiner the next day.'

'She could get out of the marriage if she really wanted to,' McKenna said. 'And she could afford the best legal brains to help her.'

'I know.' Sighing, Rene offered him what remained of the sausage rolls. 'She must *want* things to stay as they are, but God knows why.'

'Some people enjoy pain.' Janet put two more sandwiches on her plate.

'She's probably one of them,' Rene decided. 'A few days after they'd walked out, the servants went back for the rest of their things, and they took their solicitor with them, just in case. Beryl was on all fours, cleaning out the grate in the study, while Smith sat over her, dressed up to the nines like always. She can't have an ounce of shame in her body, can she?'

'Or pride,' McKenna added.

'Not like that Father Fauvel, then,' Rene said, eyes bright. 'He had more pride than was good for anybody, but folk always *did* say pride comes before a fall.' Malice coloured her voice. 'Same as it did for that reporter.' When there was no response from her audience, save for the sounds of eating, she went on: 'You do *know* her paper's paid up, don't you? Fred got ten thousand, Linda got twenty-five, and Smith's mother must've got some cash, because there was an apology and something about "undisclosed damages".'

'What are they doing with the money?' Jack asked.

'Fred went on holiday to Spain, and it near made a

new man of him. You wouldn't think he'd even been near the hospital, never mind at death's door. Linda's thinking about using hers as a down payment on one of the village houses. Craig's always had a mind to live here.'

'It's nice to know some good came out of the bad.' Janet helped herself to cake.

'It's just nice to *know*,' Rene said meaningfully, looking at McKenna. 'If you rely on what you read in the papers, you get less than half the story. And even if you put that together with what folk tell you, you still don't know if the two and two is adding up to four or twenty-four.' She put a wedge of cake in front of him, and topped up his tea. 'Some things are as plain as the nose on your face, but others – well, all you can say is there's a lot more to them than meets the eye.' Fidgeting with the table-cloth, she added: 'I mean, look at what happened with Estelle Ryman. I remember her from when she was a lass, and all you could call her for was having too much side. You'd never imagine she'd end up cracking open her husband's head like an eggshell, not in a million years.' She stared pointedly at McKenna. 'What's happening with her? Will she be going to court?'

'We don't know,' McKenna replied. 'She's unfit to stand trial at present. She's in a psychiatric hospital.'

'So likely as not, we'll never get to the bottom of it, will we?' Rene remarked. 'And we'll have to draw our own conclusions, won't we?'

'I'm afraid so,' said McKenna.

'Well, personally, I think what she did is somehow tied up with what happened at the Willows, though I can't for the life of me see how.' Rene waited for a response, again in vain. 'And what leads me to think that is what you might call a gut instinct, and it's the same with that Julie Broadbent. Some folk reckon she's gone into a convent and taken holy orders, but I don't.'

'Don't you?' Jack asked. 'Where do *you* think she is, then?'

'I think she's gone to South America with Father Barclay, and the best of luck to her if she has. She might make something of herself away from this place. There's nothing but bad memories here for her to dwell on.' She rose, rather suddenly, and picked up the teapot. 'I'll make a fresh brew. You're not in a rush, are you?'

'We're not in a rush,' McKenna agreed, gathering up an armful of used plates and following her inside. After the brilliant sunshine, the house seemed night-dark. He leaned against the kitchen counter, arms folded, while Rene stood by the gas cooker, waiting for the kettle to boil.

'It's still a rum do,' she said, 'but I suppose it couldn't be anything else. You went through this town like a dose of salts.' She paused. 'And not just the town. The police didn't come out of it too well, and for all you cleared Barry of wrongdoing his future doesn't look too bright.' The kettle began to rumble and she rinsed out the teapot. 'Did you know Colin Bowden ditched his fiancée? He's joined up with Warwick police again, and I'm not surprised, really. He never fitted in here. That silly Wendy Lewis didn't, either. She's retired sick, so I'm told.' Dropping fresh teabags in the pot, she asked: 'Is it true her solicitor's being taken to court? I saw something a couple of months ago in the *Manchester Evening News* about her getting committed for trial, but they couldn't say why. Reporting restrictions, or something.'

'The case has been dropped,' McKenna said.

'Why's that?'

'It wouldn't be worth the cost.'

'And is that why Linda didn't get done for keeping quiet about the men who replied to the lonely hearts ads?' She ignored the steaming kettle. 'She nearly had a nervous breakdown waiting to hear, then all she got was a curt little letter off the police.'

'In the end, the information she suppressed wasn't relevant.'

She switched off the gas and filled the teapot. 'Relevant to what? Who sat on Father Barclay's letter, or who killed Trisha?' There was no response. 'Or are they one and the same?' she asked, dropping a cosy on the pot. She stared at him. 'You know who killed Trisha, don't you?'

'We only have a suspicion.'

'That's usually enough. Why can't you take them to court?' Again, he remained silent. 'Why can't you *tell* me?' she demanded, tears springing to her eyes.

'You know why, Rene.'

'All I *know*,' she said bitterly, 'is that some of us have to struggle on as best we can without her, while whoever killed her is getting away with murder.'

'Not any longer.'

Both sides of her mouth clamped between her teeth, she frowned up at him. '"Not any longer"?' she repeated. 'Is Trisha's killer dead? Is *that* what you mean?' She picked up the pot and cradled it to her chest. 'So which one was it? Ryman or that damned priest?'

McKenna took the teapot from her and put it on a tray. 'You'll burn your hands.'

She began setting out clean cups and saucers on the tray. 'Julie Broadbent stayed away from the funeral, and now she's disappeared off the face of the earth. *She* knows, doesn't she?'

Almost imperceptibly, McKenna nodded.

'Then maybe you should do Wendy Lewis a favour,

and set *her* straight. Every Sunday and Wednesday,
regular as clockwork, she puts fresh white lilies on
Fauvel's grave.' Rene picked up the tray and made
decisively for the back door. 'God *rot* his wicked
soul!'

Also by Alison Taylor

THE HOUSE OF WOMEN

Alison Taylor

Lonely, ageing and chronically ill, Ned Jones is found dead on a sweltering summer afternoon in his rooms. The doctor is unable to certify cause of death, and Detective Chief Inspector Michael McKenna and his team become involved as a matter of routine. But the post-mortem findings cast new light on what at first seemed a natural death.

Frustrated by personal and professional dilemmas, McKenna returns time and again to the house where Ned lodged, home of a distant relative, Edith Harris. But fragile, neurotic Edith, addicted to tranquillizers, and her three daughters – Phoebe, swaddled with puppy fat, driven remorsely by her acute intelligence; Mina, nineteen, beautiful and blank-faced; and Annie, the eldest and an unmarried mother – spring one surprise after another on McKenna.

In search of Ned's killer, McKenna visits the sad remnants of the family, isolated in a decaying mountain farm, and comes into repeated contact with the unpleasant Professor Williams, whose place in Edith's life is far from clear. Slowly, McKenna begins to untravel a story of scholarship and greed, deceit and twisted loyalties, where the sins of the past, as well as the present, are avenged on innocent and guilty alike.

'Up there with the likes of Ruth Rendell and Minette Walters' Mike Ripley, *Books Magazine*

'With her third novel, *The House of Women*, Alison Taylor confirms her place among the new stars of British crime writing' *Sunday Telegraph*

Also available in paperback

☐ The House of Women	Alison Taylor	£5.99
☐ Fatal Remedies	Donna Leon	£5.99
☐ Road Rage	Ruth Rendell	£5.99
☐ Last Rites	John Harvey	£5.99
☐ The Reluctant Investigator	Frank Lean	£5.99
☐ Night Dogs	Kent Anderson	£6.99
☐ The Black Dahlia	James Ellroy	£6.99
☐ Silence of the Lambs	Thomas Harris	£5.99
☐ The Godfather	Mario Puzo	£5.99

ALL ARROW BOOKS ARE AVAILABLE THROUGH MAIL ORDER OR FROM YOUR LOCAL BOOKSHOP AND NEWSAGENT.

PLEASE SEND CHEQUE/EUROCHEQUE/POSTAL ORDER (STERLING ONLY) ACCESS, VISA, MASTERCARD, DINERS CARD, SWITCH OR AMEX.

☐☐☐☐☐☐☐☐☐☐☐☐☐☐☐☐☐☐

EXPIRY DATE .... SIGNATURE ....

PLEASE ALLOW 75 PENCE PER BOOK FOR POST AND PACKING U.K.

OVERSEAS CUSTOMERS PLEASE ALLOW £1.00 PER COPY FOR POST AND PACKING.

ALL ORDERS TO:

ARROW BOOKS, BOOKS BY POST, TBS LIMITED, THE BOOK SERVICE, COLCHESTER ROAD, FRATING GREEN, COLCHESTER, ESSEX CO7 7DW.

TELEPHONE: (01206) 256 000
FAX: (01206) 255 914

NAME...

ADDRESS ....

....

Please allow 28 days for delivery. Please tick box if you do not wish to receive any additional information ☐

Prices and availability subject to change without notice.